MATILDA'S GAME

Also by Denis Kilcommons

THE DARK APOSTLE
SERPENT'S TOOTH
BLOWBACK

DENIS KILCOMMONS

MATILDA'S GAME

BANTAM PRESS

LONDON · NEW YORK · TORONTO · SYDNEY · AUCKLAND

TRANSWORLD PUBLISHERS LTD
61–63 Uxbridge Road, London W5 5SA

TRANSWORLD PUBLISHERS (AUSTRALIA) PTY LTD
15–23 Helles Avenue, Moorebank, NSW 2170

TRANSWORLD PUBLISHERS (NZ) LTD
Cnr Moselle and Waiparcira Aves,
Henderson, Auckland

Published 1992 by Bantam Press
a division of Transworld Publishers Ltd

A catalogue record for this book is available from the British Library.

ISBN 0593 020510

Typeset in 11/12½ pt Baskerville
by Photoprint, Torquay, Devon.

Printed in Great Britain
by Biddles Ltd, Guildford and King's Lynn.

FOR RICHARD

Matilda told such dreadful lies,
It made one gasp and stretch one's eyes;
Her Aunt, who, from her earliest youth,
Had kept a strict regard for truth,
Attempted to believe Matilda:
The effort very nearly killed her.

                                        Hilaire Belloc

'I always tell the whole truth and nothing but the truth. And
only lie when I have to.'

                        Princess Stefanie Hohenlohe, Nazi agent

PROLOGUE

1955

Anthony Blunt, Surveyor of the Queen's Pictures and Director of the Courtauld Institute of Art, paced the living-room of his apartment above the art gallery. He made no attempt to hide his nervousness.

'Are you sure you want tea?'

He pouted and waved an arm towards an array of bottles on a side table.

'Stop flapping, Anthony.'

Kim Philby relaxed on a sofa and smoked a cigarette.

'Can't help it.' Blunt walked to the window and looked suspiciously down at the gardens in Portman Square. Eventually, he moved away, sat in an armchair and crossed extremely long legs. 'I've been flapping for three days. Ah, John.'

John Gaskin, Blunt's housekeeper, lover and procurer, carried in a silver tray that held tea for two and a plate of delicate sandwiches. He placed them on a table and retired.

Blunt watched him leave and said, 'Don't know what I'd do without the dear boy. These last few years have been hell. He's been a godsend.'

Philby smiled.

'Are you sure you have the right deity?'

'Really, Kim. He does try, the dear love.'

'He looks like a nice boy.'

'He is.' Blunt smiled tartly. 'He knows lots of other nice boys, too. Shall I be mother?' He poured tea and Philby stubbed out the cigarette. 'But you know what I mean. You most of all. It's been terrible for you.'

9

'A bit n-n-nerve wracking.' The stutter annoyed him. It always came in precisely the wrong place. 'But I've got used to it.'

They sipped tea and Philby accepted a sandwich.

Blunt said: 'It was a shock, you know. Seeing his handwriting after all this time. And Peter didn't help. He simply walked up, out of the blue, and handed me the postcard.'

The encounter that had awakened all the old fears had occurred in one of the rooms downstairs in the Institute. Blunt had completed a lecture and was dealing with the aftermath of flattery and enquiry, when an elderly man had made his way from the back of the room.

Yuri Modin was a KGB officer who had helped run the Cambridge spy ring during the war. They had known him by the codename Peter. He had handed Blunt a picture postcard of a painting and asked his opinion.

The message on the reverse was written in the unmistakable scrawl of Guy Burgess, who had defected to Moscow four years before. The shock at being confronted by the Russian after all this time, and the danger inherent in their being seen together, had been mitigated by unexpected hope.

Burgess's message had requested a meeting the next night at a public house in North London called The Angel.

Blunt now shook his head.

'I suppose I knew he couldn't be back so soon.'

Philby said, 'Guy will never be back.'

'I know. But just for a moment . . .' He smiled. 'It was so . . . so right. The Angel, for goodness sake.'

The term 'Angel' was used by the élite society of Cambridge undergraduates known as the Apostles to describe members who had taken wing and left the university. Blunt, Burgess and Maclean had all been Apostles during their years at Cambridge in the early 1930s. To be invited to join, it had been essential to be brilliant and it had been helpful to be attracted to other men. Blunt's homosexual mafia had subsequently produced a network of Soviet spies who

10

had infiltrated every level of the British Secret and Civil Service.

Philby, who had been neither brilliant nor homosexual, had not been invited to join, but he had emerged as the most effective spy of them all.

Blunt had kept the rendezvous at The Angel, his emotions torn between hope and fear. He had loved the flamboyant and promiscuous Burgess, but the man's knowledge could threaten his own very comfortable and satisfying life, and leave him open to public exposure.

Burgess had not been there.

'There was no Guy,' he told Philby. 'Only Peter. He's getting old, but then, aren't we all? I'm beginning to feel as ancient as a fairy story. An old queen in an ivory tower.'

'You've got Lady John.'

'True. They say you're as young as you feel.' His smile was a pout. 'And he feels young.'

Philby said, 'I'll see Peter.'

The purpose of the rendezvous in the pub in the Caledonian Road had been for Blunt to pass the message on to Philby that his Soviet controller wanted a meeting.

'Will you be going too?' Blunt asked.

He meant to Moscow.

'I doubt it. Five have done their damnedest but they've sweet fuck all. I'm secure enough and I still have friends in the right places.'

'Would it bother you? Going to Russia?'

'No. I've been an itinerant all my life. It would be another foreign posting, that's all.'

'What would you miss most of all?'

'Cricket. Perhaps, if the time ever comes, I'll start a Moscow eleven.'

'I'd hate it.' He was talking about exile, not cricket. 'I could never leave England.'

'You won't have to, you old poof. You're as solid as a rock. It'll be a knighthood next and a long and glorious career serving art and your monarch.'

'But after Guy and Donald . . .'

'That's old hat.'

'The newspapers still speculate.'

'About me. Not you. They have nothing on you.'

'There's guilt by association.'

Blunt was worried in case Philby had been followed.

Philby said: 'I was circumspect. Two tubes, a cinema and Harrods before I got here.'

They both chuckled.

Blunt said: 'What a ridiculous game.'

'I still find it invigorating.'

'Do you really mean that?'

'I tell myself I do. Besides, I made my choice. We all did. I have no regrets, only discomforts, and they're good for the soul. None of us could resist the challenge, Anthony. Conscience dictated our destiny, and then it was cowboys and Indians.'

Blunt ruminated.

'When you're young, nothing seems for ever. Middle age is as meaningful as the Middle Ages. When it arrives, ideals don't have the same efficacy; they've been replaced by loyalty. Loyalty to friends, relationships, routines. I miss Guy. It's strange how events have unfurled.' He shook his head. 'I could never leave England.'

Philby said: 'Melancholy doesn't suit you. Remember, few get the chance to become world players, I mean real world players, the sort who mould history. You're one of a select band and you shouldn't forget it.' He smiled. 'Not that your arrogance is ever likely to let you.'

'Bitch.'

They laughed.

'You've nothing to fear. Submerge yourself in art and the sins of the flesh. Besides, you've still got your insurance?'

Blunt nodded. 'I've still got it.'

'Then you're as safe as the House of Windsor. Even if you were blown, you'd be untouchable.'

'You think so?'

'Of course.'

The thought comforted Blunt and his mood lightened. He, too, relaxed, and they reminisced about Cambridge, when life was passion, and about loyalties that remained untarnished.

ONE

Peter Lacey was admiring the girls in bikinis by the side of the swimming-pool when Sam Bryson walked into his office without knocking.

'When do you go?' Bryson asked.

'Two weeks.' Lacey looked up from the brochure. 'Sunshine, five-star luxury and invigorating views.'

'I hope Susan understands about the views.'

'She accepts them as external stimuli.'

'A sophisticated lady.'

'Yes. She is.'

Sam offered him the fax he was holding and Lacey reluctantly put down the brochure and took it. It said:

For sale: The Blunt Legacy. Personal letters, documents and photographs are offered to serious collector or publisher interested in, among other things, peace with Germany, a royal scandal, an American connection, and the Soviet trade deal of 1964.

It was followed by an international telephone number.

He read it and looked up at his section head.

Bryson said: 'It's an advertisement that will be appearing in *The Times* tomorrow. The telephone number is an answering machine in Lisbon.'

Lacey reread the advertisement.

' "The Blunt Legacy"?' He looked up at his department head. 'There really is one?'

'We don't know. But we'd like to.'

Lacey couldn't stop himself from smiling.

14

'After all these years, the old queen is back to spook us?'

'It's not funny, Peter.'

'Not for Five. But when did they ever have a sense of humour?'

'It's not funny for us, either. We've been given the retrieval.'

Lacey stopped smiling.

'We have no one to send.'

Bryson avoided his gaze and began to pat his pocket for the comfort of his pipe but it wasn't there.

'Sam, we've no one to send.'

'It must be in my office.' He meant the pipe. He began to leave, expecting Lacey to follow, and spoke over his shoulder as he reached the door. 'It's only a two-day trip. Three at the most.'

He disappeared and Lacey held himself in check. He was determined he would not miss his holiday with Susan in Cairo in two weeks' time but he was intrigued by the advertisement and the idea of a legacy of documents left by the former MI5 agent. Lacey put the brochure away in a drawer.

The department was as claustrophobic as it was anonymous. It occupied the top floor of a Victorian office block in Charing Cross Road. The front office was protected by cameras on the stairs which were monitored by retired hooligans from the SAS; the double-glazed windows of the main office were wire-meshed, paint-sprayed mustard and net-curtained against sonar laser-beams that might pick up voice vibrations from the glass.

It was like working in a yellow submarine stranded high above the muted wheeze of London's traffic.

The sign on the outer door said, BARNABY AND ROBINSON – INVESTMENTS, but they were listed in the index at Century House as D14a. As Michael Caine might say, not a lot of people knew that.

Not a lot of people knew about them at all, in fact. They were one of the secret departments in a Secret Service that, officially, didn't exist; a department that handled the

15

unpalatable in such a way as to allow the Foreign Secretary legitimate deniability.

Lacey went into the main office and surveyed the kingdom of which he was deputy head. The wall to his left was filled with the computers, encrypters and fax machines of Harry Ryburn, who, despite a wife and three children, unashamedly preferred machines to people. Lacey, who was becoming increasingly sceptical about the games they all played, thought Harry might have a point.

Four large desks took up most of the other space. Two were for analysts and two were available to field operatives between assignments. Only one of the four was, at the moment, manned.

Malcolm – small, plump and neat in a purple velvet waistcoat – was colour co-ordinated with yards of pink print-out paper from a computer. His half-moon spectacles were on the end of his nose and his left hand hung camply from the wrist.

Middle age had caught him and he didn't mind, he had told Lacey. It was safer than catching anything else. His wild days of sexuality and the vicar from Croydon were in the past and middle age was comfortable, with an easy-to-control libido, a houseful of cats in Bow, and the occasional Omar Sharif video.

Natalie had taken the Monday off and they were all still slightly shocked that she had admitted she was going away for a long weekend with her boyfriend to celebrate her thirtieth birthday. It had been the first indication she was anything other than a beautiful android.

She was raven-haired with a shape to turn the most liberal man's thoughts to male chauvinism and had an IQ to match an IBM computer. Her cool efficiency left no room to flirt. Her desk, as usual, was at attention.

Her VDU and keyboard were regimentally aligned on the left and two wire trays were in parade-ground formation on the right. Even the two plastic beakers were symmetrically perfect: one contained four pencils, the other four pens, all diametrically spaced.

16

As he went by, Lacey exchanged a pen for a pencil to confuse her.

The two field operatives were on assignment.

Butler was not due back from Istanbul for at least a week. He was persuading a minor Muslim Fundamentalist leader that his vocation need not be jeopardized by Butler's possession of a video film that illustrated the man's appreciation of Western decadence.

Monroe was in Prague, up to his ears in delicate negotiations with a former member of the Statni Bezpecnost, the Czechoslovakian secret police that had operated as a branch of the KGB before the thaw. Like many StB officers, the man had used the information in his possession for blackmail since the Velvet Revolution of 'eighty-nine.

Funny, Lacey reflected, that it was blackmail when somebody else tried it on, and persuasion when Six were the instigators.

Bryson's office was bigger than Lacey's but not big enough for the books, boxes, files, cabinets and ashtrays. While the rest of the world was embracing high technology and visual display units, Bryson retained his faith in mounds of paper that he could shuffle and reference books over which he could spill coffee. The books had overflowed from the shelves on to the floor and cataracts of print-outs tumbled from files that had been filed on top of files.

The man's superiors across the river did not complain about his habits because he got results. Besides, the former Cambridge don would have ignored them with the same calculated eccentricity that led him to ignore the rules of fashion and wear American string ties with tweed jackets.

By the time Lacey entered the room, Bryson had found his pipe and was tamping tobacco into its bowl. His grey hair was an unruly mane around his shoulders and Lacey wondered if he had considered a pony-tail. He might suggest it, if only to create another point of antagonism for their masters to chew on.

Lacey sat in an easy chair and took out a packet of Gitanes and a box of matches. He was supposed to have stopped but when faced with Bryson's pipe he smoked in self-defence.

They both puffed out pollution and a haze settled over the desk between them.

Lacey made a pre-emptive strike.

'Why us? Five cocked up. They should clear up their own mess.'

'They don't do retrievals on foreign soil.'

'They do if it suits them.'

'They don't this time. This time, we've been asked to handle it. Besides, we don't know that it *is* a Five cock-up.'

'It is if the rumours are true.'

'Peter.' It was delivered as an admonishment. 'Rumours?'

'Yes. Those things we use to justify our budget.'

'Very funny.' Bryson puffed out more smoke. 'Tell me the rumours.'

Lacey sat back and stretched his legs.

'Let's start with what we know. Blunt was one of the Cambridge spy ring that operated for the Soviets from before the Second World War. Maclean and Burgess were the first to be rumbled and they defected to Russia some time in the 1950s. Philby had more bottle, even when he was suspected. He continued spying until he went to Moscow in the early sixties.

'Newspapers called him the Third Man and MI5 went looking for the Fourth Man. Blunt was suspected but then, everybody was suspected.' He shrugged. 'A secret service thrives on paranoia.'

He took a drag of the cigarette.

'Five eventually got the evidence to nail Blunt but they didn't. They gave him immunity instead.' Lacey looked again at the advertisement. 'That's presumably what's described here as the Soviet trade deal of 1964. Blunt kept his knighthood and his position and was still welcome at Buck House until he was publicly blown by the Great British Press in the late seventies.'

Bryson said: 'Why was he granted immunity?'

18

'Five said the evidence wasn't strong enough for a prosecution. Besides, his confession was worth more than sending him to jail. They said he told them about other spies. That's the official version.'

Bryson said: 'And the unofficial version?'

'Towards the end of the Second World War, when Blunt was with MI5, he was sent into Europe to look for documents about the Duke of Windsor and the Nazis. Evidence of collaboration would have been embarrassing for the royal family.

'The rumour is that he was very successful, but that he didn't hand over everything he liberated. He kept some back for protection. Documents that could be described, as it says here . . .' he looked at the advertisement '. . . as being connected with peace with Germany and a royal scandal.' Lacey looked at Bryson and smiled. 'The rumour is that Blunt used them to buy immunity.'

Lacey changed his position. He crossed his legs and waited for his section head to make a contribution.

Bryson took another puff at the pipe and scratched his nose. He leant forward and pushed some papers around on his desk.

He said: 'I was a member of the Fluency Committee in the sixties.'

Lacey nodded. The Fluency Committee had consisted of officers from both MI5 and MI6 and had been set up after the defection to America of Anatoli Golitsin, a senior KGB officer. He had convinced the CIA that the British had been extensively penetrated by Soviet spies. The committee had been supposed to find them.

Bryson said: 'As you say, everybody was suspect. Peter Wright was chairman of the witch hunt.'

No one in either branch of the Secret Intelligence Service had any time for the self-proclaimed spycatcher who had broken his oath of secrecy.

Bryson puffed at the pipe and thickened the smokescreen that hung above the desk before he continued.

'Blunt's confession was worthless, so it's likely there was

19

another reason they didn't go public. It may have been to save royal embarrassment because he was, so to speak, a friend of the family. The Queen Mum referred to Blunt and herself as a pair of old queens.

'It may have been to save political embarrassment. 'Sixty-three was a bad year. Philby had finally gone over, and the Profumo Affair had broken. The government was tottering. It fell later in 'sixty-four, but Blunt would have put the tin hat on it. Your theory stands up.

'In 1944, Blunt was sent into Europe to recover documents and letters belonging to the royal family. Of particular importance were those relating to the Duke of Windsor's collaboration with the Nazis. Blunt went with Sir Owen Morshead, the royal librarian at Windsor Castle. They went as members of the OSS Art Looting Investigation Unit and did a thorough job. Officially, not much has survived.

'No one thought anything of it until 'sixty-four when they finally got the evidence on Blunt. That's when the rumours started that he'd made an immunity deal before the interrogators got at him. The mission in Europe was so highly classified that when Wright got to question Blunt, he was forbidden to ask about it.

'Wright believed Blunt had something, some scandal. He thought he might leave it behind when he died. A vindictive last will and testament naming people in high places. It was a surprise that he didn't.' He shrugged. 'Now it looks as if he did.'

Lacey stubbed out the cigarette in a glass ashtray which carried the message: I LOVE CYPRUS.

He said: 'It's all very interesting, but it's also very old. Why a retrieval?'

'That's a policy decision. It doesn't concern you. We've been instructed to ensure that any deal that might have been made by Five in 1964 remains confidential and that no evidence of a royal scandal leaks to the Press.'

He puffed the pipe.

'Why the sensitivity fifty years on? What's likely to be in these papers?'

20

'That's the point. We don't know.'

'What do our files say?'

'Very little. Anything relevant is locked away in the Royal Archives at Windsor or the Public Record Office. It won't be released in our lifetime.'

'No access?'

'None.'

'Which suggests there's something to hide.'

'Quite. I can tell you what we do know and what we suspect. But first, let me put collaboration into historical context.'

He rested his pipe in an ashtray and sat back with a sigh, as if what he was going to say might be slightly painful. Lacey himself was ambivalent about the monarchy but he knew his section head had a genuine fondness for tradition and the royal family.

Bryson began.

'In the thirties, the Duke made no secret of the fact that he wanted to keep Britain out of a war. He still wanted peace, even after war started. A lot of people did.

'By May of 1940, Hitler had conquered most of Europe. What was left of the British and French armies were trapped at Dunkirk. They needed the miracle of the little boats to save them. Remember?'

Lacey said: 'I've seen the movie. Dickie Attenborough was very brave.'

Bryson ignored the remark.

'At the time, Churchill was making his famous war speeches.' He picked up the pipe and gave it a tentative puff but it had gone out. 'He was also considering the possibility of having to make peace with Germany.'

Lacey said: 'What about fighting them on the beaches?'

'Rhetoric is a valid weapon. It doesn't have to be true.'

'First rule of politics?'

'Don't be more facetious than usual, Peter. It's all words until reality sets in, and the reality in 1940 was that Hitler didn't want to fight us. He wanted to secure Western Europe

21

before he fought Russia. The point is, even Churchill was considering making peace.'

'But he didn't.'

Bryson dug into the bowl of the pipe with a match.

'No. He thought Britain was too weak to bargain at that time. He decided to fight on until he could, if need be, negotiate from a stronger position. Fortunately, he never had to. The tide turned and we stuck it out. But in 1940, all options were being considered by all sorts of people.'

'Including the Duke of Windsor?'

'Including the Duke. He was so deeply involved that the Secret Service wanted to question him about his contacts with the enemy. Churchill stopped them.'

'You mean he was a traitor?'

'If he had been anybody other than who he was, yes.'

'Royal parentage provides you with a different set of rules, does it?'

'Maybe it did fifty years ago.'

He relit the pipe.

'You're building up to something. Tell me.'

'I'm building up to the Biarritz Agreement.' He took a deep breath and continued. 'The Duke was British liaison officer at French Headquarters in Paris. Twelve days before Dunkirk, he left without authorization to take the Duchess to their villa in the South of France. He went back to Paris briefly, but left for good soon afterwards, to rejoin the Duchess.

'France fell and they went to Spain and then Portugal, both neutral countries. While they were there, Churchill and the King were worried in case the Duke made a deal with the Germans. We're working on the premise that the deal had already been made.'

Bryson paused to let Lacey know this was crunch time.

'When he first left Paris to take the Duchess south, we believe he met Hermann Goering in Biarritz. Goering also met someone else in Biarritz: Joseph Kennedy, the United States Ambassador to London and father of America's most famous president.'

Bryson had his own copy of the advertisement that was to appear in *The Times* on the desk in front of him, and he pushed it with a finger.

'We think that could be what is referred to as an American connection. We think the Biarritz Agreement could be part of Blunt's legacy.'

Bryson went back to his pipe.

Lacey said: 'They were both party to the same deal?'

'That's the assumption.'

'What was the deal?'

'Peace between Britain, America and Germany, the Duke to return as monarch, and King George VI to be sent to the Bahamas in exile.'

'Isn't that where they sent the Duke of Windsor?'

'That's right.' Bryson smiled. 'Churchill had a sharp sense of humour.'

'Churchill and the King knew?'

'Not all of it, but a great deal. They had the Ultra Intelligence.'

'Ah!'

At the start of the war, Poland had supplied Britain with the secret of the Enigma decoding machines used by the German armed forces. By 1940, a unit had been established at Bletchley Park near London, to decipher German wireless signals. The information from it was known as the Ultra Intelligence. It had played a significant part in helping win the war and it sounded as if it had helped nail the Duke of Windsor.

Bryson said: 'Unfortunately Philby had access to the traffic as well. He was head of the Iberian Section from 1941 and would have been aware of the Windsor scandal the year before. When Blunt was sent into Europe on his clean-up mission in 'forty-four, it's likely Philby briefed him on what to look for before he went. He might well have given him some of the signals.'

Lacey said, 'The Duke wanted to regain his throne. What about Kennedy? What did he want? How official was he?'

23

'He was totally unofficial. Roosevelt didn't know and wouldn't have approved. Kennedy was acting on behalf of big business. In Biarritz, he was also making a major financial contribution on behalf of American industry to the Third Reich.'

Lacey said: 'Interesting. What do you want me to do?'

'The answerphone in Lisbon has a message for callers. It says anyone wanting to bid for the Blunt Legacy should attend the conference room at the Hotel Embaixador in four days' time. So far we haven't discovered who's responsible for the answerphone. It's in an empty office. We should know by the time you get to Lisbon tomorrow.

'I want you to find out what the salesman has, and whether it's genuine or another Hitler Diary hoax. Whatever he has, we want it. We don't want the press conference to go ahead in any circumstances.'

'How do I do that?'

'In any way you can. You can even buy it. Funds will be provided through a neutral bank.'

'How much?'

'Sufficient.'

'How much?'

'*Stern* paid two million pounds sterling for the Hitler Diaries in 1983. That was for a set of books they believed to be real and an historical archive. Taking inflation into account, we've doubled that figure.'

'Four million?' Lacey was stunned. 'Who am I working for?'

'The backer doesn't concern you. Your job is to obtain whatever is on offer. If possible, without paying for it.'

It was all right for Bryson to say the backer was not his concern, but Lacey was still going through the possibilities, and there were not that many.

'So who's selling?'

Bryson shrugged.

'Who knows? An old friend of Blunt's? A Soviet out to make mischief or money? Hard currency is in short supply in Moscow. I don't know who's selling, but the feeling is someone has stumbled on the file by accident. The Lisbon connection is likely to be a middleman.'

Lacey was still coming to terms with four million pounds. 'Why is all this stuff considered so important? It's an embarrassment, nothing more.'

'It's an embarrassment the British Government, the royal family and the Kennedys would prefer not to endure.'

'Sam. Why is it such a big deal?'

'You're making the mistake of evaluating its importance by the price I've put on it.' He shook his head. 'The amount of money is immaterial.'

'Four million is very material.'

'Not if it ensures privacy for two very influential families.'

'It's not going to bring down the monarchy.'

'No, it's not, but it wouldn't put them in a good light if it was splashed all over the tabloids. The street anarchists would have a field day. In America, there's a new generation of Kennedys who wouldn't welcome the attention. The family image has been badly tarnished in recent years. A smear story about their grandfather would provide another excuse for a look at the sins of their fathers.'

Lacey shrugged.

'So? They committed a few.'

Bryson raised his eyebrows.

'What's this holier than thou attitude, Peter?'

'Maybe I'm past the age of heroes.' Lacey smiled to ease the tension. 'I'm just bitching, Sam. Nothing serious. My soul is still filed in Central Registry.'

Bryson let the silence impose a truce.

'Across the river, they think you're a character. That's why they put up with you. But one of these days, you're going to have to make a decision, Peter.'

Lacey nodded.

'I know.'

'Being in the Service is a lot like religion. You need faith.'

'Blind faith?'

'Sometimes.'

'When blind faith becomes blind obedience you're getting close to a set of ethics that didn't stand up too well at Nuremberg.'

Bryson sighed and smiled.

'Do you want to make that decision today?'

Lacey smiled back.

'I can't.'

'Why not?'

'Because you've got nobody else to send to Lisbon.'

'That's true.'

Lacey said: 'If I have to start bargaining, how do I know how much to spend?'

'You won't have to bargain. You'll have an expert with you. If it comes to buying the stuff, he'll evaluate and negotiate. Your instructions are not to look at what's on offer. When you get it, he takes charge of it.'

Lacey lit another cigarette.

Bryson watched him and waited for the reaction.

Lacey exhaled smoke.

'So. I'm just a minder.'

'No, this is your operation. You take his advice on Blunt's legacy; he takes your advice on everything else.' Lacey remained silent and Bryson added, 'It's necessary.'

'Who is he?'

'Ian Lamont-Smith.'

'A hyphen?'

'I'm afraid so.' Bryson smiled. 'You never know, you might like this one.'

'What's his background?'

'Sandhurst, Black Watch, a rugby international. His grandfather was an equerry to the royal family and he's an excellent free-lance archivist. Sotheby's use him from time to time. So do we.'

'When do I meet him?'

'Tomorrow morning at Heathrow.'

'What's my cover in Lisbon?'

Bryson held up two large brown envelopes, one in each hand.

He waved the bulkier envelope in his left hand and said, 'Briefing.' He waved the other and said: 'Cover. Lamont-Smith is travelling as Ian Alexander and you're his associate. The pair of you are representing an unnamed collector. In deals like this, it isn't necessary to reveal your principal, just to show that your principal can afford to be represented.'

Lacey took the envelopes and Bryson continued speaking.

'Further information will be at your hotel in Lisbon by the time you get there.'

Lacey said: 'What about protection?'

'What do you mean?'

'You know what I mean. I want a gun.'

Bryson frowned.

'Portugal is our oldest ally. I don't think they'll take kindly to you walking down main street packing a rod.'

'I don't care what they'll take kindly to. I want a meeting in Lisbon with someone who will provide me with proper protection. A Browning will do.'

His head of section pursed his lips in disapproval but Lacey maintained his stubborn look.

'I don't think this is necessary, you know.'

'If it isn't, I won't shoot anybody. But if this deal's worth what you think it is, there could be other professionals out there who lack your sense of fair play and generosity. They might prefer to spend a few quid on bullets rather than four million in an auction. I'd like to be prepared.'

Bryson nodded reluctantly.

'All right. I'll arrange it.'

Lacey's interest had lapsed. He was being sent to sweep up the dirt of the royal families of Britain and America. The assignment wasn't retrieval; it was garbage disposal. But that was why he had accepted the Queen's shilling; that was what D14a specialized in.

Bryson was right, the time was approaching when he

would have to make a decision about his future. But for now
. . . ? For now he would make the most of it.

He said, 'Should I wear a suit?'

Bryson smiled, relieved he had accepted the job.

'Peter. For the next few days you'll be a millionaire. You
can wear what you like.'

TWO

It was the first time Lacey had been a millionaire. Back in his own office he smiled at the absurdity of the situation. It deserved a celebration. He telephoned Susan at the antique and bric-à-brac shop in Bromley.

Lucy, her partner, answered. For once she hid the antipathy she felt for him and was almost pleasant.

When Susan came on the phone, Lacey said: 'What's wrong with Lucy?'

'Nothing.'

'She sounds human.'

Susan laughed. 'Don't start. She's just in a good mood.'

'My God. Is this a first?'

'You're rotten. She's often in a good mood.'

'Is she on a promise from Corduroy Michael?'

Lucy's husband Michael was a bearded English teacher who was as exciting as the corduroy jacket he always wore.

'I wouldn't be surprised. She wears skirts these days. She's become very feminine.'

She had started wearing skirts when Michael had threatened divorce six months before.

'That statement may be liable under the Trades Description Act.'

'Swine. She's made an effort.'

'Maybe she should shave as well.'

'You have a cruel streak that always peaks when we mention Lucy.'

'It's jealousy.'

'Hah!'

'It *was*.' He stressed the past tense. 'I always thought she fancied you.'

29

'Idiot.'

'She wore boiler suits and no make-up and read the *Guardian*. How many clues do you need?'

'Is there a point to this conversation?'

'Yes.' He remembered the cigarettes and removed the packet from his jacket pocket, swivelled in his chair, and put them back in the filing-cabinet drawer with the Jim Beam. 'I'm coming home early. Thought I might meet you at the shop and take you for lunch.'

It had been Susan's taunt that he couldn't stop smoking that had made him try. All you need is willpower, he had told her. That and your lungs removing.

'Lovely. Lucy won't mind. Why?'

He paused. He couldn't tell her he was a proxy millionaire. He told her another truth instead.

'I've got a short-notice trip.'

'All your trips are short notice.' She kept her voice neutral. 'How long will you be away?'

'Two or three days, that's all. It's nothing special.'

Susan knew he couldn't tell her any more and she knew she couldn't ask.

'What time will you be here?'

'About one.'

'I'll be waiting,' she said.

He broke the connection and opened the top drawer of his desk to look at the photograph of his wife that lay there. It was a snapshot he had taken in Greece six months before; her skin was brown, her hair windblown. She looked good for forty-two. Christ, she'd always looked good but age had improved her.

Age hadn't improved him. The bastard had subtly altered the distribution of his bodyweight so that he got out of breath if he ran for a train and had to buy trousers a size bigger. Thank God Susan didn't mind him the way he was. He'd have a hell of a job finding anyone else.

Old leather jackets and old leather faces only seemed to be attractive if they were at the sharp end of a lot of money. But he was forgetting. Today his were. He would buy Susan a present from that lingerie shop in Bromley. Something they would both enjoy.

He telephoned the minicab firm they used and arranged a car. Normally he commuted from his home in Beckenham by train but he decided he was already on assignment.

He picked up his briefcase and put both envelopes inside. The rules said that no files should be taken from the security of the office, that any documents of a high classification in current use by analyst or field operative should be locked in that individual's safe overnight. Bryson had a master-key and the sanction on who had the need to know what. In practice, Lacey knew most of what was happening in the department. He also took no notice of the rules.

Lacey left the office, cut through to St Martin's Lane, and waited for the car outside the Duke of York's Theatre. His timing was perfect. A maroon Ford moved through the traffic and stopped at the pavement.

He recognized the driver, who said: 'Traffic's a bastard.'

'The traffic's always a bastard.'

Lacey got into the back, his choice of seat indicating he wanted to be left alone rather than talk. He opened his briefcase and took out the fat envelope. It contained two background assessments: one relating to the Biarritz Agreement and Second World War collaboration; the other relating to the unmasking of Blunt as a traitor and his interrogation.

Blunt went back in the envelope and, as the car pushed its way through the traffic towards Waterloo Bridge and the road to suburbia, he immersed himself in the lesser-known perfidies of the Second World War. He was surprised to be surprised by what he read.

Lacey had spent many years as an analyst and realized truth was only self-evident to people who wished to believe it; he knew that truth had many faces and came in many shades of grey. But this document cast doubt on the popular myths of Britain's Finest Hour.

The post-war Britain he'd grown up in believed itself to be the island democracy that had stood alone against Hitler.

Dickie Attenborough being brave at Dunkirk had summed it up. He'd always viewed the war as uncomplicated history with good guys and bad guys; he'd followed its tragedies and triumphs in the company of Noel Coward and Errol Flynn. He still did, every time the movies were rerun on television.

Now he was discovering that while civilians and servicemen had made the sacrifices, puppet masters on both sides of the Atlantic had been up to their armpits in Machiavellian plots that paid no regard to morality but were governed by greed and power.

According to this, the Second World War had not been a crusade against a tyrant who wanted to exterminate Jews and rule the world. Peace with Germany had almost happened and had always been a consideration, before and during hostilities. If the percentages had been right, peace *would* have happened and the Second World War would have been fought against Russia. Some of the biggest names in commerce and government in Britain and America had been involved in the on-going treachery, deceit and dishonour.

Lacey put a hand to his pocket. Old habits. He was thinking too much and needed a distraction. He should stop thinking, stop making judgements, and wallow in the unsavoury revelations. Let them wash around him and see where they led.

By the time they reached Bromley he had almost drowned. He packed his briefcase, got out of the car, and walked the last fifty yards. He was so engrossed in his thoughts that he walked past The Lingerie Boutique.

When he pushed open the door of the shop the bell rang like the start of the first round but there was no Lucy to fight. He negotiated the elephant-foot umbrella stand that had remained unsold for four years, and looked up to see Susan walking towards him from the office at the back.

She wore a slim, black, wool dress, black stockings and high heels. He remembered he had missed The Lingerie Boutique.

He said: 'You don't look like you run an antique shop.'

'Don't I?'

32

She smiled and leant against him as she kissed his cheek.

'You look as though you run a brothel.' He held her waist to prolong the contact. 'A very high-class brothel.'

Her smile broadened into a grin.

'When you get a trip you always want to screw.'

'Make love.'

'Screw.'

He shrugged.

'Absence makes the heart grow fonder.'

'Your heart's in a funny place. Besides, you're going away, not coming back.'

'That's right. I forgot.' He ran a hand over her hip. 'I suppose that means we'll have to do it again when I get back.'

Susan laughed.

'Do I still get lunch, or are you going to have me here?'

He looked over her shoulder and saw Lucy watching them from the hatch in the office.

'It's a tempting offer but I don't trust your Alsatian. Lunch first.'

'What?' Susan looked round and waved at Lucy. 'Thanks Luce!' she called to her. 'Bastard,' she muttered to her husband.

They left, the bell signalling the end of the round.

Susan had changed her corrugated Citroën van for a Ford Transit, which was parked at the side of the shop.

She had described it as a business investment and had said it would be marvellous for the sort of house-clearance that could produce lost art treasures from the attics of Bromley residents who had died too old to realize what they possessed.

Lacey had said that sort of house-clearance didn't happen any more as the attics had long been picked over by third cousins twice removed during biannual visits to drink tea, eat cake and check the contents of their inheritance.

He said she had bought it because she liked its radio, bucket seats and paint job – it was black with a jagged red stripe down each side. It looked as if she'd got it from the A Team.

33

She unlocked her door and Lacey waited by her side.

She said: 'You want to drive?'

'No. I want to watch you climb in.'

'Pervert.'

'Yes.'

She climbed in, showing a stocking top.

'Satisfied?'

'No, but I'm getting there.'

He went round to the passenger door and climbed in alongside her.

'The Coach?' she said.

'Yes.'

The Coach and Horses was a pub in the country they kept for themselves. It sat at the side of a village green and a pond full of ducks. They didn't go there to socialize with other people; they went there to be together.

Susan manoeuvred the van into the traffic and signalled left at the roundabout. In making the turn she cut in front of a motorcyclist and caused a saloon car to brake.

Lacey watched with amusement.

'This vehicle's changed your personality.'

'Don't be silly.'

'You never did this in the Citroën.'

'I couldn't do this in the Citroën.'

The driver of the saloon accelerated alongside and honked his horn.

Susan smiled and gave him the finger.

'I'm married to a road hog.'

'I'm married to a male chauvinist pig. Do they know at the office you're a pervert?'

Lacey laughed.

'They think I'm a character.'

'I thought you were a leading man?'

'We're not allowed star billing.'

She took her eyes off the road for a moment to smile at him.

'Never mind. You're my leading man.'

'Thank God love is blind.'

'Why?'

'Have you looked at me lately? I'm overweight, my face is flabby . . . look at the brown freckles on the backs of my hands. I never had freckles on the backs of my hands. Now I've got rampant age spots. Another couple of years and they'll join up and I'll turn ginger.'

Susan laughed.

'I never thought you'd turn ginger.'

He looked at her reproachfully.

'Age is a terrible thing. I'm fifty this year. When you look at me, you see what you saw twenty-five years ago. You remember how I used to look. But to everybody else I'm past it. A boring old fart.'

'No I don't.'

'What?'

'I don't look at you and see what I saw twenty-five years ago. I see you as you are. You're not past it.' She shrugged. 'You might be a little worn around the edges and you have put on weight, but, well, that makes you cuddly.'

Lacey looked through the windscreen. This conversation suddenly put into perspective all the problems of the world he'd been dealing with since Bryson had briefed him on the Biarritz Agreement.

'Cuddly?' he said. 'Worn around the edges? What the hell does that mean?'

'You know, lived-in.'

'A block of flats is lived-in. The railway arches at Charing Cross are lived-in. What sort of lived-in?'

Susan was laughing too much to reply straight away.

'Good God, Peter, you're paranoid.'

'Yes but lived-in. Where, lived-in?'

'All right. A Bloomsbury, Bohemian type of lived-in. OK?'

Lacey was surprised that the image mollified him. He was also surprised at getting upset.

Susan said: 'Everybody gets older. It's the one thing you can't avoid.'

'Yes, but some do it better than others. Look at you. Me, I'm cuddly. You, you're bloody gorgeous.'

She laughed again and then said: 'Am I?'

'Yes, you are.'

'Thank you. You're not so bad yourself.'

'You wait till we get home. I'll show you bloody cuddly.'

The lunch and anticipation were both enjoyable but neither of them made any pretence when they got home. They went straight upstairs.

Susan pulled the curtains against the afternoon sunshine and slipped out of her dress and he slipped out of everything. They climbed on to the bed and discovered each other all over again in a shady world of urgency and caught breath.

The first ten minutes were frantic and wanton. Then the urgency was replaced by sweat and sensuality and they lost track of time. He certainly wasn't cuddly now, she thought. She'd tell him later.

It was much later when they finished and he pulled a sheet over them. She lay in the crook of his arm and luxuriated in the smell of sex they had created. Tensions had gone; tenderness remained. She let him go to sleep before she moved to make herself more comfortable.

Afterwards she could tell he had wanted a cigarette. Before settling into drowsiness his hand had gone automatically to the bedside table. She had almost told him there was a packet in the chest of drawers.

She had manoeuvred him into agreeing to give up. Part of her argument had been the dangers of passive smoking; she had deliberately made him feel guilty about damaging her lungs in order to save his. In the process she had given herself a large dose of guilt. So how could she now tell him she missed the distinctive aroma of French tobacco at times such as this?

His habit had also been an early warning system about his gremlins. Three years after the psychiatrists had put him back together again and said he was cured, he still became introverted to the point of depression. He used to blame the gremlins, and although he no longer admitted their presence she knew they still came. When they did, always

36

at night, he would get out of bed and prowl the house silently.

The gremlins, he'd told her, didn't like the daylight or French cigarettes. All he had to do was survive until dawn. In the past she would awake in the night and smell the tobacco and know he was doing his John Wayne act, calling them out and shooting them down.

Now he no longer had the cigarettes and she no longer had the warning and she had assuaged her guilt by hiding a packet in the chest of drawers just in case. Just in case what?

Susan lay on her side and looked at her hand on the pillow. The fingers were long and slender, the nails red and pointed. It was an elegant hand, a mature hand. It was a hand that was getting old. Rubber kitchen gloves and creams could protect it just so much but eventually the wrinkles would get deeper and the skin would lose its elasticity.

They were both getting old. No, not old, older. Hell, she wasn't going to give in without a fight and she wasn't going to let Peter ruin his health with tobacco. She had teased him about his age but was seriously happy about the way he looked and the way they were. Perhaps it was just as well he didn't realize how attractive he was; or was she remembering the way he was, as he had said?

She smiled.

Bloody gorgeous. He had also said bloody gorgeous. That was nice.

But was he remembering twenty odd years ago when they had been students in a flat in Durham and hadn't been able to keep their hands off each other? Maybe both their perspectives were affected by memories.

She moved a foot so that it rested on his ankle.

Lust had always been a strong bond in their relationship. At one time, it had disgusted her. She had enjoyed the sex, but afterwards had wondered why she had succumbed to such desires with a man she didn't love. Maybe if she had loved him they wouldn't have been so carnal.

That was in the wilderness years when their marriage had gone to hell and back and they hadn't even noticed. They

37

had lived in the same house, undertaken social engagements and stumbled from one anniversary to the next. Their most meaningful exchanges had been rows that were kept deliberately brief to save the embarrassment of discovering they no longer had a relationship. Rows and sex. A recipe for survival. She should have been an agony aunt.

They had both changed three years before. He had lost his apathy somewhere in Europe on an assignment that went wrong. She had lost hers when faced with the possibility of divorce and the knowledge that he had not just slept with another woman, he had loved another woman.

When he told her, in that same country pub by the village green and the duck pond, she had felt used, second-hand. When he told her the woman had died she had felt pleased.

Susan had decided that although she didn't have much of a marriage she didn't want to let it go. She fought for it and for Peter, and slowly they had found each other again.

The psychiatrists had taken the credit for putting him back together but Susan knew different. She had put him back together. They had come close to losing each other once; they wouldn't lose each other again. She drifted into sleep, still smiling.

THREE

The sound of the evening newspaper being delivered through the front door letter-box awakened him. He looked at his watch and saw it was four-thirty.

Beside him, Susan still slept. He kept his own breathing shallow and regular so as not to disturb her as he eased himself out of bed. He pulled on a bathrobe, avoided the floorboard that creaked, and escaped to the landing.

He scratched his groin as he went downstairs and smiled in memory of what had sent him to sleep. He coughed and his throat hardly hurt. It was a strange experience. Never mind, there was always caffeine.

In the kitchen he spooned coffee into the percolator and took a quick snort of its pungency before switching on the machine.

He collected his briefcase from the hall, ignored the evening newspaper that lay on the mat, and took Blunt, Kennedy and the Duke of Windsor back to the kitchen.

Britain and America had both had appeasers in the 1930s who saw more profit from an alliance with Hitler than in opposing him.

In Britain, the Duke's attempts to keep his country out of war were backed by politicians and establishment figures whose plotting changed to patriotism when the Allies started winning and a German alliance lost its attraction.

In America, big business led the fight to stay at peace with Germany. Some of the nation's major industrialists were fascists with plans that ranged from overthrowing their own government to making sure trade didn't suffer whatever happened.

The Rockefellers, Standard Oil, the Chase National Bank, Henry Ford and Irenee du Pont of General Motors all supported the capitalist domination of Europe and the destruction of the Soviet Union through alliance with Nazi Germany.

They used proxies, neutral countries, subsidiaries and foreign companies to ensure the store remained open and in profit even after war happened.

It was inevitable that Joseph Kennedy should have been involved. His position as United States Ambassador to Britain before and during the war made him an influential figure.

In 1938 he negotiated a peace agreement in London with Goering's representative that guaranteed a United States loan of between a half to one billion dollars in gold to Germany to help establish the Nazis' New Order. Roosevelt scuppered the deal.

When war in Europe broke out in 'thirty-nine, Kennedy was on hand to help smooth an arrangement between Standard Oil of America and the German chemical giant I.G. Farben, the company that later provided the poison gas for extermination camps. In the Hague Memorandum, Farben patents were locked into Standard Oil agreements to avoid their seizure by the US Government, and the two conglomerates agreed to remain in business together, whether or not the US entered the war.

Kennedy arranged for the patents to be flown by diplomatic bag to Paris, for onward despatch to the United States by special courier.

He was involved with Lord Halifax and an Anglo–German peace plan in February 1940, and in May the same year he was involved in a spy scandal when one of his cypher clerks was arrested for supplying to British Nazis copies of secret messages between Roosevelt and Churchill. They showed the President was planning to enter the war despite opposition in the US. If they had been made public they would have damaged Roosevelt's chances of re-election.

The Biarritz Agreement no longer seemed unlikely. Lacey wondered what would have happened if it had been successful and Britain and America had lined up with Germany against Russia.

Maybe Britain's special relationship would now be with Berlin instead of Washington. Maybe there would be no special relationship, just a Pax Germanica, to be endured until time eroded the Third Reich, as it had the empires of Rome, Britain and Russia.

Upstairs he heard the shower running.

He had drunk the pot of coffee and it was almost six o'clock. He was hungry and he still had more reading to do.

Lacey stretched back in the chair and stared at the ceiling. He realized he was uncomfortable and cold. The afternoon warmth had gone and the evening chill was a reminder that it was still only April.

April in Lisbon. It didn't have the same ring to it as April in Paris. He knew Paris well, and Lisbon indifferently. Maybe the reason was that he had fallen in love with Paris the first time he had been there. It was a city that bred enthusiasm. Lisbon bred indifference.

It would have been all right if he had been taking Susan but instead he had a double-barrelled royalist for company. Ian Lamont-Smith. He wondered what he would be like. Then he stopped wondering, and went upstairs to join Susan in the shower.

When they finally came downstairs they ate chicken and salad and drank a bottle of moselle. Susan wore silk pyjamas and Lacey track-suit trousers and a tennis shirt. She watched television and he listened to Mozart string quintets on a Walkman while he read the remaining papers.

When he had finished, he switched off the boy genius, removed the headphones and took the papers through to the study and opened the wall safe. In it was a bundle wrapped in soft leather that held a Heckler and Koch 9mm handgun

41

and a brown envelope that contained the passport and documents of a false identity that Bryson didn't know about. He shouldn't be in possession of either. He put the files in with them and locked the safe.

On the way to the kitchen he stuck his head round the door into the lounge.

'I'm having a beer. Do you want anything?'

'I'll have some more wine.'

He got a Beck's and a second bottle of moselle from the refrigerator and carried them back into the living-room. He poured wine for Susan and sipped the beer from the bottle. She was watching a situation comedy which involved a middle-aged couple and sexual innuendo.

'Any good?'

'Recycled rubbish. But it doesn't affect the ozone layer and it relaxes the brain.'

'You should try meditation.'

'This is meditation. For housewives.'

'You're not a housewife. You're a sex machine.'

'Maybe I should go into business.'

'You'd make a fortune.'

'Wouldn't you mind?'

'Not if I could watch.'

She laughed and threw a cushion.

'You're a bastard.'

'I love you.'

'I love you, too.'

'Then can I put a video on?'

She laughed again.

'Let me guess. *Casablanca*?'

'No.' He walked to the shelves where he kept the video editions of classic films. He pulled out *To Have And Have Not*, in which Bogart was teamed with Lauren Bacall. He held up the box so she could see the cover. 'It's the one where she teaches him to whistle.'

She nodded.

Bogart and Bacall. He was a fan of both. How could you not admire a man who said the trouble with the world is that

42

everybody in it is about three drinks behind? Another real-life love story, too.

He said, 'What's the first thing you think about the Duke and Duchess of Windsor?'

'He gave up his throne to marry the woman he loved.'

'What else do you remember?'

'She was American, divorced, and the royal family didn't like her. He bought her lots of jewels – the Windsor Collection. They were auctioned for millions after she died. Elizabeth Taylor bought some.'

'Is that it?'

She shrugged.

'Just about. It was a great love story at the time. It lasted all their lives.'

There had been a footnote in the file about the auction. Sotheby's had held it in Geneva. It had been a marketing man's dream. The mystique surrounding the couple who had defied convention to follow their hearts, had boosted the value of the gems. The wealthy had telephoned their bids from around the world; they had all wanted to own a part of the legend. The total raised had been more than thirty million pounds.

He wondered if the mystique would act as a magnet again, in the auction he had been commissioned to stop. He wondered how much people would be prepared to pay to destroy or safeguard the twin legends of the Windsors and the Kennedys, and what they would be prepared to do, to obtain the legacy left by Blunt.

What did it matter now, so many years later? Surely memories were better left the way they were. Love made the world go round much more pleasantly than treachery.

He took the cassette from its box and put it into the video machine. At least he could rely on Bogart and Bacall. The picture might be an imitation of *Casablanca* but the chemistry that sparked between the pair on screen gave it an extra quality that made their memory special.

Susan joined him on the settee and he put his arm around

her shoulders and they watched the credits roll and Bogey get ready to take on the Nazis, the reluctant hero with a strict code of honour.

Lacey wished, one more time, that life could be a movie with clear decisions, the approval of an audience and the love of a beautiful woman. He squeezed Susan's shoulder. He would have to settle for one out of three.

FOUR

Heathrow's Terminal 1 was hectic with commuting business-men and middle-aged couples escaping on three-day breaks to European capitals at bargain rates. Ian Lamont-Smith didn't fit into either category.

He was standing, as arranged, by the machine that dispensed fresh orange juice, and holding a copy of *Tatler* as if it was a sign, which it was.

The archivist was tall, with sharp, hawkishly aristocratic features, and thinning hair brushed straight back. He wore tan cavalry twill trousers, a checked waistcoat, tweed hacking jacket and a silk cravat, that all had an undefined dishevelled look. He scattered ash carelessly from a cigarette.

Lacey had been wishing it was a movie and now saw that God had a sense of humour. He had been teamed with a debonair leading man from early English talking pictures, whose age was indeterminate.

'Ian Alexander?'

Lacey used Lamont-Smith's cover name and displayed the half-naked young woman on the front of the copy of *Penthouse* he carried as identity. Someone at Century House also had a sense of humour.

The man's expression was open, his eyes twinkling. The corners of his mouth twitched in amusement. Maybe it was Lacey's leather jacket.

'Barnes?'

Lacey was travelling as Peter Barnes.

Lamont-Smith dropped the cigarette and stood on it and they shook hands. His first two fingers were badly stained with nicotine.

'Call me Ian.'

45

'I'm Peter.'

'Good show.'

The grip was firm, the accent perfect, the mannerisms sublime. He was a walking anachronism, even by civil service standards. No one would believe he and Lacey were members of the same planet, let alone the same firm.

Lacey said, 'We should check in.'

'Right ho.'

Lamont-Smith picked up a briefcase and holdall that were by his feet and they set off towards a British Airways desk. Lacey dropped the *Penthouse* magazine into a litter-bin and Lamont-Smith paused to take it out again. Lacey looked at him and the man grinned without embarrassment.

'I enjoy a bedtime read. Especially when it's got big tits. Haw, haw, haw.'

The laugh was a stage prop. What on earth had Lacey been lumbered with?

They checked their bags and went through passport control and security body checks, watched their briefcases ride a conveyor belt through a radar screen, and walked through an alarm gate to retrieve them.

Lamont-Smith looked back at the security officer who had searched him.

'Bit thorough. Hands all over the place. Reminds me of a squaddie I once knew. Big Jock McKinley. Hung like a donkey. We had to give him a transfer. His slow march in a kilt was obscene.'

It was an intriguing image.

Lacey said, 'This way.'

Lamont-Smith said, 'I say, do you think we've got time for a quick one?'

'A quick one?'

'Drink. Snifter. Hair of the dog. Met an old chum last night, hadn't seen him for years. We kept having the one we came in for until we lost count. Left me with a bit of a head.'

Lacey said, 'It's nine-thirty.'

'What? Late as that? Haw, haw, haw.' He slapped Lacey on the arm. 'Joke.'

Lacey grinned. What was it that Bacall had said? She never knew a man worth his salt that didn't drink. It appeared Lamont-Smith was worth a sackful.

'OK. A quick one.'

Lacey had a bottle of Beck's and Lamont-Smith had a pint of lager, followed by a second pint of lager.

'Dehydration,' he explained.

He took out a packet of Camels and offered them but Lacey declined.

'Do you mind?'

'Go ahead. I'll enjoy the fumes.'

'Ah. A member of the church of latter day reformists.'

'I'm still at the trying stage.'

'Keep on trying, old boy. I admire you for it.'

He lit a cigarette and drew the smoke in with a smile. Lacey waited, but he didn't seem as if he was going to let any of it out again.

Lacey said, 'Are you married?'

'Occasionally. I'm between engagements at the moment.' The smile became a grin. 'I believe the expression is resting. You?'

'I'm married. More than twenty years.'

'Good God. To the same woman?'

'Yes. The same woman.'

'By choice?'

Lacey laughed. 'By choice.'

'Incredible.'

'Lots of people stay married.'

'Yes, trapped in holy deadlock.' He shook his head. 'You don't look the type. She must be special.'

'She is.'

'I thought mine were, at the time.'

'How many have you had?'

'Four. Well, two really. I never divorced the second, so I suppose that invalidates the last two ceremonies.'

Lacey didn't think he was joking. Perhaps it was safer to change the subject. Perhaps it was time to talk business.

'How do you feel about this trip?'

47

Lamont-Smith swigged the lager and smiled.

'I always feel extremely comfortable with four million pounds in my pocket. Particularly if it's somebody else's. Of course, I would have preferred cash . . .' He grinned. 'Still, I get a free trip to Lisboa, all expenses paid. Should be fun.'

He pronounced Lisboa with extended vowels.

'You speak Portuguese?'

'Good God, no. Who on earth wants to speak Portuguese? Even the Portuguese don't want to speak Portuguese. No, old boy. I shout in English.'

Lacey nodded. It had been silly of him to ask.

'This . . . Biarritz Agreement. I've read the assessments but you're the expert. Could it be genuine?'

'Of course. The Duke of Windsor was conned into giving up his throne and wanted it back. Besides, he liked Hitler. There's a damn good chance it's genuine.'

'How about giving me some background?'

'Delighted. I like nothing more than the chance to be erudite. Too late for another, I suppose?'

Lacey looked at the electronic departure board. Their flight was being called.

'Yes, it is. Can you last until we get on the plane?'

Lamont-Smith smiled.

'I'll try.'

They talked as they walked to the departure gate.

'How much background do you want?'

'I'll tell you to stop when we get to Lisbon.'

'Right ho. Well, let's see. I suppose we should start with the Russian Revolution. The damn Bolshies of 1917. When they murdered the tsar and his family, they scared the shit out of the rest of Europe's royal houses. They were all related, you see, ran Europe like a family business.

'The Russkies also started a trend. Revolutions became all the rage and by the time the Second World War started, London was full of the uncrowned heads of Europe, all living at Claridge's and the Ritz. Churchill called them the Beggar's Opera.

'It was the Russian Revolution that made our royals change their name. They were Saxe-Coburg-Gothas until then, but the Bolshie climate in dear old blighty made them change it to Windsor. All the rest did the same. Battenberg became Mountbatten, Teck became Cambridge, and so on. They were all foreigners. The Duke of Windsor spoke German better than he spoke English; his mother was German and the Kaiser was his father's cousin.

'In the 1930s Russia was still the bogeyman, so it wasn't surprising that Hitler's rise to power was actually welcomed by a lot of the English aristocracy. He was a buffer against Russia and revolution.'

They joined a moving walkway. Beyond the windows of the corridor, aeroplanes sat on the Tarmac in the rain, being fuelled, provisioned, cleaned; disgorging and accepting passengers via the umbilical tubes that linked them to the gates and allowed people to circumnavigate the globe without once having to breathe fresh air.

Ahead of them was a bald-headed man of about forty who didn't look comfortable in his bright blue track suit. His blond wife was younger, her blouson was pink and her ski pants tight and white. Lacey admired her panty-line while Lamont-Smith picked up the thread again.

'Now, the Duke of Windsor. In the 1920s he was the most eligible bachelor in the world. Blond, athletic, handsome, and his father ruled an empire. He was privileged and he indulged himself and the British Press protected his image. He could do what he liked and get away with it. It was his favourite expression: I've got away with it.

'He was a man born to rule, but he wanted to be more than a constitutional monarch.'

They left the moving walkway at the appropriate gate, following the bald-headed man and his wife. Most of the rest of their fellow passengers waited in rows of easy chairs. A steward and a stewardess were talking by a desk near the airbridge that led to their aeroplane. Embarkation had not yet started.

Lacey pointed to an empty row of seats that were furthest away from the gate and they sat down.

He said: 'The Duke must have known there was no chance of ever being more than a figurehead?'

'Wrong, old boy. Politicians were scared of him. He was so popular he could have caused a royalist revolution. He'd seen Hitler get eight million unemployed working in Germany and he wanted to do the same in Britain. He wanted to tackle poverty with radical plans. He would have, too, but the Establishment and his family stopped him. Wallis Simpson was the excuse. You've seen photographs of her, of course?'

'Yes. Mainly when she was older.'

'She was thirty-eight when they started their affair, he was a year older. She wasn't conventionally beautiful, but striking. He was besotted with her all his life. But she wasn't suitable for a King of England. She was American, married, and had one divorce already under her belt. Royalty married royalty; that was tradition. It still is.

'When the Queen married Prince Philip it was an arrangement between royal houses. They were third cousins in descent from Victoria and second cousins on his father's side. He was Prince of Greece and Denmark, his aunt was Queen of Sweden, and his name was Schleswig-Holstein-Sonderburg-Glucksburg.'

Lamont-Smith grinned.

'Poor old Bessie Wallis Warfield Simpson of Baltimore didn't stand a chance.'

'Then why risk all to marry her?'

'Because he loved her. And because he thought he could get away with it.'

'How?'

'He believed Wallis could be his morganatic wife; that he could rule and return the throne to the house of Windsor on his death, rather than to any offspring he and Wallis might have. This was where he was stitched up.

'Edward became king in 1936 and after a few months the Establishment had had enough of his modern ways. Baldwin, the Prime Minister, played the Wallis card to get rid of him.

He got Edward to declare that he was going to marry Wallis, then told him she was unacceptable and he'd have to choose between her and the throne.

'After making the declaration, there was only one choice an honourable man could make: he gave up the throne. Baldwin knew he would, he was a clever old sod.

'Baldwin also knew that if Edward hadn't declared his intention to marry her until *after* the coronation the following year, he would have been in such a strong position he might well have been able to have his morganatic marriage. He'd still have been king, been able to bully parliament, and stay at peace with Germany.'

Lacey said: 'History is full of ifs.'

'True. But this if stayed with the Duke of Windsor all his life, particularly in the years immediately after the abdication. He believed it was only a matter of time before he was restored to his throne and allowed to get on with the job for which he'd been trained.'

A stewardess made an announcement and passengers began getting to their feet, picking up hand luggage, and moving towards the gate. Lacey and Lamont-Smith remained seated.

Lacey said: 'What about Wallis? Did she love him?'

'I think so. Of course, they got trapped by history. The Press called it the greatest love story of the twentieth century.' He shrugged. 'After losing a throne and an empire, maybe they settled for being a love story.'

'Everything you've said so far gives the Duke the motive for treachery.'

'Not treachery, old boy. Motives for wanting to return to power in the best interests of his nation.'

'That seems like a fine line.'

'Not if you're born to be king. Not if you are an honourable man.'

'Honourable men killed Caesar.'

'Dishonourable ones got rid of Edward. You really do have to accept the fact that he was not ordinary. He'd been a king, he expected to be a king again, or a president, or even emperor of Europe. He was above treachery, he was negotiating in the same way monarchs had negotiated for hundreds of years. His aim was to achieve peace and unite Europe against Russia.'

They got up and went to the end of the queue, were checked through the gate by a stewardess, and took a short walk through the airbridge to enter the plane through the forward door. Their seats were in the back row of Club Class, which was half empty.

Lamont-Smith said: 'Do you mind if I have the aisle seat? My legs need all the space they can get.'

Lacey moved past him and sat down, putting his briefcase on the spare seat. Lamont-Smith put his briefcase in the overhead locker. Lacey suddenly appreciated the man's powerful build. He carried little excess weight around his middle and moved with the physical confidence of the international sportsman he had once been. Lacey buckled the seat-belt across a flabby stomach and thought someone had got their roles mixed up. The archivist was in far better shape than Lacey to be the minder.

Lacey said: 'My briefing says Wallis had Nazi connections.'

'So did most of London's social set. Fascist supporters were everywhere. You didn't have to hide your affinity. In the early thirties, Britain had four hundred thousand fascists. Wallis's opponents tried to make out she was a Nazi spy, but a lot of it was good old propaganda. There was a spy involved, but it wasn't Wallis. It was a chap called Charles Bedaux. Do you know about him?'

Lacey said: 'I've read the name. Edward and Wallis got married at his house in France.'

'That's right. He arranged the wedding and their visit to Germany to meet Hitler. He arranged lots of things. Bedaux was a self-made millionaire. Like other American businessmen, he wanted to expand into Europe. He did it by helping the Nazis set up the Biarritz Agreement.'

A stewardess offered them newspapers, which they both declined. Lamont-Smith put out a hand to hold her arm momentarily and gave her a matinée smile that crinkled his lips at the edges. Lacey stared in disbelief but it seemed to work; the young woman smiled back with more warmth than was recommended at training school.

Lamont-Smith said: 'I hate to be a nuisance but I'm a rather nervous flyer. I wonder, when we take off, if I could have a large gin and tonic?'

'Of course, sir. No problem.'

'And perhaps a lager?'

She firmed up the smile.

'I'll see to it.'

'I'd be very grateful.'

The stewardess returned to the front of the aircraft.

Lacey said: 'I don't believe that.'

'What?'

'The simpering.'

Lamont-Smith smiled proudly.

'Charm, old boy. I always put fanny first and booze second. Used to be a Deb's Delight.' The smile became a grin. 'Still have my moments.'

Lacey shook his head.

He said: 'Bedaux?'

'Bedaux. Right. In October 1936, Wallis was granted a decree nisi. In December 'thirty-six, Edward abdicated. For the sake of propriety, they both left England to stay in separate parts of Europe until the divorce became absolute six months later. She went to Cannes to stay with friends and he went to Austria.

'Even though they supposedly didn't know him, Bedaux offered his château near Paris for the wedding through a mutual friend, and they accepted. The wedding took place in June.'

He held up his hands as if to separate what he had just said from what he was about to say.

'That's always left me asking one question: why should Edward and Wallis get married at the house of somebody they'd never met? The answer is that they had met him. In fact, they were already in league with him.'

He raised a finger.

'At the end of March, Edward left the castle near Vienna where he'd been staying and moved to a place in the mountains near Salzburg. He was able to disappear for days at a time and during April he disappeared long enough to go to Paris.

'Bedaux arranged a very important meeting in private rooms at the Hotel Meurice in Paris in April. It allowed Edward and Wallis to be reunited and to discuss their future. The men with whom they discussed that future were Rudolf Hess, Martin Bormann and Errol Flynn.'

'Who?'

'Hess, Bormann and Flynn.'

Lacey wondered why he found it more difficult to accept that a Hollywood film star had been present rather than two important members of the National Socialist Party.

'Errol Flynn?'

'Yes.'

'Why?'

'He was an agent of influence for the Nazis. He'd been a member of the Mayfair fascist set in the thirties before going to America; he knew Edward and Wallis.'

'But he won Burma single-handed!'

'That was against the Japanese. He was a racist, too.'

'He was making films in Hollywood at that time.'

'He'd arrived in Europe in early March to visit the Spanish Civil War. He went back to America in late April.'

'Are you serious?'

'Of course. He worked for the Nazis throughout the war and was under permanent FBI surveillance. He visited the Duke and Duchess in the Bahamas; so did other agents.'

The aeroplane began taxiing towards its runway and the stewardess went through the pantomime with the oxygen mask and lifebelt. The lifebelt was called a Mae West after the most famous bosom in Hollywood. Lacey wondered if she'd been a spy too.

He shook his head.

'Go on.'

'The meeting discussed Edward's future role in Europe if war broke out between England and Germany, and smoothed the way for the Duke and Duchess to go to Germany as Hitler's guests after their wedding.'

He grinned. 'Good stuff, isn't it?'

'Great. You should write the screenplay. Sylvester Stallone as Errol Flynn, Danny DeVito as Hitler. Maybe Cher will play Mrs Simpson.'

Lamont-Smith laughed.

'It sounds far-fetched but it happened. The Paris meeting in April and the confirmation by Hitler at Berchtesgaden in October of what had been agreed sets everything else in context, including the meeting with Goering at Biarritz. Edward went to the Bahamas waiting for the day when Germany finally beat Britain and he could return as king.'

Lacey shook his head.

'Why haven't I heard this before?'

'Probably because Bedaux wasn't around to tell anyone. He was eventually arrested by the Americans for espionage in North Africa. The FBI took him back to the States and he committed suicide before he could go on trial.'

'Convenient.'

'It usually is.'

The aircraft was stationary at the end of the runway; it vibrated with the power of the engines revving for maximum thrust. The pilot released the brakes and it started its run. They passed velocity one, the pilot pulled back on the control column, the nose lifted and they were airborne.

Lacey said: 'All this and Hollywood.'

'Hollywood?'

'Errol Flynn.'

'Oh, I see. I thought you meant Kennedy.'

'Kennedy?'

'In the twenties, Joe Kennedy was a Hollywood boot-legger.'

'I thought he was a banker?'

'He started as a banker but he went West for excitement. In Hollywood he supplied booze during Prohibition and became a movie mogul. Edward, who was then Prince of Wales, helped him buy a film studio, and the actress Gloria Swanson was his lover – he had the family appetite for beautiful women. He gave up both Miss Swanson and the movies when his pictures didn't make money. He went into politics instead.'

Lacey said: 'I didn't realize the Duke and Kennedy were so closely connected.'

'That particular social set were all connected.'

'Ambassador Kennedy sounds as if he was quite a lad.'

'Oh, he was. A go-getting type of chap, like Bedaux. He had a great interest in money and power and wasn't too bothered how he got them. He used to tell his sons, it's not what you are that counts, it's what people think you are. Sounds like the family motto.'

The aircraft began to level out and Lacey watched the clouds through which they were flying and hoped their air traffic controller on the ground was paying close attention to the relevant radar screens without the handicap of a hangover or emotional problems that might affect his judgement.

Clouds always made him nervous. Air travellers might be served by the best technology in the world, but when their aircraft was flying blind they were still in the hands of somebody who might be feeling like death warmed up.

Beside him, the archivist stretched his legs and let down the folding table from the seat in front. The stewardess walked down the aisle with a tray of drinks. She off-loaded on to the table two miniatures of Gordon's gin, two cans of tonic, two cans of lager and four clear plastic beakers, two of them filled with ice.

'So kind,' Lamont-Smith said.

The girl blushed.

'Anything else, just ring.'

He rewarded her with a smile.

Lacey still couldn't work it out. Was it his accent, his height, his aftershave? Some undefinable air of superiority? For God's sake, the man was wearing a cravat. He hadn't seen anyone wearing a cravat for decades.

'Drink, Peter?'

Maybe that was it, the way he phrased a question like an order.

'Yes. I think I will.'

If only to reduce his stockpile.

Lamont-Smith passed over a beaker and a can of lager, and poured himself a gin and tonic. He sipped it to reduce the level and topped it up with the second miniature, by which time Lacey had opened his can of lager.

'Cheers!' said Lamont-Smith.

'Cheers,' said Lacey.

It was still not eleven in the morning and the man in charge of a four million pound bankroll was slipping comfortably into an alcoholic haze.

Lacey had known many drunks in his life; he'd been one himself; and he wondered what sort of drunk Lamont-Smith would be. Friendly and malleable or aggressive and awkward? He would find out in Lisbon.

FIVE

From the air, the Estoril coast on the approach to Lisbon was a green circuit board upon which a lazy programmer had cast a handful of silicon chips.

The colours in the sunshine were attractive. Green hill-sides, white houses and tower blocks, a blue sea that became golden where the Tagus met the Atlantic. The gold was a con, but then so was Lisbon.

Wide sand banks at the mouth of the estuary gave the waters a false lustre. Lacey had seen the quality of the pollution that fed the river as it floated through the port. He had also seen the pretty silicon chip housing at close quarters and had not been impressed.

The suburbs of Portugal's capital city were a jungle of high-rise apartments that were purpose-built slums. It was no wonder Benfica was one of the best supported football teams in the world – the club was a diversion that provided heroes for the deprived.

The aeroplane banked over the suspension bridge that linked Lisbon with the south. Below was the giant statue of Cristo Rei that stared at the city with outspread arms from a plinth on the south bank. It was a copy of the Rio de Janeiro original and had been erected in the 1950s as payment to God for keeping the nation neutral during the Second World War.

England's oldest ally had ducked the fight against Hitler as it had ducked most fights in modern history. In a way it was still neutral, despite its membership of NATO and the European Community. Both its location and political inclination were perfect to deal with any side of any conflict, particularly if the deal involved the dubious or illegal movement of armaments and ammunition. Where there was cash there was always a way, and Lisbon was second in the league table of cities that dealt in illegal arms. He should sneer: London was top.

It was appropriate that it was here that the Duke of Windsor had prevaricated in the summer of 1940. He had stayed in a villa at the seaside town of Cascais, a few miles down the coast, had played golf, visited the casino at Estoril, and met German agents in Lisbon. He lad been loath to sail into oblivion as the Governor of the Bahamas.

As the Duchess had said: 'It's not an appointment. It's more of a disappointment.'

Lacey had first been to Lisbon fifteen or sixteen years before. The city, he discovered, had the charm of a third world colonial capital that the builders were destroying by throwing up concrete housing estates around its edges.

He'd been back since and admired the new motorways that gave excellent views of the worst slums he'd seen in Europe on the drive through Amoreiras on the way to Sintra.

He had also taken the lift to the top of the plinth on which stood the Cristo Rei. The journey had taken him a little closer to heaven and showed him that Christ had feet of clay. On that upper level, directly beneath the statue, were packed souvenir kiosks that sold everything from Our Lady of Fatima keyrings to battery-operated plastic Sacred Hearts that lit up at the touch of a button, in a gaudy display of bad taste and Mammon.

Lamont-Smith buckled his seat-belt and prepared for landing. He had managed three more gin and tonics, and two quarter bottles of red wine with his lunch.

Lacey hated airline food with a passion and had eaten only cheese and a bread roll. Lamont-Smith, displaying the appetite of a bachelor, had devoured his own food before eating Lacey's as well. Lacey found the man was neither a friendly nor an aggressive drunk; more a replete one.

They took a taxi to the Hotel Ritz and checked into rooms that had a connecting door and balconies that looked out over the Edward VII gardens. At the desk, he had been handed an envelope.

Lacey opened the sliding glass door and went out on to the balcony and looked across the greenery to the roundabout at the top of the Avenida da Liberdade, whose circumference was big enough for chariot races and which encouraged drivers to believe they were Ben Hur. He'd forgotten how the Portuguese enjoyed blowing their car horns. Maybe it had been made compulsory.

The Embaixador Hotel, where the contents of Blunt's legacy were to be revealed in three days, was a ten-minute walk away, on one of the roads that spoked out from the other side of the roundabout. They hadn't stayed there because they didn't want to be seen to be connected with the proposed conference in any way. Lacey was pleased about that; the Embaixador was two star, the Ritz five star de luxe.

He read the note in the envelope before going back into his room and shutting out the noise. Lamont-Smith knocked and opened the connecting door. He had discovered the mini bar and had a glass in his hand. Lacey guessed it was not straight tonic.

'Quite nice, what?'

'Quite nice.'

'Any plans for this afternoon, old boy?'

'Yes. But not for you.'

'Spot of cloak and daggering?'

'I'll be back about five.'

'Fine. Don't worry about me.' He waved the glass. 'Might have a bit of a snooze. See you later.'

Lamont-Smith went back into his own room and closed the door.

The weather was ten degrees warmer than Britain and the sky was clear and blue but Lacey kept his leather jacket on. He pushed a paperback copy of a Ruth Rendell mystery into a pocket, hung a small Olympus camera around his neck and left the hotel.

He walked to the roundabout and crossed the Avenida

da Liberdade, which was the city's answer to the Champs-Elysées. It was pleasant to stroll down the wide avenue that led to the Tagus, and squint against the sun after the indifferent weather of an English spring.

Halfway down he took a side street to the left to join the thoroughfare that ran parallel, and passed a familiar red pillar box, another sign of Portugal's and Britain's close links. He was below the brothels here, in part of Lisbon's equivalent to Soho, with eating places, bars, cinemas and clubs. Live crabs hung from strings in restaurant windows alongside medieval displays of fish and game.

In another side street he found a small supermarket and bought a bottle of port and a box of pretzels. The check-out girl gave him a yellow plastic bag in which to put them.

The café he went to was near the rows of blue metal shoeshine stands where black men went to have white men kneel at their feet. He sat at a table on the pavement, with his back to a wall, put the supermarket bag on a spare chair and the paperback book in front of him. He ordered a beer, watched the world walk by, and wished he had a cigarette.

An elderly street seller spotted him, moved among the tables and offered a novelty key ring that featured an entwined naked couple. The man pressed the top of the key ring and a penis jabbed out from the male figure to penetrate its female partner.

Lacey laughed but shook his head and the man dropped his price from a thousand escudos to five hundred to three hundred in rapid succession. When Lacey was still not tempted he offered an alternative: a cigarette lighter that carried a picture of Our Lady of Fatima.

Sex and religion and tramps sleeping in the sun on the benches of Liberation Avenue and the steps of the National Theatre. It summed up the city.

The man went away and Lacey watched the odd mixture of races from the country's past go about their business. Pure and cross-bred peoples from Goa, Macao, Africa and Iberia, all busy going somewhere, all inevitably carrying a briefcase,

61

while the tourists hesitated and stared and consulted Berlitz travel guides.

His attention was taken by an attractive brunette walking along the street towards him, whose hair bounced like a commercial. She wore high heels and a blue silky dress that clung to her thighs as she moved and he wished he was wearing sunglasses so he could stare more blatantly. Even so, he thought he'd overdone it when she stopped at the café, moved past the other customers, and came to stand by his table.

In English, she said: 'I see you like Ruth Rendell?'

He was surprised.

'Prendergast?'

She sat down.

'That's right. Sally Prendergast.'

She had been to the same supermarket and put her bag on the same chair as Lacey's.

Lacey said: 'We should have made it dinner.'

She smiled sweetly. Her blue eyes were big, beautiful and intelligent.

'You wouldn't be good for my image.'

'I never did appreciate honest women.'

A waiter came to her much quicker than he had come to Lacey. In Portuguese she ordered a garoto – a small white coffee. Lacey understood what she said because his rudimentary knowledge of the language was based on menus and bars.

After the waiter had gone she said: 'Don't take offence. I'm a secretary at the embassy and no one has reason to follow me. I wouldn't want to provide one. Also, my boyfriend wouldn't like it.'

'I don't blame him. My wife wouldn't like it, either.'

'Besides, you're too old for me.'

'And now you've gone and spoilt it. Just as my ego was recovering.'

'I'm sure you'll survive. I'm told you usually do.'

'Ah. Someone's talked out of turn.'

'Certainly not. I was briefed.'

The waiter brought the coffee in a glass. She opened her handbag and took out a packet of local SG cigarettes and a lighter. It didn't have a picture of Our Lady of Fatima on it. She offered the packet and he had a slight tussle with temptation before he refused. She took a cigarette and lit it.

He said: 'Don't you know it's bad for you?'

'There's nothing worse than a convert.'

'It's antisocial.'

'Not here. Tobacco is a long way down the list of health hazards. It's still a fashionable thing to do.'

'I knew there had to be something to like about the place.'

'You don't like Portugal?'

'I don't know it well enough.' He raised his glass. 'The beer's nice.'

He was trying to get a whiff of her cigarette smoke but he was upwind of the breeze.

She said: 'First things first. The advertisement?'

He nodded.

'It appeared in yesterday's *Washington Post* as well as today's *Times*.'

He shrugged. It had always been a possibility.

Sally Prendergast said: 'Anyway, your man is Enrico Latimer. He's a lawyer. He's married with two teenage children. He lives in the city; has a house up against the castle walls. His family's away at the moment, visiting his mother-in-law in Porto. He also sees a mistress at Sintra on a regular basis. His office is near the Palace Square, the Terreiro do Paco, and on his way home most evenings he stops off at a café in the Rossio for a chat with friends and a few glasses of brandy. If you plan on joining him, stick to beer. He drinks aguardente: it's strong.

'His practice is successful and well established; he specializes in international trade, he facilitates import–export licences.' Lacey smiled at the delicate way she described embargo-breaking. 'His government connections are good, but he's sailed close to the wind on occasions. I think that's all I can tell you. Oh yes, and he usually has a bodyguard with him. A large chap.'

She smiled at Lacey, as if the thought of him tackling a large chap was slightly ludicrous. He was inclined to agree with her, unless he could make his approach from behind with a hammer in his hand.

'Thank you very much, Sally Prendergast. You've been most charming and efficient.'

'We try to please.' She stubbed out what was still a cigarette rather than a butt and took another drink of coffee. 'I've got to go.'

He got to his feet when she stood up but they didn't shake hands. She picked up a yellow carrier-bag and nodded to him.

'Good luck.'

'I'll give you a call some time.'

She smiled and walked away.

Lacey ordered another beer and pulled open the remaining carrier-bag. In it was a package wrapped in cloth and an envelope. He took out the envelope.

There were half a dozen photographs that showed the outside of Enrico Latimer's home, his office, and the café in the Rossio, as well as pictures of Latimer and his mistress.

He was a small, tubby, middle-aged man in a suit that was expensive enough to try to disguise his shortcomings but which failed.

On the back of each photograph were written relevant details.

Lacey put the photographs back in the carrier-bag and enjoyed the beer. There was plenty of time to go sight-seeing.

The Rossio hadn't changed. It was still dominated by the castle walls on the hill to the east, there were still queues for the orange buses, the fountains still played in the middle of the square and, between them, the statue of Pedro IV on its tall column was still a fake.

Pedro was really Maximilian of Mexico. Max was dethroned while his statue was waiting to sail and became, in a way, war surplus. Another deal that had been too good for the burghers of Lisbon to pass up. They got it cheap and changed its name.

He noted the café that Latimer used and walked on, through the pedestrianized shopping streets of the Baixa, window-gazing at boutiques and stores that were distinctly mundane. He was surprised by an up-market Marks & Spencer with an underwear display that made him homesick. He recognized several garments from Susan's lingerie drawer.

Palace Square, Lacey had to admit, was one of the most elegant car-parks in Europe. It was bordered on three sides by government and municipal offices and on the fourth by the waters of the Tagus. In the middle, a bronze monarch on a horse watched the ferries ply the estuary.

Latimer's second-floor office was behind the square, a discreet entrance into a tall building. Lacey turned and headed towards the narrow streets that led up to the castle.

He was ready for a drink when he got back to the hotel and opened a bottle of beer from the mini bar.

The cloth-wrapped package in the supermarket carrier-bag contained a Browning power pistol with shoulder holster and two full magazines that each contained thirteen rounds. It was enough ammunition to start a war. He checked the mechanism, pushed a magazine into the pistol grip, and put the gun and the holster into a bedside drawer.

He telephoned Lamont-Smith's room and heard the ring through the wall as well as in the earpiece.

'Yes?'

'This is your early evening call. What condition are you in?'

'Oh, it's you.' Lamont-Smith breathed heavily as if getting more comfortable. 'I'm prone, actually. You woke me up.'

'How about dinner?'

'It's only six o'clock.'

'In half an hour. Dinner, and then we go to work.'

'God, you're a pushy bunny. Can't it wait until morning?'

A pushy bunny?

'The competition will be here in the morning. Some of them may be here already. Dinner's on me.'

'Dinner's on expenses, so make it a good one. What are we doing after dinner?'

'What else would we do in Lisbon? We're going to see a man about a deal.'

SIX

Ben Miller travelled by British Airways Boeing 747 from New York's J.F. Kennedy Airport to London Heathrow. He left at nine o'clock at night and arrived seven hours later at nine o'clock in the morning.

He could have taken an afternoon Concorde and cut his flying time by half but he didn't like the cramped seats and the smallness of the sideways toilets, and besides, it would have got in too late the previous night for a connecting flight to Lisbon. When he had the time, he preferred to go first class on a Boeing.

Miller was exactly six feet tall, wore a dark blue business suit, a blue button-down shirt and a patterned maroon silk tie. His shoes were plain black and laced. He never wore loafers because he couldn't rely on them to stay on his feet if he had to break someone's kneecap by kicking it.

He was a man who relied on nothing that was outside his own control because experience had taught him the fickleness of everything from a presidential guarantee to a Viennese tram timetable. If he had to rely on anything other than his wits he would pick a twenty dollar bill.

His home was in Hollywood, Florida, which often confused people, but that was their problem. He had originally gone to Key Largo after reading the novel and had intended to live there on a boat but had failed to settle because it was inhabited by tourists and no one who resembled either Hemingway or Bogart. He also discovered he got seasick easily.

He had been born, due to turbulence, in Australia thirty-two years before. His mother had been travelling from Los Angeles to visit her sister in Sydney when the aeroplane hit a sudden air pocket and started his premature delivery.

The birth hadn't actually occurred in Sydney but at Kingsford Smith International Airport in Botany Bay. He had arrived with a jaundiced view of life, much like the original criminal settlers who had arrived two hundred years before him. He had never forgotten the warm pleasure of being inside a woman and had spent a good part of his life recapturing the experience.

The birth had given him dual citizenship which, in later years, he had found unnecessary, since he always had several different identities and nationalities at his disposal.

His ability to move around the world and get things done quickly and efficiently without leaving a trail of unsolved homicides put him in the sort of comfortable income bracket that allowed him to wear Giorgio Armani, Gucci and Rolex, and afford the equivalent designer accountant. As many of his commissions were unofficial so was a lot of his income.

He declared the payments he received from the international security company of which he was a director, and the profits on his property investments and savings accounts, and lived modestly in an apartment that overlooked the sea, drove a BMW convertible, followed the Miami Dolphins during the football season, and shared roughly six months of his life at a time with various beautiful young women.

Sarah had lasted seven months and it had occurred to him that maybe this was the onset of middle age. He would have to look out for signs of senility but in the meantime he was happy with Sarah, her year-round Florida tan that made her intimate parts even more intimate, her great sense of humour, and her lack of curiosity about where he went at short notice.

This time it had been to an estate in Connecticut he had visited twice before. The Man always preferred a face-to-face with anyone he commissioned for those important little jobs he didn't want any of his friends in Washington to know about. The Man believed he could instil integrity and loyalty in his hirelings by his very presence; he declared it was important that there was this personal touch, this contact, between commander and troops.

Miller thought The Man was full of shit but he was also very wealthy and wielded enough power to make life uncomfortable for him if he said so. So far he hadn't said so, had gone along with the imperial graciousness, and taken the money. He liked money; especially twenty dollar bills.

Maybe The Man had a point anyway. Visiting him was impressive. The estate was gracious, the flunkies imported, the security tighter than the Rolling Stones, the opulence, well, opulent. Family portraits stared down from the walls as if the guy was head of a dynasty, which, he supposed, he was.

The face-to-face was calculated to inspire, all right, but not loyalty and integrity. It was calculated to let you know where your place was in the order of things, and that your place was to serve and keep your mouth shut and that if you didn't, here was the power to make sure someone else shut it, probably permanently.

The Man had told him to destroy a collection of historical documents. He had further told him to find out if the devious son of a bitch selling them had made copies and, if he had, to destroy those, too.

Miller drank no alcohol on the flight, but had several soft drinks for the liquid and the sugar, and ate sparingly. He found a country music channel on the headphones and read a paperback Robert B. Parker novel, content to trail Spenser the private eye around Boston in his mind, rather than watch a video.

He was a fan of both the character and the writer but had a problem: he had read all the other available books. Maybe he should call Parker and give him a few plots? He read slowly, to make it last.

At Heathrow's Terminal 4 he was met by a clean-cut young man in his late twenties, who wore a dark grey suit and a blank expression that the guy thought was professional, and who held a sign that said: Astor Inc.

Miller raised a hand to identify himself.

'I'm Miller.'

They walked together to an exit from the terminal. The man gave Miller an envelope and they parted and went in different directions. Miller put the envelope in his pocket and waited for a bus to take him to Terminal 1.

His flight had been delayed ten minutes on landing, immigration had taken longer than expected, and now the bus got stuck in a Heathrow traffic jam.

He didn't let it get to him but enjoyed watching the legs of the English girl who sat opposite. She wore a formal business suit and stockings. Where he came from, girls wore bikinis and tans, and he enjoyed the novelty of trying to peek up her skirt. Either his gaze made her uncomfortable or she entered into the spirit of the game, but, for one reason or another, she kept crossing and uncrossing her legs.

Miller smiled as he got off the bus and she smiled back. In other circumstances he might have stayed on. It had been a good game.

It was no surprise that he had missed the 10.25 a.m. British Airways flight and, although he didn't know it, it was probably just as well, as he would have been sharing Club Class with Lacey and Lamont-Smith. Miller switched to an Air Portugal flight and went for breakfast.

He didn't open the envelope he had been given at Terminal 4 until he was in the air on the final leg of his trip. It contained part of what he needed. The rest was in the trunk of the black Golf GTI he collected at Lisbon Airport. Its key was waiting for him along with the necessary documents in a sealed package at the main information desk.

It was three years since he had last been in Portugal. His previous business had entailed driving from the Algarve to the capital in the company of a young woman. His role had been chauffeur, guardian and protector. Their enforced close proximity had resulted in the inevitable and the trip had taken two weeks instead of two days, but she had eventually gone back to the States a lot happier than she had been when he had first prised her away from her lover by breaking both his legs.

70

Miller had no regrets, about either seducing the girl or breaking legs. She was no innocent, even though her rich daddy liked to believe she was, and the lover had been a hustler with a fishing boat and over-ambition. Instead of getting paid off he got pain. It served him right for thinking Miller would stand still and be filleted with a fish knife. It served his brother right, too.

There were music tapes in the car: some Portuguese woman with an unpronounceable name, Tom Jones, Engelbert Humperdinck, Eric Clapton, the Sex Pistols, Dire Straits and Petula Clark. This collection was the product of a sick mind.

He drove out of the airport, switched on the cassette player and stuck Clapton on. As he went under the elevated freeway he threw Tom, Engelbert, Petula and the Pistols out of the window. Dire Straits he would tolerate and he would reserve judgement on the unpronounceable name.

He went round the roundabout and headed towards the city. He had a reservation at the Hotel Plaza, just off the Avenida da Liberdade, and an itch to meet a certain lawyer by the name of Enrico Latimer.

SEVEN

Lacey checked himself in the mirror and was satisfied the leather jacket hid the shoulder holster and Browning.

Wear what you like, Bryson had said. On trips like this, he liked to wear a gun and the leather jacket. The jacket had character and discreet bullet holes. It reminded him to be careful.

Lamont-Smith knocked on the connecting door before opening it. He wore a double-breasted navy blue blazer and grey flannels. They were immaculate. His shirt was white linen and he wore a maroon cravat at his neck. Even his shoes shined as if they were patent leather. All he lacked was a cigarette holder and a line from Noel Coward.

Lacey said: 'You elegant bastard.'

'One does one's best. The valeting service here is excellent.'

At the door, Lacey sniffed and looked at the man again.

'You smell like a brothel.'

'It's Calvin Klein. I got it in the hotel shop.'

'On expenses?'

'Room account. That's what a room account's for, old boy. Shall we go?'

When Lacey had met Lamont-Smith that morning, he had looked slightly faded at the edges, as if he had seen better days. All it had taken were the services of a luxury hotel to make him brand new again. There wasn't even a hint of stale booze on his breath or his body. Maybe the secret was the Calvin Klein cologne; maybe he drank it.

They took a taxi to the café and bar district behind the National Theatre where Lacey had met Sally Prendergast that afternoon. It was still early for dinner; the restaurants were empty and some of the better ones were closed, but they found a place with a display of live lobsters in a tank in the window that amused Lamont-Smith.

Lacey's culinary tastes had always been conservative and his appetite small. He had a vegetable soup, baked cod and boiled potatoes and ordered a bottle of vinho verde.

His companion started with a fish soup big enough to hide Jaws, and a main course sea food selection that was piled in a steel tureen with a sparkler sticking out of the top. Its size and variety would have made Christ envious when he was trying to feed the five thousand. So would the bread and potatoes that came with it.

Lamont-Smith also ordered a bottle of vinho verde. It had been presumptuous of Lacey to think that one bottle would be enough.

He finished the meal with two portions of caramel custard and two glasses of port and a cigarette.

Lacey said: 'I don't think I've ever seen anybody eat that much.'

Lamont-Smith belched softly.

'Make the most of it while ye may.' He sat back and patted his stomach. 'My talents are particular and not always in demand. The time between commissions can be taxing. I eat when I can, and when somebody else is paying I eat well.'

'Can you walk?'

'What? Oh, I see. Haw, haw, haw.'

Lacey paid and explained where they were going during the walk through the back streets to the Rossio.

They sat at a pavement table at Enrico Latimer's favourite café. Lacey had beer, Lamont-Smith had port and they watched the mixed races of the waterfront city walk by in the dusk, much as they had for centuries, except that then they had worn turbans and sandals and now they wore Walkmans and trainers.

Lacey spotted Latimer coming along the pavement towards them. He was smaller and fatter than he had appeared in the photograph, his short legs taking quick, tiny steps. He carried a briefcase in his right hand. The fingers of his left were inside his jacket pocket, the thumb outside. It was an effeminate, theatrical posture that pushed his elbow out from his body. He looked like a very short chat show host in a hurry.

Lacey said: 'Here he is.'

At Latimer's side was a large black man who didn't wear suits well and who walked with a top-heavy roll to his shoulders. Lacey flexed his muscles, not in anticipation of having to use them but to feel the reassuring pull of the holster straps.

Latimer walked past Lacey and into the café. The black man followed. Lacey turned in his chair to watch them through the window. The lawyer went to a table in the corner that was already occupied by three middle-aged men; the bodyguard took a stool at the bar.

Lacey called the waiter and gave him a note with Latimer's name on it. To ensure he understood, he pointed through the window at the table in the corner where the four men were talking and laughing.

The waiter had taken lessons at the International School of Apathy and was unimpressed with the mime until Lacey pushed a five-hundred-escudos note into his hand. He allowed one hooded eyelid to rise in acknowledgement before delivering the message.

Lacey watched through the window and when Latimer looked in his direction he nodded.

A minute later, the bodyguard came out of the café. He towered over Lacey. He tore the note in half and placed the pieces on the table.

The reply was plain enough.

The note had been civil and direct but it had failed to impress Latimer. It was in English and it had said: 'I would like to speak to you about the Blunt Legacy.'

Lacey had anticipated refusal. From his pocket, he took another note, again with Latimer's name written clearly on the front.

This one said: 'I shall speak to your wife about Maria Barros.'

He handed it to the bodyguard.

'Please give this to Senhor Latimer.'

The black man shook his head.

'*Nao compreendo.*'

Lacey pointed to the name on the front of the note and hoped the man could read, even if he couldn't speak English.

'*Por favor,*' he said.

The bodyguard hesitated. A second note was unexpected. Lacey smiled encouragingly. The man took it into the café. This time Latimer himself came out, accompanied by his bodyguard.

The little man was smoking a cigarette in an ivory holder. He held it in two fingers of his right hand, withdrew it from his mouth, and let the smoke drift around his face. His left hand was back in his coat pocket. Both were mannerisms he had practised. Maybe he'd watched too many Peter Lorre movies.

He stared at Lamont-Smith who blew a smoke ring and smiled, then fixed Lacey with what he imagined was a steely look.

'English?' he said.

'Yes.'

'I don't like threats.'

'Then talk to me.'

Latimer removed his left hand from his pocket and dropped the second note on the table.

'If you threaten me, my man will hurt you.'

Lacey allowed his jacket to fall open as he reached forward for his glass of beer. Latimer's steely gaze widened at the sight of the gun.

'He can try,' Lacey said. 'But I'd prefer to be friends.' He smiled. 'Sit down. Let me buy you a drink.'

Latimer put his left hand back in the pocket and looked at the people walking by on the pavement and the other customers who were sitting outside the café. Only two other tables were occupied.

Behind Lacey, a family of fat parents and two fat daughters were eating cakes. To Latimer's right, a young couple giggled as they pulled their chairs closer together; she wore a cardigan and he wore a sweater tied around his neck and he had placed his briefcase proudly on another chair. Everybody in Lisbon carried a briefcase.

'Talking to strangers can be dangerous.'

'So can talking to your wife.'

'You are not a gentleman.'

'I've learned to live with it.'

Lacey indicated a chair and Latimer reluctantly sat down. The waiter, who had been watching from the doorway, came forward and Lacey ordered an aguardente for the lawyer; he didn't order anything for the bodyguard, who had positioned himself as an ebony partition between them and the family eating cakes.

Latimer said: 'Who are you?'

Lacey said: 'We represent a collector of historical documents. A collector with serious money to spend for exclusive rights.'

'Then be at the Embaixador on Friday.'

His English was excellent with only the faint fuzz of an accent.

'You don't understand. When I say exclusive, I mean exactly that. Our client wants to know what you're selling in advance. If it interests him, he'll buy it. He wants no press conference. He wants total discretion.'

It was Latimer's turn to smile. A curly, superior twist to his lips that didn't suit him. But then, not a lot did.

He said: 'We are anticipating a great deal of interest in the collection. The press conference will go ahead.' He put the cigarette holder in his mouth, inhaled and released the smoke to swirl around his face. 'And then, we shall have an auction.'

Lacey tapped his finger on the top of the table.

'I think we're talking at cross-purposes.' He took out the photographs Sally Prendergast had given him, and placed a snatched street shot of Maria Barros in front of Latimer. 'I'll start with simple questions. Like which Blunt are we talking about?'

The lawyer ejected the cigarette from the holder on to the pavement and put it out with his foot. His expression

76

suggested he would like to do the same with Lacey, or have his heavyweight contender do it for him. He eased his ego by taking his time before replying but Lacey was patient. The first step was always the hardest.

At last, the man said: 'The British Blunt. Sir Anthony Blunt.'

'There,' Lacey said. 'Not too difficult, was it? Let's try something else. Who are you working for?'

'That's privileged information.'

'We're privileged people. You, me . . . Maria Barros. Who are you working for?'

The waiter brought the brandy and went away.

Latimer said: 'I don't know. I receive my instructions by telephone and mail.'

'You speak to someone?'

'Yes.'

'Man or woman?'

'A man.'

'What nationality?'

Latimer shrugged again.

'He spoke English. But I don't know what nationality.'

'Have you got the documents?'

Latimer hesitated. Eventually, he shook his head.

'No.'

'Have you seen them?'

He shook his head again.

'Do you know what's in them?'

'I only know what I have been told.'

'And that is?'

'Nazi documents, photographs, private papers.'

Lacey had a drink of beer.

'You've set up a press conference on the strength of a telephone call and without any evidence that this stuff exists?'

'I was paid a retainer. A sizeable retainer. People don't waste that sort of money on a joke.'

'Why pick the Embaixador?'

Latimer shrugged and half smiled. It was the first smile that had a hint of humour.

'The retainer was not that sizeable. The Embaixador is affordable.'

'What percentage are you on?'

The man sniffed.

'That is also privileged information.'

'Ten per cent? Twenty?'

Latimer said nothing that might sully his dignity.

'How much are you expecting to make at an auction? Half a million sterling?'

Latimer shrugged. 'With the right publicity . . . who knows?'

'You may get half a million, you may not. The stuff you're selling may be phoney, in which case you'll get nothing but a bad reputation and maybe a jail sentence for fraud. Even if it's genuine it's so old it's not relevant anymore. Newspapers will take the juicy bits you give out for free, but they'll be more careful about spending money.'

The man picked up the brandy and had a sip. He maintained his silence. Lacey continued.

'If there's some way we can do a deal, we can make sure your client gets full value for his merchandise. Say a million pounds and no questions asked about where he stole it from.'

It was Lacey's turn to pause. He now had Latimer's full attention as the man waited for a figure to be put on his own personal inducement.

Lacey went on: 'Of course, making it happen is the difficult part. Don't you agree?'

Latimer concurred with a slight inclination of his head.

'If it did happen, we might be persuaded to pay another two hundred and fifty thousand.'

The lawyer didn't appear to mind having his professional integrity sullied after all. Maybe the roundness of the figure made it respectable.

Latimer said: 'Sterling?'

'Sterling.'

He took a gold cigarette case from an inside pocket and placed it on top of the photograph of his mistress on the table. He removed a cigarette from the case and fitted it into the holder. As the holder reached his lips the bodyguard reached forward with a light.

Through the smoke he said: 'Interesting.'

'And you can still claim your percentage of your client's million.'

Latimer hooded his eyes. It might have been the smoke but Lacey suspected it was a wince at the indelicate form of words.

'I need time to consider your suggestion.'

'Money's available. Time isn't.'

'I would need to talk to my client, persuade him that discretion might be better than publicity.'

Latimer picked up his cigarette case along with the photograph and put them both in his inside pocket as an unspoken sign that they were entering into a business relationship. Lacey was happy for him to do so because there was more he wanted to know before they parted company.

'How will you talk to your client, Mr Latimer?'

The lawyer went back to delayed response.

'By telephone.'

'You have a telephone number for your client?'

'An answering machine. I leave a message, he calls me back.'

'Where is it?'

The lawyer had another drag on the cigarette while he worked out whether he should tell him or not.

'London.'

That could mean that the man behind the sale lived in London. It could also mean nothing more than that he had recently been in the city, or contacted a third party there, to set up the answerphone. He could reprogramme it or pick up messages by dialling a coded number from almost anywhere in the world.

Lacey said: 'Let's get back to the conference. Who decided how to run this thing?'

'I'm following instructions. The press conference is for publicity. It will also allow me to vet the credentials of

79

those who want to bid. The bidding will take place later, in private.'

'How much later?'

'A week.'

'You can't run a press conference without something to show. When do you get the documents?'

'I don't. Not for the conference.'

'But you must have something.'

Latimer hesitated again.

'I think I have told you plenty. I think it is time for you to tell me who you are?'

Lacey nodded.

'Fair enough. This is Ian Alexander from Sotheby's,' he said. 'He's an expert in the type of documents your client has for sale. He'll know if they're genuine and what they're worth.'

Lamont-Smith inclined his head and smiled.

Latimer said: 'And you?'

'My name is Barnes. I'm an associate of Mr Alexander.'

'Where are you staying?'

'The Ritz.'

He said it as if he meant, where else?

'And you represent?'

'Strangely, our client, like your client, prefers to remain anonymous.'

Latimer smirked and did his smoke trick.

He said: 'Before our business can go any further, I need to know that you can afford to talk to me.'

'Fine. And we need to know the quality of the merchandise. What have you really got for Friday?'

The lawyer was enjoying another long pause, as if calculating how far the balance of negotiation had swung in his favour.

'There's a statement I'll read. And I have some photocopies.'

'Juicy bits?'

Latimer shrugged.

'Perhaps they'll be interesting.'

'The serious bidders will want to inspect originals. Photocopies won't do.'

The lawyer nodded.

'They will be made available at the proper time, and to the proper people.'

'A week later?'

'Possibly before. When my client decides.'

Latimer's client was playing it very close. The advertisement that had appeared in *The Times* and the *Washington Post* was clear enough to hint at scandal in high places and would attract press coverage in its own right. It would take only one story quoting a speculative historian to blow the Blunt–Windsor connection, and the tabloids would work up the rest from imagination.

The auction was even being held in the country where the Duke's treachery had almost come to a head more than fifty years before. The significance would not be lost on those journalists who thrived on sensation.

There could be a high turn-out for the press conference, which would ensure maximum publicity, as Latimer had said. It could scare more high-bidders out of the woodwork who, for whatever reasons, might prefer to let the past remain undisturbed.

Blunt had known many secrets, not just those concerning the Duke of Windsor and Ambassador Joseph Kennedy. He had been a KGB spy for three decades. Latimer's client was right to be circumspect.

Lacey said: 'When can we see the photocopies?'

'Ah.'

'Ah. If we are to make you a rich man, Mr Latimer, I think we need some mutual co-operation.'

'As I said, Mr Barnes, I need to know you are capable of fulfilling your promise. I suggest we meet tomorrow morning. At my home. You can fax your bank from there, and confirm to my satisfaction that you have the necessary funds to be the serious collector you say you are. If you are, your colleague . . .' he waved towards Lamont-Smith with the cigarette holder '. . . can have a look at what material I have.'

Lacey thought they had gone about as far as they could.

'What time tomorrow?'

'Nine o'clock?'

'All right.'

'Do you know the address?'

Lacey held up a photograph of the house.

Latimer was not amused. He got to his feet.

'Until tomorrow,' he said.

'Until tomorrow,' Lacey said.

The lawyer and his bodyguard went back into the café and Lacey paid the hovering waiter.

'What do you think?' he said to Lamont-Smith.

Lamont-Smith stretched his long legs and breathed deeply.

'That the night is still young.'

Lacey looked at the people hurrying through the Rossio, all with destinations. Going home, out to dine; groups of young people looking for action, singles waiting for dates.

Whenever he had time to pause on foreign assignments and notice the activities of ordinary citizens, he was always jealous of their domesticity and routine. Under normal circumstances he hated domesticity and routine, but when he went abroad he missed it. Mainly, he missed Susan.

Lamont-Smith got to his feet and looked into the traffic.

Lacey said: 'A few beers?'

His companion smoothed his blazer.

'Actually, I'll take a raincheck, old boy. I have a sort of date.'

'A sort of date?'

'Yes.'

They moved to the edge of the pavement and Lamont-Smith waved at a black and green taxi.

'Who with?'

'Charming little bunny. She sold me the cologne.' The taxi stopped and Lamont-Smith opened the back door. 'Drop you anywhere?'

'No thanks. I'll walk.'

'Right ho.' He gave Lacey a knowing man-to-man smile and got in the cab. 'Don't wait up. I'll see you at breakfast.'

The taxi drove off and left Lacey feeling abandoned. He wondered what Sally Prendergast was doing tonight. Out with her boyfriend or, even more cosy, in with her boyfriend?

He began to walk, more conscious than ever that the single people around him had places to go and people to meet. He went past the railway station that looked like a palace, and on to the Avenida da Liberdade that ran for a mile uphill towards his hotel. Fountains, flower gardens and palm trees lined the well-lit boulevard. Couples strolled along it.

Luxury solitude awaited him at the Ritz. He would phone home, have a few beers and watch television.

He was feeling sorry for himself and didn't notice the young couple from the next table at the café following thirty yards behind.

EIGHT

The café had been a lucky break for Ben Miller, but he was used to lucky breaks. He had the kind of positive attitude that made them happen.

He capitalized on it the next morning by sending a van from the Telephone Company to Enrico Latimer's house in the Rua da Costa do Castelo at eight o'clock.

The van had been borrowed illegally and the guy driving it was nicknamed, for some reason, Cabbage. He had been trained in electronics and signals by the Légion Etrangère at Castelnaudary in France and had served in Djibouti and Lebanon before hanging up his white kepi and opting for private practice. Miller sometimes surprised himself at the kinds of people he knew.

The street ran below the west castle wall and the houses were two and sometimes three storeys high at the front. At the back, they were built into the side of the hill

The man put a ladder against the house, climbed up, and disconnected the line through which the lawyer's telephone and fax machine operated. Then he rang the front door bell.

Latimer answered, wearing an oversize dressing-gown.

Cabbage said: 'Telephone repair.'

'I didn't call.'

'You couldn't. Something's wrong with the line.'

Latimer closed the door and made him wait while he went and checked. He came back when he discovered the line was dead, inspected Cabbage's identity credentials that were genuine but had not been issued by normal channels, and let him in.

After eight minutes Cabbage said: 'The fault might be outside. I'll take a look.'

He left the house, climbed the ladder, and reconnected the line. He rang the door bell again.

'How is it now?' he said, when Latimer answered.

Latimer closed the door, went away to try it, and returned.

'It's fine. It's working again. Thank you.'

'No problem.'

Cabbage climbed into the van and drove it down the hill to return it before it was missed.

He had placed battery-powered miniature transmitters the size of cigarette packets in Latimer's study, living-room and kitchen, to pick up conversations in the house, and had clipped a further transmitter, that was even smaller, to the telephone line outside the house to intercept calls.

At ten minutes to nine, Miller leaned over the battlements of the castle and looked down into Latimer's backyard thirty feet below.

The houses were anchored to the side of the wall by small lawns, patios, rose gardens, even vegetable patches, that had been built in terraces. It was as if the dwellings were frightened they might slide down the hill and into the city if they didn't hold on.

The American wore a set of lightweight earphones through which he could hear what was happening in the house and which were connected to a hand-held receiver. A second set of earphones were around his neck through which to monitor telephone calls and they were connected to a different receiver that was in his pocket.

The transmitters Cabbage had planted were British, a few years out of date, but still pretty good and excellent value at two hundred dollars each. The telephone tap operated on the power of the line itself, the ones inside on batteries that had a life that was perfectly adequate for what he wanted. He didn't care if Latimer eventually found them. When he did, it might scare him enough to double-deal the Brits and hand over the necessary to Miller.

He walked away from the house in case the lawyer looked out of the window and got suspicious of the early morning tourist staring back. The range was fine, the signal strong and he settled himself against a cannon thirty yards away and used the Nikon camera that hung round his neck to take tourist pictures of the city below. As he waited for the Brits to arrive, he reflected on how well the previous night had gone.

Rosita had been surprised when he paid her off at the Ritz and put her in a taxi, because she had been hired for the full night. She was a nice girl for a hooker, which was as it should be: she came from the city's top call girl agency. She had also been excellent cover, being a believable girlfriend to onlookers even though she didn't understand what was going on.

As far as she was concerned, they had had a couple of drinks and gone for a walk and she hadn't even complained despite the high heels she was wearing. So she got sore feet for a change instead of a sore something else, but she got a night off and a tip big enough to take home to mother, even though she had left with a puzzled look as she tried to work out whether Miller suffered from extreme premature ejaculation or the agency had sent the wrong sex.

In his reckless youth, Miller might have considered getting his money's worth from such a delightful package that was bought and paid for, but post-AIDS he had tightened up his personal health and hygiene habits, particularly in a port city that was so accessible to Africa and the Middle East.

She had left, content but puzzled, and he had gone back to his hotel with the briefcase.

It had been in the trunk of the GTI together with a likely itinerary of Enrico Latimer's movements. From what he'd observed in the Rossio, he wasn't the only one who knew the lawyer's habits, which must be pretty boring if two sets of spooks had got them right. He wondered if Latimer's toilet habits were as regular.

In his room he took a beer from the icebox and opened the briefcase. The electronics, including the cassette recorder and microphone, were invisibly installed in its wooden frame, beneath the leather, linings and brass fittings that made it

86

look like any other briefcase. He lifted the lining at the spine and removed the MC90 microtape.

Normal range under boardroom conditions was thirty feet. At the café in the Rossio he had been maybe fifteen feet away and there had been background noise from traffic and pedestrians, but the mike was directional and he was hopeful he would have something worth listening to. He put the cassette in a microtape player and smiled when he discovered he had.

The Brits were doing fine and he was content to let them trailblaze until the time was right to step in and assume the initiative.

He rubbed the small of his back on the cannon and looked at his watch. It was nine o'clock, the sun was shining and he listened to the front door bell ring in his headphones.

Lacey and Lamont-Smith had taken a taxi to the Rossio and walked the rest of the way, up steep, narrowing streets. Breakfast had been a silent affair and Lacey now concentrated on the climb that was yet another reminder of how unfit he was.

Lamont-Smith took it all easily in his long stride. He walked with hands behind his back and head at a high angle so that he looked down his nose. To compensate for Lacey's laboured pace, he frequently stopped to gaze in shop windows or inspect the architecture of alleyways. He looked disgustingly fit and healthy.

'When did you stop playing rugby?' Lacey said.

'I haven't.'

'You still play?'

'I turn out for an over-the-hill mob at Esher. More social than sporting. It keeps me in trim.'

'Who did you play for?'

'London Welsh. And Wales, of course.'

'Of course. Except that I thought you were Scottish.'

'Bit and bit. My mother was a Scot, and my regiment was the Black Watch. But father was Welsh so I played sports for Wales.'

Lacey paused for breath.

'Sports as in plural?'

'Oh yes. Rugby, athletics and boxing for Wales. Shooting and bob-sleigh for Britain.'

He said it as if it was perfectly natural.

'And I thought your major hobbies were drinking and women.'

'What do you think the sports were for?'

Lacey continued walking.

'How did you get on last night?'

'Ah. I cannot tell a lie, old boy. Last night did not go according to plan.'

'What?' A surge of pleasure lightened Lacey's step. 'The girl from the perfume counter turned you down?'

'The young lady took me to a discotheque. Not my forte, I'm afraid. Loud music and overpriced drinks. I was not a happy bunny. I left.'

'You bombed out?'

Lamont-Smith gave him a baleful look.

'There's no need to be hurtful, Peter. I have feelings, you know.'

Enrico Latimer was dressed for business in a grey suit, white shirt and spotted blue tie. He let them in, locked the door behind them, and led the way into the kitchen. There was the smell of fresh coffee and cleanliness. Even with his wife away, the lawyer kept an orderly home.

He offered coffee and Lacey accepted but Lamont-Smith refused.

'I don't suppose you have tea?' he said.

If he had, Latimer was disinclined to make it.

Instead he showed Lamont-Smith through to a study equipped with a computer, fax and terminal.

Lacey drank his coffee black from a white cup in the white kitchen that, on first impression, had been attractive but now began to feel oppressively clinical. He felt as if he should have scrubbed up before entering.

Through sliding glass doors he watched a Dobermann that sat on the patio. Maybe it was waiting for its master to open the doors and say something nice – like 'kill'. Saliva dripped from the corners of its mouth in anticipation.

Latimer returned carrying a brown cardboard file which he dropped on the kitchen table.

'I placed a call this morning. Asked my client to call back.'

'Good. Is this the stuff?'

'Yes. You can look at it now, if you want. You would be able to see it on Friday anyway.'

Lacey put the cup in the sink, opened the file and removed five photocopied sheets and an envelope. Two of the sheets were of photographs, two of documents in German, and one of a handwritten note or *aide-mémoire* in English.

The first photograph was of the Duke of Windsor, presumably on his 1937 trip to Germany, giving an enthusiastic fascist salute to a parade ground formation of SS troops. The second was of four men of that indeterminate age and style that categorized Lamont-Smith. It had probably been taken before the war. They wore lounge suits and their expressions showed they had condescended to be snapped.

Lacey recognized Edward, probably when he was Prince of Wales, and another looked as if he might be Mountbatten. He didn't recognize the other two, although one had the chinless look of a royal.

One of the documents was signed by the Nazi Foreign Minister Joachim von Ribbentrop and was dated July 1940, the time when the Duke of Windsor had been in Portugal. The other was on the headed notepaper of Deputy Führer Rudolf Hess and dated October 1937, when the Duke had been making his visit to Germany, and was handwritten. It finished in mid-sentence but the continuing sheet was not there. It was initialled RH in the bottom right-hand corner.

The English note consisted of only a few lines that read:

I want to be like the boys at the Packenham
And go about whackin' 'em and stickin' my jack in 'em.

Below it was added: 'Full version for Dickie!'

Lacey imagined this little treasure came from the seamier
side of Blunt's life.

The envelope was open and he took out a typed statement
that was in English.

Latimer said: 'That's what I'm supposed to read to the
press conference.'

It said:

Ladies and gentlemen, Sir Anthony Blunt had a long
association with the British royal family, the British Secret
Intelligence Service, and the KGB. He knew many royal
scandals and diplomatic secrets. He destroyed many and
took others with him to the grave. But he saved some to
save himself.

The American Michael Straight told the FBI that Blunt
was the Fourth Man in June 1963. The FBI told MI5 in
January 1964 and MI5 finally undertook the interrogation
of Blunt in April 1964. Blunt was well prepared for his
accusers for he had a collection of letters, documents and
photographs that would have caused scandals on both
sides of the Atlantic if they had been published. It bought
him immunity.

Despite the dirty tricks of MI5, Blunt's Legacy was
never found. That Legacy is now for sale. The few samples
I am authorized to show you today are simply a hint at
greater secrets yet to be revealed about world figures in
Britain and the United States.

Those wishing to bid for the collection, which will
be sold as a whole, may do so in one week's time.
Before then, and after they have registered their intention
with me, arrangements will be made for them, or their
representative, to inspect more of the collection.

Moneys raised by this auction will be used to establish
the James Russell Trust, in memory of the first victim of

the Legacy. The Trust will fund scholarships for young artists to foster Anglo–American cultural relations.

Lacey replaced the statement in the envelope. Latimer had poured himself a fresh cup of coffee and was leaning back against the sink. He was watching for a reaction. Lacey didn't give him one.

The statement and the planning hinted at something more than the auction of secrets that were fifty or sixty years old.

'Well?' Latimer said. 'What do you think?'

'I'm not paid to think. I'm paid to do a deal. My colleague will tell me whether we can proceed.'

The dog barked and the lawyer shouted at it and went to the sliding door. Lacey turned apprehensively. He had enough on his mind without having to cope with the Hound of the Baskervilles. Then he found something else on his mind . . . pieces of Latimer's brain.

For a moment, he thought someone had shaken a bottle of tomato ketchup and the top had come off.

Then he saw Latimer falling with much of the back of his head missing. For a fraction of a second he wondered where the missing part of the head had gone before realizing it had sprayed over him.

Automatic reactions took over and he fell to the floor beside the body of the dead lawyer, his right hand reaching for the Browning.

The only noise had been a punching sound as the bullet had made a neat hole in the glass door. There was an equally neat hole in Latimer's forehead which Lacey had time to study from close range as he lay head-to-head with the corpse on white tiles that would never be the same again.

The kitchen had been like an operating theatre waiting for a patient; now it looked like an operating theatre after a particularly messy surgeon had been at work with a chainsaw.

Lacey had initially thought the gunman had been on the ramparts of the castle at the back of the house, but the position of the entry wound and the exit explosion of the skull

91

indicated that the bullet had been fired along a horizontal trajectory. Nice neighbours.

He began easing himself backwards under the table when he heard the door open behind him.

'Get back!' he yelled, towards Lamont-Smith's legs.

The legs moved back nimbly.

Lamont-Smith said: 'What the fuck's going on?'

'Someone shot Latimer.'

'Badly?'

'Worse than badly.'

'Fuck!'

A scrabbling noise at the glass door gave Lacey a momentary panic and he rolled on to his stomach, gun pointing, and almost shot the Dobermann. It wagged its stump of a tail and barked to be let in. It thought they were playing.

'Did you use the fax?'

'Couldn't get through. Busy line.'

'Can anyone trace you from it?'

Lamont-Smith hesitated while he considered.

'No. All I dialled was the number of a bank in Geneva. I didn't send anything.'

'Good.' He looked at the hole in the glass door. 'The shot came from the right, same level as us. If you stay away from the windows, you should be OK. The stuff's on the table. Can you reach it?'

It had been an assassin's shot, to take out a specific target. If whoever was out there had intended to kill all the occupants of the house a rifle wouldn't have been used from long range. A sub-machine-gun would have been better and perhaps a couple of grenades.

He turned to watch Lamont-Smith's legs reappear, staying close to the fitted cupboards on the safe side of the room. He stretched and Lacey heard him scoop the papers and cardboard file.

'Fuck!' Lamont-Smith said.

'What's wrong?'

'They're covered in shit.'

'You know something? You're command of the English language definitely suffers under fire.' Then he saw the black transmitter, neatly fitted out of sight beneath the skirt of the table. He, too, said: 'Fuck!'

'What?'

'Nothing. Let's get out of here.'

Lamont-Smith's legs went through the door and Lacey crawled out after him. He went into a bathroom and washed his face and tried not to look at the bits that refused to drain down the sink. If he started thinking about it he would end up climbing into Latimer's bed and sucking his thumb. Instead, he stripped to the waist and sponged his leather jacket clean. The shirt had been cream and was a mess. He rinsed the worst of the stains out of it in the bath and wrung it as dry as possible but it was unwearable.

The first bedroom he went into had pink walls and a blue furry elephant on the bed. He'd forgotten Latimer had daughters and would be mourned as a father and husband. It had been easier to categorize him as a conniving middleman rather than credit him with a personality and a family.

He found what he was looking for in the next bedroom. Latimer kept his shirts on hangers in a walk-in wardrobe. He picked a plain blue Sergio Tecchini sports shirt, pulled it on and found the fit reasonable. It was better than wet bloodstains and, besides, Latimer had no further use for it.

He put on the shoulder holster and his jacket and found Lamont-Smith in the study, reading the contents of the brown cardboard file. Lacey remembered he still had the envelope that contained the prepared statement. It had been in his hand when he had dropped to the floor in the kitchen and he had stuck it in the inside pocket of his jacket.

Lamont-Smith looked up: 'Have you read these?'

He had wiped the file and the sheets of paper so that they were reasonably clean.

'I glanced at them.'

'Naughty, old boy. My eyes only.'

Lacey shrugged. He didn't tell him about the envelope.

'Time to go. Make sure you didn't leave smears on the kitchen table when you picked up the file, and wash the cup I used. And take your cigarette butts with you. The fewer people who know we've been here or that anything is missing, the better. See if you can find a plastic bag or something to put the file in. And this.'

He held up his wet shirt.

'Right.'

Lamont-Smith put the sheets of paper into the file and took it with him. Lacey checked the telephone. He had been right. It had a memory and digital display. Latimer had said he'd called the London number that morning.

Lacey lifted the receiver and pressed the redial button and waited for the last number the lawyer had dialled to flash up on the digital read-out. Of course, the last call he'd made could have been to Maria Barros in Sintra . . . It hadn't. The international prefix 0044 came up and Lacey reached for a pen and paper.

The call had been to London. He wrote the number down as he listened to the clicks that made the connection again. It was ringing. It rang three times, an answerphone switched on, and the featureless voice of a man said: 'Leave your message after the tone.'

Lacey hung up, went to the wall socket, and disconnected it to destroy the memory.

Lamont-Smith came back with a grey plastic bin liner into which he had already put the file. He gave Lacey a similar bin liner. Lacey put the wet shirt inside, folded it small and pushed it under his leather jacket.

It was time to go back to London, trace a call, discover the identity of James Russell, and follow the paperchase of clues that linked the Second World War to an assassin's bullet.

NINE

Whatever happened with the auction, Lacey's and Latimer-Smith's first priority was to get out of town. They did so on the 12.40 p.m. Air Portugal flight to Heathrow. Ben Miller went with them.

Lacey and Lamont-Smith went Club Class, he went Economy, taking a seat in the smoking section at the rear of the aircraft to stay well out of their sight.

He had enjoyed being an eavesdropper and had been as surprised as anyone when Latimer got shot. Well, maybe not as surprised as Latimer.

Miller had been lounging against the ancient cannon when the noise of glass, impact and falling bodies had brought him to his feet. He had looked over the battlements towards the lawyer's house.

From his position he had no clear view of the house or its backyard, but he could see a man staring over the wall that divided Latimer's patio from the next-door lawn. The man was standing on a white plastic garden chair.

Miller used the camera that was still around his neck to photograph the man as he stepped off the chair. He was carrying a rifle that was fitted with a silencer, and wore a long brown dustcoat, the type that old-fashioned storekeepers used to wear.

The man looked up and saw Miller, dropped the rifle behind a bush, and walked calmly across the garden and down a flight of steps that led to the streets below.

There had only been a handful of people in the castle grounds and none at this stretch of the wall. The hit had been professional.

95

Miller believed in flowing with the roll and the roll was taking him to London. The two Brits had leads to follow, he had the two Brits to follow, and a telephone number to trace.

He had listened to Latimer call the London number and leave a message for his client to make contact, and he had listened to the guy called Barnes dial the same number but leave no message.

That meant that Barnes had the number, but, so did Miller. The American had decoded the tones of the digital dialling. After shedding the international code it had the 071 prefix that meant it was located in Central London.

Lacey and Lamont-Smith parted company at Heathrow; Lacey to catch a tube into the centre of London, Lamont-Smith for an airport bus to take him to the long-stay car-park.

The archivist had to deliver the file to his unnamed Controller. Lacey didn't like working this way but he didn't make the rules. He would continue to work through Sam Bryson.

The street where Enrico Latimer had lived had been quiet when they arrived and left. It was possible they hadn't been noticed as anything other than tourists looking for a way into the castle. Besides, police would be looking for a killer who had shot into the house from outside rather than gained entry to commit murder.

Of course, the police would be interested in the listening devices they would find and in talking to Latimer's black bodyguard who was witness to their meeting the night before. Fortunately the man hadn't understood English but he would have been able to describe them, and Lamont-Smith was a shade too noticeable in a crowd.

It depended on how much the bodyguard knew and what other documents Latimer had hidden in his home or at his office as to whether a connection was made between the lawyer and the planned auction at the Embaixador.

Whatever happened, it had been essential for the pair of them to get out before they were picked up for questioning and became an embarrassment instead of stopping one.

At the Ritz, Lacey had made two telephone calls. The first to make the flight reservations and the second to Sally Prendergast. He and Lamont-Smith had packed, paid their bill and gone by taxi to the airport, where Sally had waited to use a public telephone that Lacey was pretending to use, and to pick up the carrier-bag containing the Browning that he left behind. They neither spoke nor acknowledged each other.

Lacey got to Charing Cross Road at four-thirty. Sam Bryson was absent. He was at a two-day seminar at Cambridge with other representatives of the Foreign and Commonwealth Office, which was a recruitment exercise. A note on Lacey's desk told him where he would be dining that night. The information was for emergencies; Bryson didn't like to be interrupted when he was dining.

Also on Lacey's desk were copies of that morning's *Times* and that afternoon's *Evening Standard*. *The Times* had carried a speculation story about the Blunt Legacy advertisement on an inside page; the *Standard* ran the same story single column on its front page. It was all nicely set up for the tabloids to sensationalize the next day.

Natalie had an address for Lacey for the telephone number he had called in from Lisbon Airport. She had also photocopied the relevant page from the *London A–Z* to show him its precise location.

'Twenty-seven, Engelbert Street,' she said. 'Named after the composer, not the singer.'

'What singer?'

It was a cul-de-sac in the tight maze of streets between Regent's Park and Primrose Hill.

He sat at his desk and she leant over him to point it out and he noticed her smell. It was perfume and talcum powder and femininity. He hadn't been noticing much for the last few hours, apart from ensuring he hadn't been followed, and he realized the ache in his shoulders was tension.

Natalie said: 'Are you listening?'

Her breath smelled of sugar and spice and all things nice. He smiled at her.

She stared at him, her eyes making an instant assessment, and she shelved her office efficiency and smiled back.

'You look as if you could do with a coffee.'

'That would be nice.'

She went to make it and Lacey at last allowed himself to relax. Death at close hand and the threat of death always left its mark. It was never glorious and was frequently obscene. Like being sprayed with parts of another human being. To cope, he did what everybody else did whose occupations dealt with tragedy and mangled bodies. He joked about it, he cracked gags – even to himself – to make the horror manageable at the time, so he could continue to function and not become a victim himself.

Later, when he was alone and had the time to acknowledge properly what had happened, he got depressed, he got angry, he got drunk, and sometimes he cried. Sometimes he fought the gremlins.

Natalie returned and put a Superman mug on his desk.

'New cups,' she said. 'The old ones were a health hazard.'

He admired the picture of Superman.

'I hope this is meant to be appropriate.'

'Of course.'

'What did Malcolm get?'

'He's a Ninja Turtle.'

'Whatever happened to Ninja Turtles?'

'They became passé, like Malcolm.'

'Cruel.'

'Ask him. He'll agree.'

He grinned at her. She was right, Malcolm would agree.

Natalie looked good. She wore a red brushed-cotton dress and didn't appear to mind, for a change, that Lacey was noticing her curves. She had the sort of radiant look that people noticed when young women were pregnant. Surely not?

'Did you have a good weekend?'

'Very good. You should congratulate me.'

My God, she was.

'On what?'

'On getting engaged.'

It was more of a shock than her being pregnant. Natalie was the sort of professional woman who could easily have arranged a marriage-free pregnancy and organized her fulfilment and career with the aid of a filofax and a nursemaid. But an engagement meant romance. It was refreshing to discover she was an old-fashioned girl.

'Congratulations.' He got up and walked round the desk to kiss her cheek and she blushed. 'I really mean it. I hope you'll be very happy.'

'Your coffee's going cold.'

He went back to his chair.

'Who's the chap?'

'He's in banking. We were at Cambridge together.'

'He's a very lucky man.'

She blushed again.

'Yes, well. The coffee mugs are my engagement present to the office.'

He toasted her and drank from Superman.

She got back to business to escape more embarrassment and checked information from her notebook.

'The telephone number is listed to a paper supply company called Zenith which went out of business three months ago. It's in a three-storey terraced house that has been office property for years. The ground floor is occupied by a video promotion company called VeeJay. They own the lease on the building. The company is registered to Veronica Jayston, hence VeeJay. She lives on the top floor.'

Lacey nodded and looked at his watch.

'I'll go there now. In the meantime, I have something else for you. A name – James Russell. Deceased.' Natalie started writing in the notebook. 'He was possibly an associate or friend of Sir Anthony Blunt. Remember him? The Keeper of the Queen's Pictures but not the nation's secrets? This bloke Russell may have had some connections with art and could have been a young artist. He has been described as a victim and could have died any time in the last fifty years.'

'Fifty years?'

Natalie paused in taking notes.

'Yes, all right. Likely periods to check are 1944–5, 1963–4, 1978–9 and 1983.'

She took down the dates but was still less than happy.

'Is that it?'

'That's it.'

'It's not a lot to go on.'

'You don't need a lot to go on. That's why you're special.'

She shot him a look that said it was almost five o'clock, before leaving his office for her own desk.

Lacey had to admit it was a tall order to find a man with an ordinary name who had died some time in the last fifty years, unless the Blunt connection paid off. That was why he had steered her towards the years when the Legacy could have been compiled, when Blunt was blown to MI5, when he was exposed publicly, and the year he died.

There was always the possibility that Russell had no connection at all with Blunt, but Lacey preferred not to think about that. Besides, the way the auction had been planned to milk publicity led him to believe that James Russell was waiting to be discovered.

Lacey was aware of the packet of Gitanes in the drawer of the filing cabinet behind him but left the office without touching them. He walked up to Leicester Square tube station and bought a packet of extra strong mints from a kiosk before catching a train to Camden Town.

When he re-emerged he gazed at the sheet from the A–Z and worked out his route. The wind had a chill factor that cut through the leather of his jacket. It had been warmer in Portugal and he had worn that very important extra layer: the Browning in its leather shoulder holster. He hadn't thought it necessary to tool up to investigate an answerphone that he guaranteed would be unattended.

He found the street. It was a terrace of substantial Victorian houses that had once been private homes. Steps led up from the pavement to the front doors.

Number twenty-seven had three bell pushes but only two had names alongside them. The ground floor name was VeeJay, the video promotion company, the slot by the top bell was blank, and the name in the middle was James Russell.

Lacey had assumed Russell was dead but the statement had been ambiguous. Maybe Russell had been a victim in some other way. Then again, maybe somebody was playing games.

He pressed James Russell's bell and a metallic female voice came out of the speaker grill alongside the door. It said: 'VeeJay PR.'

He leaned towards the grill and said: 'Detective Inspector Littlewood to see James Russell.'

'I'm sorry. Mr Russell is not available. Can I take a message?'

'Then I'll see Veronica Jayston.'

'One moment please.'

The metallic background noise was cut off and Lacey waited, alone in the street except for the parked cars and vans. He tapped his foot and began to count to five. What was taking so long? Did they think it was a raid? Were they getting rid of illicit substances or porno films?

As he was about to press the bell again the door was opened by a young woman dressed all in black. Black tights, short black pleated skirt, black polo neck shirt, long black hair and pale face devoid of make-up. She looked listless, as if she couldn't wait to get back to her coffin.

'Will you come in.'

The invitation was delivered in a low monotone, her voice was as expressionless as she was.

She closed the door behind him and pointed down a corridor.

'It's on the left. Veronica's expecting you.'

Lacey hardly liked to turn his back on the girl in case she buried her fangs in his neck, but she moved off silently to the right, opened a door from which loud rock music came, and went in.

Veronica Jayston's office door was open and she was sitting behind a large desk, wearing large tinted glasses and writing on a large pad.

The walls were white, one covered by film posters and another with shelves filled with video cassettes. A large window behind her looked out on to a garden with bushes and a patch of lawn.

She put down the pen and stood up. She was almost six feet tall, lithe, muscular and elegant, and looked mean enough to play running back for the Chicago Bears. She didn't offer to shake hands.

'Thank you for seeing me, Ms Jayston.' She had to be a Ms. 'I'm making . . .'

'Identification?'

He pulled from his jacket pocket the Special Branch card that said he was Detective Inspector Stewart Littlewood, walked to the desk and handed it to her.

She scrutinized it and looked up.

'Special Branch?'

'That's right.'

She handed the card back.

'What have I done wrong?'

'Nothing, as far as I know.' He tried a smile; it was not reciprocated. 'It's about James Russell.'

'What's he done wrong?'

'I'm sorry. I'm afraid I can't discuss that. Did you rent him the office?'

'Yes.'

'When?'

'Three weeks ago.'

'Was it a long or short lease?'

'Look. It's late and I've had a long day. Do I have to answer your questions?'

She was beginning to annoy him.

'Yes, madam, you do.' She could stuff the Ms. 'These enquiries could affect national security so I would advise you to be as forthcoming as you are able. Long or short lease?'

'It was on a monthly basis.'

'Did he pay by cheque?'

'No, cash.'

'Did you deal with him personally?'

'Yes.'

'How many times did you meet him?'

'Twice.'

'What were the occasions?'

'When he first asked to rent space and when he moved his . . . equipment in.'

'His equipment?'

'His telephone.'

It was like getting blood from a stone, almost as if Veronica Jayston had something to hide.

'Can you describe Mr Russell?'

'Not really.'

'Try. Otherwise I may have to take you into custody until you get your memory back.'

She bristled and Lacey hoped she wasn't the violent type.

'You can't do that.'

'I can.'

'I have rights . . .'

'Not when you're impeding national security. Madam.' He emphasized the word as an admonishment. 'What was Russell like?'

Her lips pursed and she developed a nervous twitch in one eye. She leant on her desk with both hands flat on its surface. At last she spoke.

'A small man. About your height.' He tried not to feel hurt. 'Grey hair at the sides, bald on top. He was thin. And he wore a fawn raincoat and tweed hat.'

'Age?'

She shrugged and said: 'Fifty? Sixty?'

'What about facial characteristics?'

103

'I don't notice the facial characteristics of old men, Inspector. I doubt I will be able to recall your facial characteristics the moment you walk out that door.'

Touché. Lacey almost grinned. She must have noticed the ginger age freckles on his hands.

'One more thing, Miss Jayston. I'd like to see the office that Russell rented.'

She knew she had no option, and led the way out of her office and up a flight of stairs. Lacey followed and approved of the sway of her hips and the tautness of her skirt and hoped she didn't read minds.

The door she went to still had a sign on it that said Zenith. She unlocked it, pushed it open, switched on a light and stepped back.

There was one room and a lavatory. The room was carpeted but totally empty, apart from dust and the answer-phone that sat in the middle of the floor. The light was flashing that indicated the machine had a message.

Lacey said: 'How much did he pay for all this?'

From the doorway, she said: 'Fifty pounds a week.'

'Very reasonable. In advance, of course.'

'A month in advance.'

'And how much did he put up front?'

'I beg your pardon?'

'Security, deposit, call it what you want.'

'I'm not sure . . .'

'I'm not interested in cash transactions that haven't been declared to the tax man, Miss Jayston. I want to know what he was prepared to spend.'

'He paid five hundred pounds for the monthly renewal option.'

'Cash?'

'Yes.'

'Did you advertise?'

'What for?'

'Did you advertise the room was for rent?'

'No.'

'Then how did he know about it?'

'He called at the office and asked. As it happens, my intention was not to rent it out again but to use this floor myself.'

'Did you know his requirements would be so minimal?'

'I knew it would be mainly an accommodation address, that he wanted somewhere secure to take telephone messages. He said his business was in Europe.' She shrugged, wanting to offer more of an explanation than there was, as proof of her innocence of whatever her tenant was involved in. 'I assumed he wanted a Central London address and telephone number. I thought he might be off-shore dealing, that sort of thing.'

Lacey nodded to show he understood. She hadn't really cared, after pocketing seven hundred pounds in readies, what the man did.

'Thank you for being so honest,' he said. 'And now, if you don't mind . . .' he pointed to the telephone '. . . a little privacy would be appreciated.'

She walked down the corridor to wait and he closed the door so she couldn't hear.

He knelt and pressed the reply button and the tape rewound, clicked, and the same toneless voice that had previously received Latimer's messages spoke.

It said: 'Well done. You made it this far. Now find the real Jimmy Russell.'

TEN

When Lacey left the offices of VeeJay he passed a parked Ford van that had a ladder on its roof and Ben Miller inside.

Miller had decided not to try following the man he knew as Barnes from Heathrow, because he would be particularly wary after leaving behind a dead body in Lisbon. Besides, he had assumed that Barnes would check out the telephone number. He had been correct.

The American had also had time to set up his own operation, using the resources of the London-based security company called Dixon Green of which he was an associate director.

A representative of the company had visited the premises of VeeJay Promotions, posing as a gas board official investigating a leak, and had discovered that James Russell had the first floor office but was away, that VeeJay occupied the ground floor, and that Veronica Jayston lived on the top floor.

The man had also discovered that the premises were all-electric and that Veronica Jayston had a short temper and a suspicious mind. He had been unable to plant any gadgetry or get any further than her office. At least that was something.

Before entering the premises, the man had fixed a bug to the speaker unit by the side of the front door that had enabled Miller to hear Barnes introduce himself as Inspector Stewart Littlewood of Special Branch.

Miller had also heard most of the conversation inside Veronica Jayston's office via a vibration listening device attached to the outside of the large window that faced on to the back garden.

He now left the van and prepared to follow the man who was following Barnes–Littlewood. They would attempt the tail with a team of three and a minicab. They were all wired for sound and wore lapel microphones and hearing-aid receivers.

It went all right until they reached the tube station at Regent's Park and then they lost him somewhere between the Bakerloo and Piccadilly lines at Piccadilly Circus.

The exercise had been useful in two respects. They had got photographs of Barnes–Littlewood, and he had shown himself to be particularly good because he had shaken the tail without appearing to notice it was there.

The team blamed itself for losing their quarry but Ben Miller didn't. He recognized quality. He guessed the guy was from British intelligence but he would like to be sure. The photographs would help. Most of the people Dixon Green employed had previously been with either the Secret Intelligence Service, Military Intelligence, Special Air Services, or Special Branch.

Private security was bigger business than most people realized. It prevented and initiated industrial espionage, protected millionaires, negated blackmail threats, negotiated kidnap deals and undertook the sort of private commissions that individuals and governments preferred to remain private.

It was fun, and Ben Miller enjoyed the freedoms and dangers of riding shotgun on the Western ranges of capitalism.

The offices of Dixon Green were in New Cavendish Street, round the corner from Harley Street. Miller thought it appropriate that they were located in an area famous for other consultants who also dealt in life, death, money, vanity and power.

He used an office in the basement that had all the essentials: computers, telephones, thick carpet, bar, a desk big enough for group copulation, swivel chair and a soft leather couch that was perfect for improper liaisons with a secretary called Gloria. It also had a backyard the size of a postage stamp through which he had access to a pizza restaurant. Who said England was uncivilized?

There was a report waiting for him at the office and, as Gloria handed it over, he winked and said 'Later', in a way that could mean either business or pleasure.

The second man from Lisbon had been followed to a long-stay car-park at the airport where he had collected a ten-year-old Land-Rover whose engine was badly in need of a tune. The vehicle licence number had given them the name of Ian Lamont-Smith and an address in Putney. A motorcycle tail had followed Lamont-Smith home.

A credit profile showed he was up to date on the mortgage repayments of his terraced house and owed more than three thousand pounds on credit cards.

An entry in *Who's Who* gave his public school followed by Sandhurst and the Black Watch, a list of sporting achievements, and his profession as archivist and historical researcher. His clubs were listed as White's and Saddle.

He had no serious motoring convictions or criminal record but an addendum to the report said Lamont-Smith's membership of both London clubs had lapsed because of failure to pay his subscriptions. More information was promised later.

The house was an end terrace in a narrow street, with a patch of garden at the front and a small concrete yard at the back surrounded by a high wall. Across a narrow cobbled lane were the backyards of the next terrace.

Two men in a dirty van that was parked near a patch of spare land twenty yards away, kept the house under observation. The Land-Rover was outside and Ian Lamont-Smith was inside. The men had earlier knocked on the front door and tried to sell him double glazing. While he was refusing, one of them had attached a miniature vibration microphone in the bottom corner of his front window.

The house was only big enough to have one main room at the front and a kitchen at the back. They had guessed the telephone would be in the front room, and although the situation was not ideal, it would do until Lamont-Smith left the house and they could break in and bug his telephone properly.

There had been no incoming calls and only one out going call. Lamont-Smith had punched a number whose tones they had been unable to record clearly. But it hadn't mattered that they couldn't decode it because after introducing himself, Lamont-Smith had asked for the person he wanted to speak to by name.

It was Leonard Oliver Chesterton, dubbed by the Press as Law and Order Chesterton, Minister Without Portfolio but with special responsibility for combating terrorism and a seat on the Inner Cabinet.

L.O. Chesterton was a close personal friend of the Prime Minister and was tipped as a future occupant of 10 Downing Street.

ELEVEN

Natalie was on the telephone when Lacey got back to the office, but shook her head when he raised his eyebrows to ask if she had traced James Russell.

Lacey used one of her pristine pencils to write a note. Alongside the top part that said: 'Voice test?' he placed the tape cassette he had taken from the answerphone.

The second part of the note said: 'James Russell – check past tenants of 27 Engelbert Street. He may have lived there.'

He put the pencil in the box that held the pens and went into his own office and gave the cabinet that contained the packet of Gitanes a hard look. He still had half a tube of extra strong mints but they were making his throat more raw than tobacco. He took them from his jacket pocket and dropped them in the waste bin.

Superman was still sitting on his desk and Lacey wondered if he ever got tired. He did. He felt like he'd been mugged with a bucket of kryptonite.

He called Lamont-Smith. The telephone rang twice before it was answered with an abrupt but expectant: 'Yes?'

Lacey said: 'Don't get your hopes up. It's only me. Are you all right?'

'What? Of course, old boy. Why?'

'I was followed this afternoon. How about you?'

'Ah. Can't say as I noticed.'

'Anything unusual happened? Any callers?'

'No, nothing. Double glazing salesmen, but . . .'

'Did you let them in?'

'No.'

'Did you go straight home from the airport?'

'Yes.'

'Have you been out since?'

'For about ten minutes. I've just got back.'

'Anything different about your house? Anyone been in?'

'Well, I'd never thought about it. It's hard to tell. I'm not the tidiest of people.'

Lacey thought about the possibilities.

He said: 'Do you know how to look for listening devices?'

'Listening what, old boy?'

'Never mind. Just assume your phone's tapped. Look, I'll come round.'

'No need, Peter, really.'

'I think you need support, Ian. I can mobilize Special Branch.'

'Good God, what would the neighbours think? I don't need anybody, really. I'm perfectly safe.'

Lacey needed to be circumspect but also wanted to get over the urgency of the situation to an archivist who seemed to have forgotten one man had already been killed in an operation that was only two days old.

He said: 'I would hate our trip to have been in vain.'

He meant he hoped the file was safe.

'Ah! No fears, Peter. Everything will be taken care of very soon. The wheels are already in motion.'

'If you're sure . . . ?'

'Perfectly sure. Thanks for the call, old boy. Let me know when you need me again.'

'All right. But take care.'

Lacey put the phone down and wondered whether he should go round to Lamont-Smith's home anyway. If they had still been in Portugal there would have been no problem; Lacey would have been in operational control. But they were back in England and Lamont-Smith was obviously about to hand over the photocopies they had obtained to his own Control.

He could only hope that whoever was running Lamont-Smith realized the archivist was strictly amateur in covert activities and might not appreciate that the opposition did not play to a sporting code.

* * *

Lamont-Smith replaced the receiver and picked up his gin and tonic. He finished the drink, put down the glass and went to the window.

He knew most of the vehicles parked in the street, even the ones that called only casually. There was a Mercedes that looked out of place twenty yards to his right and a dirty white van parked near the spare land to his left. He pulled the curtains, switched on the television and went to the bookcase in the alcove.

It was a cheap chipboard bookcase, with a black plastic laminated surface and a hardboard back. On top of it, at head height, sat his collection of P.G. Wodehouse novels. He moved ten of the books, starting at *Code Of The Woosters* and ending with *Pigs Have Wings*, and put them in an armchair. He reached over the back of the bookcase to the string that hung from a hook that was screwed into the wall, and carefully lifted out a cloth bag which he placed on a coffee table.

He put the books back, sat in the armchair and opened the bag, taking out a Smith and Wesson snub-nosed .38 revolver and a box of bullets. He released the six-chambered cylinder, checked its mechanism, loaded it and put the gun in one jacket pocket and a handful of spare bullets in the other.

His briefcase was by the television which was showing a black and white Tarzan film. If the file wasn't still in it he might as well go to Africa and join Johnny Weissmuller, except that Weissmuller was dead and had never been to Africa.

Steady, old boy. Speculation could be dangerous.

He poured himself another gin and tonic.

If it hadn't been for the lack of gin he wouldn't have left the house, and if the pub hadn't been next to the off-licence, he wouldn't have been tempted to nip in for a couple of quick pints. He had been away no more than thirty minutes.

He went into the kitchen and got ice for the drink from the refrigerator and looked at the back door. It hadn't been forced but then it wouldn't have been; it would have been

112

opened expertly by a professional who wouldn't leave a trace.

Maybe they didn't know about the file. Lacey hadn't mentioned it on the telephone in case the line was bugged. Maybe, if they had entered his home, they had only been told to bug his telephone.

Maybe Lacey was on edge after having the lawyer splattered all over him and had imagined he had been followed. Maybe the Mercedes and the white van were legitimate and no cause for concern. Maybe no one was watching him or had been into his house.

He went back into the front room, took a swig of the drink, and put the glass on the coffee table. Telephone taps were quick and easy to install; a miniature microphone could have been put into the telephone receiver itself, or the telephone wall socket could have been changed for one housing a transmitter.

His briefcase was still waiting for him as Jane prepared dinner in a cosy tree-top house. It was so much simpler then.

Lamont-Smith picked up the briefcase and took it back to the armchair and the coffee table. He sat down and placed the briefcase upright in front of him. It was an old brown leather variety that opened at the top and had a flap that came over to click into one of three catches. He always used the middle catch and that was the one in which it was still fastened.

He leaned forward to stare at the catch. It was so worn it frequently stuck and there was a knack to releasing it. He reached out and attempted to open it but it was particularly obtuse. He picked it up and put it on his knee and attempted to pressure it with sensitivity but it still wouldn't open.

With a sinking heart, he took out his keys, chose the smallest key on the ring, and inserted it into the lock. It turned and now the clasp came away.

The cardboard file was still inside and the photocopies of the documents and photographs were still inside the file. At least that was something.

Lamont-Smith considered honesty only briefly. He had been out for at least half an hour, during which time someone had entered his house, quite probably bugged his telephone and possibly the room, and opened his briefcase. He had left it unlocked but the stiffness of the catch had fooled his visitor into believing otherwise and, wishing to leave everything as he had found it, he had locked it after inspecting what was inside.

Not just inspecting. He had no doubt that each page of the file had been photographed before being replaced. Chesterton would not be a happy bunny if he found out.

He took another drink of the gin and tonic. Lamont-Smith didn't like making anyone unhappy. He wouldn't tell him.

Lacey wrote headlines down a foolscap pad. The page read:

The Blunt Legacy.
The Biarritz Agreement.
Edward–Nazis–Kennedy.
Lisbon auction.
Enrico Latimer's house bugged.
Enrico Latimer shot.
James Russell.
Boys from the Packenham, jack in 'em.
Ribbentrop and Hess.
Followed in London. Lisbon?

As an afterthought he added: Ian Lamont-Smith.

Alongside it, he laid the prepared statement Latimer was to have read to the press conference at the Embaixador Hotel in Lisbon.

That was what he had. It was not much and some of it he shouldn't have. He hadn't been supposed to look at the file that was now in Lamont-Smith's possession, and it was doubtful as to whether he should have pocketed the statement without telling Lamont-Smith.

Those few brief headings all posed questions in their own right but there were more to add. Such as who was Lamont-Smith's Control and who was Lacey working for? Was it just his own side or was he representing an Anglo–American

114

alliance? If he knew that, it could cut down the possibilities of who had put a team of Watchers on him that afternoon.

He was also bothered by the continued feeling that this was not as straightforward as Sam Bryson had made out. It had all the hallmarks of a well-constructed gameplan. But what was the game?

Natalie knocked on the open door as she walked in.

She said: 'I'm getting blanks. Everybody's gone home and there's only so much you can do by computer.'

He nodded.

'OK. Thanks Natalie. Try again in the morning, eh?'

'First thing. By the way, Sam called. He was surprised you were back so soon.'

'Did you tell him why?'

'I said that Lisbon had been a dead end.' She smiled wrily at the tired joke. 'I told him you were looking for James Russell deceased, who had become a victim some time in the last fifty years.'

'What did he say?'

'He said he hoped it wasn't another dead end.'

'Very witty.' He looked at his watch. 'I'm sorry you're late.'

'My fiancé is very understanding.'

'Good-night.'

'Good-night, Peter.' She paused in the doorway. 'You should get off home, too. You look tired.'

'It's old age.'

'You're not old. You're mature. But you're still tired. Get a good night's rest.'

He nodded and she went into the main office to collect her belongings before leaving.

Romance had mellowed Natalie. Mature, she had called him. That was the nicest thing she had ever said to him. That was the nicest thing anybody had said to him since he had started to notice the age spots on the backs of his hands.

He opened the top drawer of his desk and looked at the photograph of Susan. He should have rung earlier but he hadn't known how far he would be chasing Jimmy Russell. He would phone now.

She answered almost straight away.

'Believe it or not I'm in the office,' he said. 'I'm about to leave and come home. Warm my slippers, put out the dog and get ready.'

'You don't have any slippers and we don't own a dog.'

'Then just get ready.'

'Away one night and you're randy?'

'It's not smoking. Every time I want a cigarette I think of you. Susan wouldn't like it, I say. So Susan had better make it worth while.'

'I've had more romantic propositions.'

'But none quite so definite.'

She laughed.

'Have you really not had a cigarette?'

'Scout's honour.'

'You're trained to lie.'

'Not to lovers and friends.'

She didn't say anything to that but he thought he detected a sigh that was half embarrassment, half pleasure.

'I'll be ready. See you soon.'

He replaced the receiver, opened the filing-cabinet drawer behind him, and took out the Gitanes. He lit a cigarette, pulled the smoke deep into his lungs and coughed heavily for thirty seconds.

Ah, sweet relief. And he hadn't lied. Until speaking to his wife, he hadn't had a cigarette for two days. In fact, he had gone so long without one he felt he deserved this small reward.

From another drawer in the cabinet, he took a shoulder holster, a Walther P38 pistol and two magazines that each contained eight rounds. He took off his leather jacket and climbed into the holster, pushed a magazine into the butt of the gun, put the gun in the holster and put the jacket back on.

The Walther was a spare that he kept in the office. He preferred the Heckler and Koch that was at home in his safe

116

but the Walther could still do a job and it made him feel more comfortable. If anyone wanted to follow him now, they could do so at their own risk.

He again read down the list he had made, circled Enrico Latimer's name, and put a question mark alongside it.

Lacey didn't know why the lawyer had been killed but he needed to know who was responsible. The professional manner in which it had been done suggested more people could be targeted before the mystery of the Legacy was unravelled.

TWELVE

The death of the Lisbon lawyer was on the front pages of the newspapers the next morning.

Enrico Latimer had been identified as the man who had been organizing the auction and his death fuelled the speculation about what secrets the Legacy might hold and the lengths to which some people were prepared to go, even fifty years on, to stop them being released.

Lacey drank black coffee and crunched a slice of dry toast as he read the story in the *Mail* and the *Telegraph* before leaving for the office. He again wore the Walther P38.

It was all great publicity for the auction and he surmised that more revelations would be forthcoming before it went ahead. If it went ahead.

The next stories could feature the name of James Russell and release hordes of investigative journalists on the trail. It wouldn't take Veronica Jayston long to make the connection and see the possibility of publicity. After all, she was in the business of promotion.

He would get a real Special Branch officer round there to slap a personal D Notice on the lady to stop her talking to the Press.

Sam Bryson was still in Cambridge, which meant Lacey couldn't use him as a sounding board for ideas or, in this case, a lack of them.

While Natalie continued her search for Russell, Lacey went through the briefing file again, scan-reading much of it, taking care over other passages and reports, in the hope that something he could have missed might surface.

It didn't. All the file did was make him depressed at powerful men's abuse of power, quite often without having to justify their actions. Even when they did, they had the wealth and influence to pretend the abuse had been normal business practice or even for the common good, that reality dictated shortcuts to success in the modern world.

They hid behind jargon and position and no one called them liars because they usually owned the Press and sometimes the Government, too.

The problem was as old as history.

If it hadn't been for the machinations and ambitions of powerful men there wouldn't have been any history, any royalty or dynastic families. It had always happened and it would always happen. Lacey was uncomfortable with the possibility that he might be part of the structure that protected the right of might.

Natalie saved him from more soul-searching late in the morning.

She came into his office and said: 'I've found him.'

'Where?'

'At twenty-seven Engelbert Street. You were right, he used to live there. He also died there.' She looked at her pad. 'On the night of 12 April 1964.'

Lacey took notes as she spoke.

'How did he die?'

'Asphyxia. There was an inquest verdict of misadventure.'

He looked up.

'Any details?'

'I'm still working on it. The papers no longer exist; they've been pulped. But I've got the name of the coroner's officer at the time from Camden Town Police Station.' She looked at her notes again. 'A Sergeant Pritchard. He's retired now, but he may remember.'

And he may not, Lacey thought. A police coroner's officer in a London borough dealt with hundreds of deaths a year.

'What about the coroner?'

'He died ten years ago.'

'Shit.'

'I've got some other stuff on Russell.'

'Sorry. Go ahead.'

She checked her notebook again.

'James Russell, known as Jimmy to his friends, was an American art dealer. He was fifty-one when he died. He lived at the house in Engelbert Street with his wife, Matilda. She was a painter, known professionally by her maiden name – Mattie Purcell. She was born in Britain but took United States' citizenship after the death of her husband and is now believed to live in America. She was twenty years younger than him. There were no children.'

'Natalie. You're brilliant.'

'I know.'

'Now go and be more brilliant. Find out exactly how Jimmy died and where Mattie lives.'

She left the office and he compared his notes with the list he had made the night before and the statement he had got from Latimer.

The art connection and the fostering of Anglo–American cultural relations through a trust set up in the name of James Russell now made sense. But the most interesting fact was the date of Russell's death.

MI5 had been told by the Americans that Blunt was a spy in January 1964. Jimmy Russell had died on 12 April 1964, and MI5 had finally confronted Blunt eleven days later, on 23 April.

Somehow, that made him the first victim of the Blunt Legacy. But how?

Former police sergeant Dennis Pritchard lived in Walthamstow but wasn't answering his telephone. Natalie used her initiative and got a Special Branch officer to go to his home and find out where he was: he was in a greenhouse in his back garden tending his tomato plants.

She talked to Pritchard at twelve-twenty and put him on hold while she spoke on the internal line to Lacey.

'I'm even more brilliant and you're on a roll,' she said. 'When Pritchard left the force he took his notebooks with him. They're in his loft. He's on the line now. Do you want to talk to him?'

'Yes. Put him through.'

There was a click and she made the connection.

'Sergeant Pritchard?'

'Ex-sergeant, sir. I left the force fourteen years ago.'

'Quite. My associate has told you what we're looking for?'

'She has, sir.'

'Do you think you have it?'

'I'm sure I do. It's just a question of finding it.'

'How about if I came to see you? I could be there in an hour.'

'Fine, sir. I'll have found it by then.'

'Good man. I'll see you soon.'

Lacey came out of the office into Charing Cross Road, turned right and walked past the Garrick Theatre up to Leicester Square tube station. He went in one entrance, out of another and kept on walking up to Shaftesbury Avenue.

It was better to be circumspect than sorry and by the time he finally took a cab he was sure he wasn't being followed.

Natalie had told him that ex-sergeant Dennis Pritchard, former coroner's officer, had served thirty years in the police force and was a widower, his wife having died six years before. He had been pleased to get the call – Natalie had got the impression he was lonely.

He lived in a neat bungalow in a quiet cul-de-sac, which would probably have been perfect if his wife had still been alive. But, for a man living alone, Lacey imagined it could be solitary confinement.

A small Volvo was parked in the drive and a Ford Sierra outside on the road. Lacey paid off the taxi and rang the doorbell. The small front garden was full of rose bushes and Pritchard had even teased some into climbing up the wall by the side of the door.

A thick-set man in his thirties opened the door. He said nothing but simply stared at Lacey. It was good to see that Special Branch still used the same charm school.

Lacey showed his Foreign Office security card and the man stepped aside to let him in. A tall, thin bloke with a

121

bald head and droopy moustache was standing in an open doorway along a short corridor. He wore slippers, old blue cord trousers and a baggy sweater that had holes in the elbows. Lacey guessed that if his wife had been alive she would have made him smarten up for visitors.

'Mr Pritchard?'

'That's right.'

They shook hands.

Lacey told the Special Branch man he could go, and he and Pritchard went into a comfortable but untidy living-room at the back of the house.

On a table were cardboard boxes of notebooks, albums and memorabilia. In going through them, Pritchard had pulled out a black-and-white photograph of a group of rowdy men in a pub. It sat on top of what looked like a wedding album whose cream leather cover was grained with dust.

Pritchard saw Lacey looking at the album and tried to be offhand.

He said: 'It's amazing the stuff you find in a loft.'

Lacey picked up the photograph. He stared at it and pointed.

'That's you, isn't it?'

'That's right. My leaving do.' He chuckled. 'I was legless. They brought me home in a Black Maria. Edna wasn't amused.' He turned back to the door. 'Cup of tea, sir?'

'Lovely.' Lacey put the photograph back where he'd found it. 'And let's cut out the sir, eh? The name's Peter and this call is unofficial. You know how it works.'

'Fine by me, sir . . . Peter. Glad to be of help.'

He went into the kitchen and switched on an electric kettle that, from the instant sound of building steam, had only recently boiled.

Lacey sneaked a look in the wedding album. Pritchard had never been handsome and the new grey suit he wore looked as if it had been bought in a rush, but the pictures captured the humour in his eyes. Edna had been a small and pretty girl with her dark hair caught for ever in a beehive.

122

In the kitchen, the kettle switched itself off with a whoosh and he heard Pritchard pouring the boiling water into a teapot. He closed the album guiltily as if he had been stealing the man's memories.

'You've got quite a collection here,' he shouted through the open door.

There was a rattle of cups and Pritchard appeared carrying a tray.

'I suppose I've always been a bit of a hoarder and I didn't like the idea of a good part of my life's work ending up in a council incinerator.' He put the tray down on the table. It contained teapot, milk jug, two mugs and a plate of mixed biscuits. 'That's where most of the official records ended up, you know, the statements and reports. Until they started using computers and microfilm.'

He put milk in both mugs, picked up the pot and swirled the tea to speed its brewing.

Pritchard said: 'I know it sounds daft, but I kept them for another reason, as well. I always meant to write a book. There's a lot of humour, you know, in death.'

'I suppose there must be.'

He poured the tea.

'I'm sorry,' he said, 'but I don't take sugar so I don't buy it.'

'That's all right. I don't take it, either.'

'Have a biscuit.'

'Thank you.'

Lacey accepted the mug and took a biscuit to make it a tea party and sat at the table. Pritchard got his spectacles and a notebook from the top of the television set, and sat at the other side of the table.

'This is what you've come about.' He put his spectacles on and opened the notebook at a section that was marked with a piece of paper. 'James Russell.'

Lacey took out his own notebook and a ballpoint pen. He crunched the biscuit in his mouth and waited expectantly.

Pritchard looked at Lacey over the top of his spectacles.

'As it happens, I'm glad it's you I'm giving the details to, and not the young lady I spoke to on the phone.'

'Why?'

'Well, I know the inquest verdict was misadventure, but that was to save the feelings of the family. It was one of those funny ones, if you know what I mean. You know, a sex case.'

'What sort of sex case?'

'A carotid nerve job. They're more common than people imagine, but that's usually because coroners never give them a lot of publicity.'

Lacey still didn't understand.

'You'd better give me all you've got, Dennis. And slowly. I don't write shorthand.'

'Right.' He looked at his notebook. 'James Russell, an American gent, but he'd been resident in London for five years. His wife found him when she got home from a concert. He was in his study on the second floor. Mr Russell had a noose round his neck and was hanging from the door.

'Ingenious really, but they always are. He'd tied the rope to the door handle on the outside and thrown it over the top so the noose hung down to the right length.' He paused. 'You know, it's amazing how it brings it all back. One of so many. I couldn't remember him until I started going through the notes.'

Lacey said: 'I'm glad you kept them. Maybe you should write that book.'

'Yes. Maybe I will. Anyway, back to Mr Russell. We can't leave the poor sod hanging there for ever, can we?' He laughed, without malice.

'He'd been standing on a foot stool. It was lying on its side a couple of feet away. It often happens like that. The pleasure gets too intense, their feet kick out, and bingo ... instead of experiencing sexual delight, he ended up hanging himself.

'The coroner, it was Mr Beatty at that time, he used to be discreet about them and return a verdict of misadventure. If there was any doubt about it – you know, that it might be suicide – he'd give an open verdict.'

Lacey nodded.

'There was no mistake?'

'No mistake. Mr Russell had taken his trousers off and folded them on a chair. His underpants were round his knees, and there were open magazines on the floor all round him. Art books. Pictures of naked women.'

Ex-sergeant Pritchard had retained his delicacy by describing them as art books.

'And this sort of death is normal?'

'Well, not normal, but pretty frequent. I had a bank manager once. His wife found him hanging from the bedroom door. Stone dead and dressed in her pink knickers and nightie. And there was a bloke whose body we pulled out of the canal. He'd got all the gear on. Frock, stockings and suspenders, and a rope round his neck.

'Apparently he'd tied the rope round a rock, dropped the rock in the water and let it pull him under. He got a kick out of nearly drowning and at the right moment he cut the rope with a pair of scissors. Only he dropped them. A diver went down and found the scissors. He found dozens of other rocks with bits of rope tied round them as well. He'd been doing it for weeks. It makes you think.'

It did. Lacey was sidetracked into imagining how the man got dressed up in women's clothes, threw himself in a canal and then went home soaking wet with a smile on his face and a bruise on his Adam's apple. It was surreal.

Lacey said: 'This isn't what I was expecting. You've taken me into areas I didn't know existed.'

'People are funny, Peter. And everybody's got secrets. They might hide them when they're alive but they have a habit of sneaking out when they're dead. And it's the loved ones that get hurt, the people they leave behind.

'I remember with Mr Russell, his wife was in shock for days. Couldn't speak to me, not properly. But we put a statement together and tidied him up. There was no mention at the inquest of magazines or the state of his clothes. It was a formality. Mr Beatty had all the statements and he called me to swear on oath that the circumstances were correct,

Mrs Russell gave the identification and that was it. They never took more than three or four minutes when it was a straight-up-and-downer.'

Lacey said: 'Were there any press reports?'

'A paragraph in the local paper, that's all, just to record the coroner's verdict.'

'At the time, Dennis, you had no doubt this was a straight-up-and-downer?'

'No doubt.'

'Have you ever had any cause to think differently?'

'Until your young lady called, I never had any cause to think of it at all.'

'Yes, of course, you said.'

'But since she did, and since you're here, of course I'm thinking differently. If you're interested in it all these years later, perhaps something was wrong. But if it was, I didn't see it.'

He held up the notebook.

'According to this, there was no evidence of anybody else being there. No booze or drugs lying around. No signs of an orgy or a kinky party, if you know what I mean. He was on his own and his wife's shock was genuine. You can tell, after a while, them that put it on.'

Lacey nodded, and had a drink of tea.

Pritchard added: 'It's not that I can remember it that well, of course, it was so long ago. But I can tell from the way I wrote the notes.'

'I trust your judgement, Dennis. And I appreciate the help.'

He shrugged.

'It makes a change from the bloody greenhouse.'

'Write the book.'

'I might at that.'

'But I'm afraid you'll have to do it without this particular notebook. Do you mind?'

He held out his hand and Pritchard handed it over.

'I thought you'd want it.'

'I doubt whether you'll get it back.'

126

'I've got plenty more.'

'It's also my duty to remind you of the Official Secrets Act.'

'Of course.'

'I can't tell you any more but, well, you might read about it in the papers before too long. Some of it, not all. Discretion is essential.'

'I understand.'

Lacey nodded, took another biscuit to show business was over, and prepared to lead Pritchard through it again, but this time encouraging him to reminisce in the hope that it might spark more memories.

Pritchard had confided he had a title for the book he had never written: *A Funny Thing Happened On My Way To The Morgue*. After listening to his stories for an hour Lacey believed him, and found that it put his own profession into a strange perspective.

Lacey had seen people killed, had been responsible for killing, and had come close to being killed himself. His experiences had given him a healthy respect for life and the knowledge that there was little dignity in death. He hadn't realized there was so much obscene humour in it.

Pritchard had insisted on driving him to the nearest tube station when they finished talking, and all the way there Lacey watched the man's big, bony hands on the steering-wheel of the Volvo.

These were the hands that had handled the secrets of a thousand corpses, as well as pretty young Edna. How could anyone who did such a job lead a normal life? How could they grow tomatoes and make tea for two?

Very easily, of course.

Man adapted quickly, as Lacey himself had done. The first time he had killed had been the worst, but when he had to do it again he had sensed a terrible arrogance lurking at the back of his conscience that enjoyed playing God.

He and Pritchard made an odd combination, a professional and a tradesman involved in the same business.

But Pritchard was the normal one, the acceptable one, who had carried out an unsavoury job on behalf of society, while Lacey had operated beyond its bounds and snuffed life as he would snuff a candle for the sake of Queen and Country.

Pritchard's conscience would be clear, but what about his own?

He was glad to leave the ex-policeman to his loneliness and join the anonymous bustle of the underground. It was more conducive to constructive thought.

His notes were becoming a dossier but they still didn't make sense. How did an accidental sex death make James Russell the first victim? Was it accidental?

Pritchard, who had described it as a straight-up-and-downer, now had second thoughts, not because of what he had found at the scene, but because it had prompted an investigation so many years later.

The ex-policeman had stated the obvious. The whole point of what had happened so far had been to lead Lacey to James Russell. The man's death was important, and if it hadn't been accidental it had been deliberate.

In his office, Lacey filled another sheet of paper with headings, arrows indicating possible links, exclamation marks, and words written in capital letters encased in circles. He stopped when the lead in his pencil broke. He accepted the hint that he wasn't getting anywhere.

He opened the drawer behind him and stared at the packet of Gitanes. The packet stared back, daring him. He closed the drawer and made coffee instead.

Natalie took hers black, like he did, but Malcolm preferred his milky with three sugars. Lacey put the turtle mug on his desk and Malcolm, who was wearing green cords and a matching roll-neck sweater, looked at him over the top of half-moon spectacles.

'Thank you, love.'

Lacey toasted him with his own mug.

'Do I look as much like Superman as you look like a turtle?'

128

Malcolm surveyed him with deliberation.

'Probably,' he said.

'Bitch!'

Lacey went back to his notes and frustration. Half an hour later Natalie saved him from the Gitanes he hadn't yet earned. She came through the open door of his office in a rush. Her face was flushed and she was smiling.

He said: 'Don't tell me. We're still on a roll?'

'I've found Mattie Purcell.' She handed him a piece of paper with an address on it. 'She lives in Cannon Beach, Oregon. It's a town on the Pacific Coast, a sort of artists' colony.'

He read the address, sat back in his chair and stretched his legs.

'Natalie, I love you.'

'I'll tell Susan.'

'Never heard of polygamy?'

'I don't like parrots. What are you going to do?'

Lacey had no option but to go to Oregon. He believed the death of Mattie Purcell's husband was pivotal to finding the Blunt documents and he didn't want to jeopardize his chances of solving the mystery with a telephone interrogation.

She might not want to speak to him, and if he was six thousand miles away she didn't have to: she could simply put the phone down. Face to face, he could be more persuasive.

'I'll go. If she's there. Maybe she's on holiday? Maybe she's visiting a sick aunt in Sacramento?'

'You want me to find out?'

'Yes. Be devious.'

It took her ten minutes before she came back into Lacey's office.

'Miss Purcell wasn't at home. She was at a gallery she owns, in the town.'

She handed him another address.

'Does she suspect anything?'

'No. I was Jessica Fulbright from San Francisco?' She switched to an American drawl. 'Wanted to know if Mattie

Purcell was Mattie Defreitas that was? From Jackson Heights?'
She reverted to English. 'She wasn't. She's the genuine article
and she's alive and well in Cannon Beach. It sounds like a
nice place. Maybe you'd like me to go?'

'Your fiancé and my wife wouldn't understand. You keep
telling me.'

'I didn't mean with you.' She checked the notebook she
carried. 'There's a British Airways flight from Heathrow at
two forty-five tomorrow afternoon and there are plenty of
seats. You change planes at Seattle for Portland, Oregon.'

Susan was understanding, as always, when he told her in bed
that night that he was going away again.

'It's just an excuse,' she said. 'You're getting too old to
manage it two nights in a row.'

'Don't you believe it. I've been learning new tricks. They
involve a rope and dressing up in a frock.'

'I always dress up in a frock.'

'I don't.'

She laughed softly in the darkness.

'We'll try the rope if you like, but let's keep the frocks
where they belong. You don't have the legs for high heels.'

'Agreed. I'll bring you some duty free hemp back.'

'I'd prefer Nino Cerutti. It smells better and it doesn't
leave marks on your wrists.'

'I'll get soft hemp. And Nino Cerutti.'

'You sweet-talker, you.'

She stroked his naked groin beneath the sheets and for a
few seconds he thought that images of bondage and the soft
caress might raise his enthusiasm. But it was late, he had too
much on his mind, and besides, he was too tired and too old.

130

THIRTEEN

The instructions were simple, which was exactly how Danny Harper liked them.

He wasn't paid to do complicated things because he couldn't do complicated things. If he had been able to, then he would be breaking complicated things down into simple things and paying someone like himself to do them.

Shit, then he'd have everything from man-management to the price of chowder to worry about. It was best he stuck to doing what he did well.

The job was a thousand miles from the City of the Angels, which pleased him because it gave him a chance to run the white Caddy with red upholstery he had just bought from Billy the Fish. It was a beautiful car and he loved it more than Lulu's black ass.

When he got back he would lay Lulu's black ass inside the white Caddy and combine his lusts, whether she objected or not. Maybe he'd get Billy the Fish to drive the car while he did her. Just like the car, she was his to use and she better believe it. He had discovered life was for the takers and he took.

He had driven out of the city through Beverly Hills, just to remind himself he was a part of the glamour, the hustle and the sleaze, and took the road north through Ventura and Santa Barbara. He crossed the coastal mountains at Gaviota Pass and kept to the coast even though the road was slower, to drive through Big Sur and Carmel and Monterey, because the names still gave him a kick.

The views of the Pacific to his left and the stands of redwood and pine to his right he could take or leave. Sure it was nice. He saw it on TV all the time. But what really charged him was the area's wealth and extravagance.

131

Back there was San Simeon where William Randolph Hearst had built a castle. Danny had been there once, as a tourist, to see how millionaires lived. The place was full of crap they pretended was art but he had to admit the guy had style. It would have been a hell of a place for a party.

Danny had no illusions.

Growing up on the wrong side of the tracks in Flagstaff, Arizona, with a mother who was a sometime waitress and a part-time whore, had taught him to expect little and get less. He had survived childhood on a diet of chilli burgers and sleepless nights, when he had tried to ignore the noises coming from his mother's room through the paper-thin walls of the apartment.

He was bright enough to realize he was the product of one of those nights of casual fucking and, judging by the men in stained vests with sagging guts who had wandered around the place the morning after, he was glad he had never known his father.

Shit, any illusions he might have had would have been right down the pan if he had actually seen the son of a bitch. And anyway, who said fathers were compulsory? He was happy to be a casual fuck. It had a ring to it. Don't fuck with the casual fuck. Or you'll get fucked. He liked that.

He liked the reputation he had and the employment it had brought him. The people who mattered trusted him and their confidence and money had given him opportunities that a guy who was short, with red hair and the sort of white skin that never tanned, couldn't have gotten any other way. Especially not in California, land of the suntanned beachbums who all looked like extras from Federation Wrestling or Mr Universe.

People had called him punk in Flagstaff. They had called him punk in Vegas, too, for a time, until he had started building his reputation. It was like showbusiness. You got your name known around the right people and the offers came. And he was a good performer. Never missed an entrance. No one called him punk now.

He was twenty-eight years old, looked ten years older because of the tinted spectacles and receding hairline, and because he took his work seriously. He had come a long way from Flagstaff, Arizona.

The noises in the night had been the spur to get him started on the road to hell.

He grinned. That's what a cop had told him one time, that he was on the road to hell. Well, he'd been to hell and he liked it.

The noises in the night had led him to start staying out as soon as he was old enough. It was no hardship after a while. He would break into places to find somewhere to sleep. If he found a good place, in a factory or some place where no one knew he'd been, he'd go back and use it on a regular basis.

He'd save his trashing sprees for those houses he didn't like. Those houses with the smug expressions and the stereo and the three TVs and the drapes that matched the sofa that came new from J.C. Penney's.

He got a kick out of messing up those places and a kick out of imagining the reaction of the owners when they got back to their suburban respectability and found he'd shit in their bed and pissed and masturbated in the wife's underwear drawer.

Danny grabbed his crotch at the memory. It still made his dick go stiff.

He joined the 101 north of Salinas and would stick on it through to San Francisco to make up time. It was a highway that ran from Mexico to Canada, a highway with the good life in abundance in the towns and cities it linked, with opportunities for advancement for anybody with the nerve to try.

One thing Danny Harper had was nerve. Shit, he'd had fuck all else when he finally left Flagstaff for Vegas, one step ahead of the law, with a juvenile record of delinquency and two terms in the joint, for burglary and theft, that had rounded off his education.

The police had been interested in talking to him about a burglary and attempted rape, but he knew damn well they wouldn't have been interested in listening to him explain that

133

it had been the bitch's own fault for coming home early and he hadn't been raping her, just spilling his seed in her face.

He chuckled and felt his crotch again. Memory lane was a turn-on.

Now he was a businessman who worked for a major organization, a professional in a suit and tie who knew how to be polite, a regular guy, to whom people said have a nice day and then forgot his face.

When he was working, personal pleasures, like Lulu's ass, stayed at home. Except this time. This time, the job was going to be a personal pleasure. His instructions told him to make it just that.

It was something to look forward to on the long drive and it reminded him of the first time he had made it with Lulu.

She had not been so eager for him to have his sexual way with her but he had been persuasive by locking the door and pulling most of her clothes off.

'I'm not that kind of girl,' she'd said.

'You will be,' he'd said.

She'd excited him, standing there defiant in a torn shirt and little white panties that made her black skin look so much blacker.

He had undressed slowly to enjoy the power, to enjoy the moment, and when he was finally naked she'd laughed and pointed at his dick.

'Who the hell do you think you're going to please with that?' she'd said.

'Me!' he'd said, and they'd both grinned and her resistance had melted.

That first time had been a disappointment, but she'd learned to fight when he fucked her, to cry and plead until he subdued her, and sometimes tied her wrists.

Lulu often called him a dirty son of a bitch and he agreed and he'd tell her the dirty things he'd done as a kid, and when those stories were exhausted he'd tell her stories of things he'd maybe done and rapes he'd maybe committed and watch her eyes glaze and her lips dry out so that she had to lick them and then they'd go and do it and he'd maybe hit

134

her some and she'd enjoy it and admit she was a dirty son of a bitch too.

They were good for each other: Dirty Lulu and Casual Fuck. It was a union made in sleaze and, in between the fights and the accusations, they revelled in it.

But for now he was Mr Respectable, a businessman checking out a real estate deal up north, and missing the wife and kids he'd left at home.

He took the Bay Bridge out of San Francisco and round about Fairfield he stopped and ate at a Denny's. Then he headed up to Interstate 5 and settled back for the tedious run through the Sacramento Valley, up through the mountains and into Oregon and down into Grants Pass where he turned off the freeway.

At a store he bought a six pack and a bag of potato chips before driving to the Shilo Motel.

He had stayed once before and liked the informality, the affordable rates, the cable TV and the fact that a large number of its guests only stayed one night, travelling south to Disneyland and the wonders of Hollywood or north to Seattle and Vancouver. With so many one-nighters he wouldn't be noticed.

Harper showered, had a beer in the lounge and dinner in the restaurant. After the meal he went straight to his room, watched TV, drank beer and ate the potato chips.

Before he finally went to bed he checked the map one more time and worked out the distances. He got between the sheets and smiled as he anticipated the job ahead. He slept soundly.

FOURTEEN

Jimmy Russell was all over the front pages of the morning newspapers.

The statement that Lacey had taken from Latimer's house had been sent to the Press Association news agency in London. He had no doubt copies of it had also gone to Associated Press of America and all the other agencies that served the world. They didn't know who Russell was, but the statement was used in full in all the papers and kept the story bubbling.

At least Sam Bryson was back from his recruitment drive in Cambridge and sending out smoke signals from his office.

Lacey made himself a coffee and stuck his head round the door.

'Got a minute?'

'Just the man. Come in and tell me what went wrong in Lisbon.'

Lacey sat and they faced each other across a desk that was for once clear of clutter. He told Bryson about the aborted Lisbon trip and the answerphone in Engelbert Street; he didn't tell him he had seen the documents and photographs that Lamont-Smith had.

He told him about James Russell and Mattie Purcell and gave him a copy of the statement that mentioned the James Russell Trust which had been reprinted in the Press. Before going home the previous night he had underlined phrases in the statement that might be significant.

Bryson read it and puffed smoke.

He said: 'Do you want to talk me through it?'

Lacey shrugged.

'Most of it is pretty obvious. In the first paragraph, for instance, it says Blunt knew "royal scandals and diplomatic secrets". We're presuming this relates to the Duke of Windsor and Joseph Kennedy making a deal with Goering in Biarritz. Are there any other scandals we should watch out for?'

'I haven't been specifically warned about any in this context.'

The answer didn't resolve Lacey's doubts.

He said: 'You see, Sam, when you briefed me, you were very specific. You told me what the scandal was – the Biarritz Agreement – but then you told me I shouldn't see any of the papers involved. Why not, if all they referred to was a Biarritz Agreement?'

It was Bryson's turn to shrug.

'Need to know.'

'But if this agreement is so sensitive, maybe there was no need for me to know even that much? Maybe I should have just been sent to get Blunt's papers without being given a hint about what was in them. Do you get the point I'm making?'

'Tell me.'

'Maybe there are other things in the Legacy that are also sensitive. Maybe I was told only so much to stop me looking any further.'

'There may be. But they don't concern you. We just want the whole bloody lot back here where they belong, and not splashed across the world's press.'

'But they do concern me. They could tell me who killed Latimer and who tried to follow me yesterday. Having only half a story is dangerous.'

'You were followed? Here in London?'

'Yes. I lost them. But they know about Engelbert Street. Which is why I think you should tell me everything.'

'Peter, you know better. In this game you're lucky to get half a story. You complete your assignment and walk away. Not only don't you need to know why, it's safer not to know why. This job doesn't have a finished product; it provides strands for somebody else to weave.'

What Bryson said was acceptable 90 per cent of the time but what angered Lacey was the 10 per cent when bureaucrats and politicians used field officers as pawns. That was when field officers became as expendable as the truth. He hoped it wasn't happening on this occasion.

'OK, Sam. We'll move on.' He looked at his copy of the statement. 'Second paragraph. The FBI knew Blunt was a spy in June 1963 but didn't tell MI5 for seven months. Five then waited another three months before finally tackling Blunt.' He looked across the table at Bryson. 'Why did it take so long?'

'Several reasons. The chap who blew the whistle was Michael Straight, an American whom Blunt tried to recruit when they were both at Cambridge. Maybe the Americans wanted to debrief Straight at leisure so that when they finally passed on the information there would be no more cock-ups. Don't forget Philby had warned Burgess and Maclean only a decade earlier and the Yanks were still concerned about the penetration of our secret service.

'Anyway, by then Blunt was no longer a major threat. He'd left MI5 and had been suspected for a long time. But he was close to the royal family. That would have caused Five to move cautiously. The situation had to be discussed with the Palace, apart from deciding how to actually make an approach.' He shook his head. 'I don't think the time lapses are too extreme in the circumstances.'

Lacey offered no comment but moved on to the next part of the statement he had underlined.

'The next paragraph intrigues me. It says Blunt's papers were never found "despite the dirty tricks of MI5". The inference is that Five tried something. Do you know what it was?'

'I think all they tried was to get Blunt to confess. He did confess, but whether or not he did so with an ace up his sleeve I don't know. It doesn't matter whether Five tried anything or not. What matters is what is for sale now.'

Lacey nodded. Bryson was uncomfortable and on edge; he didn't want to discuss the case as they normally would, but wanted to know how far he had got with it. Bryson was undoubtedly reporting back to the same Control who was running Ian Lamont-Smith, someone with very important connections.

'Who am I working for, Sam?'

'Her Majesty's Government.'

'Who in particular?'

'You don't need to know, Peter.'

'Is this a solo operation? Or am I representing the interests of our Cousins, as well?'

'Same answer. Let's not play games.'

'I'm trying not to. But one man is dead in Lisbon and I was followed here in London. Maybe it was the killer from Lisbon. Maybe another interested party. Whoever it was, it would be nice to know who I'm working for. If I'm solo, the killer and the tail could be a Cousin. I'd hate to kill a Cousin in the line of duty.' The two men stared at each other. 'Am I solo, Sam?'

'I'm sorry. I still can't tell you. This affair is extremely delicate. It's best you know as little as possible.'

Lacey let his silence register his protest. At last, he nodded and got to his feet.

'OK, we'll do it your way. I hope it works.'

'So do I.' Bryson tapped the bowl of the pipe in an ashtray. 'Where do you go from here?'

'To Oregon this afternoon. To see Jimmy Russell's widow. To find out why he's so important.'

'Tread carefully. And clear up behind you. No loose ends on this one.'

Lacey smiled. There were always loose ends. The important thing was being able to deny them.

He had a Club Class ticket for the ten-hour polar flight to Seattle, where he would change planes for the forty-five-minute commuter trip to Portland.

In the departure lounge he sat on a bench seat and felt underdressed flying Club Class to America in his old leather jacket. Maybe people would think he was an ageing rock star,

139

except that rock stars went First Class. An ageing rock star of intermediate means, then.

Lacey watched a particularly attractive stewardess walk across the departure lounge and stop to talk to the middle-aged woman who was waiting at the gate to collect boarding cards. She had nice ankles, nice legs, nice everything and was twenty years outside his scope of possibilities, even if there hadn't been Susan to consider.

The two women spoke to each other and the stewardess handed over a piece of paper. The middle-aged woman spoke into a microphone.

'I have a message for Mr Peter Barnes, travelling to Portland. Mr Peter Barnes?'

Shit. This was all he wanted. Starting a covert trip by taking a bow in front of his fellow passengers.

As he began to stand up he felt someone staring at him and it wasn't the curious gaze of a bored traveller. His scalp prickled and his armpit felt empty after carrying a gun for two days. He had had to leave the Walther P38 in the office. British Airways were particular about that sort of hand luggage.

The man was sitting further along the row of bench seats.

Where the hell did he know him from?

He wore a blue suit and had a briefcase but he didn't look like a businessman. Aged about thirty, good looking, if you liked dark hair, clean-cut features and a suntan, and self-confident. The bloke was expensive but his confidence didn't come from money. He was smiling.

The man eventually chuckled, as if he had made a decision, and got to his feet. He walked towards Lacey and held out his right hand. There was no gun in it; he wanted to shake.

'Hi. I think it's time we introduced ourselves. My name's Ben Miller.'

He spoke in an American accent.

Lacey shook the hand and remembered.

'Lisbon. The café.'

140

'That's right. Also the castle wall the morning after, the same flight back to London, and a van parked in Engelbert Street.'

'Jesus Christ.'

'I thought your name was Peter Barnes? Or is it Lacey?'

'I'm not sure any more.'

'Look, get your message. Then we'll talk.'

Who the hell was Ben Miller?

The man had been in Lisbon and now he was heading to the West Coast of America with Lacey. Was he a Cousin? Or an assassin?

Lacey went to the middle-aged woman, identified himself, and was given a slip of paper. It said: 'Trip cancelled. Ring the office.'

What the hell was going on?

There was a public telephone at the entrance to the lounge. As he started towards it the middle-aged woman announced that First and Club Class passengers could now start boarding.

Ben Miller grinned at Lacey as he went past and said: 'We'll talk on board.'

Natalie answered the phone.

'What's wrong?'

'Your luck ran out. Sam called. He says to forget James Russell. It will be taken care of. He says the trip, the whole operation, they're cancelled.'

'Why?'

'He didn't say. You've scratched someone in a sore place, Peter.'

'Bastards.'

He was angry. He'd had a feeling about this one; about someone else pulling the strings, about not being trusted with a full story.

'Where is Sam?'

'He's still out. He had a luncheon appointment at White's. He's still not back.'

Bryson had probably been briefing the real Control over lunch at the club. Jimmy Russell's name had obviously been

141

discussed and Lacey's trip to see his widow, and Lacey's position had been reconsidered. The decision to cancel had perhaps come with the pudding, when it had finally been decided he wasn't trustworthy enough to handle this particular royal scandal. Maybe his old school tie had let him down again.

'Who was Sam having lunch with?'

Natalie hesitated. She wasn't supposed to know and she definitely wasn't supposed to tell.

'Leonard Chesterton.'

Law and Order Chesterton, also known as the Smiling Viper. The hardman of Westminster with a reputation for ruining the careers of rivals. It was said he had perfected the art of mugging his opponents from the front while they were still expecting to shake hands. That was why the PM kept him so close: to watch him.

It sounded right that Chesterton would be the man briefing Bryson. He was perfect for the role of intermediary between the Palace, Number 10 and the SIS.

But why call the operation off and stop him going to see Mattie Purcell?

Maybe Ben Miller had the answer. And he was already on the Boeing 747. Economy passengers were boarding now, and he didn't have much time.

'I can't cancel. Somebody else knows about Jimmy Russell's widow and they're already on the plane. I'm going with them.'

'Peter! Sam was specific. There's no choice.'

'There's always a choice. And I've made it.'

FIFTEEN

There were eighteen seats in First Class in an area that would have accommodated fifty seats in Club or eighty seats in Economy.

After take-off, Ben Miller fixed for Lacey to be upgraded to First Class and came to escort him to the front of the aircraft. Maybe now people would think he was an ageing rock star.

The seats were in pairs; three rows of two pairs and a final row of three pairs. There were only four other people in the section, two men on the back row where smoking was permitted, who could have been diplomats or gun-runners, and an unmistakably English couple in their well-coutured sixties, who sat on the starboard side and whose body language indicated total disdain for their surroundings and each other. It looked like the only thing they had in common was wealth.

Miller led him towards the nose of the plane and they sat in the first two seats on the port side. The seats were wide, long and very comfortable.

A stewardess appeared as if someone had rubbed a lamp and Miller looked at Lacey.

'You want something?'

'Only an explanation.'

Miller waved her away.

'I guess I owe you one at that.'

'Go ahead. We have ten hours.'

'OK. I'm on the same job as you. I've been hired to find the Blunt papers. I also believe we have the same objective when we find them? To see they're destroyed?'

Lacey smiled. He had forgotten that Americans frequently talked in questions.

143

'Tell me about Lisbon. Tell me how you know me and why you're on this plane.'

'Sure. Have you heard of Dixon Green? It's a security company.'

'I've heard of it.'

'Thought you might. Graham Lee works for us. I believe he's an old . . . chum? . . . from Century House?'

'We were never "chums". He thought I was a prat and I thought he was a bigger prat.'

Miller laughed.

'He said something similar. Anyway, I'm an associate director of Dixon Green. We're one of the biggest companies of our kind in Europe and probably the best. We do pretty well in the States too.

'Lisbon was straightforward. I knew Latimer's movements and hired a girl to take to the café. You may or may not recall I was carrying a briefcase?' Lacey recalled. Everyone in Lisbon carried a briefcase. 'It was bugged. A directional mike picked up everything you and Latimer said.' He shrugged. 'I was quite happy with the way you were arranging things so I let them go ahead. I was on the walls of the castle the next morning, above Latimer's house.'

'Did you shoot him?'

'No. But I saw it happen.'

Miller picked up the briefcase that was by his feet, opened it and took out a large brown envelope which he handed to Lacey.

Lacey took out half a dozen ten by eight colour photographs. They showed a man in a brown overall standing on a chair in the garden next to the lawyer's house. He was holding a rifle. He was also photographed after he had got down from the chair. In one of the pictures, he stared blatantly at the camera. The last was an enlargement of the man's head and shoulders.

He had grey hair at the sides and was bald on top. His face was thin; drawn, as if he was ill. His age was difficult to tell because of what looked like a weight loss. From the other shots, he judged the man to be about five foot seven or

144

eight. He fitted the description given by Veronica Jayston of the man who had rented her second-floor office.

Lacey said: 'Do you know him?'

'No. We're looking, but it's not an exceptional face.'

'Did you bug Latimer's house?'

'You saw them?'

'There was one under the kitchen table. When people get shot, I have a habit of crawling under kitchen tables.'

'I had that done. And his phone.'

'So you had the answerphone number?'

'Sure did.'

'That was when I sussed I was being tailed.'

'You were.'

'How far did you get?'

'We lost you on the tube. But we got your picture.'

'Did you talk to Veronica Jayston?'

'Didn't have to.'

'Don't tell me. More electronics?'

Miller grinned.

'We live in an age of advanced technology.'

'And policemen are getting younger. Did you hear everything?'

'Enough.'

Lacey shook his head.

'I think you owe me wages for being your legman.'

'Maybe we can work something out.'

'Maybe.'

Miller flicked with a finger the photographs that Lacey was still holding.

'The description the Jayston woman gave you fits this guy.'

'It does.'

'So why does the guy set up an auction then shoot his auctioneer?'

'Best publicity in the world.'

Miller nodded.

'I came to the same conclusion.'

'Bully for you.'

'Rancour doesn't suit you, Pete.'

145

'It's Peter, not Pete. In fact, you can call me Mr fucking Lacey.'

Miller laughed.

'OK, I'd be pissed too. Let me make it up to you.'

He opened the briefcase again and took out another envelope that he handed over. Inside were photographs of the documents that Lamont-Smith had.

'How did you get these?'

'He went to the pub before you warned him.'

Lacey sighed.

'You tapped his phone too?'

'Of course. And I've had a full biography done on him. Did you know he served with the Special Air Services?'

'Really?'

Lacey tried to make it sound as if the information was of no interest, although it interested and surprised him greatly.

'Another piece of information I'll give you for free. He's working for Leonard Oliver Chesterton.'

'I know.'

At least being able to say so with authority gave him satisfaction.

Miller pointed at the documents.

'The one by Hess is a report for Hitler. The Duke saw Hitler at Berchtesgaden on 22 October 1937, and he and Wallis had dinner with Hess and his wife the same night in Munich. It seems the Duke continued discussions with Hess that he'd started with Hitler. Part of it relates to a "solution to the Jewish problem". No, he wasn't suggesting gas chambers. He preferred mass emigration and deportation. So did Hess.

'The one by Ribbentrop was also to Hitler, written when the Duke was in Portugal. It's confirmation that fifty million Swiss francs had been deposited in a bank in Geneva on his behalf and it refers to a list of British politicians that the Duke wanted in his government. It seems they had finally made a deal.'

Lacey wondered if the documents were real or fake. He also wondered if the deal had been made in Biarritz.

146

Miller pointed to the picture of the Duke giving a fascist salute to German troops.

'That was taken on his visit to Germany in 1937. He was inspecting the Death's Head Division of the SS at their training headquarters at Crossensee.

'The other one is a line-up of royals, probably taken in the mid-1930s. That's the Duke, when he was Prince of Wales, and the others are Mountbatten, the Duke of Kent and David Bowes-Lyon. Bowes-Lyon was the brother of the Elizabeth who married George VI. Your Queen Mum.'

Lacey held up the page of doggerel verse.

'And this?'

'It's in Blunt's handwriting. We presume it's from a diary or notebook. It could be included to prove the rest of it really does come from the Blunt papers.'

Lacey put the photographs of the assassin and the photographed copies of the documents in their respective envelopes and offered them back to Miller.

'Keep 'em. Gesture of goodwill.'

'Who are you working for?'

'Sorry. I can't tell you.'

'CIA?'

Miller just smiled.

'The Kennedys?'

The smile widened.

Miller said: 'I think you know something I don't.'

'Well, that makes a change.'

'Want to tell me?'

'No.'

They appraised each other.

Miller had been open and friendly so far, or had appeared to be. Lacey had no reason to doubt that he was who he said he was. This was the sort of job that would not go through the normal channels of any government agency; which was why D14a had got it and were apparently under the personal control of Chesterton. If D14a had not been available Chesterton could have commissioned Dixon Green instead.

147

But Chesterton hadn't, and Miller had intimated he had not been hired by the Kennedys. So who was he working for?

Lacey said: 'Why are you on this plane?'

Miller shrugged.

'I'm going to Cannon Beach, same as you, to see Mattie Purcell.'

'So you found Jimmy Russell?'

'I found his death certificate. Our American office found his widow.'

'Do you know how Russell died?'

'I know what was on the certificate. Do you know more?'

'Yes. I know.'

Lacey smiled at his own foolishness. He was actually feeling smug.

Miller said: 'Are you going to tell me or make me wait until I can ask the widow?'

'I talked with the police sergeant who handled the death. Russell apparently strangled himself with a noose while trying to get some kind of sexual high. His wife found him hanging from a door. There were dirty magazines on the floor and he had no trousers on. The sergeant says it happens all the time. When it does, coroners don't publicize the facts to save the feelings of the family.'

The American nodded.

Lacey said: 'Have you spoken to the woman, to this Miss Purcell?'

'No. But I had her checked out. She has a gallery and takes classes. In the summer she's a leading light in an adult arts programme in the town that's sponsored by Portland State University. She's lived in Cannon Beach fourteen years. I have an appointment to see her tomorrow morning. She thinks I'm a reporter from the *Oregonian*. How about you? Did you call her?'

'No. I just made sure she'd be there.'

They exchanged more meaningful stares.

Lacey said: 'How are we going to work this?'

'I think that for the time being we'd better work it together. We both know where we're going and why, and we'll be

148

asking the same questions. Maybe we'd better wait until we reach a conflict of interests before declaring war.'

'Sounds reasonable.'

'Good. I've rented a plane at Seattle. Instead of Portland we'll fly direct to Clatsop County Airfield. With luck we'll be able to see Mattie Purcell tonight.'

Lacey didn't sleep but it was possible to stretch out and worry in comfort. Now the talking with Ben Miller was over he had time to consider his position and the last-minute instructions to abandon the mission that he had ignored.

Sam Bryson wouldn't like working under Chesterton, but he would do so out of loyalty. Bryson was a staunch monarchist, despite disliking many of the institutions and practices of the establishment.

If Lacey explained his reasons for continuing his trip to the United States he had no doubt Bryson would accept them. The situation had called for an instant assessment not covered in standing orders.

That's what Lacey was supposed to be good at; that's why he had been moved from Century House and put in a department people preferred not to know about because they had a habit of making decisions that sometimes caused a mess.

The reason why Lacey, D14a and Chesterton were involved was deniability. From the point of view of Number 10 or the Palace, Chesterton was a perfect choice to run the retrieval. He was ruthless, got things done and would ensure discretion. But he would also be watching his career and would be wary of taking risks which made him and his judgement vulnerable. That made Lacey vulnerable.

If Lacey's trip resulted in a swift breakthrough maybe Chesterton would accept it; if it didn't, the politician was not a forgiving person. Any blame would fall on Lacey's head. That he didn't mind. It was the other type of vulnerability Lacey didn't like, vulnerability to being killed, although it now appeared as if the mysterious gunman who was stage-managing the proceedings was out for publicity rather than a death toll.

149

Lacey also wondered why the names of Jimmy Russell and Mattie Purcell had triggered the decision to take him off the hunt, for it surely had.

That was the only new piece of information Bryson had taken with him to lunch, and it had proved particularly unpalatable.

SIXTEEN

They landed on time at Sea-Tac International Airport, and from their privileged position at the front of the plane Lacey and Miller were among the first passengers to disembark. Neither had to wait for suitcases to be unloaded; they both carried only hand luggage.

Miller was waiting for Lacey on the other side of immigration and customs. With him was a man in a suit that was cut like a uniform who escorted them on to the runway. The air was crisp but hardly fresh, as it was mixed with the fumes of a taxiing Alaskan Airways jet.

They climbed into a jeep which the man drove to the far side of the airport. They were heading towards a small aeroplane with an engine on each wing and a third mounted on top of its tail fin. It looked clumsy, as if someone had constructed it from a kit and put the pieces together wrongly.

Lacey said: 'We're going in that?'

Miller said: 'It's a Trislander. Perfect for this coastline. Short take-off and landing.'

At least they were comfortable. The interior had ten seats set around tables in an executive business layout and a stewardess who brought them coffee. Turbulence was slight, and Lacey enjoyed the view of the ocean on the starboard side and the snow-capped mountains on the port. The stewardess pointed out Mount Rainier and Mount St Helens, the volcanic peak that had erupted in 1980. She also provided them with road maps of North-west Oregon and tourist pamphlets of the area they were heading to.

The small airfield they landed at was near Warrenton, a town across the estuary that led into the Columbia River. The pilot taxied to the low terminal building and when they climbed out they were met by a young man in slacks and sports jacket, who had a wholesome toothy grin.

'Welcome to Clatsop County.'

He said it like he meant it and he probably did.

Lacey told himself to forget his cynicism; he had been away too long. It had come as a shock on his first visit to the United States to discover that what you saw was what you got. The friendliness was genuine.

The young man handed over the keys to a Buick Century hire car he had just unloaded from a trailer.

They said thank you, Miller signed a form accepting delivery, and they were on their way with the minimum of formalities. They joined the coastal Highway 101 and drove into logging country.

Roadsigns pointed down turn-offs towards the sea to places called Sunset Beach, West Lake and Surf Pines. A sign said the next town ahead was Seaside.

Natalie would be jealous as hell, thought Lacey. It was perfect, apart from the rain.

It was fine drizzle, the sort that confused windscreen wipers and made them screech in frustration. The light was also going fast. They went through Seaside, a long straight street with clapboard houses, closed shops and directions pointing off to the right to its attractions on the coast.

'Cannon Beach is next,' Lacey said.

A few miles further on, Miller turned off Highway 101, took a couple of narrow bends and crossed a bridge, and they were driving down Hemlock Street, the main road through town.

'This is nice,' Lacey said.

Cannon Beach had sidewalks, log cabin buildings, small wooden houses with front gardens, art galleries among the shops and restaurants, a small theatre and a lot of character. This was a rural American community conceived and built by Disney – except that it was real.

Lacey followed their progress on a town street guide as they went through Downtown, Midtown and out on to the southern stretch of Hemlock where there were cabins for

152

rent, motels that seemed unchanged since the fifties, and developments that, although newer, had not been allowed to go higher than three or four storeys.

The address they had for Mattie Purcell was on a dirt road among the trees, a block past the Tolovana Inn, the first modern resort hotel Lacey had seen.

Mattie's home was a wooden bungalow set back from the road. It had a porch at the front and the grass was protected by a white picket fence. A gravel driveway ran alongside the lawn to a double garage. Lights were on in the house and two electric lanterns lit the porch.

They stopped the car on the road, opened the gate and walked down the path to the front door. Miller rang the bell.

A woman opened the door with the words: 'Where's your key?' before she realized they were not who she was expecting. She was about forty years old, slim, and wore slacks and a sweater. Her auburn hair was short and she had that fresh-faced, tanned American look that needed little make-up.

Miller said: 'Hi. We're looking for Mattie Purcell?'

'She's not in right now.' Her look was suspicious. 'Who shall I say called?'

'We're from the *Oregonian*. My secretary made an appointment for tomorrow, but we got here early so decided to say hello. I hope we've not come at a bad time?'

'Actually, you have. I'm in the middle of making dinner.'

'I'm sorry . . .'

A car turned on to the gravel from the dirt road, its headlights giving them fleeting stardom as it swept the porch. The three of them looked towards it.

The woman said: 'Here's Mattie now.'

The car was a yellow Japanese compact. Its lights were switched off and Mattie Purcell got out, slammed the door, climbed the three steps at the end of the porch, and walked towards them.

She was a small woman in her mid-fifties, her hair a natural steel grey, cut short and swept back. Her skirt was loose and ankle-length in maroon cotton that flowed as she walked; her suede boots were flat-heeled like moccasins. The blouse was white cotton and she wore a multicoloured shawl around her shoulders and carried a satchel instead of a handbag.

She said 'Hello?' as she approached, in a way that called for an explanation for their presence.

Miller said: 'Ms Purcell? I'm Ben Miller, this is Peter Lacey. We've come from England to see you.'

The woman at the door said: 'You said you were from the *Oregonian*.'

Miller shrugged in apology.

'I lied.'

Mattie Purcell looked from Miller to Lacey and didn't appear impressed by either. Eventually her gaze settled on Lacey.

'You must be Jessica Fulbright from San Francisco.'

For a moment, Lacey wondered what she was talking about. Then he remembered the name Natalie had used in making sure Mattie Purcell was in Cannon Beach.

He nodded.

'That's me.'

'Mattie, what in hell is going on?'

The younger woman was even more confused.

'Don't worry about it, Linda. I'm sure these gentlemen will tell us. You'd better come inside.'

She led the way, Linda hovering to close the door behind them, still unsure about the intrusion.

The front door led straight into a big living-room with comfortable armchairs and a sofa. Original paintings hung on the walls and the alcoves were filled with books. To the left, steps led up to a dining area and a kitchen. The smell of a roast reminded Lacey he was hungry for real food. To the right was another door that, presumably, led to the bedrooms.

Mattie flung her bag on to the sofa, walked to a fireplace which housed a potted plant, and turned to face them and the room.

'Well?'

Miller said: 'We'd like to talk to you about James Russell.'

'I thought you might.'

Lacey said: 'Why?'

'I watch the news.'

Lacey again: 'It's been on TV?'

She didn't answer but stared at them, as if making up her mind whether to carry the conversation any further.

She said: 'Who are you working for?'

Lacey and Miller exchanged glances.

Miller said: 'Maybe if we told you why we're here?'

'No. Tell me who you're working for.'

'That's difficult,' said Miller. 'I represent a private security company. I can't tell you the name of my client.'

'How about you?'

She looked at Lacey.

'I'm with the British Foreign Office.'

'And it's taken you all these years to get interested in how Jimmy died.' She smiled mirthlessly. 'Linda? Get me a whisky sour?'

'Sure, honey.' The other woman started for the kitchen and hesitated. 'What about . . . ?'

Mattie said: 'Do you want a drink?'

Miller said: 'Coffee?'

Lacey was still dry from all the travelling.

'Do you have a beer?'

Linda asked Miller: 'How do you take your coffee?'

'With cream, no sugar.'

She continued to the kitchen and Mattie waved at the chairs.

'You'd better sit down.'

They sat in armchairs and Mattie went to her satchel and took out a packet of menthol cigarettes. She took one out and lit it without offering the packet. She continued standing and went back to the fireplace and faced them like an inquisitor.

'When Jimmy died I went into shock.' She pulled hard on the cigarette. 'It took me a long time to get over it, to get over my conscience. Then I worked things out and I got angry, but I learned to live with the anger.' She stared at Lacey.

155

'I've made my own life now. I'm an American citizen. And you people can go to hell.'

Lacey raised his eyebrows.

'Me in particular, or both of us?'

'You represent the British Government, don't you?'

Lacey nodded.

'Then take it personally. And if you're here to warn me to keep quiet, forget it.'

Lacey said: 'Miss Purcell, the last thing I want you to do is keep quiet. I want to know how your husband died. We need to know. Won't you tell us?'

She took another long drag on the cigarette before stubbing it out in the back of the fireplace and dropping the butt in the grate.

'Jimmy's death was no accident. And it was no sex trick, either.'

Lacey said: 'I spoke to the police sergeant who investigated the death for the coroner. He told me that kind of accident is more common than people realize. It was unlikely your husband would have told you about what is, after all, a very private act.'

'I agree. And Jimmy enjoyed very private acts. But with boys, not girls. Jimmy was gay. If he was going to get his kicks looking at pictures with a noose around his neck, the pictures would have been of young men. Not my lesbian art collection.'

Pritchard had said art books: it was Lacey who had interpreted it as a euphemism for men's pin-up magazines.

Miller said: 'Then your marriage . . . ?'

'Was convenient. He came from a very respectable family and they would never have understood his preferences. They were relieved when we got married, and he stayed in the will. We got on fine together, we were compatible. We had affection for each other but there was never anything physical. I also had respect for Jimmy. He knew art, and he helped me a great deal.'

Lacey gave her the prompt for which she was waiting.

'So how did he die?'

'He was murdered.'

Her stare challenged him to keep on asking the questions.

'Who by?'

'My guess is the British Government.'

Linda came back from the kitchen with a tray. Lacey got a bottle of Budweiser Light and a glass. The bottle was perspiring with cold but Mattie's accusation had taken the edge off his thirst.

It was not that it was unexpected but he had been hoping for a different answer. Enrico Latimer's statement had referred to MI5's dirty tricks and this fitted the bill, although he still didn't know why they might have topped Russell.

Linda hesitated and looked from one to the other before settling her gaze on Mattie.

'What about dinner?'

'We'll have dinner when it's ready. These gentlemen will be going soon. They're almost through.'

'Oh. Oh, OK.'

She smiled nervously and returned to the kitchen.

Mattie sipped her drink and stared over the glass at Lacey.

She said: 'I suppose you want to know why I think your government killed my husband?'

'Yes, I do.'

'I don't know why. I didn't suspect it then, nor for a while afterwards. The death was a shock and the police were helpful. At least, I thought they were. I told you his family were respectable. His mother was still alive and I didn't want her to get hurt any more than was necessary. Death by misadventure was the best way out. If I'd yelled murder I'd have had to explain why.' She shook her head. 'I was in shock and I guess I still hadn't grown up. I'd relied on Jimmy a lot. Instead, I relied on a Man from the Ministry.'

She said it in derisory tones.

Lacey said: 'What ministry?'

'The Home Office. He came to see me because Jimmy was American. Helped smooth things out, dealt with the undertaker, the coroner. At the time, I just let him. It was

157

a relief. I didn't feel like I could talk to anybody else about it, any friends. But I could talk to him. He was an outsider, someone who wouldn't make personal judgements. Know what I mean? And he had authority. He'd know what to do. I tried telling him it wasn't an accident and he listened but he didn't appear to take it seriously. He said maybe Jimmy had been playing games with a friend and things had gone wrong. He said misadventure was the least messy verdict.

'Later, I wondered if his interest was normal. I began to suspect it wasn't, that he was there to cover things up. It wasn't until 1979 that I was sure. When the newspapers said Anthony was a spy. I read all I could about it and the dates made too much sense. I guess Jimmy was killed because of Anthony, but I don't know why. I guess it's connected with this new bunch of stuff that the TV are calling the Blunt Legacy?'

Miller said: 'You've got it in one.'

Lacey said: 'Jimmy and Blunt knew each other?'

'Yes.'

'Business?'

'No. Anthony was an academic. He gave opinions on art, authenticated paintings. He couldn't do business with art dealers, it would have devalued his reputation. His relationship with Jimmy was social. They were friends, but not lovers. Jimmy did the occasional favour for him in Europe. Jimmy went to Europe a lot.'

Miller seemed content for Lacey to continue asking the questions.

'What did they call this Man from the Ministry?'

'Briggs. Frank Briggs.'

'You seem very sure after so long?'

'I've had time to remember.'

'What did he look like?'

'Now that is asking a lot, even for an artist.' She pulled a face. 'At the time he'd be in his late twenties, maybe a little older. Not too tall, about five eight. I remember his height made me feel comfortable.'

158

Miller got to his feet.

'If you'll excuse me a minute, there's something I need to get from the car.'

'Sure.'

Miller let himself out of the house and Lacey drank some beer.

It was beginning to look as if Five had made some kind of cock-up during the original Blunt investigation and Russell had died in the process. Maybe Chesterton hadn't wanted him to come to Oregon and find out. Maybe Jimmy Russell had been a spy, too? A courier? Mattie said he had travelled to Europe a lot.

'Where did your husband go in Europe?'

'What?'

'You said he travelled. Favours for Blunt?'

'Oh. Well, he went to shows and galleries, of course. But he liked Hamburg and Amsterdam.' She shrugged. 'There was literature there, magazines, he couldn't get in England.' She scowled at him for making her reveal her late husband's tattier secrets. 'Another reason why I knew he wouldn't have used my art collection.'

'Ah.'

He sipped more beer and suddenly felt tired. Even First Class couldn't dissipate totally the effects of jet lag and an eight-hour time difference.

Mattie lit another cigarette.

Miller came back into the house, carrying his briefcase. He put it on the chair in which he had been sitting, opened it and took out a batch of photographs.

He held up a copy of the head and shoulders of the gunman from Lisbon. Mattie squinted at it and he walked across the room so she could see it more clearly.

'Do you know this man?'

She stared at it.

'It was a long time ago.'

He held up another, a photograph that showed the man standing in the garden after getting rid of the gun.

Mattie said: 'It could be Frank Briggs.'

159

Lacey looked at Miller and Miller stared back. Lacey wondered which of them was Alice and which the White Rabbit.

The casting didn't matter; it was the way they kept dropping down holes that was interesting, and the way that this whole damn affair got curiouser and curiouser.

SEVENTEEN

Danny Harper had not been able to stop himself laughing out loud. The sea lions had looked just like the men who had wandered round his mother's apartment the morning after.

Mouths yawning and grunting, bellies wobbling, heads moving carefully as if they were trying not to spill a hangover. He wondered which one was his father.

He had found them after rejoining 101 on the coast, a few miles north of Florence.

VISIT THE SEA LION CAVES, the sign said. He had the time, so he did. He wouldn't have missed it for the world.

He paid his money and took a lift two hundred feet down into a series of caverns linked by duckboard walkways. It was dark down here, and he liked the subterranean feel, and the weird echoing noises. Small groups of people stared through the wire mesh to where the Pacific Ocean splashed the rocks of the caves.

At first, he couldn't work out what the interest was. Then he realized that those weren't rocks, those were sea lions. Hundreds of the stupid bastards.

They slept, they fought, they splashed in the water, they did courtship stuff, and they waddled round like those beer-bellied one-night stands his mother told him were Uncle Mike and Uncle Roy.

He fed coins into a set of binoculars that were fixed to a plinth and took a close look at the big daddies down there, who were as oblivious to their audience as drunks to danger.

Hi pop, he shouted in his mind, and giggled.

Then he didn't feel like giggling any more and he didn't

like the memories of the fat-bellies that had pounded his mother.

He slouched against a corner of the cave in the darkness to let the anger cool. The past was past; it was now that was important. He anticipated the night and felt his good humour returning.

Two girls were leaning over the binoculars. One was overweight and shouldn't have been wearing stretch pants. The other was trim, with a neat little ass in tight shorts, long legs and white socks and sneakers.

This was a prick-teaser made in high school heaven and his dick responded. He straightened it in his trousers without anybody noticing and, as their money ran out, joined them. He reached over and put more coins in the slot.

His thigh brushed casually against the girl's thigh.

He grinned his inoffensive grin and pointed.

'Did you see that big guy over there? He looks like the daddy of them all.' The girl put her head back to the binoculars and he leant further over. 'You can move it in and out of focus here.'

She didn't move when he brushed against her more deliberately, but kept on looking.

Harper moved against her some more as he fed coins into a second set of binoculars for the fat girl. Both of them exchanged a glance, giggled, and went back to staring at the sea lions.

A prick-teaser made in heaven, all right, as he pushed his stiff little dick against her butt. Maybe it was the size she didn't identify, maybe she thought he had a bottle in his pocket, what the hell did he care.

He had a neat little throb on by the time the money ran out and she knew damn well what he'd been doing and was flushed and embarrassed and too young to know how to complain.

Another inoffensive grin to make her think maybe she'd been wrong, and then get out of there before she told the fat girl and the fat girl made the complaint because he hadn't rubbed it against her.

162

Back up top he didn't buy anything in the gift shop but got back in his car and headed north, stroking himself through his trousers at the favours he could have done for the girl he'd left behind, and wondering what favours he could do in the job ahead.

EIGHTEEN

The Haystack Motel was named after the third largest free-standing monolith in the world. It said so in the complimentary copy of the *Cannon Beach Magazine* that was in Lacey's room.

Haystack Rock rose two hundred and thirty-five feet out of the sea offshore from the town and was a protected wildlife sanctuary. Judging by the pictures in the magazine, it was also one of the most painted and photographed pieces of natural history in the area.

The motel was less imposing than the rock but more than adequate after the stretched day of surprises that Lacey had endured. The first-floor room even had an ocean view, when it became light enough to see, if you counted looking across Hemlock Street and the car-park of the Tolovana Inn.

They had booked into the Haystack at Mattie Purcell's suggestion, after she had finally accepted that they really were interested in the truth about her husband's death.

Lacey hadn't liked to tell her that it was unlikely anything would be done even if they did discover why Jimmy Russell had died and who had killed him. Maybe it was enough that she had shared her secret and her anger after all these years, with people who believed her.

It was too late to telephone Charing Cross Road. In London, it would be the early hours of the morning and the only person in the office would be the retired hooligan on duty. He didn't even want to leave his number; he would prefer to remain uncontactable until tomorrow, after they had talked to Mattie Purcell again.

Then he would go home, because there would be nowhere else for him to go, and he would take with him another piece of the mystery: Frank Briggs, Man from the Ministry . . . or MI5?

Maybe someone else would be commissioned to track Briggs down after Lacey's disobedience. Maybe not. Maybe Lacey knowing was one too many already, which meant that Lacey would keep the job of tidying up loose ends.

Another reason he didn't want to phone was that he didn't know what to tell Bryson about Ben Miller.

The young American was personable, friendly and very confident. He reminded Lacey of how he would like to have been himself at that age.

Instead, when he had finally been let off the leash, Lacey had been past forty, past his best condition, and with an in-bred inferiority complex from not having the right school tie.

But he was off the leash now and had no intention of going back to fetching and carrying at Century House. He still had the feeling that this case would reach a make or break point. He was looking forward to it, when it arrived.

He and Miller drove into town, which was quiet this early in the year, and had dinner in a log cabin restaurant with blazing fires, attendant waiters, excellent Oregon wine, and a very comfortable lounge with the sort of leather armchairs that encourages Jim Beam to sneak up on you.

Jim Beam did, and made a wicked combination with the jet lag. When they left the lounge and stepped outside Lacey enjoyed the cool night.

Miller said: 'Maybe we'll go whale spotting in the morning.'

'What?'

'Whales. They migrate this time of year. It's a Pacific Coast sport.'

Lacey could think of nothing appropriate to say.

'Really?'

They walked down the street towards their rented car and Lacey stroked the paintwork of a white limousine that was parked at the kerb.

He said: 'Nice.'

'Cadillac. America's dream machine.'

Dream machine was right. It seemed to sum up the country. A land of amazing variety and beauty, wealth and poverty, where everything was available and anyone could make it. That was the theory.

It was how they made it that sometimes spoiled the dream.

Lacey didn't sleep. He lay in bed, aware of the strangeness of his surroundings. His body was tired but his mind wanted to play. At least the gremlins stayed away.

He imagined the previous transient occupiers of his room: tourists piling their seashore gear in the bathroom, salesmen watching lonely late-night television, senior citizens farting and belching in the comfort of their long-term relationship, young couples screwing.

It didn't have to make sense, it just had to fill the void in his head.

Then it picked on the Blunt operation. It scanned, traversed, assessed and disputed the whole damn thing, while Lacey sat outside himself as a non-participating observer.

He hit a period of calm where tiredness took over but knew it wouldn't last and that the jet lag would be back. It was; this time bringing the whacky races, that state of mind named by Susan when the brain becomes hyper-active, sparking without reason from one idea to another, creating anxiety where none existed, building tensions, like the count-down to a brain haemorrhage.

When the telephone rang he sat straight up in bed and wondered where the hell he was and why the telephone was in the wrong place.

Then he wondered who the hell was ringing him at this time of night when no one knew he was there. No one except Mattie Purcell.

He switched on the light, saw it was two o'clock, and picked up the receiver.

'Hello?'

Mattie said: 'Lacey?'

166

He blinked his eyes wider open and worked his mouth for saliva.

'Yes.'

'Is your friend with you?'

What was she implying?

'What do you mean?'

'I mean is Miller there? At the motel?'

'I think so. He's got the room next door.' He was suddenly wide awake and realized Mattie was speaking in an unnaturally low voice. 'Why?'

''Coz we've got a prowler. I heard . . .'

The line went dead.

He looked at the room number on the telephone. He dialled the number for the room next door. Miller answered it on the first ring.

Lacey said: 'Mattie's got a prowler and her line just went dead.'

'I'll see you outside.'

It took him less than a minute to get dressed and regret that British Airways and immigration were not more understanding about shoulder luggage that contained a handgun.

Miller was waiting.

They ran down the outside stairs to the car-park and got into the rented car. Miller drove it quietly into Hemlock Street and turned it towards Mattie Purcell's house.

The American said: 'You knock on the front door. I'll go round back. If they run, they'll run to me.'

Lacey nodded. It was Miller's country after all, maybe he was entitled to call the shots.

Miller turned the car into the dirt road but stopped short of the white picket fence. They got out, leaving the doors partly open to avoid making a noise. Lacey guessed this was the wrong time to tell his athletic companion that while he was really pretty good with a gun, he was pretty useless in a physical confrontation.

Lacey ran up the road on the grass verge and stopped when he reached the picket fence. He looked round but Miller had already disappeared.

167

He went through the space into the driveway, stepped on to the lawn to avoid making a noise on the gravel and stared at the house. All the lights were out, including the two on the porch.

Maybe it had been the jet lag but since the phone call he'd been reacting without thinking. Now the tension of the situation started to get to him. Two women were inside that house and in danger, and once he banged on the front door he would be in danger himself.

He ran across the grass, staying parallel with the drive-way, his eyes scanning the gloom ahead by the closed doors of the garage for something he might use as a weapon. There was a rake for leaves but nothing else. He got hold of the pole of the rake and as he moved it, saw a garden fork sticking in the ground. He abandoned the rake, pulled the fork free and took it with him. He ran along the porch, no longer trying to hide his footsteps.

At the front door, he rang the bell and listened to its echo in the silence of the house. He rang it again and pounded on the door.

'Mattie!'

He checked the windows for light and wondered which would be easier to force open, a window or the door. The windows were double-glazed and would prove a problem. He went back to the door, banged on it again and stepped back to give himself room to kick, when it opened. It was the one thing Lacey hadn't expected and he was caught cold.

'Move and you're dead.'

The voice was low and matter-of-fact, almost tempting him to move so that the death threat could be carried out.

Lacey remained where he was, arms by his sides. He couldn't see the speaker.

The man said: 'Drop the gun.'

'I haven't got a gun.'

'Drop what's in your hand.'

He dropped the garden fork.

The man laughed.

'What you doing? Digging mushrooms?'

168

The snigger stopped at a noise behind him in the house and Lacey took a dive off the porch and on to the lawn.

There was no gunshot as Lacey crawled away from the view of the open door back towards the garage. The man was a professional who wasn't going to waste bullets until he knew they would hit someone.

The man must be on his own, otherwise he wouldn't have been distracted by the noise from inside the house. That meant the man believed neither Mattie nor Linda had been capable of making the noise – were they already dead? Which left Miller.

The unarmed American must be inside and involved in an unfair stalking contest.

He rolled to the corner of the house, grabbed the rake and went back on the porch. From inside the house, he heard a piece of furniture fall over as if someone had walked into it. He tapped the window with the curved metal spikes but no one shot the glass out.

Lacey moved towards the front door, feeling foolish with the six-foot rake in his hand, when a door slammed inside the house and three muffled shots from a silenced handgun thumped out.

Furniture crashed and the voice of the unseen man, no longer calm, cursed loudly.

'Fucking shit bastard!' Another crash. 'I'll be back, whore. Hear me? I'll be back!'

Lacey placed the rake, prongs down, on the porch so that the pole lay across the open doorway. He grabbed the garden fork from where he had dropped it and rolled back on to the grass by the three front steps.

Someone came running and he hoped it wasn't Ben Miller.

It wasn't. It was a small man wearing luminous tight white trousers who shouted 'Shit!' as he tripped over the pole and fell down the steps.

Lacey had raised himself to a crouch and thrust upwards with the garden fork as the figure came towards him and discovered the man wasn't wearing tight white trousers. He wasn't wearing trousers at all.

The man screamed and the pair of them rolled in different directions, then bullets were coming at Lacey and the silenced handgun sounded extremely loud and dangerous from this close. The screaming continued as Lacey made himself small in the dirt and darkness beneath the porch. He wondered whether any of the aches he could feel was the result of a gunshot.

There was a scampering from the garden, heavy breathing, yelps like a wounded animal, crunching gravel, but no more gunshots.

Footsteps creaked the boards above his head.

'Peter?'

'Down here.'

He crawled out and Ben Miller stepped off the porch to help him.

Miller had climbed into the house through the same rear window that had been forced by the intruder and found himself in a bathroom. He had opened the door and been taking time to get his bearings when Lacey had rung the bell.

The sound had startled him in the silent house but it had startled someone else more.

A door along a corridor to his right opened and he ducked back into the bathroom and listened to a man's footsteps go by.

Lacey was now banging on the door and shouting, which, Miller figured, should be diversion enough to allow him to move on.

The corridor led off from the living area of the house. There were three doors down here, as well as the bathroom, plus one that sealed off the corridor itself from the living-room. He went to a door that had been left open.

It was a bedroom. No light was on but the curtains had been pulled back to let in the moonlight. Linda, Mattie Purcell's companion, was on the bed. She lay on her back, her hands tied above her head to the brass bedstead; a gag was around her mouth and her night-dress had been pushed up above her breasts.

Mattie, still in pyjamas, was also gagged and tied by her hands and feet to a chair but was already half-way to getting her right hand free.

Miller was embarrassed by Linda's nakedness. His first act was to pull down the night-dress whilst trying not to look at her body. Then he turned to Mattie and helped her free both hands, whilst listening to what was happening along the corridor and in the living-room.

As Mattie pulled her gag free, he heard the man threatening Lacey.

He whispered: 'Is he alone?'

Mattie nodded and pulled the rope from her legs.

Miller said: 'Lock this door.'

He left the room. It was his turn to cause a diversion.

From the corridor he could see, above the intervening furniture, the torso of the man outlined in the open front doorway. The guy was standing well back but he had Lacey covered with a handgun.

Miller looked round for something to throw and saw an ashtray on a three-legged table behind him. He picked up the ashtray and lobbed it down the side of the room towards the fireplace.

It bounced on the carpet before skittering on to the stone flags. The man turned and from outside came the sound of Lacey making the most of it.

Christ, this was hide-come-seek with a nasty pay-off.

Miller eased back into the corridor. The man walked into something that fell over; he cursed, and Miller slammed and locked the door, sealing off the corridor from the lounge.

He sat, legs straight, back against the wall as three bullets slammed into the woodwork, and he thanked God this was lumber country and that the carpenter hadn't stinted on quality.

Now the guy was cursing again and making threats.

Miller was happy for him to make all the threats he wanted, just as long as he went away. Next time they could be better prepared than ashtrays at thirty paces.

The crash confused Miller but the screaming and the bullets from outside caused him to react.

He unlocked the door and went into the living-room low, taking cover behind a sofa, but in here it was quiet. Had that been Lacey screaming?

The room was empty and he rolled to the window, pulled the shades apart and risked a look outside. He saw the shape of someone turning the corner by the gravel drive.

Outside it was quiet. He stepped cautiously on to the porch and found a broken rake pole. A blooded fork lay on the garden path, and the Englishman was beneath his feet.

Lacey said: 'Has he gone?'

'He's gone.'

'The women?'

'They're OK.'

'Jesus Christ.'

His right hand was covered in blood.

Miller said: 'Are you hurt?'

Lacey patted himself at the points on his body that ached but found no wounds.

'I don't think so. I think the other bloke might be. I stuck a garden fork in him.'

They both looked towards the picket fence and the gloom of the unlit and tree-lined road.

Miller said: 'Take a look?'

Lacey, still high on adrenalin, shrugged.

'Why not?'

They ran to the road, staying in the shadows, and looked down towards Hemlock Street. Their car was where they had left it.

Miller ran to the far side of the dirt road and they moved down cautiously, one on either side, Lacey realizing with every step how stupid they were, hunting a wounded

172

man who was armed with a gun. If he was too badly hurt to run he could be lying in wait for the chance to get his own back.

Lacey approached their car cautiously, but it was empty, the doors partly open as they had left them. Miller was moving on more quickly the closer they got to Hemlock. He turned and waved for Lacey to join him. When he did, the American pointed to what looked like an oil spill on the ground.

'Blood. You got him good.'

They reached the junction and heard a car engine start from the car-park past the Tolovana Inn. The driver was not being quiet.

Maybe he was in too much of a hurry, Lacey thought. Or too much pain.

A white Cadillac came on to Hemlock and drove fast towards them, making them instinctively crouch in case the driver saw them and detoured into the shrubbery at the side of the road. But the driver was concentrating too much on keeping the car straight to bother with them, his face white and etched as the car went past.

They watched him head south towards the highway, the tension suddenly leaving them with the danger.

Lacey licked his lips and took three or four deep breaths.

'The American dream,' he said. 'It just lost its trousers.'

They exchanged their stories as they went back to the house. Lights were on now, and when they knocked on the front door Mattie shouted for them to come in.

Miller opened the door and they stepped inside to find themselves staring down the barrel of the shotgun that she held.

Lacey raised his hands and said: 'Just us.'

Miller said: 'He got away. But Peter hurt him.'

She lowered the gun and motioned with her head to the kitchen and they followed her.

Beyond the kitchen was a small den with a pair of armchairs, a television and a table stacked with books and magazines. Linda, dressed in a blue bathrobe, sat curled in one of the armchairs. She clutched a glass and didn't look at them.

Miller said: 'Is she OK?'

'She will be after enough vodka. Coffee?'

They both nodded and she indicated high stools at the breakfast bar.

Mattie laid the shotgun on the bar top, filled an electric jug with water and plugged it in.

She said: 'It's not what the bastard did, it's what he said.' She took mugs and a jar of instant coffee from different cupboards. 'He enjoyed talking. He has a sick mind.'

Lacey said: 'He didn't appear to be wearing any trousers.'

She said: 'They're in the bedroom. I didn't want to touch them.' Her face was white with both shock and anger. 'He is some sick son of a bitch.'

Lacey got off his stool.

'I'll get them,' he told Miller.

The lights were on down the corridor and in the bedroom. The women had wanted to scare away the nightmare by banishing the shadows.

He looked at the rumpled bed and got angry. The two women had been close to becoming the worst kind of statistics; those that made salacious reading in the Press, victims of a rapist and killer who took his time and enjoyed inflicting suffering.

Jesus Christ. Another part of the dream?

The trousers had been hung carefully over the back of a chair to keep their creases sharp. They were tan in colour, made of a lightweight material and very ordinary. There was nothing in any of the pockets. Also on the chair were a pair of boxer shorts: white with a blue stripe.

What sort of a rapist was this, who took off his trousers and underpants but kept everything else on, including his jacket and tie? Christ, how should he know? He didn't know any rapists.

174

Lacey didn't inspect the shorts too closely but picked them up by the waistband and folded the trousers around them.

He took them into the living-room and placed them behind a chair near the front door. He guessed the women would not want to look at them again.

Miller said: 'Anything?'

Lacey shook his head.

'From the way he emptied his pockets and folded his trousers, it looks like he's done this kind of thing before.'

Miller said: 'A hitman with a trademark.'

Lacey looked at Mattie, wondering how she would take the reference to a hitman.

Mattie was smoking a cigarette and Lacey almost asked her for one. She placed a mug of coffee in front of his empty stool, so he sat down and let the steam from the drink rise into his face instead of tobacco smoke.

She sat down and placed the packet of cigarettes and a lighter in front of her and said: 'I'd guessed this wasn't random.'

They sat in silence and sipped coffee.

Eventually Lacey said: 'I don't think he'll be back. I don't think anyone will be back.'

She looked at him.

'Why?'

'Let's assume he was sent to silence you.' He shrugged. 'In such a way that it would look like a . . .'

He hesitated because he didn't want to upset her, but she supplied the missing words.

'A sex killing?'

'Yes. A sex killing. Whoever sent him will now know that you've talked. There's no longer any need to silence you.'

'That guy was a weirdo. He said he was coming back and he just might.'

Lacey nodded.

'That's true. He might. But he was hired for a job and he'll be told it's cancelled. I think it's unlikely.'

175

'You go ahead and think.' Mattie looked worried as well as angry and moved her head to indicate Linda. 'It's us who are going to have to live with the possibility.'

She was right. The nightmare was not going to go away and there was nothing else he could say.

Mattie pulled hard on the cigarette and stubbed the end out in an ashtray in front of her. She took another cigarette from the packet, lit it and drew in a lot of nicotine. After what she had almost been through, Lacey didn't blame her.

She said: 'Who hired him?'

He was afraid she was going to ask that.

'I don't know.'

She looked at Miller.

'I don't know either. We're fishing in muddy waters, Mattie. There's a lot we don't understand; competitors we haven't identified. But I think Peter's right about the hit. The contract will be cancelled.'

Mattie blew smoke and looked over her shoulder at Linda, in the den and too far away to hear their speculation. She got up, took the empty glass from the other woman, replenished it and put the glass back in her hand. She squeezed her shoulder before coming back to the breakfast bar.

She said: 'What about the police?'

Lacey said: 'Do you want the police?'

'I don't know.' She looked back at Linda. 'This is a small town. The people are good but they still talk.' She took another deep pull on the cigarette. 'God, I don't know. I guess it wouldn't help you two either?'

Miller and Lacey exchanged looks.

The American said: 'If you want the police, I'll go call them now. Of course, you could always call them later, after we've gone? Give them his pants. Maybe say you scared the guy off with the garden fork.'

She shook her head and Lacey felt deeply sorry she had been dragged into a chain of events not of her making. She had been an onlooker and now she was a participant.

'I don't know,' she said. 'Maybe I'll wait until morning.'

Lacey also felt guilty.

176

He and Miller had been led to Cannon Beach by the clues provided by a man who could be Frank Briggs. Lacey still didn't know what game Briggs was playing but he remembered what Natalie had told him before he had boarded the plane at Heathrow.

Sam Bryson had cancelled his mission and his trip to see Mattie Purcell. Sam Bryson had said it would be taken care of.

By a rapist in the night?

NINETEEN

He was bleeding all over the upholstery. Jesus fucking Christ where did all the blood come from? Had he pissed himself as well?

This wasn't supposed to happen. A fucking hick with a garden fork? A motherfucking hick with a garden fork in the middle of the fucking night?

It had been going like a dream and he had to get the fucking village idiot.

He gripped the wheel and whimpered through clenched teeth at the pain and the fear.

How far was he from home? Too fucking far, he knew that.

His car! Look at his car! All this fucking mess all over his car. But, oh sweet Jesus, it hurt. This mess was his and it hurt.

If only he'd been wearing his pants maybe it wouldn't have been so bad, but his pants and his shorts were back there in the fucking bedroom and here he was in the middle of fucking nowhere with his balls and his dick bleeding into the dust cloth he'd got from the glove compartment to wrap them in.

When he got fixed up he'd go back and he'd really mess those women up before he killed them. He'd stick something up them and it wouldn't be his dick.

He'd find that motherfucker with the garden fork and do a job on him too. A slow slicing job between his legs to make him wish he'd never been born.

And it had been going so well . . .

The highway was empty and the road straight and he let himself believe speed was important and that it was taking him somewhere he could get fixed up.

Lulu had better not laugh when he got home and saw where he'd got stuck or he'd make her pay. He'd make her pay anyway.

Maybe he'd pick up some free-lance hooker, too, some unaffiliated bitch that nobody would be bothered about, that he could beat up real good, make a real mess of, make her really hurt just to get his own back for the way he hurt now. A lot of people were going to pay for the way he hurt now.

He winced, and the car swerved and he wondered why he was tired. Too much blood. He was losing too much blood.

So what the fuck do you do about that, big shot? Stop at a 7-Eleven and say fill me up?

Signs went by, trees went by, the stars in the fucking sky went by, then there were no stars, just walls like a tomb, and he panicked and the car swerved and he realized he was in a tunnel.

Where were the fucking stars?

He hated the tunnel, hated being pressed in by bricks, and just as the panic was getting as unbearable as the pain he was through it and the sky was there again, vast and stretching all the way to LA.

Shit! What a mess. The job had not been done and the people he worked for would not be pleased and maybe they would cancel any more contracts or maybe they would just cancel him but at the moment he didn't give a fuck because the pain and the fear and sickness he felt from thinking about what had been done to him were bursting his head.

The car slid off the road and kicked up stones and the rattle made him pull on the wheel to straighten it. He wanted no stones kicking shit out of his paintjob.

Oh, sweet Jesus, how long did this road go on?

A sign he picked up in his headlamps said he could stop up ahead and he realized that that was what he needed to do.

He slowed, and when the turn came he pulled off into a wide parking bay and his headlamps read another sign that said from here he could view the ocean.

The car was pointing out to sea, its front wheels up against a row of rocks. He switched the engine off but left the

179

lights on to blaze silently across the water as a marker to tell people where he was, and he cried and wished he was back in Flagstaff, Arizona, and that things had been different and the jobs his mom had tried for had worked out.

But the pain twisted again and kicked out of focus his search for good-time memories he didn't have, and he bared his teeth and screamed out loud whilst inside he cursed his whore mother and his walrus father.

Music. He had to have music. He had to have some fucking thing. But all the radio played was country.

He fumbled at the dash and stuck a cassette in the player and turned it on loud.

Marvin Gaye had heard it on the grapevine with that sense of black rhythm that ran all the way to Lulu's ass, and he was crying again and rocking gently in his seat because the dust cloth had become so soaked in blood it had become part of his genitals and he daren't touch it, daren't touch himself at all, and he knew damn well he would never see Lulu's black ass again.

The gun was on the seat next to him and he picked it up and pointed it at his face.

He looked over it and along the beacons of his headlights at the eternity of night.

'Fuck you,' he shouted.

Then he put the end of the gun in his mouth and pulled the trigger.

TWENTY

The morning news on the local television station solved one problem and posed another.

Lacey and Miller watched it on a portable TV on the breakfast bar with the sound turned down low.

The women were asleep in the armchairs in the den. Vodka martinis might not have mended Linda's shattered nerves, but they had anaesthetized them. Mattie had eventually succumbed after smoking her last cigarette a half-hour before dawn. The shotgun lay at her feet.

Miller had been back to the motel and, Lacey guessed, had made a few telephone calls. Lacey still didn't know who to call or what to tell them. The American had also parked the rented car on the gravel drive, and put the garden fork and the broken rake under the porch.

They were ready for the next round and it came right after the weather as Lacey was eating bacon and eggs he had cooked himself.

A newscaster gave the local headlines. They included a suicide in a beauty spot near Manzanita, twenty miles down the coast.

The newsman said: 'Death came in the night to the viewpoint overlooking the Pacific Ocean in what police have termed the Cadillac Killing. But officers are being coy about the precise circumstances surrounding the death and identity of the white, male victim who was alone in the car, which was found with lights blazing and radio playing.

'The man had a fatal gunshot wound to the head and a gun in his hand, which might seem pretty conclusive evidence of suicide, but police are still looking for the answers to two questions: where are the victim's pants and

181

who inflicted severe knife wounds to his naked groin and abdominal region?

'One theory is that the suicide could be the result of gangland retribution that started in Los Angeles.'

The newscaster moved on to something else and Miller said: 'You really got him.'

Lacey felt no regret or elation.

'Mattie will be relieved,' he said, and continued eating.

The latest revelation from the Blunt documents was the third item on the networked coast-to-coast news broadcast that followed. It spoiled Lacey's appetite.

A woman reporter presented the story, which was accompanied by photographs of the people it named.

'The Fifth Man of the notorious Soviet spy ring headed by British agent Kim Philby in the forties and fifties is said to be alive and well . . . and a prominent American.

'The claim has come from the unnamed vendor of the Blunt Legacy, documents left by disgraced Britisher Sir Anthony Blunt, who was unmasked as the Fourth Man in the 1960s.

'It was thought the KGB spy ring, launched from the hallowed halls of England's Cambridge University before the Second World War, was a purely British affair. Diplomats Guy Burgess and Donald Maclean were the first to defect to Moscow, followed by Third Man Philby. Then Blunt, the holder of the ancient title of Keeper of the Queen's Pictures, was said to be Number Four.

'Spycatchers at the CIA and the British MI5 long suspected the trail didn't end there, but their search for more traitors was concentrated in England.

'Now, a statement issued by the owner of the Blunt Legacy claims they reveal the identity of the Fifth Man and describes him as, and I quote, "a prominent American, who has received his country's highest honours," unquote.

'The Legacy has already caused one death when the lawyer organizing its auction was shot dead in Lisbon, Portugal. The statement says the auction will go ahead regardless at a date to be announced in the next few days. And we'll have

182

to wait until then to find out which veteran United States citizen was a KGB spy.'

Lacey put down his knife and fork.

The Fifth Man?

This was getting bizarre.

Was this who Miller was working for? Had the Fifth Man hired the services of Dixon Green to ensure he remained a prominent American?

Miller turned off the television set.

Lacey took his plate to the sink, scraped what was left of his breakfast into the waste disposal, and washed it clean under the hot-water tap. It was getting close to make-your-mind-up time. He needed help and didn't trust getting it from his own side.

He turned from the sink and faced Miller.

'What do you know about the Biarritz Agreement?'

Miller thought about it and shook his head.

'Nothing. Should I?'

'Maybe. Maybe not.' Lacey picked up the cigarette packet from the breakfast bar without thinking, but it was empty. He poured more coffee instead. 'What do you know about the involvement of Joseph Kennedy in the Blunt Legacy?'

'Nothing.'

Lacey sat on a stool and sipped coffee. Blunt's documents could contain many secrets; the fact that Miller knew nothing about the one Lacey was chasing didn't mean it didn't exist. He had already discussed that very possibility with Sam Bryson. But how much did he trust Sam Bryson?

He had always regarded him as a friend, but Bryson was now operating under the instructions of Leonard Chesterton. It had been Bryson who had ordered him to abandon the case, and who had said Mattie Purcell would be taken care of.

'OK.' He put down the mug of coffee and stared at Miller. 'If I tell you what I know about the Biarritz Agreement and Joe Kennedy can you check it out for me?'

'Check out what?'

'If it exists. As fact, rumour or possibility.'

Miller nodded.

183

'I can do that.'

'Good.'

Lacey told him and Miller took notes without comment. He gave him a potted version of the briefing he had received, about the Duke of Windsor and the Ambassador of the United States to wartime Britain, plotting a peace with Hitler.

When they had finished, the American left to make more telephone calls, and Lacey remained to continue wondering whether he had done the right thing.

Miller called his Washington office collect from a public telephone and asked for first-base run-downs on several subjects, including what Lacey had told him. He wanted something quick but accurate. Then he went to the motel, ran a bath and soaked in it.

He was glad of the chance to get his thoughts in order.

The more powerful men got, he reflected, the more dangerous became their peccadilloes.

Deification of Jack and Bobby Kennedy had ensured the political survival of their lesser brother Teddy, in the long years that followed when no one had tried to kill him too.

Maybe would-be assassins thought Teddy's antics at Chappaquiddick devalued the effort, and he'd done nothing since to change anybody's mind and make them take him seriously.

The Kennedy name was still an aphrodisiac to the media, though. A scandal about big daddy Joe would be gleefully savaged and no one would be left out in the catalogue of sordid indiscretions and dubious deals that would be rerun and revamped.

But, Miller thought, it was unlikely that the Kennedys would be the ones to make the headlines this time, if Blunt's documents ever saw the light of day. He suspected the prominent American would make them. He also suspected he might be working for him.

Orville B. Bross didn't have the international fame of a Kennedy, but then he'd never been President, he'd never been assassinated and he'd never been to bed with Marilyn

184

Monroe. But The Man had been a power in American politics for fifty years.

Bross had been born to money and, in a long and illustrious career, he'd made more. Billions more. He'd studied at Harvard and Oxford in the 1930s, had majored in Economics, dabbled in art and had a natural flair for languages. His father had got him a job at the State Department in 1941 but that had been the only help he'd needed. One thing Orville hadn't lacked was ability and ambition. He'd built a reputation and a power base by the time he left the State Department in 1947 to make his own fortune in finance and to start his political career.

Elected to Congress in 1954, he became an influential power broker and earned his nickname: he was The Man you saw if you wanted to get things done. One of the committees on which he'd served was the House Appropriations, which dealt with the Defense Budget. He'd also been chairman of the Intelligence Committee, which received the reports of America's secret services and approved their funding.

His eldest son was continuing the tradition in Congress, while his youngest son was heading, and part-funding, the President's latest anti-drugs campaign. His daughter was an assistant district attorney.

The Man had eight grandchildren, four great-grandchildren, a Palm Beach holiday home, a golf course in Georgia, an art collection the envy of New York's Metropolitan Museum, and an estate in Connecticut. Among other things.

Orville B. Bross had been close to four presidents and a confidential adviser to two of them, and at the centre of Western power for most of his active life.

Could he also have been a KGB spy?

Peccadilloes Ben Miller could overlook, but, Jesus H. Christ, what did he do if his client had been a traitor since before the Second World War?

When Mattie woke, Lacey told her about the suicide down the coast that had been reported on television but she didn't believe him until she saw it herself.

She watched the newscast in silence and when it had finished she said: 'Good.'

He couldn't be sure, but he thought a smile of satisfaction moved her lips.

Linda, who was still unaware of the reasons why someone had tried to kill them, woke with a hangover but wouldn't go to bed where she would be alone. Mattie made her a bed on the couch in the living-room, before going for a shower and a change of clothes.

Lacey stretched and smelled his armpits. He could do with a shower himself.

Miller returned. He had washed and changed but he had no news.

'We have good access, but it'll take time,' he said. 'I'm calling my Washington office in an hour. Why don't you go and freshen up at the motel.' He threw him the car keys. 'I'll stay with the ladies.'

It was a bright, fresh morning with a chilly breeze from the ocean. In London it would be mid-afternoon and probably raining, and Bryson would be wondering where the hell he was.

Lacey showered and dressed and then made the call.

Bryson said: 'I hope you have a good excuse, Peter, because this time your career's on the line.'

'I don't have any excuses, Sam. But I do have reasons. They might interest you.'

'Did you see our friend?'

'I saw her.'

'And?'

'She was helpful.'

'Will she stay helpful?'

'You mean, will she stay quiet?'

'Yes.'

'You knew more than you told me, Sam.'

'I didn't then. I do now. Will she?'

'I don't know. But I do know she's written out her story and put it in her lawyer's safe. Just in case.'

If Chesterton or Five had been behind the hitman, and

186

Lacey was by no means sure they were, the lie might dissuade them from trying again.

Bryson said: 'You told Natalie you had company on the plane.'

'That's right. An interested party.'

'Is he still interested?'

'Very much so.'

'Is it a serious conflict of interests?'

'Not yet.'

'What does that mean?'

'I'll tell you when I get back.'

'When will that be?'

'As soon as I can.'

'Come straight to the office, Peter. And if anything happens, call me. I'll be staying in the annexe.'

The situation had to be serious for Bryson to stay in one of the small annexe bedrooms at Charing Cross Road with nobody but a retired hooligan for company.

When Lacey got back to the house Mattie was wearing a shirt and Levis. She looked ten years younger than she was. Linda had been persuaded to go into the bathroom.

'We're taking a trip,' she told Lacey. 'We have friends in Vancouver.'

'Sounds like a good idea.'

Miller said: 'Mattie will report a prowler and ask the police to keep an eye on the house while she's gone. I've fixed the window.'

She said: 'Linda can do without this sort of publicity. Or the world's Press descending on us if they ever make the connection. I can cope. But it wouldn't be fair on Linda. Maybe it will all be over when we get back in two weeks.'

Lacey said: 'I hope so. When will you leave?'

'As soon as we've packed and I've arranged for someone to run the gallery. We'll be away by twelve. How about you?'

Lacey looked at Miller.

'I don't know,' he said. 'How about us?'

'Back to London, I guess.' The American looked at Mattie.

187

'There's a flight early evening from Seattle. We could drive with you part way to Vancouver.'

'That'd be good. Thank you.'

Lacey wondered what reason Miller might have for volunteering their services as bodyguards all the way to Seattle. Then the thought struck him. Maybe there was no other motive than offering the women reassurance. He'd been in this game too long.

Miller went off to call Washington again. When he returned, he still had no news.

They all left the house before noon. Mattie reversed a big old Ford out of the garage and left her Japanese car on the driveway. Linda was still quiet but looked better and seemed pleased to be leaving.

Lacey sat in the back of the car while Mattie drove it round to the Haystack Motel where Miller was making a final telephone call before checking out.

He was waiting for them outside reception.

'One more stop,' he said. 'At the US National Bank in town.'

Lacey transferred to the rental car, which Miller drove down Hemlock, behind Mattie's Ford, towards the shopping area.

'Run out of money?' he said.

'No. I've arranged to use their fax machine. Washington are sending some stuff that might interest you.'

Mattie led the way to a public parking area behind the shops. Lacey stayed in the car while Miller went to the bank carrying his briefcase. The two women also took the opportunity to make last-minute purchases before the trip.

After fifteen minutes the women came back, but it was another ten before Miller reappeared.

He got in the car and took five flimsy waxed sheets of fax paper from his briefcase. He put the briefcase on the rear seat, gave the flimsies to Lacey, started the engine and waved Mattie Purcell out of the car-park ahead of him.

'Read 'em and weep,' he said, in a joke voice.

Miller followed the old Ford north out of Cannon Beach towards Highway 101.

Lacey didn't even take a last look at the town that had impressed him so much when they had arrived the day before. He was already engrossed in the faxed reports.

The top one was headed: JOSEPH P. KENNEDY, AMERICAN BUSINESS AND THE NAZI PARTY. It read:

Joseph P. Kennedy had many contacts with members of the National Socialist Government of Germany, both before hostilities started in Europe, and after Germany was at war with Great Britain. He used his position and influence for the benefit of those sections of American business that often had no qualms about trading with the enemy and, in some cases, were themselves supporters of fascism.

He was also noted for his lukewarm support of the British cause and, after the fall of France, his belief that the British were on the brink of defeat. This, in itself, should not be misconstrued as the British Government and Roosevelt also thought defeat was a possibility. If it had happened, Roosevelt intended to keep the United States at peace with Germany at all costs, until America was strong enough to fight a war it could win.

It is confirmed that the companies and consortiums mentioned in your original message were involved in business with the Nazis and that Kennedy played a part. The depth of this trading with the enemy may never be known because of the death of the agent Charles Bedaux.

However, it is doubtful that Kennedy and the Duke of Windsor were ever involved together in a peace conference with Hermann Goering or anybody else. Kennedy and Windsor followed different paths of appeasement, and there is no reason why they should have negotiated in concert.

There are, though, two items relating to Goering, Kennedy and Windsor which may be relevant. One is

189

a persistent rumour that says the Duke of Windsor met Goering at Biarritz on 16 May 1940, during Germany's invasion of France. The other is a report from J. Edgar Hoover to President Roosevelt, dated 2 May 1941. Copy follows.

The second sheet was headed: FBI REPORT FROM HOOVER TO ROOSEVELT. It read:

Information has been received at this Bureau from a source that is socially prominent and known to be in touch with some of the people involved, but for whom we cannot vouch, to the effect that Joseph P. Kennedy, the former Ambassador to England, and Ben Smith, the Wall Street operator, had a meeting with Goering in Vichy, France, and that thereafter Kennedy and Smith had donated a considerable amount of money to the German cause. They are both described as being very anti-British and pro-German.

This same source of information advised that it was reported that the Duke of Windsor entered into an agreement which in substance was to the effect that if Germany was victorious in the war, Hermann Goering, through his control of the Army, would overthrow Hitler and would thereafter install the Duke of Windsor as King of England.

Lacey's briefing was beginning to fall into place and the FBI report was the hinge on which it hung. On its own, it was less than persuasive, but the British SIS could have additional information not known to Ben Miller's sources. Of course, there was the other possibility: that the whole briefing was a clever fake to hide the real reason he had been asked to find Blunt's documents.

There were still three sheets to go. The next one was headed: THE DUKE OF WINDSOR AND THE NAZIS. He read on:

190

There is no doubt the Duke and Duchess of Windsor were fans of Hitler and the Nazi Party and made one or more agreements to return to the English throne after Germany's victory. The photocopied documents you sent could be real or could be forgeries based on known facts.

Fact: Windsor was in favour of deportation to solve Germany's 'Jewish problem'.

Fact: Windsor was offered a large amount of money by Hitler to defect to Spain in 1940.

In fact, he didn't defect, probably because he feared being shot by his own secret service, and because of moral cowardice. Even so, the offer remained and was to be collected when he returned from the Bahamas to rule England for Germany when it was safe for him to do so.

The Windsors were under permanent surveillance by the FBI and continued their associations with known Nazis, Nazi agents and Nazi sympathizers in the Bahamas.

Next came: ASSESSMENT OF POSSIBLE KENNEDY/WINDSOR PLOTS IN RELATION TO BLUNT.

The two don't correlate. There is no reason why Blunt would have detailed knowledge of Kennedy's activities, or of a Biarritz Agreement if it had existed. There is no reason why Blunt would have knowledge of much that you posed in your questions relating to the Duke of Windsor.

Blunt joined MI5 in August 1940, after the Duke of Windsor's European plotting had finished, and after the date of the so-called Biarritz Agreement.

He did have knowledge of the Ultra Intelligence: that is, he knew Bletchley Park was using the Enigma decoding machine to read German wireless messages; and he had access to selected summaries of Abwehr messages. But neither he nor Philby, at MI6, was in a position to themselves select intelligence, or have access to past messages, that might have related to the time Windsor was in France and Portugal.

Blunt's mission in 1944 was mainly to recover archive

letters written by Queen Victoria and Queen Mary of England to their German relatives, which were viewed as an embarrassment, and certain items of royal jewellery. These were stored at the Schloss Kronberg, a castle near Frankfurt, which was the home of the Hesse family. Before the war, Prince Philip of Hesse had acted as go-between for the Duke of Windsor and Hitler. It was thought there might also be incriminating papers about this relationship.

It is fact that many German and Portuguese records relating to the Duke of Windsor's Nazi connections have been destroyed or have gone missing. Blunt's mission into France, Austria and Germany provided him with the opportunity to destroy or obtain some of these records although it is doubtful if any would be in the form of a signed contract.

At the most, they might intimate collusion and plotting, but would be unlikely to provide concrete proof of a Windsor–Hitler plot.

The screws were coming out of the hinge that held up his briefing. He turned to the last sheet and got a surprise. It was headed: LEONARD O. CHESTERTON.

Chesterton was born in Bristol in 1934, the only son of Reginald Chesterton and Lady Jane Chesterton. His father was in aeronautics and his mother was a member of the English aristocracy. He was educated at Marlborough public school and Oxford, where he graduated with First Class honours in modern languages. He went to Sandhurst and served in the Army. His party political biography says he was with the British Civil Service until he went into business and eventually became a Member of Parliament in the mid-1970s.

Chesterton saw action in the Army in Cyprus in 1958 and 1959 during the EOKA emergency. He worked with military intelligence, organized ambushes and interrogated captured terrorists. He was ruthless but effective. Peter Wright, a former Assistant Director of MI5, was also on the island in 1959. Wright was running Operation Sunshine, an attempt to find, trap and eliminate the EOKA leader Colonel Grivas. It is possible that Chesterton met Wright, but whether he did or not, Chesterton was recruited to MI5 from the Army the following year.

Chesterton was a member of MI5 until 1972, and when he left the service, his family and professional background attracted the offers of directorships of several companies, including Worldwide Private Security. He travelled, particularly to the Middle East and America.

During the mid-1970s, when Harold Wilson was Prime Minister, union trouble and strikes were rife in Britain, and some right-wing establishment figures feared a socialist take-over. They prepared by planning a counter-coup.

Two private armies were thought to have been formed. David Stirling, the founder of the SAS, was behind GB75, which probably never existed and is likely to have been a semi-official Psychological Operations scam. The other was Civil Assistance. This was fronted by General Sir Walter Walker and G.K. Young, former Deputy Director of MI6. Among those who gave support were Lord Mountbatten, several senior retired military personnel, and Chesterton.

Chesterton was also involved with The National Association for Freedom, which was inaugurated in 1975 by industrialists, businessmen and members of the British right-wing Monday Club. Among its members were three Conservative MPs who later became cabinet ministers.

Chesterton was already active in politics and was part of the Tory Action group that got Margaret Thatcher the leadership of the Conservative Party.

Lacey felt cogs begin to slot into place in his head.

Peter 'Spycatcher' Wright had led part of the debriefing of Blunt in 1964. If Chesterton had been a protégé of Wright, maybe Hollis, the head of MI5, had given him first bite at the Keeper of the Queen's Pictures. A first unofficial bite to assess what damage the spy could still do.

Maybe Blunt warned Chesterton that he had secrets to bargain with, and maybe Chesterton traced the secrets to the apartment of Jimmy Russell. Chesterton, 'being ruthless but effective', could have gone too far in his attempts to make Russell talk.

The speculation didn't tell Lacey what secrets Blunt had been holding, but it did provide a reason for Chesterton taking personal control of the present operation.

Maybe Lacey's job was two-fold: to keep a royal secret for which a large budget had been provided; and to cover up the fact that Law and Order Chesterton, a possible future prime minister of the United Kingdom, was a murderer.

TWENTY-ONE

They both had plenty to think about as they trailed Mattie
Purcell's Ford on the journey north. They had crossed from
Oregon into Washington and joined the Interstate 5 freeway
before Lacey felt like talking about anything other than the
migration of whales, the San Andreas Fault or the activity of
the volcano on their right.

'How did you get into this business?' he said.

'Security?'

'Yes.'

'I started out wanting to join the FBI.' He grinned. 'I
guess I watched too many reruns of Eliot Ness as a kid.'

'Did you join the FBI?'

'Sure. Passed the entrance exam, trained, learned the
tradition and history, and decided it hadn't changed enough
since Hoover, so I left.'

'And?'

'And I started my own business with an ad in the
Washington Post. No office, just an ad saying I was available
for commissions abroad, payment on delivery. I figured I'd get
hired if the guy wanting a job done didn't have to pay for it
up-front. That way, if I was unsuccessful or dead, it wouldn't
cost him anything. It worked. The first job was in Mexico,
the second in Beirut. After that, I started getting recommen-
dations. Pretty soon I didn't have to advertise any more.'

'What sort of jobs?'

'Collections, deliveries, retrievals. Goods, contracts, people.
Sometimes the people had to be persuaded.'

'It sounds dangerous.'

'Sometimes it was. That was part of the fun. Trying to stay
alive. It was also a great learning process.' Miller laughed.

'Look, I wasn't a total amateur. I'd done survival courses, martial arts. I was educated, single and had two years with the Bureau. And I learned quick. I became a success. So much of a success that Dixon Green made me an offer three years ago.'

'What about ethics?'

Miller laughed.

'What about them?'

'Do you break the law?'

'Dixon Green is a respectable company. Sixty per cent of our work is white collar and computer fraud in banks and investment funds; protection of companies involved in hostile take-over bids. We have forensic chemists who are expert at identifying forged documents, former cops from the Fraud Squad. The guy who runs the fraud division used to be an investigator with British Customs and Excise. They operate within the law. They have to. When they crack a case, they provide evidence good enough to hand over to the police. They get convictions.'

Lacey said: 'That's sixty per cent. What about the rest?'

'We have a security advice section. It provides assessments, equipment and bodyguards for the extremely wealthy or extremely vulnerable. And there are a lot of rich, vulnerable people in the Middle East. Italy's good, too. Kidnapping is still a way of life there. We employ a lot of guys from the SAS.'

'And what do you do?'

'I do the jobs that a respectable company like Dixon Green doesn't like to profile in their brochure.'

'The illegal jobs?'

'Not necessarily.'

'But you break the law? Telephone taps, bugs?'

'I have the greatest respect for the law. I've seen it used like a stiletto and like a club, as a punishment and a threat. Sometimes I've even seen it used for the furtherance of justice.' He grinned. 'Wherever possible, I avoid it.'

Lacey understood his philosophy.

'Why do Dixon Green bother with the less than respectable?'

196

'Market forces. They need to provide every type of service, particularly if a good client wants something other than a fraud investigation. The unusual also pays well. For instance, we're investigating a three hundred million dollar corporate fraud in Dallas? The contract for the first year is half a million dollars, with another half million for expenses. It'll take a lot of man hours to earn that, going through files and account books. My contract for the Blunt papers is two hundred and fifty thousand dollars, plus expenses.'

Miller glanced at Lacey to see if he had caused a reaction.

Lacey chewed his lip as the familiar urge for a cigarette returned and he comforted himself with the thought that at least his Civil Service pension was index-linked.

'How were you supposed to get the papers? Buy them? Steal them?'

'I'm not supposed to get them; I'm supposed to destroy them.'

'Sight unseen?'

'That's right.'

'For money?'

'Is there a better reason?'

'That depends if the bloke you're working for is a Soviet spy.'

'And your reasons are better? Because you work for your government?'

Lacey didn't answer. It was a question he'd been asking himself and still hadn't resolved.

Miller said: 'Have you ever heard of I.F. Stone?'

'No.'

'Crusading American journalist. He had a pertinent way with words. One of the things he said was all governments are liars and nothing they say should be believed. I guess I tend to go along with those sentiments.'

They drove in silence for a while.

Lacey felt he was in no position to argue morality. He was comfortable swapping cynicisms with Sam Bryson but Ben Miller didn't sound cynical; he sounded honest.

There had been many times in the past when Lacey had been faced with difficult decisions of conscience. He had been deceitful and he had killed; that was the nature of the work in which he was involved, but he had passed the blame on to the government that employed him. A minister who preferred not to know how a result had been achieved, as long as it was achieved, carried far more guilt than he did.

Miller said: 'How do you feel about Chesterton?'

'The man is a bastard.'

'You think he had something to do with Jimmy Russell's death?'

'He could have. He's capable of it.'

'And how do you feel about keeping that a secret?'

'I don't like it.'

'I don't like the idea I'm covering for a Soviet spy, either.'

A mile went by.

Lacey said: 'What are you going to do about it?'

'Fucked if I know. You?'

'I think I'll take my wife to Cairo.'

'You don't sound happy with your work?'

'I'm not. I'm beginning to wake up from a lie.'

'We all live them.'

'You seem remarkably well adjusted to yours.'

'Until now, I always had a choice.'

'And now you don't?'

Miller shrugged.

'There's still a choice. Maybe it just gets harder when you're used to First Class.'

'That's something I don't have to worry about.'

'You could.'

'What do you mean?'

'If you don't like what you're doing, resign. Come and work for Dixon Green. Join our expanding department of the unusual.' He grinned. 'All expenses paid.'

Lacey grinned in response. It was a long time since anyone had offered him a job.

'Are you serious?'

'Sure am. Think about it.'

Mattie Purcell signalled early, and they followed the Ford off the freeway and into a complex of roadside restaurants and gas stations. The four of them ate at a grillhouse, filled the cars with petrol, and said their goodbyes.

They were still a couple of hours from the airport but had no further reason to stop. It was an awkward leave-taking. Lacey and Miller shook hands with Mattie. Linda, whose recovery could be measured in the miles she had put between herself and the memory, was friendlier and gave each of them a hug.

'Thank you both. So much.'

She got into the Ford and Mattie gave them a final look.

'I hope your trip was worth while,' she said.

Lacey said: 'I think so.'

'I'll keep watching TV to see what happens. I hope I'll think it was worth while too.'

She climbed behind the wheel and drove the Ford back on to the freeway. Lacey and Miller followed them all the way past Olympia and Tacoma until they saw the signs and peeled off for the airport, south of Seattle.

Miller got rid of the car with the rental agency, while Lacey went ahead and checked in. They met up again in a bar overlooking the runway. Lacey was sitting at a table by the window, drinking a cold Mexican beer straight from the bottle, and watching a Hawaiian Airlines Tri-Star, with bright orange and purple markings, taxi into position for a flight to paradise.

The American dumped his briefcase on the seat opposite and Lacey held up his boarding card.

'Club Class. I'm back working for the Government.'

Miller nodded.

'Think about what I said. When this is all over you might want to leave.'

'That could depend.'

'On what?'

'On what we both do.'

Miller held up his boarding card.

'Change of plans. I have to see a man on the East Coast before I go back to London. Depending on what he says, I may not go back to London. Here.' He gave Lacey a Dixon Green business card with a telephone number written on the back. 'That's my home number in Florida. Just in case.'

Lacey nodded and put it in the pocket of his shirt.

The American pointed at the beer.

'You want another?'

'Why not.'

Miller went for the drinks and Lacey went back to looking at the aeroplane preparing to fly to the ultimate holiday destination. Maybe, if he went private, he could afford to take Susan there. But first there was Bryson and Chesterton, and who the hell knew what secrets to sort out.

Lacey felt in the mood to get drunk. He had a ten-hour flight in which to do it and in Club the drinks were free. There was time for an alcoholic stupor after the in-flight movie and he would be able to face Bryson with the benefit of both hangover and jet lag when he got back to London tomorrow afternoon.

He wondered who would be calling the shots then and whether he would still be chasing Blunt's bloody legacy, or even whether he would still have a job.

Miller returned with two beers, placed one in front of Lacey, sat opposite and toasted him.

'To the future.'

Lacey raised his own bottle and wondered if he had one.

TWENTY-TWO

Sam Bryson was in a wary mood. Lacey suspected his appearance contributed to it.

He had chosen not to shave on the plane but had concentrated on drinking, giving both bourbon and beer an equal chance to fuzz his mind. His eyes were red, and appeared to have retracted deeper into their sockets in protest at both the booze and the abuse he had wrought on his body-clock by hopping backwards and forwards through an eight-hour time zone.

Lacey was punch-drunk and didn't care; it gave him an edge that Bryson recognized.

They sat either side of Bryson's desk, Lacey drinking his way through a second Superman mug of coffee. He had recounted in full the whole of the trip to the north-west coast of America, including working in concert with Ben Miller and the intrusion of a rapist intent on murder.

He had handed over the photographs of the gunman from Lisbon, who, he had suggested, was Frank Briggs, and had told Bryson that Jimmy Russell had been murdered. He had not revealed the contents of the faxes he had received from Ben Miller as they left Cannon Beach.

Bryson remained silent and began packing his pipe with tobacco.

'That's what is called a full and frank report,' Lacey said. 'Now, how about giving me one?'

The department head raised one eyebrow and paused from tamping down strands in the pipe bowl.

'I don't know if that's possible.'

He continued packing the bowl.

'Am I still on the case, Sam?'

'Yes. I think you are.'

He struck a match and lit the pipe.

'Does that mean you have to get confirmation?'

In between puffs, Bryson said: 'Yes.'

'From Chesterton?'

Bryson raised both eyebrows to stare at him over the pipe which he continued to puff.

'How do you know about Chesterton?'

'Something Lamont-Smith said.'

'Sometimes,' Bryson blew out smoke, 'you're too clever for your own good.'

'Do the job and walk away, right?'

'That's what the manual says.'

'I never did like the manual. It takes no account of initiative.'

'Initiative is a dirty word.'

'How about truth? Is that a dirty word?'

'It can be very dirty.'

'It can also be essential, especially on a case like this.'

'I disagree. Truth is only ever a technical advantage.'

Lacey smiled and decided to try a different tack.

'What about the Fifth Man?'

'Yes. A bit of a turn-up.'

'Any suspects?'

'Not really. This has come out of the blue, not at all what we were expecting.'

'Could there be a Fifth Man?'

'Good God, there could be a Twelfth Man. There could be enough to form sides and play cricket. Peter Wright had a list of forty British names: eight undisclosed KGB agents in MI5 and MI6, and the rest in universities or government. He even suspected Harold Wilson.'

'How come they've never been named?'

'Some have. But not in the way the Press can hang a good title on them. And there must have been Americans as well. A lot of Yanks went to Oxbridge and the London School of Economics in the thirties. After Michael Straight confessed,

202

he spent a month identifying possibles to the FBI. It's likely they found a few but they didn't publicize the fact. The last thing they wanted was a spy scandal. That was the British disease.

'We'd had Burgess and Maclean, and then Philby. And in 'sixty-three, while Straight was singing to the FBI, we had Profumo, Christine Keeler and Stephen Ward.'

Lacey said: 'So you wouldn't rate catching this prominent American as being of particular importance?'

'I would rate it less than that. Philby, Burgess and Blunt were the ringmasters, all the rest were minor players. Of course, from the point of view of the American concerned, it's a revelation that could destroy him, just as Blunt was destroyed. Particularly if he gets lumped with a title. The Press love them and "The Fifth Man" is so emotive.'

'Like "the Blunt Legacy".'

'Yes.'

'Or "the Biarritz Agreement".'

'Ah.'

Lacey finished the coffee.

'I need some more of this.'

He raised the mug and Bryson nodded.

Lacey went into the main office to spoon Nescafé into the mug and add boiling water. Natalie watched him from her desk, looking for clues as to how the meeting was going. He gave her a wink.

He went into his own office and took out the packet of Gitanes. Going to America and back without benefit of nicotine was easy; you sat in non-smoking and let someone else enforce the ban. But this was different. He lit one, inhaled deeply, and had a coughing fit.

God, had he ever enjoyed this?

He inhaled again, just as deeply, and felt light-headed. Of course he had enjoyed it. The sensation was marvellous.

Lacey went back to Bryson's office with the cigarette and coffee, sat down and smiled disarmingly across the desk.

203

'Now, Sam, give me some answers.'

'I'll try.'

'Let's start with the Biarritz Agreement. Was there ever any such thing?'

'No. Not really.'

'Not really?'

'We think something happened there, but not an agreement as such.'

'The FBI report?'

Bryson widened his eyes.

'Yes.'

'I've seen the FBI report. So you made the rest up to give me an acceptable scandal to chase?'

'Yes.'

'A bit extreme, wasn't it?'

'No, it was very easy to do. Lamont-Smith provided most of it. It was all factual and there could have been an arrangement made at Biarritz with Goering. All we did was give it a title. We needed something that fitted the advertisement in *The Times* that could have been true. We didn't think the sod would start splashing clues all over the world's press about what he's really got.'

'Why do you think he's been doing that, Sam? It's not just for the publicity, is it?'

'No, it isn't. Although that's part of it.'

'So what's the other part?'

'In a word, disaffection.'

'Go on.'

'Frank Briggs was with Five until 1981. He was never a high-flyer, always a plodder. He was recruited from Special Branch in the late fifties. He was with A Branch for years. When his health began to deteriorate he was put on admin duties with F Branch, maintaining files on trade unions and left-wing teachers, that sort of thing.'

Lacey noted that Briggs had been in the right section at the right time. The A Branch of MI5 was the technical operations section, the dirty tricks brigade that burgled and bugged properties and ran surveillance operations with

204

teams of Watchers. His work at F Branch had been much less influential.

'Briggs took early retirement because of ill health, although he didn't want to go. He also wasn't happy with his pension and took it to a review board twice, without success.

'Four years ago he invested in a time-share development in Spain. The business was a con and Briggs lost most of his money. He applied for another pension review but the Treasury turned it down. His wife died about the same time and Briggs blamed Five for most of the misfortune. We now think he's doing a Peter Wright, but with knobs on.'

Wright had revealed all in his book Spycatcher after a dispute about pension entitlements in which he accused MI5 of failing to keep promises. Frank Briggs had the added incentive of a dead wife.

Lacey pointed to the photograph of the Lisbon gunman that lay on the desk.

'Is that Briggs?'

'That's him.'

'How did you know about him?'

Bryson hesitated.

'An alternative source.'

'Chesterton?'

Bryson didn't reply but stared at Lacey through the smoke.

Lacey went on: 'I know Chesterton was with Five at the same time as Briggs.'

'You know a great deal.'

'Clever sod, aren't I?' He took a last pull at the cigarette before stubbing it out in the I LOVE CYPRUS ashtray. 'Chesterton rumbled it was Briggs who was selling Blunt's legacy as soon as the name Jimmy Russell cropped up, didn't he? That's why you tried to stop me going to the States to see Mattie Purcell. Right?'

'Partly. Because Chesterton had identified Briggs as being responsible it was no longer necessary for you to go to America.'

'That's not all of it, Sam. He didn't want me to find out Russell had been murdered. Right?'

'Go on.'

'Five went in with clogs on as usual, and ended up with a body on their hands. Isn't that what happened?'

'It's interesting speculation.'

'It's more than interesting if the team who did it were Briggs and Chesterton. You said the Press like neat packaging. How do you think they'd react if they found out Law and Order Chesterton was guilty of murder?'

'You're letting your imagination run away with itself, Peter. Five don't deal in death. You know that.'

'It happens.'

'This is dangerous speculation.'

'What about Colin Wallace of military intelligence? He tried to talk about dirty tricks in Northern Ireland and was accused of killing his best friend.'

'He was found guilty and sent to prison.'

'But did he do it, Sam? Or was it a frame?'

'Good God, Peter, you're in the realms of fantasy.'

'What about Hilda Murrell? The anti-nuclear campaigner? She walked in on a botched burglary at her home and paid for it with her life.'

'That wasn't Five.'

'No, but it was somebody working for them. A private mob on a dirty-tricks commission? Deaths happen, Sam. You know they do. Unattributable, accidental. But occasionally there are cock-ups. Occasionally, suspicion gets out.'

'Suspicion! Bloody press sensationalism.'

'Jimmy Russell was murdered. Quite possibly by Chesterton. Did Chesterton also send someone to Cannon Beach to kill Mattie Purcell?'

Bryson slammed the hand holding his pipe on to the desk. The stem broke. He pushed the two halves dismissively to one side.

'I seem to recall you've been responsible for a few deaths yourself, Peter.'

'I don't want to be Prime Minister.'

They stared at each other. A pulse was prominent in Bryson's neck. Eventually they both relaxed and eased off to positions from where they could begin talking again instead of shouting.

Lacey wished he had another cigarette. He had known Bryson would remind him of his own past and he still couldn't reconcile the killing he had done with the outrage he felt about Chesterton.

What made it right for Lacey to kill and wrong for Chesterton? Was it just the ambition to high office?

Lacey had mostly killed in self-defence; once he had executed a terrorist. He had preferred not to dwell on his actions afterwards; if you attempted to analyse what couldn't be analysed you ended up drinking too much and sharing the night with the gremlins.

There had only been one death he had regretted, and it had been forced back into his thoughts by the murder of Jimmy Russell and the attempted hit on the two innocent women in Cannon Beach. It was the one death that could be classed as cold-blooded murder, when he had pushed a man who knew too much from a cliff top on the Costa Brava.

At the time he had told himself the killing was necessary, that there was no alternative.

Had Chesterton used the same reason?

Bryson opened a drawer and took out another pipe. He began filling it with tobacco.

'What do we do with you, Peter?'

'I don't know. I think you'll probably send me after Briggs.'

'Will you go?'

'It depends why you want me to find him.'

'We want the papers he's got. The Blunt papers.'

'Not to silence him about Chesterton?'

'That's still only your speculation. I don't think the British Press would be too interested in unsubstantiated allegations against a senior politician, even if Briggs was to make them.'

207

'Sam, did Chesterton arrange the hit at Cannon Beach?'

Bryson struck a match and paused before putting it to the tobacco.

'I don't know.'

He lit the pipe.

Lacey said: 'If he didn't, who did?'

'Frank Briggs? He shot the lawyer to get attention. He pointed the finger at Russell. Perhaps he put the contract on the woman for more publicity and, maybe, to get people thinking Chesterton was responsible.'

'Neat.' Lacey smiled, despite himself. 'Very neat. We're back to looking in mirrors, like Alice.'

He finished the coffee before continuing.

'If there's no Biarritz Agreement, what's in the Blunt Legacy that makes it so important?'

'I'm sorry. That's still restricted.'

'Because Five are so sensitive?'

'It's not Five that's sensitive.' He closed his mouth as if he had already said too much. 'It looks as if Briggs is trying to embarrass Five and Chesterton to get his own back. In the process he appears to be prepared to damage the royal family. Take the documents away from Briggs and he loses his power. He'll simply become a vindictive old man that people will not take seriously.'

Lacey knew how that would work. The intelligence community would do a character assassination, as they had with Colin Wallace and Fred Holroyd when the two Northern Ireland specialists had tried to go public about psy-ops and dirty tricks. By the time they finished, the only people who would take Briggs seriously would be the sort of extreme left-wing politicians who gave credibility a bad name.

'What do I do now?' he said.

'Go home to Susan and wait. When we find Briggs we'll tell you.'

And then he would go hunting again, for a dirty tricks expert from Five who had killed in Lisbon and had maybe, just maybe, put out a particularly dirty contract in Cannon Beach.

It could be leading to another inevitable conclusion, where Lacey would once again stare along the barrel of a gun at his conscience.

TWENTY-THREE

The meeting had taken twenty-four hours to arrange. Miller had flown to New York, where he'd spent the night in a Fifth Avenue hotel. He had waited there until lunch-time the next day before Orville B. Bross had agreed to see him. He had made the trip to the estate in Connecticut in the Bross chopper from the Wall Street Heliport.

An English butler had led him past the family portraits to a study where he was told to wait. Miller passed ten minutes estimating the value of the paintings and drawings on the wall. They were old and they were originals and two of the paintings were of semi-nude girls.

The door opened and Orville B. Bross made an entrance.

A big man, he had a distinctive mass of white hair that swept back at each side of his head like the helmet of a winged messenger from the gods, which Miller thought was appropriate considering how friendly the guy had been with four presidents.

He wore blue checked slacks, loafers, an open-necked shirt and a red cardigan and looked exceptionally young for a man approaching eighty.

Bross stopped in the middle of the room and pointed at the nudes.

'Jean-Baptiste Greuze. French, eighteenth-century. Do you like them?'

'Very nice.'

'Yes, they are. No more, no less than very nice, but I like 'em.' He took a cigar from a box on the desk, cut off the end, and lit it with a Zippo lighter.

He held up the cigar.

'Rolled on the thighs of Cuban maidens.' He laughed out

210

loud. 'Cigar snobs get scandalized every time I torch one with a petrol lighter. My doctor gets scandalized every time I torch one, period. He says they're killing me. Bullshit. Old age is killing me.'

Bross sat in a leather armchair and waved at a second armchair.

'Sit down, Ben. Tell my why you're here.'

Miller sat down. He wasn't fooled by the act of *bonhomie* and all guys together. No one made the money The Man had made or survived in politics as he had, without knowing how to manipulate people.

'I think you know why I'm here, Mr Bross.'

The Man puffed smoke and nodded.

'I guess I do, at that. You want to know if I'm some kind of Russian spy. Right?'

'Right.'

Bross continued to smoke his cigar and his eyes strayed back to the paintings of the women on the wall.

'One thing I learned in politics is that there's never an absolute. Whatever you're dealing with – issues, contracts, wars, people – they're hedged with options, interpretations. Nothing is as clean cut as it appears to be. You know what I'm saying?'

'I know what you're saying.'

'Even presidents have faults.' He laughed again, a boom of sound that expected his audience to join in. Miller smiled. 'JFK was a womanizer. Johnson had no breeding and Carter had no friends. Reagan wasn't clever enough but Nixon was too damn clever. Nobody has come out of the White House without trailing shit on the porch. Everybody's got some weakness, some skeleton they'd rather the world didn't know about.'

He smoked the cigar some more and Miller remained silent and let him tell it the way he wanted.

'When I was young, I had a chasm for a mind. It devoured everything. I spoke four languages by the time I was eighteen, not counting English, and learned two more by the time I was twenty-three. I enjoyed learning, and Europe

211

in the thirties was a great place to learn, full of knowledge, great minds. Anthony Blunt was one of them.

'He taught me about art. He loved Poussin, had copies of his work all over the place. *Narcissus, Apollo and Daphne.* He had an original he bought with eighty pounds that Victor Rothschild lent him in the thirties. When he died, it was valued at half a million. He liked Greuze, too, but not the nudes. We disagreed about the nudes.

'Hell, he was a great guy back then, had all the right connections. I guess, maybe I was somewhat impressionable at that time as well, still in awe of titles and English accents. Anyway, we became friends.'

More smoke before The Man tapped an inch of ash from the end of the cigar into an ashtray on a stand next to his chair.

'Anthony was older than me. I met him in 1938, when he was at the Warburg Institute and writing his first book on Poussin. He introduced me to a part of London society I hadn't known. As I said, his connections were phenomenal. The aristocracy, theatre, literature, art. I knew Guy Burgess, too, but he was never a friend.

'After Oxford I lived in London for a time, and travelled in Europe. Paris, Brussels, Berlin, Lisbon. I saw fascism and oppression and everything that was rotten. It made me frustrated that I couldn't change things. That all those terrible things that were going to happen, were going to happen no matter what the hell I said or did. I guess that's why I went into politics.' The Man puffed his cigar. 'You know what I'm saying?'

Miller nodded.

'Don't get me wrong. It was also the most exciting time of my life, although maybe being young had something to do with that. But it was exciting. The war made life sharper. It made anything possible. You felt that if you didn't grab it you might never get a second chance. You know?'

He paused again and stared back at the paintings through the smoke. The silence lengthened, as if he were lost in memories.

212

Miller said: 'Did Blunt recruit you?'

'What?'

'Did you become a communist agent?'

'Hell, no. I guess the most I did was pass on stuff I'd heard at the US Embassy. Gossip, you know? Something to talk about. My father knew Joe Kennedy so I visited from time to time. I talked politics with Anthony, sure, and I knew where his sympathies were, but I didn't know he was involved in any of this spy stuff.

'After I came back to the States I didn't see him until 'forty-eight. I was in London on business and he'd been made director of the Courtauld Institute the year before. I visited with him there. We looked at pictures and talked art.

'Burgess tried calling me a couple of times when he was in Washington in 'fifty-one but I didn't want to see him. I had a family and he wasn't the sort of person you introduced to your family. The next I heard he'd gone to Russia and there was talk of a Third Man. That's when a lot of stuff fell into place; that's when I suspected Anthony was involved.

'The FBI knew the Third Man was Philby and they told the British to get rid of him. He was fired the same year, 'fifty-one. After that, I made it my business to know what was happening. I knew they were looking for others from the same sort of circle. As far as I was concerned, I didn't want even to be reminded of that period in my life. But I was, in 'sixty-three.

'Anthony was in the States taking a summer course at Pennsylvania State University. He called and asked to meet. The thought of meeting him after all that time made me nervous but, hell. We saw each other in Washington and he was more nervous than me. His left eye drooped; some kind of paralysis. He didn't look good.

'That was the year Philby finally went to Moscow and the year Burgess died there. Anthony talked about Burgess and about other people from before the war; about motives, beliefs. He quoted Aby Warburg, the founder of the Warburg Institute. God lurks in the detail, he said. Hell, we both knew what he was talking about.

213

'He said Michael Straight had visited him in London. Straight was going to be offered the chairmanship of the Advisory Council on the Arts by President Kennedy. The appointment had to be ratified by Congress and that meant an FBI investigation. Straight told Anthony that when the offer became official he'd have no choice but to turn it down and tell them about his Communist connections at Cambridge.'

He got rid of more ash and then looked at the cigar as if he had lost track of his narrative.

Miller prompted again.

'What did Blunt want?'

Bross took a pull on the cigar and looked across at Miller.

'Help. Any help he could get. I had influence and I knew people. Maybe he thought I could get the offer withdrawn, save Straight from having to make his confession. But he was too late. The offer had been made official and Straight had already seen the FBI.

'Even then, Anthony didn't let go. He said, at times like this you needed friends. He wanted me to remain a friend, use my influence, mitigate the damage. He said if he went, others would go as well. He had names, events, photographs. A bookful of stuff. He said I was in it.' He shrugged. 'He wanted a deal and I told him he was talking to the wrong person. He said think about it. Maybe I could arrange something.'

He smoked the cigar again.

'And did you?'

'Hell, I sure thought about it. All sorts of things went through my mind. I thought maybe I could arrange to kill the son of a bitch, but that wouldn't have found his damn book. In the end I did nothing but wait and sweat and see if he got a deal.' More smoke. 'He got a deal from the British.

'I heard nothing more about it and nothing more from Anthony. When he died, I thought maybe something would happen then, but it didn't. Then the ad appeared in the damn paper and now this talk of a prominent American. Shit!'

214

Miller said: 'He calls the prominent American the Fifth Man.'

'That was a joke. A bad joke he made in 'sixty-three because I was known as The Man. If he was the Fourth Man, he said, I'd be the Fifth. Well I'm not, son. I've told it like it was. I'm no damn spy.'

'Then what the hell had he got on you?'

The Man puffed more smoke, tapped more ash and looked again at the semi-nude ladies by Greuze.

'This is strictly between you and me, Ben. Client confidentiality.'

'Of course, Mr Bross.'

'Because if it isn't . . .'

He left the threat unsaid.

Miller said: 'I know.'

Bross nodded.

'You have to remember the period. It was the thirties when everything was available for those who could afford it, and everything went. You felt you had to try everything at least once, and I did.'

He pulled on the cigar again and seemed to hold the smoke inside himself for strength.

'You see, Anthony was a collector. He collected souls at their most impressionable. He collected mine with a camera, committing a sexual indiscretion. Of the homosexual kind.'

Bross stared straight at him. His chin had firmed up in the defiant way Miller remembered from TV and newspapers in his days as an aggressive politician, fighting a cause. A small tick in his left eye showed the inner emotion, the nervousness, as he waited for a reaction.

Miller stared back and nodded. It was a revelation he had not expected. Bross had been linked with many beautiful women before he met his wife, including a film actress from Hollywood. He had been married to the same woman for forty-three years, until her death.

A homosexual connection with Blunt and the Cambridge spy ring would have destroyed his career if it had become known in 1963. It might have destroyed his marriage, too. It could still destroy his special place in American history and damage his whole family if it became public now.

Bross said: 'I tried it, and I didn't like it. A lot of young men did at that time. I discovered I wasn't queer. You want the details? You want me to explain?'

Maybe he thought Miller's silence was a challenge.

Miller shook his head.

'No. I don't need an explanation, Mr Bross.'

There was the possibility that Bross was lying but Miller felt it was unlikely. He was the kind of man who would probably have preferred to be called spy sooner than homosexual.

'You believe me?'

'I believe you.'

The Man was no longer an intimidating patriarch. He seemed relieved to have made the confession and to have had it accepted. He relaxed enough to draw life back into the cigar.

'Are you still with me, Ben? Still on the team?'

Miller smiled at the terminology with which The Man had cushioned his life and career, terminology that had flattered people into taking his point of view.

'Yes, Mr Bross. I'm still on the team.'

You got through the bluster and instead of The Man you found a guy with a secret who had lived with the possibility of its discovery for a large part of his life, and with the thought that maybe he had been a contributor to treachery by not running straight to the FBI as soon as he had suspected Blunt.

But that didn't make him a bad person; an asshole maybe, who liked power too much to be totally trustworthy, but not a bad person. A man who, through an ego trip of a career, had made a valid contribution to the strength and wealth of America, whilst making the odd million or ten for himself.

'And will you find the Blunt Legacy for me?'

'I'll find it, Mr Bross. And I'll burn it.'

'Thank you, son. And thank you for your courage and honesty in coming here today, to put your doubts on the

216

line.' He puffed the cigar. 'That courage and honesty has just earned you a bonus.'

They smiled at each other.

Miller knew that The Man was happy because he believed he had won him over with the strength and warmth of his personality. He hadn't.

He was happy to be able to continue with a job that would be one of the most profitable he had undertaken, because, while he objected to working for a traitor, he didn't mind one bit working for an asshole with an ego as big as the Grand Canyon and a bank balance to match.

TWENTY-FOUR

Lacey found the cord from a dressing-gown neatly coiled on his side of the bed when he got home.

Susan had remembered; he had forgotten the perfume.

He had arrived at the house before she had got back from the shop. He felt dirty and tired. The alcohol, lack of sleep and disorientation were reducing reality to flashes of ten seconds out of every minute. He undressed and showered and brushed his teeth. The embryo beard could wait. He wondered, in one of the flashes of clarity, whether it could be classed as designer stubble.

Bed was a life-raft and he climbed in and pushed off. He was asleep within seconds of laying his head on the pillow.

He awoke in the dark and tensed at a sound somewhere in the house before he realized where he was. He relaxed and dozed for a while, content to lie in the warmth and familiarity of the bed, with the smell of Susan that still clung to the silk night-dress lying on the pillow next to him.

At least he had nothing else to figure out. All he had to do was wait until the combined resources of Her Majesty's Secret Intelligence Services found Frank Briggs, then go and persuade him to hand over a bundle of documents. Easy. Like always.

Just as long as Briggs hadn't taken refuge in Reykjavik. Lacey didn't like cold weather.

'Are you awake?'

'Mmm?'

Susan came into the room carrying a cup of coffee. She left the light off.

'I thought you must be. The snoring stopped.'

'I don't snore.'

218

'Then there's a pig in the wardrobe.'

She put the coffee on the table at the side of the bed and bent down to kiss him and he held her for a moment.

'What time is it?'

'Eleven. Hungry?'

'Yes.'

'Steak? Eggs and bacon? What?'

'How about a corned beef sandwich?'

'Are you sure? Just a sandwich?'

'With brown sauce.'

'OK.'

'And a beer.'

She went downstairs and Lacey sat up, pushed the pillows back and reached for the remote control of the television set that sat on a table at the end of the bed. He switched it on and channel-hopped away from a discussion programme and found a rerun of *Monty Python*. The bizarre humour suited his mood.

Susan returned with the sandwich and a bottle of Beck's.

'I'll switch everything off downstairs and come to bed,' she said.

He had finished eating by the time she came back and he watched her undress in the glow from the television to the accompaniment of laughter and a naked man playing a piano.

She put on the night-dress and got into bed, pushing her pillows up close to his, and lying thigh to thigh. They held hands.

'Good trip?'

'Tiring.'

'Still tired?'

'Yes.'

'Never mind. The rope can wait.'

Monty Python finished, and he reached for the remote control and channel-hopped again until he was back to the same station.

He said: 'I always think I'm missing something.'

She squeezed his hand.

'I don't think you miss much.' They watched the screen and waited for the next programme. 'Is the job over?'

'Not yet.'

'Will you be going away again?'

'Yes. Just for a couple of days.'

'What about Cairo?'

'Don't worry. We won't miss Cairo.'

'And if the job isn't over?'

'It'll be over. One way or another.'

'That sounds very final.'

'It might be. I'm thinking of resigning.'

'You've thought of resigning before.'

'This time I'm serious.'

The credits for a film came on the screen. It was Michael Caine in *The Ipcress File*.

'I like this,' Susan said. 'He was handsome when he was young.'

'Weren't we all.'

She squeezed his hand again, as if she thought he needed reassurance.

They watched Caine introduce Harry Palmer to the world. She said: 'What will you do?'

'I've been offered a job. A private security company.'

'What?' She took her eyes off the screen to stare at him. 'The sort where you wear a uniform?'

He laughed.

'No. I wouldn't have to drive a van either. But I would travel First Class.'

She continued to watch the screen.

'Is it a good job?'

'It sounds like it.'

'Who made the offer?'

'An American I met.'

'Where is it? The job, I mean.'

'The company is based in London, but the work would involve travel.'

'First Class.'

'First Class.'

'Will you take it?'

'I don't know. What do you think?'

'I think you'll make up your own mind.'

They watched television for a while.

She said: 'What's brought all this on? The male meno-pause?'

'I'm long past that.'

'What then? I know there are bad times but, well, I thought you believed in what you did.'

'I suppose I used to. I'm not sure any more.'

'Would you be sure if you went private?'

'I don't know. Maybe I'll find out before this job's finished.'

On the screen, Harry Palmer was displaying working-class prejudice towards officialdom.

Susan said: 'He reminds me of you.'

Lacey laughed.

'I don't know why,' he said. 'He always wins.'

'I'm sure you win without knowing it.'

'I do a lot of things without knowing it.'

Susan fell asleep half-way through the film with her head resting on his shoulder. He moved her so that they would both be more comfortable and watched Michael 'Harry Palmer' Caine work his way through a complicated plot to a neat conclusion.

Easy. Like always.

He got up early, showered and stayed in his dressing-gown. He repressed the nicotine craving with black coffee. At seven-thirty he took Susan breakfast in bed.

Sleepiness made her crumpled and vulnerable. He felt a sudden burst of companionship for her; not love, or passion, but friendship. They had been through a lot together, seen each other at their worst and most selfish, and their relationship had survived.

It had started at university in Durham, a city of narrow roads, spires and turrets, a railway viaduct and a lazy river. Romantics might have remembered the rowboats on

221

the river but what he remembered most was the single bed in his room where they had spent hours at a time. He remembered the smell most, that heavy, intoxicating smell of sex they created and in which they wallowed.

The memory made the feeling of companionship change to something more intimate.

He waited until she had arranged the pillows behind her before he put the tray on her lap.

'Nice,' she said, sipping tea.

He leant against the dressing-table.

'Do you remember that bed in Durham?'

She smiled and crunched toast.

'I was young and innocent.'

'You were a quick learner.'

'Lucky you.'

'Yes, I was.'

She continued eating and he continued watching her.

Susan said: 'What are you thinking?'

'I'm thinking how much I'd like a cigarette.'

'Sod.'

She laughed and he grinned.

'I love you,' he said, conversationally.

'I love you too.'

She smiled again and bit into more toast.

Lacey stayed in the dressing-gown while Susan got ready to go to the shop. He sat in bed and read the morning newspapers and drank coffee.

'Too much of that stuff is bad for you,' she said, walking in from the bathroom where she had been putting on her make-up.

'I need one vice.'

'You've got one vice. A very nice vice. Drink too much coffee and you won't be able to practise it.'

'I need the coffee for my nerves.'

'Michael Caine didn't have nerves.'

'He didn't have to work out what to do next. He read the script.'

'You'd rather have a script?'

222

'That's the trouble. I've got one. And I don't like it.'

He watched her get dressed. He had always enjoyed watching her put on and take off clothes; she did it well, aware of his interest. He felt his libido rise. But his mind was still too clogged with doubts about other things.

She said: 'Will you be here when I get back?'

'I don't know.'

'It's a good job I trust you. You could have another woman.'

'I don't need another woman.'

'God, you really are getting old. I'll buy you slippers for your next birthday.'

'Maybe I'll wear them.'

'That'll be the day.'

She sprayed perfume and came over to the bed and gave him a kiss and a long look.

'Don't get careless,' she said. 'And call me.'

'I won't, and I will.'

She left for a day of bric-à-brac and Lucy, and he went downstairs and made more coffee. He took it back to the bedroom and dropped the dressing-gown on the floor to enjoy the comfort of nakedness. Susan wouldn't have minded him walking around without clothes but he had regard for her sensibilities and his ego; nudity was rarely attractive, particularly on him.

He looked at himself in the mirror on the dressing-table and considered the meaning of life for the over fifty. Not just his belly sagged, everything sagged.

Lacey pulled in his stomach and raised his chin to force the flesh taut but he still wasn't impressed. This was a body that could still fool people when wearing Levis and a leather jacket; this was a body that didn't look too bad in the dark; but, in the cold light of day, this was a body that might, just might, interest medical research.

Maybe he should opt for slippers and a dog to take walks. If he wore a baggy cardigan maybe Susan would let him smoke a pipe in the garden shed he would have the time to build in early retirement. She might also find

223

herself a young gardener to ease him out of other duties as well. Maybe it was not such a good idea.

He sprawled on the bed and switched on the television but it held nothing but banality. He left the picture on but turned the sound off. Maybe he could become a quiz show host?

Your starter for ten: Who really did kill Hilda Murrell? Correct!

Now double your money: Who really did frame Colin Wallace?

It was a shame that it was a job with no future. Tam Dalyell and Ken Livingstone had tried it in the House of Commons but found it didn't lead to anything much but a career banging your head against the Establishment wall.

Which left Dixon Green.

Lacey had always been suspicious of private security companies. He knew they were used by all branches of the secret services and that some had been specifically set up by former employees to undertake jobs that even department heads could then deny.

So where did Dixon Green fit into the scale of things?

It was an international company with a solid reputation that was enhanced by good public relations: the acceptable face of private security.

But what was acceptable? Did the size of the fee Ben Miller commanded make a difference? Did the fact that they were sometimes employed by governments make them more legitimate? He was employed by a government now and was pissed off.

What had Miller said? All governments are liars.

Christ, pretty soon he was going to be wrestling with morality and it wasn't even nine o'clock in the morning.

Lacey decided that all he could do was follow his instincts, in this job and any future job. He would do what he felt was right.

He would tell Sam Bryson that, too. But not yet. Not until afterwards.

TWENTY-FIVE

Malta is a speck of an island that floats in the Mediterranean between Sicily and Libya. It is about sixteen miles long by six miles wide and, with the adjoining islands of Gozo and Comino, has a population of three hundred and thirty thousand.

Frank Briggs was one of them.

Lacey and Lamont-Smith took an evening Air Malta flight from Heathrow to Luqa Airport. The arrangements, Bryson had told Lacey on the telephone, would be the same as before.

They had reservations at the Dragonara Hotel, where a message would be waiting with all available information on the whereabouts of their quarry.

'What about the other arrangements?' Lacey had said.

'What other arrangements?'

'Regarding Mr Browning. I found his presence a great comfort in Lisbon.'

'Peter. This time we know what we're after. Mr Browning won't be necessary.'

'Sam, you're not listening. I find his presence essential. Fix it.'

There had been a pause before Bryson replied.

'All right. There'll be a message at the desk.'

Lacey had met Lamont-Smith at check-in. The former international sportsman and spinner of amazing yarns wore the same clothes and the same grin as he had when they had first met six days before. This time they didn't shake hands. This time Lacey would treat him with all the scepticism an employee of L.O. Chesterton deserved.

After they had gone through the airport formalities,

225

Lamont-Smith had said: 'We have things to say to each other. How about we say them over a drink?'

Lacey had allowed him to lead the way to a bar and to buy the drinks, but he hadn't helped forge a new relationship.

'Look,' Lamont-Smith had said, 'I'm sorry about the subterfuge but I was under orders, just like you.'

'That's all right.' Lacey had smiled. 'You tell a good story. It was all very interesting.'

'It was all true. I mean, it's not as if I was lying.'

'True but irrelevant.'

'Yes. But it was rather good, actually, wasn't it?'

'It had me going.'

Lamont-Smith had smiled.

'Look. I really am sorry. I hope we can still get on. I mean, we are on the same side, after all.'

'Yes. We're on the same side but I'm wearing blinkers. Why not tell me now, Ian? Why not tell me what we're really after?'

'No can do, sport. Sorry, but . . .'

He had shrugged.

Lacey had shrugged in reply.

'Of course not. Silly of me to ask. Another beer?'

The time would come when Lacey would find out whether the secrets they were engaged in finding and hiding were royal or Chesterton's. When he did, he would then have to decide whether he and Lamont-Smith really were on the same side.

They walked out of the aeroplane and into a summer night. The taxi that took them to the hotel at St Julian's Bay was an old Peugeot that rattled and had never had a test for roadworthiness since it had rolled out of the showroom thirty years before. The driver handled the wheel with careless bravado and caressed the column-change gear stick into places it didn't want to go.

Lacey had forgotten how old most of the cars on the island were, and how magnificent the green buses, with their small

226

dashboard shrines to saints. The island was a paradise for the lovers of veteran vehicles.

Ten years before he had spent three weeks in August attached to the United Kingdom High Commission in Floriana, the business and diplomatic area on the outskirts of the capital of Valletta. He had been waiting for an intelligence drop from an oil worker from Benghazi and had stayed in the splendour of the nearby old colonial Phoenicia Hotel.

The heat of mid-summer had been extreme and the island had been scorched of vegetation. Parts of it had still shown damage from the Second World War, when it had survived the aerial bombardment of Italy and Germany. The Maltese had been as stubborn under siege against the Axis forces as they had been against the Turks four hundreds years before.

Lacey had found that the Maltese remembered things like that. They were an island race on an island with little to commend it but tradition, history and a thousand churches. They took all three seriously; so had Lacey.

Because the place was so small, everywhere was accessible, and he had discovered prehistoric sites, catacombs, places of worship, bars, and the silent city of Mdina that rose from the central plain of Malta like a fairytale castle from Hollywood.

He had also discovered driving the Maltese way.

Their taxi driver was an expert. He displayed a healthy disregard for motoring laws of any kind that might impede his progress or sully his pride, and took delight in carving up the opposition, which was every other vehicle on the road.

Driving was passion and flair without malice, and the old cars and vans with gleaming renovated bodies seemed to love it. Lamont-Smith didn't appear to share the enthusiasm.

Lacey sat alongside the driver in the front and looked over his shoulder at the archivist who was in the back with the bags, jaw set and lips twitching disapprovingly at the shriek of tyres and the groan of old metal as corners were taken too fast for comfort but just right for fun.

The main roads were quiet and the driver built his speed on the down-slopes of dual carriageways so that he could make the up-slopes without dropping too many gears. They left the main highway, made further turns through quiet and darkened streets, and were abruptly surrounded by discos, noise, neon lights and young people.

Their driver nosed his vehicle through the crowds and found peace again on a narrow road that curved around a bay of fishing boats. At the top of the hill the view to their left was cut off by a wall. Further along, the car manoeuvred through the gateway in the wall and they were at the Dragonara Hotel.

It was an imposing palace of a building, set in palm-treed gardens with floodlit fountains, on a promontory that was surrounded by the sea on three sides. Beyond it, along a private road, was the island's only Casino, also floodlit against the night sky.

They checked in at reception in a high-ceilinged marble hall. The sound of a trio playing light music came from a bar that overlooked the sea. Lamont-Smith picked up his key and his bag and hesitated, as if drawn by Circe towards the music. Lacey accepted his key and a padded envelope but shook his head at his companion. Neither the music, nor the bar, was that tempting.

'I'm going to bed. You please yourself.'

Reluctantly, Lamont-Smith followed Lacey to the lift. The rooms were in a wing of the hotel on the third floor. Lamont-Smith's overlooked the swimming-pool while Lacey's was across the corridor and overlooked St Julian's Bay and the road to the casino. They said good-night and parted company.

There was a breakfast card on the bed and Lacey filled it in, requesting coffee and rolls be served at seven-thirty. He opened the door of his room to hang the card outside and was in time to see Lamont-Smith walking jauntily along the corridor. He had succumbed to Circe – or was it Bacchus?

Lacey took a can of Cisk lager from the fridge, kicked off

228

his shoes and sprawled on the bed. He opened the padded envelope and shook out a car key attached by a metal ring to a white plastic tag with a number printed on it.

He took out three sheets of paper and read that the car key belonged to a white Ford Escort that was parked in front of the hotel. He also read that there was still no address for Frank Briggs.

Briggs was one of many British expatriates who lived on Malta and Gozo. He had been here almost three years, and had been a security consultant at the casino for the first year. He had rented an apartment in St Julian's Bay until he had given up the lease four months before. It was known he had still been living on the island because he had continued to visit his usual haunts, although not as frequently, and the strict immigration controls showed he had made two recent trips to Europe.

He had flown in from Rome four days before and, unless he had used another identity to leave, he was still on Malta.

Lacey guessed there would be no other reason for flying from Rome other than that it was an international airport with a service to Malta. He had checked and found that you couldn't fly to the island direct from Lisbon.

Although there was no current address for Briggs, there was a list of his regular haunts in and around St Julian's. They included a bar on the waterfront, the San Giuliano Restaurant that overlooked the fishing harbour, and the exclusive Reef Club. The letter told him he could see it from the balcony of his room.

He went out on to the balcony and located the Reef Club on the other side of the road that led to the casino. It appeared to be built into the rocky coves at the mouth of St Julian's Bay, but it was closed and it was too dark to see clearly.

The final sheet of paper held a message that was brief and unequivocal.

229

Regret to inform you that Mr Browning unavailable on Malta. Also, he has no local contact. You are expected to rely upon your own resources. When business complete, leave car key with hotel reception in envelope provided.

Lacey felt a surge of anger that he quickly controlled. He should have expected it. Bryson had given in too easily, and anyway he had probably been right.

They knew what they were chasing now, and Briggs would know they were closing in. Lacey suspected that Briggs had calculated everything down to the imminent meeting and would be ready to make the deal he had intended to make all along, whatever it might be.

Lacey had enough complications to deal with as it was, but he feared there might be yet another to overcome, and that depended on whom Briggs intended to deal with.

He had drip-fed clues to arouse interest in Europe and America. British intelligence might have been expected to gain the advantage once he had been identified, but what if he had foreseen the possibility and evened the odds by giving additional information to other interested parties?

The permutations were becoming more complex and far-fetched, and Lacey knew he had to safeguard against falling into the disease endemic amongst those involved in secrecy, where secrecy bred fantasy, and fantasy bred more fantasy.

He switched on the television and watched an old Western that had been badly dubbed into Italian on a station beamed from Sicily.

This was fantasy he could handle, with a body count that mounted at a comfortable Sicilian rate. Lacey hoped it wasn't an omen.

230

TWENTY-SIX

The rolls were soft Maltese bread and the coffee excellent, and the view was of the Mediterranean sparkling in the clear morning air.

This island, Lacey thought, was too friendly for anything nasty to happen.

While he ate, he read *The Times of Malta*, a thin tabloid newspaper with charming parochial contents that reflected the pace of a tiny nation that appeared to be still living in 1950.

He had anticipated the DO NOT DISTURB sign that hung on Lamont-Smith's door and at nine o'clock he left the hotel to check out his stalking ground alone, wearing Levis and a short-sleeved shirt to blend in with the holidaymakers.

A ten-minute walk took him to the harbour and he was pleasantly surprised to find it had retained an old-world charm despite the tourist development. He went down steep stone steps to reach the waterfront. Small and brightly multicoloured boats were tied to iron rings and between them shoals of silver fish darted in the clear water.

The northern side of the harbour had been paved and the old warehouses had been converted to pizza places and cafés. The bar that Briggs used was along here, with tables placed almost to the water's edge.

He strolled past it and sat on a bench and looked back at the way he had come. The bar, with white and green umbrellas, was to his right. Past it were a couple of inexpensive eateries, the first with red umbrellas, the next with orange, and then steps that led to the entrance to the Giuliano Restaurant.

231

The restaurant was housed on an upper floor of a stone building that sat elegantly above the harbour, its picture windows providing an uncluttered view above any smells of gutted fish. He had checked it in a guide book and knew it was one of the best Italian restaurants on the island.

He walked back towards the hotel past the Hilton and along a street of more restaurants. Among them were gift shops that sold cut-price pirated audio and video cassettes and fake designer sweatshirts that were guaranteed to self-destruct after the first wash. In one of them he bought a book for the day ahead: Nicholas Monsarrat's *The Kapillian of Malta*, the fictionalized story of the wartime siege that had won the island the George Cross.

Lacey remembered the book from his previous visit and had bought it then too, but had never got past the first fifty pages. The reason had nothing to do with the quality of the novel but more with the nature of Lacey's job. He had used it as a prop and had lost it in a forgotten bar.

Lamont-Smith was awake and using room service when Lacey got back to the hotel. He was chewing as he opened the door to Lacey's knock, and indicated a full English breakfast laid on the table on the balcony of his room.

'It's a rather good hotel, old boy. A certain old-fashioned style, you know.'

'I'm glad you approve. I'm going over to the Reef Club. Briggs goes there sometimes. Why don't you stay around the hotel in case there's a message?'

'Right ho, sport. Rely on me.'

Lacey let him return to his food and, in his own room, changed into shorts and a T-shirt and took a towel from the bathroom. He took the lift to the lower ground floor, which was at pool level, and walked past the first-comers who were staking territory around its edge.

An extended family of bronzed Italians with beautiful women, fat men and screaming children, had commandeered a larger portion than their numbers merited but it was unlikely anyone would argue. Beyond them were a Nordic blond husband and wife whose physiques appeared to have been attained on the rack, and, nearby, a group of Londoners with unmistakable East End accents rattled an extensive collection of heavy gold jewellery around their wrists and necks. Lacey hoped they didn't drown when they tried to swim in it.

He left the grounds through a side gate and crossed the road to the Reef Club. His residency at the Dragonara gave him membership.

It was in several sections. A restaurant and bar to his right, and dance floor and stage for Saturday night cabarets. To his left a path wound around the coves of the promontory and led to a scuba-diving club and, beyond that, a swimming-pool and high diving board and another bar. In front of him was the area Frank Briggs was supposed to prefer, a paved slab of rock jutting into the sea lined with maybe a hundred sun-loungers and umbrellas. Past it, down at sea level, were more water sports.

Lacey picked a position near the entrance and a boy erected the umbrella and brought him a foam mattress which he spread on the plastic lounger.

It was still only ten-thirty and sunbathers were thin on the ground. The weather was warm and this early in the year the sun lacked the scorching power he remembered from August. It was more like a pleasant English summer day and he wouldn't even need suntan lotion.

He took off his shirt and sprawled on the lounger, his head in the shade and his body in the sun. He still had a tinge of tan left from last year's holiday but in direct light he had to admit he looked anaemic. He hoped a family of bronzed Italians didn't decide to sit next to him. They might mistake him for a white salami.

Lacey read for a while, dozed for a while and kept note of all who entered. The loungers began to fill up, although it was never going to be really busy.

An elderly couple took loungers near the bar, where they could get instant waiter service. The man was white-haired and had a clipped military moustache. His khaki shorts and shirt suggested a British expatriate. They were obviously known by the staff. He took off his shirt to display a well-tanned but extensive belly; she shed a sundress, underneath which was a one-piece swimsuit, but she kept her thighs tastefully covered by a sarong.

They were joined by an older woman with wrinkled face and red lips, who spoke Maltese to the staff and English to the couple, flipping backwards and forwards from one to the other as if performing a high-wire language act. An older boy came forward to set her up with umbrella and mattress and she took several opportunities to touch his arm or thigh and call him a darling before tipping him a coin.

She stepped out of her sundress to reveal herself in a high-cut swimsuit: a thin, brown and old body with so many hanging wrinkles it looked as if she had been badly deflated. The handsome youth, Lacey thought, deserved all he got, and if that's what sunbathing did for you, maybe he should go and put some trousers on before he turned into a walnut.

This group could easily be one of the reasons why Briggs frequented the place, to talk about England, the weather and the rate of sterling exchange.

Two young women restored his good humour when they made a striking entrance just before noon. They were twins, maybe in their late teens, with short blond hair and delicate features.

'Excuse?'

Lacey sat up startled. He had been watching them over his book but hadn't expected one of them to speak to him.

'Yes?'

'These are vacant?'

She indicated the two loungers to his left, upon one of which he had thrown his shirt. He retrieved it.

'Yes, they are.'

'Thank you.'

The two girls conversed in German while a boy brought them mattresses; they declined to have the umbrellas raised. They were serious sun-lovers.

234

Lacey realized they were really serious when they removed T-shirts and shorts to reveal the smallest of bikinis. Then they removed the bikini tops and lay down.

He had coped with worse distractions on worse assignments but their presence only an arm's length away destroyed his literary concentration. Maybe this was why Briggs liked the Reef Club.

An hour later he went into the shade of the restaurant-bar, not quite sure whether it was the sun or the girls that had given him hot flushes. He had a toasted sandwich and fries and a cold Cisk lager and thought maybe he had misjudged Bryson on this one. Maybe he should send him a postcard saying, having a nice time.

He stuck it out for most of the afternoon on the lounger next to the girls, and even managed to read a few more chapters of the book despite the distraction. He talked to them a couple of times, in English, rather than letting them know he could understand anything they might say about him in German: once when he retrieved the bottle of sun oil that the nearest one dropped beneath his lounger, and again when her companion asked him the time.

Lacey told her and held his wrist out for her to see his watch. She leaned forward, across the buttocks of her twin, and lightly held his arm, before smiling and saying thank you nicely. His smile was painful because of the proximity and the view.

The elderly team left about three-thirty and he stayed another half-hour before deciding to call it a day. The sun was no longer hot and the sea breeze was becoming uncomfortable rather than cooling.

He said goodbye to the German girls and they politely said goodbye to him, one adding a comment in German to her sister that he didn't hear but which caused them both to smile.

They could have been discussing his attributes as a sex symbol but Lacey thought it more likely they were giving him a one to ten rating as a dirty old man. He tightened his paunch, summoned his dignity, and left.

The sun and inactivity had tired him and in his room he lay on the bed for ten minutes. Two hours later the ring of the telephone woke him. It was Lamont-Smith, enquiring about dinner.

Lacey was surprised it was six-thirty. He arranged to meet his companion in the bar at seven.

The shower was the second indication that the sun had been stronger than he thought. The first indication had been the cover on the bed that irritated his skin. He now realized there was nothing wrong with the bedcover, but that his body was red and burned.

His condition wasn't serious but it was itchy. He needed suntan lotion after all.

He and Lamont-Smith had a drink in the hotel bar before strolling to the harbour and having another drink at the place with the white and green umbrellas. They ate at the Italian restaurant and went back for another couple of drinks at the harbour bar.

The evening was cool and calm and they watched the lights of the coast road and the traffic that wound round Balluta Bay to St Julian's Point with its fortified tower.

This was a nice place to be in April, Lacey decided, but he would rather be here with Susan. Or maybe, even, the German girls. Did thought-crime count as infidelity? He would ask his wife when he called her.

They went back to the hotel and had another drink in the bar where the trio was playing pleasant background music. The gregarious Lamont-Smith smoothly joined the conversation of a mixed middle-aged English group from Swindon, but Lacey excused himself and went to his room.

He switched on the television and found a football match on an Italian channel. He turned the sound down, got a lager from the fridge, and lay on the bed to telephone Susan. It was eleven-thirty in Malta, ten-thirty in England.

Susan was also in bed, watching television.

'The toyboy couldn't come tonight,' she said, and laughed at the unfortunate choice of words.

236

Lacey said: 'There must be something wrong with him. I never had any trouble. What are you doing instead?'

'Indulging my second passion. Eating garlic bread and gorgonzola cheese.'

'I've never seen you eat garlic bread and gorgonzola cheese.'

'I only eat it when you're away. Garlic doesn't just repel vampires, you know.'

'How considerate.'

'Yes, I am. What are you doing?'

'Watching football and drinking beer.'

'What an exciting life you lead. You can do that here.'

'I went sunbathing this afternoon.'

'You sure you don't mean window shopping?'

'Are you suggesting I'm a dirty old man?'

'Yes.'

'Dirty old men don't make conquests.'

'And you did?'

'Well, not exactly a conquest.'

'You mean you thought about it.'

'Are you jealous?'

'I trust you. Who was it?'

'Who were they? Twins. German, nubile and topless.'

'Were they female?'

'Funny. Extremely female, or they've been taking the wrong steroids. They chatted me up.'

'Really?'

'Well, they asked the time.'

'I suppose that must be a boost to someone pushing fifty.'

'They smiled at me a lot.'

'You sure they weren't giggling? Maybe they noticed the age spots on the backs of your hands.'

For an illogical moment, Lacey regretted holding out his wrist for the girl to read his watch.

'You're probably right. It was a pleasant fantasy at the time.'

'Save it for Cairo. I'll pretend to be eighteen and you can wear a blindfold.'

237

He laughed.

'I'll look forward to it.'

'Make sure you're back in time to go with me.'

'I'll be back.'

After he hung up, Lacey drank lager and wondered if it would be over by then. It was now Wednesday night and their flight to Cairo was Sunday. If there was no further word from Bryson tomorrow about the whereabouts of Briggs he would have to start asking questions.

TWENTY-SEVEN

Lacey was back at the Reef Club at ten the next morning, armed with a sunburn protection cream as well as his book. Bryson hadn't called and he left Lamont-Smith sitting by the pool bar.

The German girls arrived at ten-thirty, said hello like old friends, and again took the adjacent loungers. They talked little, but concentrated on the sun. The one immediately next to him lay on her stomach and her twin rubbed oil on her back. Then she rubbed oil on her own front and lay down to read a magazine.

There were more people than the day before and they formed little groups beneath the umbrellas. The place was half full by eleven-thirty but the elderly trio still hadn't shown up. The girls turned over on the sunbeds and went through the oil rubbing bit again. Lacey guessed it would have been presumptuous of him to offer to do it for them to save them messing up their magazines.

A large bronzed Italian with very small swimming trunks walked past to the bar. He returned carrying an iced bottle of lager and sat on the end of a vacant lounger opposite the girls. He wore a thick gold chain around his neck and he stared blatantly at the girls' bodies. He asked the one sitting next to Lacey if they were English.

'No.'

She gave him no encouragement and continued to look at the magazine she held.

'Norway?'

'No.'

'German?'

'Yes.'

In fractured German, the Italian said he liked German girls. German girls, he said, were friendly. They were very friendly. He liked being friendly and he thought these two girls were very fine. Their bodies were very beautiful bodies. Were they sisters?

What was he? Lacey thought. Blind as well as pushy? If they weren't sisters somebody had perfected cloning.

The girl ignored the Italian's attempts to charm her but he wasn't deterred. He continued talking and he continued staring.

Maybe, if the girls wanted to be friendly, they could join his friends and they could all be friendly together. They would take them out in their jeep, give them a good time, maybe disco? He moved his arms like a corpse doing the twist. And then, maybe, they could all be very friendly.

Lacey decided that friendly just wasn't translating well from Italian into German. The girl thought so too.

She told him, in simple words, that they didn't want to go out and that, if he had seen enough, perhaps he would like to leave before their father got angry.

The Italian looked at Lacey.

Lacey looked at the girl, then at the Italian. Maybe the Italian mistook his confusion for a parental glare.

'*Mi scusi.*'

He held his hands out in a gesture of pacification, grimaced to acknowledge you can't win them all, and left.

Lacey said to the girl in English: 'Your father?'

'Oh. You speak German?'

'Yes.'

The girl blushed, then laughed and said in German: 'Forgive me. He was an idiot. I wanted to be rid of him.'

'Yes. He was an idiot.'

Lacey smiled. So much for his sex appeal. These girls simply felt safe with him around.

They talked some more, and the girl said she was Magda and her sister was Ursel and they were eighteen and staying in an apartment in St Julian's. They both had boyfriends at home and had come to Malta for the sun and were not

240

interested in casual sex, although her smile, when she said it, suggested they might be open to romantic offers if they met the right young men.

Lacey said he had come to Malta on business but his client had not yet turned up. He didn't tell her his age.

A little later, when he turned over, Magda offered to rub lotion on to his back. He accepted graciously and decided he definitely would send Bryson a postcard.

The elderly trio arrived together at noon and occupied the same positions. The older woman went through the same touching process with the youth who brought her mattress and put up the umbrella. Even Lacey wouldn't like to be touched by her, never mind the teenager. He wondered if Magda had had similar thoughts when she had rubbed lotion on his back.

Magda put his mind at rest when she turned over. She asked him if he would put cream on her back. Lacey sat up and complied with the request. Was she still feeling safe, or was she teasing? He didn't care, he applied the cream from her shoulders to the curve of her buttocks without once letting his fingers stray. It was as exhilarating as off-piste skiing but he was relieved when he had finished.

He sat back and read his book and, at twelve-thirty, Frank Briggs walked in.

Briggs wore a straw hat, tan cotton slacks and a matching short-sleeved shirt that looked too big for him. Maybe it hadn't been at one time; he looked as if illness had shrunk him.

The elderly trio greeted him and he shook hands with the expatriate and gave each of the women a kiss on the cheek. The old wrinkled woman called him darling.

He stood while he talked to them and as the conversation moved from him, he glanced around at the people near by and saw Lacey watching.

Briggs nodded to Lacey, and Lacey nodded back. After a few minutes of further conversation, Briggs excused himself from the group and approached Lacey.

He held out his hand and they shook.

241

'Frank Briggs,' he said. 'I've been expecting you.'

'Peter Lacey. I thought you might be.' He nodded towards the bar. 'Can I buy you a beer?'

'Why not?'

Lacey got up and put on his shirt. He left his towel, book and sunburn lotion on the lounger, and they walked to the bar. As they passed Briggs' friends Lacey smiled and nodded and they nodded back but gave him curious looks.

They sat at a table in the shade and Lacey had a Cisk lager and Briggs a Hopleaf Pale Ale.

Briggs held up his glass and said: 'One thing the British taught the Maltese – how to brew decent beer.'

They drank, set their glasses back on the table and exchanged looks of evaluation. The suntan couldn't hide the ill-health that showed in Briggs' face; even his eyes looked tired.

'Are you with Five?' Briggs said.

'No.'

'Six?'

'Yes.'

'Is Chesterton involved?'

'He's running the operation.'

'Is he? I thought he'd be involved, but I didn't expect him to be in charge. He left the Service a long time ago; except, of course, you never really leave the Service, do you?'

'You did.'

'Enforced retirement. Two more years and I'd have had a decent pension, but the Service has never been run on sentiment.'

'So now you're getting your own back?'

He smiled.

'There's more to it than that.'

'What?'

He took out a box of small Henri Winterman cigars and offered them but Lacey declined. Briggs took one from the box and lit it with a book of matches.

242

'Chesterton will say I'm a crank. I've gone rogue out of bitterness, I blame the Service for everything from my dandruff to the death of my wife. Right?'

Lacey nodded.

'Something like that.'

'Well, I was bitter. Still am. About a lot of things, not just getting turfed out. Bitter about life. I've had time to think in the last few years, especially since Nell died.' He chuckled disparagingly. 'My ever-faithful. What a motivation she was.'

'In what way?'

'She was a nagger. Know what I mean?'

Lacey nodded and Briggs continued.

'Nothing was good enough. The size of the house, the age of the car, the bloody pension. It was her who wanted to move to Spain, not me.' He grinned, drank his beer and nodded towards the German twins. 'Then I saw the advantages. Tits and bums. It had to be better than bloody Bognor.'

'Bognor?'

'That was the alternative. So we went to Spain.'

'You lost money and she died?'

'That's right. I got screwed by some sod who lives in a penthouse in Park Lane who was selling villas he didn't own. He's probably still doing it; different site, different company name. The usual thing.' He pulled on the cigar and raised his eyebrows. 'The rich get richer . . . ?' He left the saying unfinished.

Lacey had tried not to have preconceived ideas about Briggs but the man was not what he had expected. He still hadn't formed an opinion about him, and when he did he would be careful not to let it show. His role was to be as amenable as possible to Briggs, to entice him into a deal.

He said: 'We all have problems, Frank.'

'Problems are all right if you have the money to buy your way out. I never had the money or the pull. Until now.'

'I can arrange the money. You know that from Lisbon.'

'I know.'

'Do you want me to?'

243

'Maybe.' He smiled and smoked the cigar. 'Maybe I want something else as well.'

'What? To embarrass the royal family?'

'Yes. I'd like that.'

'Why? They've always struck me as being pretty innocuous.'

'Oh, they are. Until you look at how much they own and how much they cost and how much tax they don't pay. They're a prime example of everything about Britain that pisses me off.'

Briggs wanted to be prompted so Lacey prompted him.

'What do you mean?'

'Ninety-eight per cent of the country is owned by two per cent of the population and it's that two per cent that sits right at the top. The rest of us take our chances depending on what we're worth, and God help the poor sod at the bottom of the pile. He's just there to shovel the shit.'

Lacey sensed Briggs had been brooding on this for a long time. It was something he wouldn't have been able to say to his expatriate friends. He continued to feed him lines.

'It's called a democracy. People can vote to change things.'

Briggs laughed.

'They change nothing. Democracy's just a word used by the politicians. They buy it by the sackful at Sainsbury's.'

Lacey grinned and quoted Ben Miller quoting someone else.

'All governments are liars and nothing they say should be believed.'

'That's true. Who said it?'

'An American.'

'Well he got it in one. But in Britain we've got the monarchy as well. A right bunch of spongers and parasites.'

'The people like them.'

Briggs laughed out loud.

'The people are fed a myth. The system owns the media and the media feeds the people royal glamour. It's self-perpetuating. They talk about what they do for charity,

244

show them opening youth clubs and mingling with ordinary people for as much as five minutes at a time. It's so patronizing, it's sickening. And what do they really do? Fuck all, that's what.'

'Do you think the Blunt Legacy can change it?'

'It might make people think twice.'

'By saying the Duke of Windsor was a Nazi?'

'No. Not that. That was a come-on for the Press.'

Lacey drank some of the lager.

'And the Fifth Man?'

Briggs smiled.

'A slight exaggeration. For the American press.'

'So what is it that you've got?'

'A very unsavoury cake.'

'Blunt's Legacy?'

'Blunt's diary. His secret diary.'

'What's in it?'

Briggs shrugged, finished the cigar and stubbed it in an ashtray.

Lacey said: 'What are you going to do with it?'

'I'm still not sure.'

He finished the beer and waved to a waiter to bring more drinks.

Lacey said: 'The easiest thing would be to sell it to me.'

'That might also be the easiest way to end up dead.'

'You think I'll kill you?'

Briggs stared at him but didn't say anything until the waiter had brought fresh bottles.

'Possibly. If not you, maybe somebody else. Do you know Chesterton's background?'

'Some of it. He tried to stop me going to America to see Jimmy Russell's widow.'

'I remember her. Mattie. She was a nice girl. I quite fancied her, until I found out she was the other way.'

'Someone tried to kill her. Was it you?'

Briggs looked up in surprise.

'No.' He shook his head. 'I didn't think he'd go that far.'

'Chesterton?'

'Yes.'

'Because he killed Russell?'

'You work that out by yourself?'

Lacey nodded.

'Does Chesterton know you know?'

'Probably.'

'Then watch your back. If he has any doubts you could become a target. Chesterton doesn't like leaving jobs half done. Is Lamont-Smith with you?'

'Yes. You know him?'

'I know him. Old ILS. So does Chesterton. They're members of the same club. He was with Five for a while. After he left, he was used as a free-lance.'

'He's supposed to authenticate the Blunt Legacy.'

'My guess is he's also supposed to make sure you don't step out of line.'

'You're talking as if you think I might.'

'I live in hope of a lot of things, as well as tits and bums.' He drank some beer. 'Tell you what. Why don't we get rid of Lamont-Smith first. Then talk some more.'

'How do we do that?'

Briggs smiled.

'Bring him to my house at Mosta and I'll give him the Blunt Legacy.'

TWENTY-EIGHT

Ian Lamont-Smith looked bigger than ever in shorts and a polo shirt. Lacey could well imagine him running through Australians and South Africans in his glory days as a rugby player. All these years later he was still an imposing figure, despite his apparently excessive drinking.

Was he something else, besides an archivist?

Lamont-Smith sprawled in one of the leather armchairs in the reception hall of the Dragonara, fresh from the shower and smelling of yet another aftershave he had bought on his room account. Lacey sat on a leather sofa that was placed at right angles to the chair.

This was the coolest room in the hotel, with a domed ceiling that went the height of the building and from which hung huge chandeliers.

Briggs walked in five minutes late at one thirty-five and they stood up. Lacey exchanged nods with the elderly agent but Briggs and Lamont-Smith exchanged stares.

Lamont-Smith said: 'It's been a long time, Frank.'

'Yes, it has. You haven't changed one bit.'

The men didn't shake hands and Lacey guessed the comment had not been intended as a compliment.

They followed him out into the sunshine and Briggs pointed to an old Hillman Minx that was in immaculate condition.

'That's mine,' he said.

He got into the Hillman Minx and Lacey and Lamont-Smith got into the rented Ford Escort and followed him out of the grounds of the hotel.

They turned right on to the coast road that dipped into St George's Bay to provide another picture postcard view, and

247

inland past the now closed nightclubs, discos and roller-rinks that provided late-night and early-morning entertainment for young people.

Briggs took the two-lane highway north before turning inland along roads that got progressively narrower and which were badly maintained. Eventually they reached another, more modern road, and followed it into Mosta.

Lacey remembered the town from his previous visit. It was famous for its domed parish church, which had suffered a direct hit from a bomb during the Second World War. To the relief of the congregation, the bomb had slid across the tiled floor and failed to explode. The Maltese had first given thanks and then turned it into a tourist attraction.

They drove past the church and out to the town's western suburbs. Briggs led them a zig-zag trail off the main road and along a street that ended in a secluded cul-de-sac that served one house.

It was an imposing building, with steps up to double doors that were flanked by Doric columns. They got out of the cars and Briggs unlocked the doors and led them into a circular tiled hall that had the sort of marble staircase Fred and Ginger used to dance down.

The hall was cool and dim and would have been impressive but for the odd mixture of furnishings. Ancient oil paintings hung on the walls in peeling gilded frames, while antique sideboards stood alongside cheap, modern, vinyl-covered furniture.

Briggs went into a room at the back that was filled with the clutter of living. A settee and easy chairs were placed around a low table upon which were newspapers, magazines, an ashtray and a dirty coffee mug. On a sideboard was a small pile of mail, letters and circulars that had been opened, read and left lying on their envelopes, as if they hadn't been important enough to throw away. There were two photographs in a double leather frame that opened like a wallet.

A small kitchen led off the room and Briggs went into it and switched on an electric kettle.

'The house belongs to a friend,' he said. 'A Maltese friend who's in Europe for six months. He's with the Government.'

Lacey said: 'It's great.'

Briggs said: 'It's free. And it's hard to find. Now, if you'll excuse me a moment, I'll get the stuff you've come for.'

He left them and went into the hall. They listened to his footsteps going up the marble staircase. He didn't sound as nimble as Fred or Ginger.

Lacey looked at the photographs on the sideboard. They were snapshots of the same woman, presumably Briggs' wife, but taken maybe thirty years apart. When she was young, she had been pretty and blonde; in later life, she had put on weight and become dumpy. Her expression, and the grip on her handbag, suggested she was tolerating being photographed.

Back in a London suburb, the policeman, Dennis Pritchard, was also alone in his retirement bungalow. He had propped up the structure of his life with gardening and pleasant memories of his dead wife.

Briggs had propped up his with a mission, tits and bums.

Lacey opened french windows and stepped through them on to a paved patio, equipped with plastic furniture and a barbecue. Beyond it was a small square swimming-pool. Running off the patio and alongside the house was a narrow strip of garden. Grapevines hung from above the french windows and climbed a trellised arch from house to wall.

Briggs returned with a cardboard shoebox which he placed on the living-room table and Lacey went back inside.

'How do you have your coffee?' Briggs asked Lamont-Smith.

'White, actually.'

'Sugar?'

'No, thank you.'

Briggs went into the kitchen, poured hot water and returned with a mug of coffee. He pointed to the box.

'You'd better bring that,' he said to Lamont-Smith. 'You can look at it in the study.'

Lamont-Smith picked up the box and followed Briggs across the hall and into a room near the front door. Briggs came back.

He said to Lacey: 'Beer or scotch?'

'Scotch.'

While Briggs got a bottle and two glasses from a cupboard, Lacey pointed to the photographs.

'Your wife?'

'That's right. That's Nell. She was a lovely-looking girl when I met her.' He pointed to the french windows and led the way outside. 'But she seemed to think she didn't have to try after we got married.' He put the bottle and glasses on the patio table. 'Know what I mean? The paint and the feathers were for snaring a mate. After she'd got me, she was quite happy to look like her mother.'

Lacey sat down but the man went back into the kitchen to return with a jug of water. The whisky was ten-year-old Glenmorangie single malt. Briggs poured a measure into each glass and added water to his own. Lacey did the same.

Lacey said: 'Was it a happy marriage?'

'We got used to each other.'

Briggs sipped his drink.

'Now,' he said. 'Where do we begin?'

'How about Blunt?'

'It started before Blunt. It started with Stephen Ward and the Profumo Affair.'

'Jesus Christ. Is everything linked?'

'Just about. The Secret Service is a small world. Anything can happen and usually does. You should know that.'

'I do. That's why I believed the phoney briefing I was given when all this started.'

Briggs laughed.

'What did they tell you?'

'That Joseph Kennedy and the Duke of Windsor were involved in a Nazi plot.'

He laughed again and took his tin of small cigars from a pocket.

250

'It wouldn't surprise me. The Kennedys were involved in most things. They were involved in the Profumo Affair.'

'They were?'

'When Joe Kennedy was ambassador in England before the war, John F. made plenty of friends. He knew the Astors and the Cliveden set.'

Lacey nodded. 'They were the aristocratic and wealthy circle to whom osteopath Dr Stephen Ward had introduced girls like Christine Keeler and Mandy Rice-Davies. Sex parties had frequently taken place at Cliveden, the country home of Lord Astor.

'The President and his brother Bobby, the Attorney General if you don't mind, both screwed Ward's young ladies. JFK was involved with Mariella Novotny, who became London's orgy queen. The CIA thought it could be a Russian honeytrap. When the Profumo thing broke, both JFK and Bobby could have been dragged into it.'

Briggs lit a cigar.

Lacey said: 'Nobody comes out clean in this, do they?'

'No one.' He puffed smoke. 'Hypocrisy rules. Always has.'

'Tell me about the Profumo Affair.'

'In 1963, Arthur Martin ran D Branch.' D Branch of MI5 specialized in Soviet counter-espionage. 'He ran an officer called Keith Wagstaffe. Wagstaffe ran Stephen Ward. They wanted to catch a Soviet naval attaché, a bloke called Ivanov, in their own honeytrap. Christine Keeler was the honey. Unfortunately, Keeler was also screwing John Profumo, who just happened to be the Minister of War.'

He shrugged.

'The whole thing was a security nightmare. The Minister of War and a Russian sharing the same mistress. President Kennedy and a whole host of aristos waiting on the sidelines to be named. Ivanov was recalled, Profumo was disgraced, and Five abandoned Ward and denied all knowledge.'

Lacey said: 'Where's the connection with Blunt?'

Briggs ignored the question.

251

'The sex scandal needed a scapegoat and the Establishment picked on Ward. He went on trial for running prostitutes.'

He sipped whisky, before continuing.

'A year later, Arthur Martin – the man who ran Wagstaffe who ran Ward – was the MI5 officer sent to interview Blunt.'

Lacey said: 'Martin was a senior officer. It's natural he would get Blunt.'

Briggs shrugged.

'Maybe. But it gets better. Both Ward and Jimmy Russell died.'

'Ward took an overdose.'

'Overdoses are convenient. Particularly as Ward had written a three-page letter to the Home Secretary, naming all those prominent names, the night he died. A *Daily Express* photographer took pictures of him writing the letter. He arranged to meet Ward the next morning to take it to the Home Office.

'Fortunately, after the photographer developed his film, he left it at the *Express* and went home. In the morning he was surprised Ward had taken an overdose. He was more surprised that his film had disappeared. He shouldn't have been; we had people working at the *Express*.'

Lacey said: 'How did Ward die?'

'An overdose. He was on sleeping pills so it was easy. A friend kept waking him up and telling him to take his pills. Once you get them drowsy they lose count. They'll agree to almost anything.'

'Who was the friend?'

'A Pole, one of the Eastern European immigrants Five were using at the time.'

'He was killed to stop the letter being delivered?'

'That was part of it. Ward also had a collection of photographs of his girls, doing their stuff at Cliveden and at a safe house in London. They included one of a prominent royal. It wouldn't have been published here, but it could have caused a scandal in Europe and the States. The pictures were retrieved as well.'

252

Briggs pulled on the cigar and they both watched the smoke.

He added: 'The Pole was being run by Chesterton.'

Lacey stared at Briggs, who stared back and drew on the cigar. Lacey sipped whisky to help assimilate being told that one of Britain's most powerful politicians had organized the death of Stephen Ward.

Briggs went on.

'Blunt and Ward had mutual friends; their social circles overlapped. Blunt learned from Ward's mistakes. He also had something to bargain with, but he hid it. Unfortunately, we thought Jimmy Russell had it.'

'We?'

'Chesterton and me. There was a three-month gap before Arthur Martin went to see Blunt. Hollis sent us first. Blunt had contacted him and said he knew he was blown and wanted a deal. He said what he had was sensitive and would be hurtful to the royal family.

'We went and talked to him. Well, Chesterton did the talking. He thought of himself as a royal, some sort of cousin, twice removed. He tried his bully boy tactics but they didn't work. We had a tap on Blunt's phone. Blunt made a call to Jimmy Russell and Chesterton read it wrong. Russell was holding some art prints for him and Chesterton thought it was a code word for the blackmail stuff.'

Briggs had another sip of whisky and this time kept hold of the glass.

'Russell was supposed to be out the night we broke into the house. We didn't find anything, but he came home early and found us. Chesterton didn't mind. He put a rope round his neck and tried to make him talk but the poor sod didn't know anything.' He finished the whisky and licked his lips. 'We killed him.' He shrugged. 'Chesterton killed him, but I was there. Then we made it look like a sex thing with the pictures of naked women. We didn't know he was queer.'

He poured himself another scotch and offered the bottle to Lacey, who allowed him to top up his glass. They again added water.

'The killing didn't bother Chesterton. He used it to threaten Blunt, told him the same thing could happen to him. Remember what happened to Stephen Ward, remember what happened to Jimmy Russell, he said. I did those, I can do you, too, he said. What Chesterton didn't know was that the old queen was taping the whole bloody lot.

'Eventually, Chesterton gave up and told Hollis we couldn't break him and we couldn't find his dossier of secrets. So he sent in Arthur Martin to make the immunity deal.'

Earlier, Briggs had told Lacey that Blunt's diary contained embarrassing secrets about royals and powerful Americans. The diary might, or might not, still be relevant, considering how old it was. But a tape recording of Law and Order Chesterton boasting he was responsible for the deaths of two people in two of the most sensational spy scandals of the century was extremely relevant. It was bloody incredible.

Lacey nosed the whisky, appreciating its distinctive smell.

He said: 'Does Chesterton know about the tape recording?'

'He knows.'

Maybe Chesterton had forgotten about it, over the years. People had the capacity to put out of their minds events they preferred not to remember. Lacey knew that from personal experience. Perhaps he hadn't been too worried about it at first; after all, in the sixties and seventies it was the sort of allegation that Five covered up very successfully.

The tape's authenticity could be denied, its allegations discredited, and if it had been offered to a British newspaper there was more than a fair chance the story could have been suppressed.

But now the climate of investigative journalism had changed, Five was still living with the reputation provided for it by Peter Wright, and Chesterton was no longer an obscure civil servant but a national figure.

Lacey said: 'What's the stuff that Lamont-Smith is looking at?'

'A complete set of documents that show the Duke of Windsor sold out his country to the Nazis for a down payment of fifty million Swiss francs and a guarantee to be put back on the throne by Hitler.'

'Are they real?'

'Some are. But intelligence – people like Blunt – did a clean sweep after the war. The crucial ones are forgeries, based on fact. They should give old ILS a headache or two. I enjoyed making them.'

'So where's Blunt's diary?'

'In a safe place.'

'How did you get it?'

'Blunt gave it to me. I went to see him when it became obvious he was going to be blown publicly in 1979. Five were already trying to get rid of me, so I decided to take out insurance.

'When Chesterton and I saw Blunt in 'sixty-four, we did the usual nice and nasty routine. Chesterton was nasty – he was a natural at it – and I was nice. In 'seventy-nine, Blunt needed a friendly face. He was panicking; an old man whose life was in ruins. His diary had become an embarrassment. If he'd released it then, his life wouldn't have been worth living and no one would have believed it anyway.

'The diary was a liability but the tape recording was a lifeline. I offered to take care of both and to make sure he was left alone, that there'd be no arranged suicide.'

'He believed you?'

'Not fully. He gave me the diary – he just wanted to get rid of it. But he kept the tape. He sent me that in 1982, a few months before he died. I wrote to him when I was eventually pushed out of the service, and he sent it to me. He said he no longer needed it, and maybe I'd like it instead of a pension. Maybe he thought I could make trouble with it. He was a vindictive sod, you know.'

'Why did you wait so long to use it?'

Briggs shrugged and stubbed out the cigar.

'I don't know that I ever intended to use it. I just wanted to own it; to have something on Chesterton. He'd been the golden boy – the right background, the right career moves. Public school, Oxford, his mother landed bloody gentry. My father was a printer and I went to a polytechnic.

'I suppose you could call it jealousy, but it isn't as simple as that. He and I, what we did, the opportunities we got, seemed to sum up the system. It worked for him, and it screwed me.

'When Nell died I did a lot of thinking and decided I didn't like my country much any more. Chesterton was making headlines, becoming a public figure. The system was taking care of its own again. Then, about a year ago, a doctor told me I was dying. Oh, it's nothing dramatic. But bits of me are wearing out and can't be replaced. He gave me a couple of years and I decided to do something with them. I decided to take a kick at the royals and get Chesterton.'

He smiled at Lacey.

'One small step for Frank Briggs.'

Lacey said: 'Why the advertisements? The auction?'

'To make them all sweat.'

'Why kill the lawyer in Lisbon?'

'To get attention. To make them sweat more.'

'Didn't it bother you? The killing?'

'Latimer was a toad. He got the pay-off he deserved.'

Briggs sounded rational, as if he had reasoned everything out many times. It sounded as if he saw himself as Don Quixote taking on Chesterton and the monarchy, but it was more likely he was motivated by a combination of reasons. He had already admitted bitterness and jealousy, maybe there was a touch of madness too.

Lacey said: 'This all started because of Blunt's diary. If it's not Hitler and the Duke of Windsor, then what's in it that makes it so special?'

Briggs lit another cigar, coughed through the smoke, and sat back.

He said: 'Blunt didn't have to go to Europe for his insurance. He collected most of it in London and Ireland. Have you ever heard of The Gang of Four?'

'No.'

256

'Before the war, when Edward was still Prince of Wales, he went around with his younger brother, the Duke of Kent, David Bowes-Lyon, and their cousin, Lord Louis Mountbatten. They were The Gang of Four.'

Lacey said: 'There was a photograph of them in the file I got from Latimer.'

'That's right. Blunt was often with them. He recorded their activities. The line of poetry?'

'Something about Packenham.'

'I want to be like the boys at the Packenham, and go about whackin' 'em and stickin' my jack in 'em.'

Lacey nodded. He didn't like what he anticipated.

Briggs said: 'The Packenham was a pub in Knightsbridge that young guardsmen used to visit. The Gang of Four, and Blunt, went there as well. The four royals were bisexual. They picked up soldiers for sex.'

TWENTY-NINE

Lacey sipped scotch and thought of England.

Briggs said: 'Shocked?'

'I don't know.'

'People think sex and drugs were invented by rock and roll. They weren't. The privileged have been enjoying them for generations. English gentlemen learned about sodomy at public school. Still do. And those wealthy sods who had everything, tried everything. They weren't totally queer. Well, some were. But there were plenty who didn't care who they went to bed with.'

'But the Duke of Windsor gave up his throne for a woman?'

'Wallis Simpson was not just a woman. She was a sexual expert, studied it first hand in Hong Kong brothels. She got him to perform where other women had failed. You know his nickname was Little Man? That he suffered from premature ejaculation? They played sex games together; very kinky. It must have been a great relief when he found someone who could fulfil him in a proper relationship.'

Lacey said: 'What about the others?'

'What about them? David Bowes-Lyon was only a minor royal, he was never much good for anything, but the Duke of Kent was well known for his affairs with men and women. Noel Coward was one of his lovers. He was the real black sheep of the family, not because he behaved worse than the rest, but because he kept getting found out. He was totally over the top.'

Lacey said: 'And Mountbatten?'

'Yes. The war hero. But there was another side to him,

and his family. Have you heard of the Milford Haven pornographic collection? His father started it and the next two generations added to it. Seven volumes of everything from incest to bestiality.

'Mountbatten swung both ways, but he preferred men. Did do all his life. It didn't stop his wife enjoying herself. Many of her friends were lesbians and she had a liking for black men. When Mountbatten went to India as Viceroy, she went as Nehru's mistress.

'Blunt got on particularly well with Mountbatten and they were part of a gay county set in Ireland, going to parties and orgies at country houses on both sides of the border. Mountbatten was very active homosexually in Ireland. It's possible that's one of the reasons the IRA picked him as a target.'

Lacey drank the whisky and helped himself to another. This was distasteful and dynamite. The Duke of Windsor had been discredited years ago, although never in outright terms. He had been presented for public consumption as the golden prince who had opted for love rather than a kingdom. The suggestion he could have contemplated treachery during the Second World War had been suppressed for years.

Evidence that proved he had been a traitor would have been bad enough, but this was worse because of its cast of four. The Duke of Windsor, the Duke of Kent and David Bowes-Lyon might be history but they were royal history, and when combined with the final name the weight of tarnished glory was immensely significant.

Briggs smoked the cigar and watched Lacey.

Lacey said: 'Are you really going to publish this stuff?'

'Why not?'

'It would hurt a lot of people.'

'When Lord Denning wrote his whitewash report about the Profumo Affair, he called Stephen Ward the most evil man he had ever met, because Ward had introduced a few girls to aristocrats, including a royal. Ward was the scapegoat. He had his character destroyed and he died. Yet all he did was help the Establishment have a good time.

259

'They didn't suffer. They closed ranks. They never suffer. They live and breathe by double standards. They have this high-profile role as defenders of respectability and the public good, and a private life that's in the gutter. Why not publish?'

Lacey changed the direction of the conversation.

'Who's the American involved?'

'Orville Bross. Also known as The Senator, or The Man.'

'I know him. What's his connection?'

'Sexual. He's in the diary; a picture, too. An unfortunate adolescent romance, except that Blunt also saw him in America just before he got burned. There's an entry that uses his nickname – The Man – with Fifth written over the top of it and a question mark. It's all a bit obvious, but Bross held pretty high office in the States.'

A homosexual affair alone would have been unlikely to turn Bross into a KGB agent, and association with Blunt would only have become embarrassing after Blunt had been unmasked in 'sixty-four. There was a possibility that The Man had been an agent, but Lacey was prepared to accept that on a probability scale the evidence weighed in favour of acquittal. It was certainly too flimsy to warrant a witch hunt so long after the event, but disclosure of the connection could have a devastating effect on Bross's reputation.

Briggs added: 'There are other scandals in the diary, other names. Titled, theatricals, people from the arts. A former prime minister, Sir Anthony Eden. Also the name of the person who tipped off Burgess and Maclean that it was time to run.'

'That was Philby.'

'Someone else provided the crucial tip.'

'Why?'

'To stop a sex scandal. Why else?'

Lacey shifted in his seat and watched leaves floating on the swimming-pool. It looked just about big enough to hold all the reputations Briggs was threatening to drown.

'I don't think you can publish and I don't think you can damage Chesterton.'

'Why?'

'Because the Establishment will do what you say they do: close ranks. They'll produce experts to say the diary's a fake. Newspapers, particularly in Britain, may not even run the story. They'll make out you're a crackpot. And Five'll discredit the tape recording. They're good at this sort of thing; you know that.'

Briggs stared at Lacey.

'You're probably right. And you're going to make me an offer.'

'Frank, you've made a lot of important people in London and America uncomfortable. Maybe caused a thrombosis or two. But there's not a lot else you can do. We know where you are and you can be taken out any time, with or without the goods. You told me yourself, that's what might happen. Alive, and in possession, you're an embarrassment. Dead, you're not going to make waves, even if you've fixed some way of releasing the stuff after you're gone. There's only one thing you can do, and that's give it to me.

'Look, they'd prefer to get it without paying anything but I'm in the bargaining seat, not Lamont-Smith. I'll get you a million pounds sterling and a guarantee you'll be left alone. If you've got a year, you might as well enjoy it. A million pounds will let you do more than just look at the tits and bums.'

Briggs chuckled, but he was thinking.

'You're good, Lacey. Now tell me how you'll guarantee my safety?'

'I'll keep a copy of the tape and tell Chesterton to leave you alone. You can enjoy yourself and know he's still sweating.'

'You try that and your career is finished.'

'I never had much of a career to start with. Wrong school, wrong background. I went to a polytechnic too,' he lied. 'I'm even with the wrong department. Have you ever heard of D14a?'

'No.'

'It's where they send the bad lads, the ones who are expendable.' He smiled. 'I'm fifty this year. If I don't take out insurance now, I'll end up fighting for pension rights. I've been waiting for something like this for a long time. Instead of finishing my career it could cushion it. Besides, I don't like Chesterton.'

Briggs finished the whisky.

'You make a good case. But then you would.'

They heard Lamont-Smith approaching and turned their heads to watch him come through the french windows and on to the patio. He was carrying the shoebox, which he put on the table.

He looked at Briggs and said: 'Garbage, old son. Very interesting, very nicely done. But garbage. Now, where's the real stuff?'

Briggs smiled at him.

'I've just been telling your friend. We've come to an arrangement.'

Lamont-Smith stared down at Lacey. He was no longer a languid eccentric; he was a tall muscular man with a mean expression.

'What sort of an arrangement?'

Lacey said: 'I've bought it.'

'How much?'

'A million.'

'Sight unseen? You must be joking.'

'We both know what's in it, Ian. I don't particularly want to see it.'

Lamont-Smith was angry. His lips were compressed and he was breathing loudly through his nose. He looked from one to the other of them before settling his glare on Briggs.

'What about the other item?'

'The tape recording is included.'

'He knows about it?'

'Mr Lacey knows all about it.'

Lacey guessed that Lamont-Smith was not a happy bunny.

'This has been a cock-up from start to finish,' Lamont-Smith said. 'You've got a lot to answer for, Briggs. You'll . . .'

He shut up abruptly and turned to Lacey.

'When do I take possession?'

'You don't, Ian. I'm dealing with Chesterton myself.'

'That's not in the rules.'

'Fuck the rules.'

'Chesterton won't like it.'

Lacey smiled at being presented with the perfect opportunity.

'Fuck Chesterton.'

'So what the hell am I here for?'

'To put a million pounds sterling into the bank of Frank's choice.'

He prompted Briggs with a look.

Briggs said: 'The Valletta branch of the Mid-Med Bank. It's in Republic Street. It opens at four this afternoon.'

Lamont-Smith glared some more and looked on the verge of becoming physical, but thought better of it.

He told Lacey: 'I'll be in the car,' turned on his heel, and went back through the french windows.

They listened until the front door opened and then slammed.

Briggs chuckled.

'I enjoyed that,' he said.

'So did I. Do we really have a deal?'

'A million is a nice round figure. What made you pick it?'

'Nominal damages for a life. Stephen Ward's, Jimmy Russell's . . . yours?'

'You're a smooth bastard but I still don't know.'

'Think about it. It's the only way out.' He sipped whisky. 'Where is the stuff, Frank?'

'In Ireland.' He smiled. 'Blunt left it there for safe keeping. I went in 'seventy-nine to collect it and liked the place. I've been a few times since. When I started this I took it back there, along with the tape.'

'To Blunt's friend?'

263

'No. He's long dead. To someone else.'

'Are you going to tell me?'

He knocked ash from the cigar and evaluated what was left to smoke.

'Come back at ten. Without ILS. I'll tell you then if we have a deal.'

THIRTY

Lacey drove back to the Dragonara Hotel not knowing two things.

He didn't know whether Frank Briggs would tell him the location of the diary and the tape; and he didn't know what he would do with them if he got them. Briggs had talked about hypocrisy and had hit a nerve.

Lacey had been responsible for death. Had Chesterton only been doing what Lacey had done?

When Lacey had taken life it had been on operations where events had dictated themselves. If Chesterton had been involved in ensuring the silence of Stephen Ward, as Briggs had said, it had been sanctioned and planned, not to serve the state, but to serve the 2 per cent. It had been a perversion of justice.

Jimmy Russell had been one of the accidents that happen. He had come home too soon and walked into a situation from which he could not be allowed to walk away, if Five was to maintain security. The distasteful manner in which his body had been left was irrelevant. The important thing, in department terms, was that they had got away with it. Almost.

The attempt on the life of Mattie Purcell only days ago in America was again different. It seemed certain that Chesterton had been responsible for arranging a hit that would look like a sex killing, to ensure silence. But for whose benefit?

Was the Minister still operating in what he saw as the best interests of Crown and Country, or was it now a personal crusade to protect himself? And was either reason good enough to justify the death of an innocent woman?

On the way back to the hotel, Lamont-Smith maintained his stiff-upper-lip sulk, while chain-smoking cigarettes until they were on the two-lane highway close to St Julian's Bay. The smoke, as well as the man's presence, began to irritate Lacey.

Lamont-Smith said: 'Have you really made a deal?'

'Yes.'

'How does it work?'

'You get me proof the money has been transferred, and I do an exchange with Briggs for a letter of authorization.'

'Has Briggs got the stuff?'

'He's got it.'

'Here?'

'No.'

'He's told you where?'

Lacey smiled at him.

'Yes.'

'Look. There's still time to do this right, Peter. Give me the authorization. I'll get the stuff and give it to Chesterton and we both get commended for a job well done.'

'No. I'm doing this my way.'

Lamont-Smith's anger finally spilled over.

'My way! Who do you think you are? Frank Sinatra? I was told your fucking ego has a habit of taking over, but for Christ's sake. You work for the Government.'

'No I don't. I work for the people. For the security and well-being of the country. In case you forgot, it's the people who elect the Government.'

Lamont-Smith threw the stubb of a cigarette out of the window.

'You'll regret this, Peter. You'll bloody regret it.'

There was still an hour's heat in the sun, so Lacey went back to the Reef Club and rejoined Magda and Ursel. The view and the company were pleasant and he didn't have to take any telephone calls from London. Neither of the girls asked him to rub oil on their backs, but he could live with that.

The whisky, and finally finding out what everybody had been trying to prevent him from finding out, made him relaxed, and when the girls allowed him to buy them Coca Cola he pushed his luck and invited them to dinner.

'Just dinner,' he stressed. 'I have a business appointment later.'

They laughed and giggled, but he didn't think it was at his age spots, and they agreed. It made him inordinately pleased with himself.

When he got back to his room there was a message under the door, instructing him to call Sam Bryson immediately. He took a cold beer from the refrigerator, sat on the bed and dialled the number.

'Hello, Sam.'

'What the hell are you playing at?'

'According to my international archivist friend, I'm playing at Frank Sinatra.'

'What is it? Personality conflict? What?'

'It's not that.'

'Then what is it?'

'I don't like being screwed, and I don't like being taken for a mug. You should know that, Sam. You should tell Chesterton that.'

'Lamont-Smith is his man. Give the goods to him.'

'Lamont-Smith is extraneous to my needs. I'll deliver them myself.'

Bryson didn't speak for a moment.

'You're upsetting powerful people.'

'I've been doing that all my life.'

'Don't overestimate your importance. You're a minor player; Chesterton could knock you off the board.'

'There you go, Sam. Just when I was beginning to get some self-confidence.'

'There's still time to change your mind.'

'I won't do that.'

'Then for God's sake don't do anything else that's stupid. Just bring the goods home.'

'You're the boss, Sam.'

'I wish I was.'

Lacey showered and his sunburn tingled. He rubbed cream on to his shoulders before putting on a shirt. He wore blue to make the most of his glow. Blue shirt, blue slacks; the leather jacket that he hoped gave him character, and Kurt Geiger moccasins for that indefinable touch of class.

As Lacey was leaving his key at reception, Lamont-Smith came into the hotel lobby. He was wearing slacks, a shirt and tie, and carrying a briefcase.

'I've got it,' he said, and Lacey followed him to one of the leather sofas.

'You've got what?'

He opened the briefcase and handed Lacey four documents. The first was telexed affirmation from the Union Bank of Switzerland of the transfer of one million pounds sterling to the Mid-Med Bank of Valletta. The second was a copy of a fax from the Mid-Med Bank to Geneva, confirming the transfer. There was also a statement in the name of Frank Briggs, showing that his account had been credited with the money, and a letter to Briggs from a bank vice-president, assuring him of personal assistance at all times.

Lacey said: 'I'm impressed.'

'It was a simple transaction. When will you see him?'

'Tonight.'

He folded the documents and put them in his jacket pocket.

Lamont-Smith said: 'I'll be waiting.'

'Don't hold your breath.'

He left the hotel and drove the car to the harbour. People in London were wetting themselves, Lamont-Smith was pouting himself silly, and still nothing had been decided. The daftness of the situation put him in a good mood.

The girls were already at the bar and, after a drink, he took them to the Italian restaurant with the view, where he had dined the night before.

Magda and Ursel enjoyed the food, the waiters enjoyed serving them, and he enjoyed the envious looks of every other man in the place. By the time they had finished a second bottle of wine, he had the distinct impression that Ursel was flirting with him. Or was it Magda?

Maybe it was his rugged good looks, his world-weary sophistication, the magic of the old leather jacket. Maybe it was because he was paying the bill.

Whatever the reason, they had a thoroughly good time.

Outside the restaurant they both gave him the friendly sort of goodbye kisses that the Italian had been hoping for earlier in the day.

Tomorrow, they said.

Maybe, he said.

He drove through the night towards Mosta with a smile on his face. Almost fifty and flirting.

The smile slipped when he turned off the two-lane highway on to unlit country roads. He got lost once, tracked back and rejoined the correct route. He arrived at Frank Briggs' house at ten minutes past ten.

After a long wait Briggs opened the door and led him into the back room. The whisky bottle was on the table, and from the way he steadied himself on the door jamb as he went through it looked as if the elderly agent had continued drinking all day.

He collapsed in his chair and pointed an invitation at the bottle, which, Lacey saw, was almost empty. Lacey shook his head. He took the documents from his pocket and laid them out on the table in front of Briggs.

Briggs leaned forward, fumbled to put on a pair of spectacles, and peered at the pieces of paper.

'It's no good,' he said. 'I'm too pissed. What's it mean?'

'It means you're a millionaire, Frank. The money's been transferred.'

Briggs sat back, his mouth open, spectacles on the end of his nose, and barked a laugh like a walrus.

'Bloody hell. All those years I asked them for money and got bugger-all. You snap your fingers.' He tried to snap his fingers but failed, even when he concentrated. 'You snap your bloody fingers and there's a million. Just like that!'

'What about our deal, Frank? Is it on?'

Briggs blinked and tried to sit forward to reach for his glass but the effort was too much and he sat back again. He took off the spectacles and dropped them by the side of the chair.

'I'm pissed,' he said.

Lacey went into the kitchen to make coffee.

Briggs shouted: 'Not for me. I like being pissed.'

Lacey came back and, when the drunken man tried to get out of the chair, he helped him. Briggs picked up the four documents, folded them and staggered into the hall.

'No peeking!' he shouted over his shoulder.

He didn't bother to see if he was observed. Lacey watched him go to an oil painting of a seventeenth-century knight and slide the documents into the torn backing canvas.

When he returned, Lacey was studiously reading the label on the bottle of Glenmorangie. He put the bottle down and looked at Briggs.

'Well?'

Briggs slumped back into the chair and focused on Lacey's face. He tried to snap his fingers again and this time it worked and he grinned at his hand as if it had performed magic.

'Just like that,' he said.

'Frank, are you going to tell me where the diary is?'

He breathed deeply, close to sleep.

'Tomorrow,' he said. 'Arrangements have been made.' He blinked his eyes to aid his concentration. 'Have you been to Ireland?'

'No. I never have.'

'You'll like it. Lovely place. Full of soul.' He grinned foolishly. 'And booze. Course, you don't get the tits like you get at the Reef Club. But there's Bushmill, Paddy's, Jameson and Tullamore Dew. There's a gang of four, for you. Eh? A real gang.'

'What happens tomorrow, Frank?'

'I'll tell you where to go in Ireland. I'll tell you the arrangements. Deal?'

He held his hand out and Lacey took it.

'It's a deal.'

'You're a good man, Lacey.' He grinned. 'At least, I hope you are. Now pour me another drink before you go.'

Lacey emptied the remnants of the bottle into the glass.

This time, Briggs didn't take any water.

Lamont-Smith was waiting in the lobby of the hotel when Lacey got back. He was sitting in an armchair with a gin and tonic on the table in front of him. Lacey got his room key and walked across to him.

'What do you want?' Lacey said.

'Was he satisfied?'

'He commends your efficiency.'

'But it went all right?'

'It went all right.'

'When do we leave?'

'I leave tomorrow. You can please yourself.'

'Don't make it difficult, Peter.'

'I'm not. Consider our association terminated.'

'You'll regret it.'

'You're wrong.'

Lacey walked to the lift. The doors opened when he pressed the button and he stepped inside. He turned and looked back into the lobby as he keyed the panel for the second floor but Lamont-Smith had already gone.

The gin and tonic remained on the table like a broken date.

271

THIRTY-ONE

The offer had come with the brandy at the annual dinner of the Special Services Association at the British Museum, after their patron, Queen Elizabeth the Queen Mother, had departed.

Ian Lamont-Smith had been approached by Roger 'Wheels' Wellington and Clive 'Umpire' Meadows. Everybody in special forces had a nickname; it was part of the Boys' Own camaraderie. Wellington had been dubbed Wheels because of his skills with motor cars on nocturnal missions around the streets of Derry, and Lamont-Smith was known as Bunny.

Meadows had a gallows sense of humour and Lamont-Smith had been with him the day he had acquired the name Umpire. They had been members of a four-man team flown from undercover duties in Northern Ireland to undercover duties in the North of England.

The mainland police had been hunting a former para-turned-murderer who was armed with a small arsenal of deadly weapons. When they jumped out of the helicopter on the Yorkshire Moors, the man had already been cornered on the outskirts of a village.

Lamont-Smith had known there was more to the mission than helping the local constabulary catch a murderer: they'd been given shoot-to-kill orders. The buzz was that before turning criminal the para had been employed by some shady department for covert work of a violent nature. Such a claim might make an interesting mitigation plea in court but would be embarrassing to the Government. It would be best if he didn't make it to court. Yet, in a way, he did.

Task Force officers and armed constables had the man contained and were capable of doing the job; their team had been sent to direct tactics and make sure. Everybody knew the bloke was too dangerous to take chances with; that he had to be put down. Politics aside, this could only have one conclusion.

The ground chosen for it was perfect. The armed men took up positions behind two walls facing into a field; the walls ran away from each other at a right-angle so there would be no chance of them being caught in cross-fire. Their target was in a wood and his expected line of retreat from helicopter harassment was across a municipal tennis-court.

Lamont-Smith and Meadows were at the end of the wall closest to the tennis-court. The ex-para broke cover. He was carrying a rifle. They let him get into the middle of the court before opening up, everybody joining in for the Bonnie and Clyde finale. Afterwards, thirty-eight bullets were removed from his body.

The last shot died, smoke curled from above the walls, the man lay crumpled against the net-mesh fencing, and policemen who rarely used guns looked grey in the eerie aftermath. Meadows broke the tension, speaking in the deep, resonant tone of a Wimbledon official:

'Game, set and match.'

It had become a story to relate in select company, usually at the brandy stage of reunions.

This time, at the British Museum, Meadows had laughed at the retelling, before moving the conversation on to a more serious note. Lamont-Smith had agreed that he missed the old days of controlled wildness and was still willing, no, eager, to contribute to the nation's security. He had been recruited into Group 13.

The Group consisted of former Special Services officers and men, who made themselves available to handle specific missions that could not be publicly or even covertly sanctioned in the normal way, and which could not be dealt with through existing departments of MI5 or MI6.

They were Britain's totally unofficial and highly efficient assassination squad.

Their talents were not required on a regular basis but, when they were needed, retired hooligans now running pubs in Hereford and Worcester, or archivists living quietly in London, would be reactivated, take out the totally illegal guns they still possessed, and undertake a termination with no questions asked.

Usually the jobs were dressed up as accidents or suicides, but occasionally the order would be given for a wet operation so that the victim's colleagues, family or accomplices would get the message.

Lamont-Smith sat in the shadows beneath a palm tree in the gardens at the front of the Dragonara Hotel, smoked a cigarette and remembered other excitements with Meadows and the chaps; excitements that had been more enjoyable because they had been less complicated than the present operation.

He had foreseen problems in being teamed with a regular intelligence officer from Six, but there was little alternative. Lacey, and the resources of a department that could tap into Century House, had been needed to do the groundwork to track down and negotiate with Enrico Latimer and Frank Briggs. Lamont-Smith's genuine talents as an archivist, and his unique family background and friendship with Chesterton, had made him the natural choice to accompany him.

It was unfortunate that Lacey had chosen to go his own way. Lamont-Smith liked the man, envied his home life and the way he was comfortable with silence and his own company. He recognized strengths in him that didn't need flippancy or unnecessary talk. He hadn't liked being deceitful in Portugal but it had been necessary, as much for Lacey's sake as anything else. There had been an edge of paranoia about Chesterton the last time they met that had made Lamont-Smith uncomfortable.

Lamont-Smith stubbed out the cigarette and got to his feet. He walked to a small, blue Fiat car that he had hired without Lacey's knowledge, got in and wound down the window. He had moved the driver's seat as far back as possible but it was still a tight squeeze for his legs. He laughed at being uncomfortable again. It was a state he'd got used to from being a child.

His parents had divorced acrimoniously when he was nine. For a long time, rather than make a choice between a father in Wales and a mother in Scotland, he'd relied on the stability of his boarding-school. He had grown up with a sense that he lacked something, although he hadn't recognized that it might have been affection.

After school and college he had found refuge in the military. The orderly male world that came complete with tradition, drunkenness and chums, suited him, and his marriages and liaisons with various ladies had taken second place.

Home was a word that had always lacked intimate meaning. Home was dear old Blighty and the white cliffs of Dover, but nothing more personal.

Lamont-Smith viewed life as a mysterious party to which he'd been invited. He didn't know why it was being held or when it would end, and he suspected his invitation had been mixed up with someone else's and he was at the wrong venue. But while it lasted he would accept whatever was on offer, be it food and drink, a dalliance with a lady, the thrill of a challenge, or the comradeship of a drinking pal.

He drove out of the hotel car-park and threaded his way through the narrow streets. Couples walked hand-in-hand between the brightly-lit restaurants and bars. Back at the hotel, Lacey was probably on the telephone right now to his wife. Lamont-Smith felt the familiar pang of envy.

Perhaps if he'd received the correct invitation he would be a complete person with a stable relationship, like Lacey, rather than living with this feeling of discomfort, waiting for someone to find him out and peel away his postures and reveal the stranger that lurked inside.

The invitation to join G13 had been a godsend. It kept him in touch with danger and stopped him thinking too deeply and regretting too much. It gave him a role to hang on to while he lurched between civilian commissions in an

275

occupation that was less than successful. His army pension cushioned him from poverty but sapped ambition. He might be considered a failure as a civilian, except that failure was not a word in his vocabulary. His marriages hadn't failed; they simply hadn't worked.

It was an attitude that had made him good at sport, successful as a soldier, and an efficient member of G13.

Having his house entered and the contents of his briefcase photographed had been an affront to an ego and a self-image that was getting rockier the older he got. He was determined there would be no more. Chesterton had stressed he wanted this left like Mother Hubbard's cupboard, with no bones for anyone to pick over. Tonight would be a demonstration of his efficiency.

He reached the dual carriageway, turned north and headed for Mosta.

THIRTY-TWO

Clouds blanketed the island and made the morning chilly. They had gathered in particular strength over Mosta and Lacey drove into a rainstorm that was brisk but brief and which stopped as he approached the cul-de-sac where Briggs lived.

He was about to signal the left turn when he saw a police car among three or four vehicles parked in a cluster outside the house. He drove on.

Further up the road he took a right and did a three-point turn in a side street. He drove the car back on to the main road and parked thirty yards from the entrance to the cul-de-sac.

After a few minutes a van came out of the street and headed towards the centre of Mosta. Ten minutes later, the police car went in the same direction.

Lacey drove down the road, turned right and stopped the hire car. He walked the rest of the way to the house. Outside was an old black Mercedes and, beyond it, the Hillman Minx that belonged to Briggs. The Mercedes did not look like a police department vehicle.

He knocked at the door and it was opened by the expatriate with the trimmed moustache from the Reef Club.

Lacey smiled.

'Hello again. Frank's expecting me.'

The man hesitated. Eventually he opened the door wider.

'You'd better come in.'

Lacey stepped into the hall and the expatriate closed the door. He stared at Lacey, unsure what to do next.

He said: 'You're a friend of Franks?'

'Well, friend and business colleague. Where is he?'

'Look, I'm sorry. Frank's had an accident. He's . . . he's dead.'

He had started trying to be tactful but had given up at the hopelessness of being tactful about death. He shrugged.

Lacey had expected complications after seeing the van and police car, and this was a possibility he had considered while he waited on the main road, but the news was still a surprise.

'Oh, no,' he said, adopting a role of commiseration and sadness he did not feel. What he felt was anger at not foreseeing it might happen and at being left out on a limb. His feelings towards Briggs didn't count and he didn't immediately have time to allow himself to have any. 'How?'

'Drowned. In the pool. It looks like he'd been drinking and fell in.'

He shrugged again. His words were as clipped as his moustache.

'God.' Lacey walked slowly towards the painting of the seventeenth-century knight. 'I was with him yesterday. It's such a shock.'

'Were you close friends?'

Lacey shook his head, not in answer but in a small gesture of how cruel life can be.

'Look, I'm sorry. Do you think I could have a drink of water?'

'Of course.'

The man left for the kitchen and Lacey moved to the painting. The documents were still inside the loose canvas but, to his disappointment, there was nothing else. He put them in his pocket before walking into the living-room where he met the expatriate coming back with a glass of water.

'Spot of whisky, or a gin perhaps? Frank has a well-stocked cupboard.'

'No, thank you. This is fine.' He sipped the water. 'Look, I'd better introduce myself. I'm Peter Lacey.'

'Bill Fullshaw.'

They shook hands and Fullshaw's grip faltered.

'Hang on. Did you say Lacey?'

'Yes.'

278

'Bloody coincidence. I posted a letter to a Lacey yesterday. For Frank.'

'To a Peter Lacey?'

'Yes. The name was Peter Lacey. Why would he write to you in Ireland if he knew you were here?'

Lacey didn't answer straight away. He walked to the sideboard and looked at the two photographs of Nell, and then to the french windows, which were open, and out at the swimming-pool where Briggs had died.

When he had left him last night, Briggs had been incapable of getting out of a chair unaided. Yet he had gone for a walk, fallen in the pool and drowned. Another convenient death that had occurred only hours after Lacey had told Lamont-Smith the deal was settled.

Lamont-Smith didn't know he had arranged to see Briggs this morning; he had expected Lacey to take an early flight out of Luqa Airport, and to remain unaware of the accidental drowning of a well-known inebriate that wouldn't even make a paragraph in British newspapers.

Bryson had told him not to leave any loose ends behind. Lacey now wondered whether, if he did get the diary and tape, he would himself become a loose end.

To stay in front and alive he had to act quickly.

'When did you post the letter?'

'Yesterday afternoon. I called in to see him after the Reef Club. It was stamped and addressed and I put it in the post on my way home. He was in a rum mood. He gave me a package, too. Almost as if he had a premonition. To be opened in the event of his death, he said. And then this.'

'A package? What did he say about it?'

'He told me to open it when he died. He played it down, said it was a bet he had with his doctor.'

What the hell had Briggs been up to? Lacey had no alternative but to take risks and hope he could persuade Fullshaw to hand it over.

'Bill.' He moved on from feigned distress to a more suitably grim expression. 'Were you in the forces?'

'Yes. A regular for twenty years. Rank of captain.'

279

'Good. What's your connection with Frank?'

'We're friends. Were friends. My wife and I met Frank and Nell, Mrs Briggs, in Spain. We were on holiday there. He lost some money in property and we suggested they move to Malta. We've lived here for years. Nell died before they could both come out. What's all this about?'

'I think you already suspect what it might be about.' Lacey was making a calculated bid to boost his ego and at the same time stop him asking awkward questions. 'Did you find Frank's body?'

'No, the cleaner did. Mrs Bologna. She came for me. I live in the next road.'

'And you sent for the police.'

'Yes.'

Lacey nodded. Fullshaw's training in the Army had been to accept authority, as well as use it. If Lacey could impose his right of command he could get co-operation.

'Did Frank talk about his job?'

'Not a lot. I gathered he'd worked in security; Ministry of Defence.' He straightened his shoulders. 'It's not the sort of thing you chat about.'

'Exactly.'

Lacey indicated the chairs and they sat down, either side of the table, and he took out his wallet and showed Fullshaw his Foreign Office identification. Fullshaw's eyes widened, he opened his mouth to say something, changed his mind, and shut it again.

'I've no alternative, Bill. I'm going to have to involve you.'

Fullshaw nodded, unsure what he was agreeing to.

'At least I know you're clean – we have reports on all Frank's contacts – but I still have to warn you that what I'm going to tell you is covered by the Official Secrets Act. OK?'

'OK.'

'Right. First, as far as the Maltese authorities are concerned, Frank's death was accidental.'

'You mean . . . ?'

'I mean Frank was with MI6. His cover was to pretend to be disaffected with the terms of his retirement. In fact, he

280

never retired. But it helped him infiltrate an operation being run by, well, let's call it a hostile force from the Middle East.'

Fullshaw nodded. Libya was only two hundred miles to the south and Malta had been used as a crossroads for intrigue for centuries. His moustache bristled.

Lacey said: 'Frank suspected he'd been rumbled. That's why I came to Malta. That's why I'm going to Ireland today. Getting you to post the letter to me in Ireland, and giving you the package, was insurance in case anything happened. Something did.

'That package cost him his life. He must have trusted you to put it in your care.' Or maybe Briggs didn't have anybody else to give it to. 'Where is it?'

'In the boot of my car.'

Fullshaw regretted the statement as soon as he made it. His eyes left Lacey and moved around the room, looking for somewhere safe to think.

'It sounds far-fetched, Bill. I know that.' Lacey held out the Foreign Office identification again, and allowed the man to hold it and inspect it more closely. 'You're right to be cautious, but if the opposition hear about the package they'll come back. I have to ask you to give it to me.'

'I'm not frightened, you know.'

'You should be. These blokes don't mess about. Look. I could telephone the Foreign Office in London and get them to call the High Commissioner in Floriana. They could get him to call you and vouch for me. But that would take time, telephone calls on an island like Malta could blow my cover and implicate you, and the bloody High Commissioner could be having a day off on Gozo.

'We haven't got that luxury, Bill. We haven't got the time. I need to get that package off the island before they know I'm here.'

Fullshaw went to the drinks cupboard and poured himself a large gin and tonic.

'You sure you won't?' he said.

'I'm sure.'

281

He went into the kitchen and Lacey heard him put ice cubes in the glass. He came back, stood in the doorway and took a large swig.

'Bill. Frank gave his life for this. Let's not fuck it up.'

Fullshaw nodded, put the drink on the sideboard and walked into the hall. Lacey followed. If he tried to get into his car and drive away, Lacey would have to stop him and unarmed combat had never been his strong suit.

Ankles and knees, the SAS instructor had said. They can't run without ankles and knees. Stamp on them or kick them in the right place and the biggest bastard will fall over.

That was probably true if you were wearing boots in which to do the stamping and kicking; Lacey was wearing his Kurt Geiger moccasins.

Fullshaw went to the rear of the car, opened the boot and took out a bulky brown envelope. He closed the boot and handed the envelope to Lacey and they went back into the house.

Lacey took it into the living-room and put it on the sideboard but didn't open it.

'I'll have that drink now,' he said. 'Gin and tonic?'

Fullshaw made the drink and topped up his own, taking both glasses into the kitchen for ice. When he came back, Lacey toasted him.

'Cheers, Bill. Thank God you were here.'

Fullshaw's moustache twitched again, at the praise.

He said: 'It may be a dirty word to some people, but I know my duty.'

They drank.

Lacey said: 'I've also got to go to Ireland and get the rest of it. Can you remember the address on the letter?'

'It was an hotel, but that's all I can remember.' He looked puzzled. 'Don't you know?'

'We were using a cut-out system. This was a thirty-three?' Lacey lied, hoping Fullshaw enjoyed jargon. 'Top priority. He would have phoned me with the address.'

'Ah. Of course.'

'Which doesn't help, unless . . . did Frank have an address book? A filofax?'

'An address book. He kept it in here.'

Fullshaw opened a drawer in the sideboard and took out a black book with an A to Z index in the margin. It had been lying on top of loose documents, letters, leaflets and photographs; the usual bits and pieces of paper that categorized and summed up a life.

'Go through it, Bill. See if any of the addresses mean anything.'

'Right.'

He took it to the table with his drink and sat in a chair with his back to Lacey, who pulled from the inside pocket of his jacket the documents he had earlier retrieved from behind the painting. He dropped the documents in the drawer and closed it. Maybe a distant cousin of Briggs would get a nice surprise when his estate was sorted out.

Finding the address didn't take long.

'Here it is.' Fullshaw held up the book. 'The Glen Hotel, Delgany, County Wicklow.'

'Bloody marvellous.'

Lacey gave him a true Brit smile and took the address book. He picked up the package from the sideboard and Fullshaw got to his feet, once again unsure about whether he had done the right thing.

'Well,' he said.

'Thanks, Bill.' Lacey stuck his hand out and tried to remember how David Niven had done it in all those old war movies. 'Frank may have died, but he won't be forgotten. Not with this. You don't know how much . . .'

Lacey nodded to emphasize rising emotion as they shook hands and Fullshaw put his shoulders back.

'You don't have to say anything. Just get the job done,' he said.

They spent a few more seconds nodding at each other before Lacey judged the time was right to leave. He didn't look back but walked to the hire car, assessing other parked

283

vehicles and pedestrians on the way. It didn't look as if he was being watched.

He got in to the car, held his breath and started the engine, but it didn't blow up. That would have been unsubtle, but he had a feeling that if Lamont-Smith was part of this team they would be working quickly and taking chances.

No one followed him on the way back towards St Julian's and he stopped the car on a stretch of road that was open and empty and which gave no other vehicle a reason to stop behind him. Most of the clouds had gone and those that were left remained clustered in mourning over Mosta. Elsewhere on the island the sun was back in command and the sky was as blue as the Mediterranean.

He opened the bulky brown envelope and took out two small padded envelopes and a short note.

The note said: 'Bill, do me a final favour. No questions – just post these. Thanks for being a friend, Frank.'

Lacey felt guilty. Maybe he had misjudged both Briggs and Fullshaw. Maybe a rogue agent and an ex-pat could have had a friendship.

The padded envelopes were addressed to *The Times* of London and the *Washington Post* in the United States. Each contained an audio cassette and a typed and signed note that explained the conversation on the tape was between Blunt and Chesterton, and that he, Frank Briggs, was a witness to the truth of the contents.

Briggs had gone along with the deal that had made him a millionaire but he had taken out his own insurance in case Lacey reneged or an assassin took him out. Even if neither of those possibilities had happened, and if he had spent his final year of life surrounded by tits and bums, he would still have had a last laugh from the grave.

Now Lacey had time for feelings but they were difficult to assess. Briggs had said he had originally obtained the diary and tape for no other reason than that he wanted to possess them; to have something Chesterton hadn't got.

Chesterton had had the connections, the promotions and, Lacey suspected, the ability, and Briggs had been

284

made to feel a second-string legman from Special Branch, a low-ranking gofer to be ordered about by an aristocrat not famed for his tact.

The bit about hypocrisy seemed to be something he had tagged on to his motives for the sake of respectability after finally deciding to get his own back on the politician, not because of a poor pension but because he felt life had dealt him a poor hand.

As Briggs lost money in Spain, Chesterton's star was beginning to rise in the public sector. Being told how long he had to live had probably been the incentive he'd needed to threaten to unleash the scandal.

Briggs had been a cynical exploiter who had gone along with the dirty tricks brigade while he had worked with Five. He was no born-again saviour of the common man. His jealousy had prompted a final mission that had been a diversion from thoughts of his own mortality. He had probably enjoyed his last few weeks of power.

Lacey put the car in gear and continued towards the hotel. He wouldn't mourn for Frank Briggs but men like Bill Fullshaw still gave him a jolt.

Fullshaw had talked of duty and meant it. He hadn't had to think twice about saying it, with sincerity and without embarrassment. For him, duty had been clear and unequivocal.

Now Lacey had to consider duty, a package and a letter. He screwed his eyes against the sun as he turned the car off the main road.

Maybe Chesterton and Bryson considered him to be nothing more than a blind postman, but he intended to deliver a few surprises before the game was run, and the first one involved Ben Miller.

THIRTY-THREE

Ben Miller was not in his London office when Lacey
telephoned. He was in the Hilton Hotel which Lacey could
see from the window of his room, on the next curve of the
bay beyond the Reef Club.

He had arrived the previous day and was about to take a
trip to Mosta. Lacey told him not to bother and suggested
Ireland instead. They discussed details and agreed Miller
should go through Heathrow, while Lacey would take a route
through Manchester.

It was reassuring to know that Miller had still been on
the trail, even if it had taken his organization longer to find
Frank Briggs. It was reassuring that the SIS could still find
one of their own before an outsider. It was not reassuring to
suspect that Lacey himself was now being tracked by his own
side as he left Malta. He had not seen Lamont-Smith since
the previous night but he had no doubt his movements were
being monitored.

Air Malta does not have the greatest reputation for
efficiency so it was a surprise that the early afternoon flight
left on time. It arrived in Manchester four hours later. The
transfer to one of the frequent shuttles to Dublin was smooth
and the wait minimal.

Aer Lingus, Lacey discovered, had a charm all of its own.
Ireland started with the smiles and beguiling accents of the
stewardesses.

The flight was an elongated funfair ride. No sooner did the
aircraft reach cruising height than it was time for its descent
to Dublin. As it broke cloud cover on its final approach,
he looked out of the window and was disappointed. There
were no horses pulling jaunting cars and no leprechauns:

286

just housing estates, slow-moving traffic and wet fields. It looked depressingly like England and a lot colder than the Mediterranean.

He hired a two-door Ford at the terminal, spent ten minutes studying a map and a hotel guide-book that showed him the location of the Glen Hotel, and decided the only way to get there was straight through Dublin. He jotted down the street names he should follow and prepared to get lost.

The traffic jam started where the short stretch of motorway ended. It was aided and abetted by roadworks and office home-time.

He followed Dorset Street into Bolton Street, a wide but clogged main road that cut through the northern edge of a city in disrepair. Then into Capel Street where he became lodged in chaos.

Cars were parked on both sides of the road in total disregard of prohibitory signs, as if abandoned in haste. Some had been, as drivers nipped into shops that looked like a left-over set from a pre-war film, in between the traffic lights changing.

At last he crossed the Liffey and negotiated bends round civic buildings and a castle wall. The city centre remained a mystery, hidden back in the traffic. Dublin, he decided, was a compact capital whose road problems deserved somewhere bigger.

Lacey got lost as expected, but not badly, and an hour and a half after leaving the airport he was ten miles south of the city and nearing his destination. The Wicklow Mountains were to his right and the countryside was beginning to fit the tourist image, despite the drizzle.

The hotel was a converted manor house on a hillside. Access was along a narrow dirt track through a small wood. When he checked in, he met his first leprechaun. He was behind the reception desk and begrudged handing over a room key. Maybe that was where he had hidden the pot of gold.

Lacey carried his bag to the first floor. His room was at the front with a view down the glen to the south. The rain had stopped and late sunshine had broken through the clouds, slanting into the mist that rose from the valley to make the hills beyond float like legends.

It was beautiful, except that Lacey was here to collect a package that could destroy legends.

The hotel was busy with weekend guests and the leprechaun had undergone a change of humour with a change of duties. Being behind the bar suited his temperament better. Lacey climbed on to a stool.

'And will you be having a drink before dinner, sir?'

Lacey knew what drinks before dinner led to. They led to drinks with dinner and after-dinner drinks. He had the album, knew the lyrics and, just like Loudon Wainwright, he'd been there more than once.

But this was a night when he knew he was in no danger. No one would move against him until they were sure he had taken possession of the goods. He ordered a pint of Guinness and wondered why the leprechaun was serving someone else.

The answer was in the stout. The barman left the tap running with a pint glass beneath it and was able to put two whiskeys on the bar, take the money and provide change, before he wiped the head off the pint with a wooden spatula and topped it up.

'The name's Pat, sir. And what room number are you?'

The Guinness was wonderful enough for him to have a second before he went into dinner where he had a third with the finest fillet steak he could ever remember eating.

An obligatory priest was dining with two sober-suited men at the table on his left. Lacey wondered if the clergy's views on sodomy had changed much since Oscar Wilde had left Ireland's shores for British persecution of a different kind to the sort that was usually handed out to Irish heroes. Ben Miller and a beautiful girl with legs that went on for ever were at a table to his right. After Lacey finished his meal he had a second Irish Mist purely on account of the way she kept crossing them.

288

Miller and his girlfriend followed him into the bar. Lacey took a different stool, drank Guinness and watched the room fill up with hotel residents, diners and local people on a Friday night out. Miller and the girl were at a table against a wall that gave them a view of the entrance.

A band was setting up. A large bearded man wearing a guitar moved behind one of the microphones that had been erected in front of two speakers. He was joined by a girl with a fiddle and a youth with another guitar.

'Hello dare,' the bearded man said. 'And welcome to the Glen Hotel. We're The Charlie O'Malley Quartet, only dare's only t'ree of us tonight, cos Liam had to work.'

The man said it as explanation and not as a joke.

Lacey stayed and was surprised that the music was so good. Maybe it was because the songs were articulate, gentle and funny, and the tunes were instantly recognizable, even though he'd never heard them before. 'The Rare Oul Times' was followed by 'The Cliffs of Dooneen' and 'The Rose of Allendale' and the sentiment and the Guinness made everyone an Irishman.

By the third song, people were joining in with the chorus and the atmosphere was heavy with friendliness and alcohol. There was no challenge in this bar, just good humour.

Lacey stayed longer than he intended. Both Blunt and Briggs had enjoyed Ireland, although for different reasons, and he felt as if he'd come home, which was odd since he had been born and bred in England. Maybe this was the key to the country's tourist popularity.

He left the bar at the end of the band's first set after he had found himself singing along to 'The Fields of Athenry'. If he'd stayed he'd have drunk too much, and he needed a clear head for the morning.

In his room, he checked the fridge to make sure it held two essential items: a can of Coca Cola and a cloth bag that contained a Walther PPK automatic handgun and spare magazine. He went to bed with the gun under his pillow and half a dozen love tunes in his head, thinking of Susan.

* * *

The cold coke dispelled any hint of a hangover when he woke up. He pulled the curtains back and stood naked at the window staring out at a morning fresh with spring sunshine. Dew glistened on the shrubbery in front of the hotel and a thin mist floated further down the glen.

He breathed in deeply and didn't cough. There was also no burning urge for a cigarette.

Look, Susan: no addiction!

He showered and dressed and went for a walk in the grounds before breakfast, crunching across the gravel car-park towards a path that led into the mist. The grass was wet and virginal, and for a while he wondered what he could smell before he realized it was nature. The only sounds were birds and a breeze that moved the top branches of the trees.

If the Watchers were watching they would wonder what to do in all this countryside. They were more at home in an urban landscape.

The walk was enjoyable, but the further he went the more the back of his neck tingled. Rather than Watchers he could be being tailed by the same specialists who had been in Malta, and there was always the chance they were short of patience or had been badly briefed. He wondered how good his insurance was and whether, perhaps, he was pushing his luck a few hundred yards too far. He went back to the hotel.

A mail van arrived at the same time he did but there was no letter for him. The middle-aged woman in reception told him Feargal brought a second delivery on Saturdays on his way home at lunch-time.

Ben Miller and the girl were already having breakfast and both were eating heartily. Lacey wondered what they had been doing to sharpen their appetites.

After breakfast he read the newspapers and watched television in his room until eleven-thirty, when he went down to the bar. He was greeted by Pat the leprechaun like a long-lost relative and introduced to Fin and Mick, large-boned men with red faces who wore rough suits, their trousers tucked into wellington boots.

Lacey was careful not to be seduced by the company and took his time over a pint of stout while the two men quaffed and the leprechaun sipped halves. They talked about the pig with three legs that had been born to Liam O'Connell in Kilcoole, but Lacey didn't know if they were serious or having a joke at his expense.

'Sure, it's all that nuclear fall-out stuff from across the water,' Fin said. 'No offence, sir.' He raised his glass at Lacey. 'But we send England our young men and they pay us back with three-legged pigs. Now isn't that an English way of doing things? Couldn't they make the fall-out that bit stronger to give the pigs foive legs and make us a profit?'

Lacey grinned.

Feargal arrived at noon in a blue Bedford van, although he was still wearing his uniform. He joined Fin and Mick and ordered a pint of Guinness. Lacey excused himself and went to reception.

A bundle of letters held with a rubber band lay on the desk and the middle-aged woman was nowhere to be seen. Lacey checked them and saw one with Maltese stamps. He pulled it from the bundle and read his name.

He went to his room, locked the door and opened the envelope. It contained the torn half of a one pound Irish banknote and a sheet of paper upon which was a name, a telephone number and the message:

There's a £100 sterling redemption fee.

Lacey dialled the number. It rang several times before it was answered. A girl said: 'The Model Shop.'

'Can I speak to Gerry O'Sullivan, please?'

'Mr O'Sullivan's busy right now. Can I help?'

'I'm afraid not. This is a personal matter and it's rather urgent.'

'Well, can you hold on a mo?'

'I'll hold.'

Lacey waited a full minute before a man picked up the receiver and announced himself.

291

'This is Gerry O'Sullivan.'

'Mr O'Sullivan, my name is Lacey. I arrived in Ireland yesterday from Malta where I saw Frank Briggs. He asked me to collect a package from you.'

'Did he, now? And did he say how it was to be paid for?'

'Yes. He told me one hundred pounds sterling.'

'And do you have the pawn ticket?'

'I do.'

'Would you read the number to me?'

'Of course.' Lacey read the number from the half bank-note. 'It's FLK 050856.'

'Will you hold on a moment more?'

'I'll hold.'

This time the wait was no more than thirty seconds.

'Mr Lacey?'

'Yes?'

'I have your package. When can you collect it?'

'That depends on where you are. I'm staying at the Glen Hotel in Delgany.'

'My shop is in Bray. You're only a few miles down the road. Do you have a car?'

'I have.'

'Park it at the bottom of the town, near the shopping precinct. There's usually space there. Then walk up the hill, past the Royal Hotel on your left. There's some traffic lights, and just past them, on the right, is The Model Shop. There's an alley at the side that goes down to the pawn shop at the back. We're very discreet.'

'I'll be there within an hour.'

Bray was a sizeable seaside town that clung to the curve of the coast. He drove around it, to familiarize himself with its layout in case it was necessary to know where to run, and to see if he was being tailed. He was.

The promenade was tatty and still waiting for a fresh coat of paint for summer, and the town itself had lost a lot of character by having a concrete shopping precinct grafted on to its lumbar region.

292

He parked the Ford at the precinct and walked up the hill. The sky had become grey and he turned up the collar of his leather jacket against the cold. Cars and vans were backed up nose to bumper from the traffic lights and the narrow pavements and the pubs were busy with people.

Toy electric trains lined shelves in the window of The Model Shop and model aeroplanes hung from the ceiling on strings. The main display was of British soldiers in red tunics and rifles with fixed bayonets facing a French artillery battery on a green felt field. Napoleon and Wellington watched with detachment on their respective cardboard boxes and Lacey wondered who won Waterloo in Irish war games.

He went down the alley at the side of the shop, the brick walls providing a refuge from the noise of the main street. Towards the rear of the premises there was a frosted glass window that was protected by wire mesh, and a door above which hung three brass balls. The alley ended at a gate that was locked.

Lacey went inside the pawn shop. The room was small and dark and dominated by a counter that was at least five feet in height. This was an establishment built by a cautious pawnbroker who had taken care that awkward customers couldn't attempt to influence his assessment of the value of their goods.

The floor was flag-stoned. Behind the counter a passage ran towards the shop. An electric bell push was badly fitted to the wall and a sign said: RING FOR ATTENTION. He rang.

He heard its tone in another part of the building, breathed ancient dust and waited. A door opened down the passage and a big man with a grey beard appeared. He stepped on to a raised platform of some kind on the other side of the counter and looked down. It was like being in a courtroom waiting for sentence.

The man said: 'What can I do for you?'

'Mr O'Sullivan?'

'That's me.'

'I'm Peter Lacey. We spoke on the phone.'

'We did.'

293

O'Sullivan got off the platform and disappeared from sight. He reappeared and placed a brown paper parcel on top of the counter.

Lacey offered the half banknote, which O'Sullivan took and, out of sight on the counter top, presumably compared with the other half. When the man looked down again Lacey offered five twenty-pound notes.

They were accepted and counted and O'Sullivan handed down the parcel.

'Will you be seeing Frank again?' the man said.

'Not for a while.'

'Well, if you see him before me, tell him he owes me a pint.'

'I'll do that.'

O'Sullivan nodded and Lacey nodded back and left the shop for the real world.

The alley looked narrower than when he went in but no one turned the corner from the road to block his path and the gate didn't open from the yard behind him. He wondered what it would be like to wander round a town without watching for reflections in shop windows and assessing routes of evasion and escape.

He reached the road and headed down the hill, the direction of the precinct and the parked car. Before he returned to the hotel he would go shopping and buy a present for Susan.

THIRTY-FOUR

He collected a message with his key when he got back to the hotel. It said:

See you in the bar.

Lacey left a plastic carrier-bag of purchases with the receptionist and walked down the corridor to the bar, carrying the brown-paper parcel. Fin, Mick and Feargal had gone, but sitting by a window was Ian Lamont-Smith. His long legs were stretched out, and a pint of lager was on the table next to him, along with his cigarettes and lighter. A newspaper was in his hand.

He looked up, saw Lacey, and waved.

At another table was Ben Miller and the girl with long legs. They were leaning towards each other, staring into each other's eyes. She held one of his hands in both of hers, while his free hand stroked her knee.

Lacey went across to Lamont-Smith and sat down. He put the parcel on the table between them.

The archivist grinned, looked at the parcel, and put the newspaper down next to it. It was the *Daily Telegraph* and it was folded at the crossword.

'Can I get you a drink?' he said.

Lacey ignored the offer.

'I told you I was going solo.'

'Look upon me as your conscience.'

'I look upon you as a pain in the arse.'

Pat had come from behind the bar to take his order but Lamont-Smith held up a hand and shook his head, and the leprechaun went away.

Lamont-Smith nodded towards the parcel.

'Is that it?'

'That's just dirty washing.'

'Haw, haw, haw. Very droll.' He let his false humour relax into a smile. 'What's to stop me taking it?'

'Me.'

'I don't think you could.'

'I don't think you'll try.'

'Quite right. Not my style. I really have been sent to nudge your conscience. As they say in the movie, phone home, Peter. Bryson needs to talk to you.'

'I don't need to talk to Bryson. The only person I want to talk to is Chesterton.'

Lamont-Smith reached for the cigarettes on the table and lit one. His voice had lost its flippancy when he spoke again.

'Are you sure you want to do this your way, Peter?'

'Quite sure.'

'Then I'm authorized to arrange a meeting.'

'Good. Somebody's listening at last.'

'This is not going to do your career any good. You've still got time. Give me the stuff,' he nodded towards the parcel, 'and your tantrum in Malta will be forgotten.'

'I can't do that. I promised Frank Briggs I'd deliver it personally.'

Lamont-Smith blew smoke and waited for it to dissipate. Maybe he meant it to be allegorical; Lacey's last chance fading into thin air.

'All right,' he said. 'I'll fix it.'

'When?'

'Now.' He smiled. 'Bryson said you wouldn't change your mind. Leonard flew to Ireland with me this morning.'

Lacey raised his eyebrows.

'I'm honoured.'

'Don't be. He has horses in training in Kildare. He's combining business with pleasure.'

'Which am I?'

Lamont-Smith's smile was a faint reprise of his earlier *bonhomie*. Now he no longer had to pretend.

'I'll drive. It's not far. Straight across the Wicklow Mountains. An hour at the most.'

The mist was wet as fine rain and they had to use the windscreen wipers of the old four-door Vauxhall that Lamont-Smith was driving. The wipers groaned on the upstroke and screeched on the downstroke as if a couple were having tired copulation beneath the bonnet.

They cut across the Glen of the Downs and towards the hills they could no longer see because of the weather, along empty, narrow country roads that cut through trees and lush green fields. On the back seat the brown-paper parcel sat like a bomb.

They went through dense forest and the road narrowed even more. As they approached a crossroads, Lacey could see a dilapidated truck coming from the opposite direction. If they had met it a mile back there would have been no room for them to pass.

Lamont-Smith turned left and Lacey read a signpost that said they were heading towards Sally Gap. They were leaving the trees behind and climbing on to moorland that was wildly beautiful but inhospitable in weather that had worsened. The mist had now become rain.

The road twisted around steep outcrops of rock, dropped dramatically and climbed again. It was a switchback ride through the clouds and Lamont-Smith drove carefully. He also began to fidget in his seat.

'I'm sorry, old boy, but I'm going to have to stop.'
'What?'
'I was waiting in the bar for an hour. I need a pee.'
'Where are you going to stop? The road's too narrow.'
'The next lay-by. There's plenty of them up here. People come to look at the views.'

A rock face was solid on their right, the drop steep on the left as they climbed the next hill. From the top, the road began a long descent. A third of the way down, the ground had been banked to provide a parking or overtaking bay at

297

the edge of the drop. Lamont-Smith drove on to the space and stopped.

He got out, the cold and damp momentarily invading the warmth of the car until he shut the door. The wind buffeted the vehicle. Two hundred yards below, another car had parked where the road levelled along the floor of the valley.

On a clear, sunny day the views might be spectacular, but in this weather there was little to see except wet turf and the occasional sheep.

So why was the car parked two hundred yards below?

Lacey unfastened his seat-belt and turned to look out of the window. Lamont-Smith was at the rear of the car facing up the hill. Peeing into the wind?

Another car came round the top of the hill and slowed as it approached. Lamont-Smith turned and came back to the car. He opened the rear door and stared at Lacey with the total confidence that came with holding an automatic pistol in his right hand.

'I'll take the parcel.'

Lacey nodded.

Lamont-Smith said: 'Less complicated this way. Don't make me use it.'

Lacey poked the Walther PPK between the front seats.

He said: 'I won't if you won't.'

Lamont-Smith's smile was without humour.

Lacey said: 'What now?'

'I'm sorry, Peter. Now you're on your own.'

He slammed the door and ran round the back of the car carrying the brown-paper parcel towards the other vehicle, which had stopped ten yards away. The driver, wearing jeans and a windcheater, got out. He was carrying a sub-machine-gun.

It was all extremely logical to Lacey. He was about to become the victim of a terrorist ambush. His identity as a British intelligence officer would be leaked to the press and the IRA would be blamed. Getting the parcel wasn't enough; Chesterton wanted him dead.

298

Lacey clambered into the driver's seat but the keys were missing.

'Shit!'

In the rear-view mirror he saw the man priming the sub-machine-gun. He was walking sideways to get a better shot. Down below, two other men had climbed out of the parked car and were watching.

Lacey fumbled for the seat-belt, snapped it across him and did the only thing he could. He released the handbrake and let the car roll off the side of the hill.

THIRTY-FIVE

A burst of gunfire shattered the rear window as the car went over the edge. Lacey ducked and hung on to the steering-wheel.

Its nose dipped with the weight of the engine and hit the side of the hill with a fierce blow that had him straining against the bite of the seat-belt. Trying to steer was impossible as the vehicle careered down the steep hillside.

Colour and shapes of sky, grass and bracken were kaleidoscopic; bits of car flew off, and his ears were filled with the sounds of tearing metal, shattering glass and a continuous yell that he realized was his own. The hill began to level and the floor of the valley was hurtling upwards when the car was detoured by a boulder that caved in the front off-side and made it roll.

He blacked out.

Something was on his hand and he flicked his wrist to get rid of it. He opened his eyes and saw the grass and smelt the damp earth. The car was upright but half the size it should have been and Lacey was hanging out of the open door, still restrained by the seat-belt.

The irritation was back on his hand and he looked down and saw it was blood that was dripping from his head. He must be hurt but he didn't feel it. He pushed the release button on the seat-belt but there was too much tension for it to work. The pain came when he moved into a position to ease the belt, pain that came from his back, not his head. Now the release button worked and he crawled out into the grass and looked up the hill.

The gunman was following the trail the car had left, jumping from one outcrop to the next. The other car was

300

driving down to the bottom of the hill, where it stopped. Lamont-Smith got out and he and one of the two men waiting there ran across the valley towards the wreck. The other remained by the cars.

Lacey had lost the Walther PPK. He crawled away from the Ford, rolled over a small rise and kept on rolling into a stream. It had not been a planned move but it was well-timed. The car blew up behind him.

The water was ice-cold. He dipped his head in it to wash the blood from above his ear and to numb the ache that was beginning to start.

He ran, crouched double, along the stream-bed. It curved across the valley floor until it went beneath the road near the parked cars. His back continued to hurt because of the uncomfortable position. When he guessed that Lamont-Smith and his team might be close he crawled into a gulley, lay still and listened.

Behind him the water gurgled pleasantly, but he was freezing and hurting and in no state to appreciate it. He heard the thud of boots and the rasp of a man's breath getting closer. The boots stopped but the man continued breathing heavily, taking in huge gulps of air.

From somewhere more distant a voice shouted.

'Six o'clock!'

It was an instruction, not a time, and Lacey's heavy breather started moving again, splashing across the stream ten yards away and heading towards the rear of the burning car.

Lacey had always hated the refresher courses at Fort Monkton and had never seen the value of crawling through mud when his life was spent in cities. He still hated it, now that his life depended on doing it well. He went forward twenty yards before risking a look through the grass.

Three of them had formed a triangle around the wrecked Ford on a fifty-yard perimeter and were slowly walking towards it. Ian Lamont-Smith was the closest to Lacey. Over at the road, the fourth man still waited by the parked cars.

301

Lamont-Smith had been in the SAS, Lacey remembered, and they were operating as a classic four-man SAS unit. The archivist had obviously kept up his association. Lacey also remembered that the SAS motto was Train Hard, Fight Easy. Considering he was middle aged, unarmed and knackered, the odds seemed a little unfair.

His only chance was at the road. There were a hundred and fifty yards to crawl without being seen and an armed man to overcome when he got there, but maybe something would turn up on the way. It did, almost immediately.

Three motorcycles appeared at the top of the hill. The first had a single rider, the other two had riders and pillion passengers. They stopped and revved the engines of their machines as they stared into the valley.

Lacey peeked through the grass at the three men surrounding the burning car. They, too, were staring at the hillside. Lamont-Smith looked back at the wreck and waved to his colleagues and they moved in quickly, tightening the triangle.

The motorcycles went down the hill fast, before slowing at the parked cars. They stopped and their riders talked to the man standing there. Lacey kept watching. The conversation at the car ended abruptly with a shot and the man fell to the ground. The engines of the bikes were revved again, and their riders drove them across the turf towards Lacey and the others.

Lamont-Smith fired two shots at the bikers and one of the pillion riders responded with a burst from a sub-machine-gun. Ben Miller had brought the bloody cavalry.

Heavy Breather shouted from behind Lacey.

'Re-group at the stream!'

The man ran forward and Lamont-Smith scuttled sideways to join him. The motorcycles with the passengers veered away to attempt to cut off the third man on the far side of the wreck.

Lacey waited until he heard the two men splash into the water behind him before getting to his feet and running. He heard an exchange of sub-machine-gun fire away to his

302

right, and a sub-machine-gun burst and two single shots from behind but he kept going, the turfs and lumps of heather and grass giving him a natural zig-zag path to follow, making it more difficult for anyone shooting at him.

The solo motorcyclist rode in from the flank and skidded his bike alongside him.

Miller said: 'Sorry we're late.'

Lacey climbed aboard. He was too tired to say anything.

Miller carried Lacey a safe distance from the guns of the men in the stream before stopping. The other bikers had dismounted and were carrying a variety of weapons including handguns and a Thompson sub-machine-gun. They were stalking the man they had separated from Lamont-Smith and Heavy Breather.

'They're professionals,' Lacey said. 'They look like SAS. Call your blokes off before they get hurt.'

'They're professionals, too. They wouldn't listen.'

'What sort of professionals?'

'IRA.'

'Jesus Christ!'

'You said you wanted protection. At short notice, this was the best I could do. Maybe I struck lucky.'

'You've got yourself cowboys and they won't stand a chance. Get me out of here.'

Miller rode the motorcycle to the parked cars and stopped and they both got off. Lacey thought Miller was going to abandon the motorbike for a car but the American opened the back door of the vehicle Lamont-Smith had driven down the hill and reached inside.

The body of a man was lying at the rear of the car, a snub-nosed Magnum revolver in his hand. Lacey took the gun from him, just in case the man was not dead and came round long enough to blow him away.

Miller straightened and held up the parcel.

'There's a coat inside if you want it,' he said, and walked back to the motorcycle.

Gunfire still came from the valley but the battle couldn't go on for ever. The area was isolated and Ireland was underpopulated but some vehicle was bound to come along whose occupants would see what was happening and raise the alarm.

Lacey reached inside the car and pulled a raincoat from the back seat. He draped it over his gun arm, closed the door and froze.

Ian Lamont-Smith was crouched by the bonnet of the car, covering him and Miller with a handgun. He no longer looked like a matinée idol or an alcoholic archivist. He looked exactly what he was: lethal.

His clothes, face and hair were caked in mud, but, unlike Lacey, he wore it naturally, as if he'd spent his life surviving. Only the gun was clean and only his eyes showed expression: they were bright and calculating.

'That's mine,' he said to Miller, moving out from the car to see them better.

In the corner of his eye Lacey was aware of Miller, already astride the motorcycle. He held the parcel in front of him.

Lacey said: 'It's not worth it, Ian.'

The mud creased as the man smiled and he changed the direction of the gun slightly towards Ben Miller. Lacey read his intention to shoot the American first.

'Ian?' he said, but Lamont-Smith was concentrating on the kill and didn't see Lacey point the raincoat and fire the Magnum.

The one shot was enough. The gun's owner had loaded it with dumdum cartridges. The bullet hit Lamont-Smith in the chest, blew him backwards off his feet and turned the mud into tomato soup.

Lacey stepped away from the car, the gun held at arm's length in case he needed to use it again. He didn't.

He looked back at where the stream ran under the road but Heavy Breather had stayed on the battlefield to help his colleague.

Ben Miller's voice was low but calm.

'I guess he wanted it pretty bad.'

Lacey dropped the raincoat, handed the gun to Miller and took the parcel.

'He can have it,' he said.

He walked back to Lamont-Smith, unfastened the string and pulled off the paper. He threw the contents at the feet of the body.

They were old *Playboy* magazines from the 1960s that Lacey had found in a second-hand bookshop in Bray when he had gone shopping.

Their pages unfurled in the wind and stuck into still-life papier-mâché sculptures as they became saturated with rain. Only one centrefold spilled out. It was Miss May of 1969.

Lamont-Smith had failed to kill him or gain possession of the Blunt Legacy, but at least he had ended up with a happy bunny.

Lacey rode pillion and at the top of the hill they paused to look into the valley.

The IRA gunmen had retreated to their machines and were preparing to leave. Two of them were wounded. What had seemed like good odds hadn't turned out that way.

The bikes roared and they headed for the parked cars. As they slowed to regain the road, a figure stood up from the stream-bed and fired a short burst from a machine-pistol at close range.

The first motorcycle screamed as a hand twisted the throttle and its front wheel rose high in the air before it fell backwards on top of its riders. The other bike turned away and headed back across the valley and towards open country, rather than risk the same fate. One of the bikers lay still but the second tried to drag himself free of the machine. He was reaching for something in the road.

'Jesus Christ,' Lacey said.

The man walked from the stream-bed, gun held straight out in front of him, and fired two single shots without ceremony into the heads of the two men on the ground.

Both Lacey and Miller had been holding their breath. They now let it out in sighs, as if bullets had punctured their own bodies.

305

At the scene of the killings, the gunman stared up the hill at them. His companion climbed out of the stream-bed, a hundred yards from the road, and began to run towards the car. He was limping.

What they had taken part in and what they had witnessed was vicious and cold-blooded. Lacey had done it and seen it before and had kept his head in one piece by refusing to analyse or dwell on the act of killing. It happened, and philosophy had nothing to do with who survived. Being a mean bastard did.

Unfortunately being a mean bastard didn't cut much ice with the gremlins at night. That's when they sneaked in with doubts, questions and fear of dying. That's why he would get drunk tonight in the hope he would be unconscious when they came.

Miller was still shocked.

He said: 'What a mess.'

'It's always a mess.' The wind blew squalls of rain at them and moaned through the Wicklow hills. 'Now get me somewhere warm. I'm freezing my bollocks off.'

THIRTY-SIX

Miller took him to a holiday cottage near the promenade in Bray that he had rented as a safe house. The girl with long legs was there and he introduced her as Gloria, his London secretary. Miller gave her no explanation as to where they had been or what they had been doing.

Lacey had a hot shower and put on dry clothes provided by Miller. The shirt and sweater were OK, but the Levis were too long. Gloria tucked the excess material up inside each leg once he had them on, and tagged them with a stitch.

She also cleaned the wound on his head and suggested it needed stitches. Miller agreed and produced a medical kit in a black leather case but Lacey balked at the sight of needles and thread. Instead, the American smeared on a heavy duty congealant.

The three of them went by car to the shopping precinct. Gloria drove and Miller sat in the passenger seat. Lacey had the back to himself. He felt like lying down and going to sleep. The girl parked the car and went to buy Lacey a hat to cover his wound and an anorak to cover the state of his leather jacket.

When she had gone, Lacey said: 'Thanks.'

Miller said: 'I didn't know it would be like that.'

'Neither did I. I didn't really think they'd do it.'

They watched people walk by being normal, hiding from the rain under umbrellas.

Lacey said: 'You lost two men. Will that be trouble?'

Miller sighed, as if he didn't like being reminded that two people he had recruited had died.

'They were well paid and they were free-lancing. Dublin

Provos who wanted to prove they were as hard as the Belfast and Derry brigades.'

'They weren't. Where did you find them?'

'You meet all sorts of people in my profession.' He tried a laugh that didn't work. 'I know a mercenary in Lisbon called Cabbage.'

They watched the people again.

Miller said: 'Are you going to be OK now?'

'Who from? Murder Incorporated?'

'Yes.'

'They're a programmed unit. The operation failed and they took two casualties. My guess is they've loaded their dead and are already across the border. First priority was me and the package, second was leaving no evidence they'd been here.'

'Can you be sure?'

'No. That's why I kept this.'

He patted the Magnum that was pushed inside the jeans against his stomach, beneath the baggy sweater.

Gloria returned and handed Lacey a paper bag that contained a blue anorak and a tweed hat. He put them on, pulling at the hat.

He said: 'I never wear a hat. It feels odd.'

Gloria said: 'It looks great. You look like a proper country gent, just back from the shoot.'

Lacey got out of the car and went looking for a taxi.

At the hotel he retrieved his carrier-bag from reception, went to his room and changed into his own clothes. He did it slowly because of the pain in his back. Once again he told himself he was too old to be doing this sort of thing. He checked the age spots on the back of his hands but they hadn't got any bigger.

Phone home, Lamont-Smith had said. It was time he did. He dialled the office in Charing Cross Road.

Malcolm answered and for once he wasn't flippant.

'I don't know what the hell's been going on, duckie, but your arse is in a sling.'

'Is Sam there?'

'No. But he's available. Are you all right?'

'I'm always all right. You know that, Malcolm.'

'You sound tired.'

'It's been one of those days.'

'Well, watch what you say. He's not in a good mood.'

'Neither am I.'

'I'll patch you through.'

Lacey waited while Malcolm made the connections. Thirty seconds later, Bryson was on the line.

'Where are you?'

'The Glen Hotel in Delgany, County Wicklow. I have a problem.'

'How clever of you to notice.'

'It will be easier if you listen, Sam. You have to sort it out.'

'Go on.'

'Where's Chesterton?'

'Why?'

'Just tell me.'

'He's at his home in Buckinghamshire for the weekend.'

It was no surprise to learn that the Minister was not in Ireland.

'Call him. Tell him I want to meet him in the morning.'

As he talked, Lacey checked timetables for British Airways and Aer Lingus.

Bryson said: 'You can't deal with Chesterton like that. He has engagements. Besides, he won't see you.'

'He'll see me.'

'Why?'

'Because I have a delivery to make.'

'You've got the package?'

'Yes.'

'Then bring it home. That's all you need to do.'

'Sam, I'm getting tired of people telling me what I need to do. This time, I'm doing the telling.' He read flight times. 'Chesterton can buy me breakfast at Heathrow. I'll be landing at Terminal 1 at ten-thirty. If I miss the flight, tell him to wait.'

309

'You can't deal with ministers like this.'

'On this occasion I can. Don't worry, Sam. He'll be there.'

Bryson paused before speaking.

'What's happened?'

'I'll tell you when I get back. Just call him and fix the meeting.'

'Peter, are you all right?'

'All of a sudden, everybody's concerned for my health. I'm fine, I'm not cracking up and I'm not having delusions of grandeur. I'm having delusions of reality. Tell Chesterton the time is non-negotiable. I'm going on holiday tomorrow afternoon. Call me back to confirm.'

He gave him the number, hung up and dialled again.

Susan was at the shop and answered at the first ring.

He said: 'What's wrong? No customers?'

'The weather's kept people at home. I think they're building arks.'

Lacey laughed.

'Never mind. Sunshine tomorrow.'

'Will you be back in time?'

'I'll be back. I'll meet you at Gatwick at two o'clock. You'd better pack some stuff for me.'

'A noose and a dressing-gown cord?'

'Forget the noose, but we might try the cord.'

She giggled. Sophisticated women weren't supposed to giggle but Susan did. It sounded girlish and he was glad he had her instead of twin Germans.

In a more serious voice, she said: 'Is it over?'

'It will be in the morning.'

'Take care.'

'I always do.'

They enjoyed a comfortable silence before he spoke again.

'I'm going to have to hang up. I'm expecting a call.'

'OK. See you tomorrow.'

'You certainly will.'

'Love you.'

'Love you.'

Bryson phoned back twenty minutes later.

310

'He didn't like it, but he'll be there. I hope you know what you're doing, Peter.'

'Christ, Sam, I haven't known what I've been doing for years. Maybe now I'm beginning to.'

'When will I see you?'

'When I get back from holiday.'

'But your reports . . .'

'You won't want reports on this one. This one never happened.'

'All right, but be careful tomorrow. Chesterton carries a grudge. He makes a bad enemy.'

'That I've already found out.'

Lacey met Ben Miller on the path into the woods at the side of the hotel. The drizzle was persistent and no one else was daft enough to be out for a stroll.

Thirty yards down the track was far enough. There was a clearing and, in the middle of it, the blackened remains of an old fire.

Blunt's diary was in three volumes. They were the size of thick exercise books and were leather-backed. As well as being filled with handwritten entries, the books contained loose pieces of paper, photographs and letters.

Lacey crouched round the embers that had previously burnt rubbish and ripped the books apart. He stacked the pieces on the damp ashes and Miller poured over them a tin of fuel for lighting barbecues. They looked at each other.

'Be my guest,' Lacey said.

Miller took a box of matches from his pocket, used one match to light the box in a blaze of fire, and dropped it on to the pyre of memoirs.

They caught immediately, the flames curling photographs that hadn't seen the light of day for years and now never would, and turning into ashes pages of the past that would never be read.

Lacey moved one of the covers deeper into the flames with his foot.

311

He hadn't read the diaries. He hadn't even opened them until he had ripped them apart for burning. Their destruction had not been prompted by a loyalty to the Crown but by a sense of what could be achieved.

'I'd better get back,' he said.

'OK. I'll make sure there's nothing left.'

Miller hadn't asked to look, either. He had been content to be told that the books they were destroying contained the secrets of Orville B. Bross.

Lacey walked back to the hotel through the gloom of the late afternoon. He felt no satisfaction, no elation. His mood matched the weather and he needed a drink.

THIRTY-SEVEN

The man tipped to be the next Tory Prime Minister didn't buy Lacey breakfast at Heathrow the next morning. Lacey tried not to let his disappointment show.

He was met by two men wearing suits and expressions that were regulation Special Branch issue. They called him Mr Lacey in the sort of tone that implied that if the three of them were ever alone in a dark alley they would enjoy kicking seven shades of shit out of him.

In return, he smiled and admired the suits.

'And people say you don't have a sense of humour?'

They viewed his leather jacket with distaste.

He was led away from the rest of the passengers, through a no-entry door, along a corridor and into an office.

Leonard Oliver Chesterton sat behind a desk in a high-backed leather swivel chair. He wore a Pringle golf sweater, green cord trousers and brogue shoes. His legs were crossed in the same languid fashion adopted by the late Lamont-Smith, and he only used the bottom half of his eyes as if Lacey wasn't worth opening them the whole way. The smile was a sneer of power and wealth.

He didn't get up and he didn't offer to shake hands.

The two heavies left them alone and closed the door. The room had bare green walls and no windows and was perfect for strip searches or detaining illegal immigrants without food and water. It was hygienic and anonymous and almost exactly right for the business that was to be conducted there. The only place more suitable that Lacey could think of would be a lavatory.

There was one other chair in the room on Lacey's side of the desk. It was the sort of upright, uncomfortable wooden chair that had featured in a thousand police films, usually occupied by a criminal who was surrounded by intimidating detectives who shone a light in his face.

Lacey looked at the ceiling. Chesterton had got it wrong. He couldn't do much with tube lighting.

Chesterton said: 'You have something for me.'

It was a statement, not a question.

'Yes.'

Lacey put both his travel bag and his briefcase on the desk. From the briefcase he took an audio cassette and placed it in front of the politician. The man looked at it but didn't move.

'The games are over, Lacey. Where's the rest?'

Lacey smiled.

'Somewhere safe.'

Chesterton uncrossed his legs and sat upright. He picked up the cassette and held it in his right hand and looked Lacey in the face, although he still kept his eyes hooded.

'Extortion?'

'Blackmail.'

'Don't even think it.'

'I've not only thought it, I've planned it.'

'I despise traitors. You will be taken care of, Lacey. You will get no money and you will have no life.'

'You already tried that. Besides, I don't want money.'

Chesterton sat back in the chair.

'Then what do you want?'

'Your resignation from politics.'

The eyes opened all the way.

Lacey grinned. He was getting there.

'You want what?'

'Your removal from public office. Go back into banking, or off-shore trading. Make yourself a billionaire or breed pigs. I don't care what you do, I just don't want you in politics.'

Chesterton's back stiffened.

'You don't want? You? Who the fucking hell are you?'

'I'm the man with the royal dirt and the high-quality reel-to-reel tape recording of your confession. You should call me Mister.'

The man appeared to be about to suffer lockjaw. His chin quivered, and a vein in his neck seemed to be pumping far too much blood to his head. He raised his arm and threw the cassette at Lacey, who moved to one side. The cassette hit the wall behind him with a clatter and the plastic box smashed. The door opened and one of the off-the-peg Special Branch men stepped into the room.

He waited for the order to kill but Chesterton regained his control and waved him away. The door closed and they were alone again.

Lacey said: 'That's a nasty temper. I don't think politics suit you. You'd be much better off pig farming.'

Chesterton was taking deep breaths to calm himself down. Lacey now sat in the chair and stretched his legs.

He said: 'You can't frighten me, Chesterton. Check my record. You can only kill me, but if you do that, everything spills. Now. Do you want to hear my plan?'

'Go on.'

'You resign and I guarantee to destroy the diaries – there are three of them, by the way – and the letters and the photographs. I also guarantee not to release the tape recording where you boast about certain indiscretions. That's it. Clean and simple.'

'Why?'

'A lot of reasons. Maybe I'm getting old and looking for a grail. Maybe I just want peace of mind for once. Maybe I'm a wee bit cross that someone tried to kill me. But the main reason is because you piss me off. Jesus Christ, we've had some crooked bastards running the country, but you're a class apart. Let's just call it one small step for mankind.'

'You're mad.'

'Actually, I'm not. I haven't felt this good for a long time.'

'Why should I give up my career because of you?'

'One, you're a royalist. Look upon this as a sacrifice for the Crown. It'll probably bring your knighthood that much quicker. Two, if you don't give up your career, I'll destroy it. And I'm much better than Frank Briggs.'

'You're a man without honour, Lacey.'

Lacey laughed.

'How often I've heard that word. People like you use it as justification. Well in your mouth it's shit. You eat it.'

He got up and picked up the travel bag and briefcase. Chesterton's eyes widened even more.

'Where are you going?'

'For some breakfast, and then on holiday.'

'We haven't finished.'

'Oh yes. We've both finished. You've got two weeks to announce your resignation as a Minister and a Member of Parliament. Give whatever reason you like, but resign with a declaration that you have no further interest in politics.'

The lids of Chesterton's eyes were slipping back to the half-way mark.

'And if I do?'

'There'll be no scandal, no tape. I'll keep my end of the bargain. Check my file.' He smiled. 'I may not have your sense of honour, but I keep my word. Think yourself lucky I'm not a bastard like you. Now, if you'll have a word with your goons, I'll be on my way.'

He kicked the door. It opened and the same Special Branch officer filled the empty space, ignoring Lacey and staring intently at Chesterton for a word of command. Maybe they went to training classes with Dobermanns.

'It's all right. He can go.'

Lacey turned and gave Chesterton a last smile.

'Have a nice day,' he said.

He walked down the corridor and through another door and rejoined the crowds of Terminal 1.

There were never happy endings, just endings, and at least this one had concluded on time and with a percentage of success. It would never have been possible to make Chesterton pay fully for all he had done, but making him pay at all had been a worthwhile experience.

Lacey felt good and he felt hungry and he went in search of bacon and eggs.

316

POSTSCRIPT

George Blake and Sir Anthony Blunt were members of the British security services who were both spies for the KGB.

MI6 officer Blake was sentenced to forty-two years in jail in 1961, yet only three years later, in 1964, Blunt was granted immunity, his treachery was kept secret by the authorities, and he was allowed to retain his knighthood and his position as Keeper of the Queen's Pictures.

The question has been asked many times why the two spies were treated so differently, without a satisfactory answer ever being given. It was left to the media eventually to unmask Blunt in 1979.

Before that happened, in 1971, Blunt survived a dangerous illness that caused panic in Whitehall and at MI5 headquarters.

According to Peter Wright, former Assistant Director of MI5, Prime Minister Edward Heath and Victor Rothschild, a lifelong friend of Blunt and head of the Government Think Tank, were worried the spy might leave a last will and testament to be published on his death.

In Spycatcher, *the best-selling book the Government tried to ban, Wright said:*

> *Victor knew better than any outsider just what damage Blunt could do. Both he and Heath were obsessed with the damage the Profumo scandal had done to the last Conservative Government, and were terrified that Blunt could bring them down in the same way.*
>
> *It was not just the problem of the immunity; there was the horrendous possibility that he might name fellow conspirators, both living and dead, as well as the chance that he might choose to leave a more intimate record of the halcyon days of the 1930s.*
>
> *More than a handful of reputations stood to suffer if their sexual peccadilloes from that time were circulated on Fleet Street.*

* * *

Matilda's Game *is fiction based on truth and, as is often the case, it is the truth that is stranger than the fiction.*

The facts upon which it is based have been culled from many sources but prime among them are the following books: Honey Trap *by Anthony Summers and Stephen Dorril;* Spycatcher *by Peter Wright;* Conspiracy of Silence *by Barrie Penrose and Simon Freeman;* Mask of Treachery *by John Costello;* Wallis, Trading With The Enemy, *and* Errol Flynn: The Untold Story, *all by Charles Higham;* The Crown and The Swastika *by Peter Allen;* The Men Who Would Be King *by Nicholas Shakespeare;* The Cambridge Apostles *by Richard Deacon;* Hollywood Babylon II *by Kenneth Anger; and* My Silent War *by Kim Philby.*

Also invaluable have been Lobster, *the British magazine of covert intelligence, and, in particular, Stephen Dorril, author and co-producer of* Lobster, *and Richard Donkin of the* Financial Times.